THE HUMMINGBIRD AND THE SEA

BOOK 1 THE DAWNLAND CHRONICLES

JENNY BOND

PART I

EASTHAM, MASSACHUSETTS
SUMMER 1716

1

E*ven in the shade of the colossal oak, there was a light around Maria, a glow. Leah had it too, but she wore it differently. No newcomer to Eastham took them for sisters. There was a simplicity to Maria; Leah was harder to understand. Standing under that tree, Maria appeared bewitched by something. She seemed out of place and time, still and silent, almost petrified. Perhaps I'm reading too much into that expression of hers. Remembering that day and everything that's come since has made me do so. Did I even notice it then? It was the quarterstaff bout that had captured and fixed her attention. I look back now and think, what if she'd never seen it? That day was back in July and it was hot, hot as Jove. It was the kind of day that just made you want to lie down until it was over. The air was thick as wax and the rank stench of bodies rolled right over you.*

But Maria looked cool under that oak. I recall the image so clearly because I never saw her look quite the same way again.

~

MARIA STOOD near the meeting house green. More a dusty, rutted, manure-covered square of dirt than a green, the area in front of the white building was where most of Eastham's dramas played out. It was set with a whipping post, a pound and a watch house. On this particular summer's day, the space was playing host to a lively quarterstaff bout. Maria could barely hear the staves connecting over the din of the cheering spectators. Most were yelling the name of Judah Doane, a young man of twenty whose family she knew well. He was the grandson of one of the first settlers in Eastham. Maria was the granddaughter of another. The two families had forged their lives in the wilderness side by side.

Maria wore her most becoming dress. Although it featured no lace or embroidery, the mulberry-coloured bodice fit perfectly, accentuating her neat waist and compact bosom. She liked the contrast of its bold white cuffs against the vivid purple. Wiping her brow with her gloved hand, she looked towards the unblemished sky through the leaves of the oak. The tree was one of only a few survivors when the township (consisting of little else than a tavern, blacksmith and meeting house) was carved out of the forest seventy years earlier. *Grand and glorious; a true gift from heaven*, Maria thought, as her lips curled into a contented smile. Her gaze drifted towards the ocean. The bay was quiet of all activity. Boats lay anchored, dormant, as their captains and crews enjoyed the festivities in the town. Even nature itself refused to toil on such a day, refusing to produce a single wisp of cooling breeze.

Craning her slender neck to view the man Judah was fighting, Maria saw her sister's husband, Palgrave Williams, among the bystanders. The town's silversmith, he stood at least a head taller than those that surrounded him. He watched the bout pensively, but on noticing Maria, lifted his spider-like hand and cast a gentle smile in her direction. Palgrave had a particular economy of gesture, as though he had worked out just how little movement he required to sustain him. She'd never seen him hurried. He was never in a rush. He always walked with a slow, fluid stride, like the roll of a boat over an easy swell.

The crowd parted slightly. She could now see Judah's challenger, an opponent whose name no-one was crying. A raven-haired man, older than her friend, flourished his weapon grandly, intending to impress the onlookers. His broad grin, directed at both Judah and the spectators, was taunting. As he engaged the audience with his skill, his eye caught Maria's. His smile disappeared, although he continued to look at her while sweeping the stave in large arcs across his body. She felt her face flush. She turned away, albeit grudgingly, and feigned interest in a stall where cider was being sold. Maria did not recognise him. He was not from Cape Cod, she was certain. But there were many unknown faces in the town this Thursday. He was probably a crewman from one of the merchant ships docked in the harbour. He wore nothing but breeches and a thick leather belt.

A moment later, the town's beadle, Arthur Earl, came into view. Maria had noticed him before as he patrolled the area at a meditative pace, his close-set green eyes taking in the town. She saw him glance briefly at the two opponents. As he passed Maria, he tipped the brim of his hat with his forefinger. 'May I share a little of your shade?' he asked, as he stepped beneath the bowers of the tree. 'You looked so cool in this heat that I thought I might join you.'

Maria moved sideways, one step only. She never knew how to take Arthur Earl. He was at once stern but friendly, shy but forthright; handsome in his own quiet way, yet never overly solicitous of her, or indeed any woman's, company. Apart from Leah's, of course – they had been childhood friends.

They were silent as the men fought. Arthur finally cleared his throat.

'How is your sister, Mistress Hallett?'

'She is well,' Maria replied. 'Leah is here with Palgrave and the children.'

Earl nodded thoughtfully. 'I'll seek her out, say hello.'

'She would like that.' Maria hoped he would move on.

'Have you seen Silas?' he said. 'He arrived in Eastham last night.'

Maria's voice caught in her throat. 'Nay, I have not.'

Surprised, the beadle assessed her response briefly before continuing.

'Perhaps he is weary from his journey. Good day to you, Mistress Hallett.'

'Good day, Mister Earl.' She allowed her eyes to be drawn back to the bout.

The chest and arms of Judah's opponent glistened in the noontide heat. The stranger's movements, his expression and his very presence were grander than all of Eastham – he had the look of a man who had seen the world. She was aware of the impropriety of staring so blatantly. There would certainly be gossip.

But she couldn't look away.

'Maria.' A voice from behind startled her. She recognised it immediately and turned to face her old friend. Silas held out his hand and took her fingertips gently in his own. She lowered into a curtsey. The formality of their gestures made Maria uneasy. She and Silas, companions since childhood, had never stood on ceremony.

'I see you're enjoying the bout,' Silas said, as if sensing

her unease. 'It's a feisty match, to be sure, but I have seen no man best Judah Doane at quarterstaff.'

'Neither have I.' The crowd cried out. Maria's gaze returned to the fighters for an instant. Judah had been hit.

'I'm pleased to see you've arrived home safely, Silas,' Maria said, turning back. Her friend's narrow face had filled out in the past six months and he now wore a close-cropped beard, the same shade as his chestnut hair. He was clothed in a striking suit of taupe-coloured silk, the likes of which Maria had never seen before. It didn't hang comfortably on him. To Maria, it made him appear less than the man she recalled.

'I trust your journey from Cambridge was uneventful?' she asked.

'Aye,' he answered, straightening his vest. 'It was tiring ... but on seeing you, it seems my fatigue has quite disappeared.'

Maria smiled uncertainly, turned towards the fight again, her blonde hair fanning out from her bonnet. Silas breathed in deeply, hoping to catch a hint of its scent. Perspiring, he reluctantly removed his hat, fearing the absence of his headwear would ruin the effect of his appearance. The felt hat, wide-brimmed and brass-buckled, completed his carefully chosen ensemble of coat, breeches and vest – attire he felt befitted his new position.

While Maria watched the bout, Silas stood behind her observing the way the dappled sunlight danced and glinted off her hair.

They both started at a sudden roar from the crowd.

Judah rushed his opponent and thrust his stick wildly towards his adversary's face. His assaults were parried consistently. Then, in no more than four blows, Judah was face down on the ground. The victor stood holding his staff above his head, one foot pinning the vanquished man in the dust. As the spectators applauded, Judah's opponent pulled him to his feet then offered him his hand. Judah shook it, at first reluctantly, then more convincingly after the dark-haired stranger uttered something in his ear. With the left side of his face caked in dirt, Judah laughed and nodded. Within seconds the crowd and the competitors had dispersed.

'That was an outcome I didn't predict,' Silas said as Maria scanned the crowd.

'Who are you looking for?'

Maria faced her companion. 'My sister.'

He stared at her intensely, taking her in. When she lowered her blue eyes to the ground, he lifted her chin with his finger.

'Your father announced the news of your posting last Sunday during his sermon,' Maria began, easing away. 'I'm pleased for you. A ministry in Beverly is an achievement, but we all had hopes you might relieve your father of his congregation here.' She paused before adding pointedly, 'Our congregation is dwindling, Silas.'

'That had been my hope as well,' he replied, disappointed that her remark was not more intimate. 'But father is not yet ready to retire and believes I'll make a better fit in Beverly. He's pleased with my position, even though I'm merely the minister's assistant.'

'But for one so young ...'

'Not so young,' Silas cut in. 'The Reverend Cotton Mather began at Harvard College when he was twelve and delivered his first sermon at sixteen. By those standards, I'm an old man!' He smiled.

Maria laughed, relaxing into their conversation, finally

recognising her friend of old. 'You must have worked very hard.'

'I did. Maria ...' He was glad to be able to say the rhythm of her name aloud again – *Ma-rye-ah*. 'Might we take a walk?' he suggested. 'It's hot and the forest is cool. We could find some moss and sit down. Do you remember how we used to do that as children? Cool ourselves by stretching ourselves flat on the moss?'

Maria nodded.

'I have so much I want to tell you! Harvard is such an interesting place, full of like-minded men with the same calling as myself ... I have such plans for the future, Maria ...'

'But Silas, I must find my sister ...' she said. 'I told her I would help with the children.'

'Then later? We could meet at Boat Meadow River at three, by the willow?'

'Aye,' she finally agreed, regretting her earlier hesitation. 'By the willow at three.'

'Do you promise?'

'Aye, I promise.'

2
____

Maria found her sister and the children by the harbour watching four local men who stood playing music. With violins, a flute and a lute, the foursome produced a merry jig. They were farmers, like her father. The children danced and skipped to the tune while the adults stood by, motionless. Leah had her hands behind her back and her delicately rounded chin lifted in interest. Her children ate sweet cakes as they danced, the sticky crumbs glued to their lips and chin. Maria took a place by her side and eyed her sister's profile.

'Did Arthur find you?'

'He did.'

'Are the sweet cakes from him?'

Leah nodded.

At twenty-eight, Leah was beautiful still. There were light traces of lines around her eyes and mouth, but her slim nose, sculpted cheekbones and pink, straight lips were perfect. Her hair was concealed beneath a cap and hat, but Maria envisaged her sister's honey-coloured locks falling to her shoulders in obedient waves. It was as though God had taken special care when he had created her. Every aspect of her appearance was so carefully etched and defined; all was in startlingly perfect proportion. Maria believed her own features too large, her mouth and eyes overcrowding her round face.

She noticed Leah was wearing her most appealing dress. It was dark olive green with a wide white collar. Three small black bows travelled down the middle of the bodice. The children applauded vigorously when the music ended. Happy sounds were not commonplace in Eastham.

'We're meeting Palgrave by the tavern,' Leah explained once the noise had quieted. She instructed her children to settle and walk on. She picked up the youngest, Joshua, and placed him on her hip. 'He's doing business.'

Maria nodded.

'I pray that his haul will be bountiful,' mused Leah.

'You'll get by,' Maria said. 'You always do.'

'Aye.' Leah studied her sister closely. 'We do.'

Maria frowned, thinking. The sisters walked for a time in silence. When Maria did not try to fill the space between them with words, as she would typically do, Leah began. 'You're quiet.'

'Silas has returned.'

'And that has made you quiet?'

Maria shrugged.

'He loves you, Sister.'

'I know.' Maria stopped walking. 'But what if I don't love him?'

Leah stopped too. 'It never occurred to me ...' She placed Joshua on the ground and watched as he ran after his siblings. 'But there is a fondness ...?'

'I want to feel something more than *fondness* for the man I am expected to marry,' Maria said. 'Am I asking too much?'

Maria gazed at her sister earnestly, waiting for a reply. Before Leah could answer, Palgrave called to them from outside the tavern. He was counting a few coins into Giles Upton's hand. He opened a sack that rested at his feet and the man placed a tarnished vase into its depths. As they farewelled, a woman exited the tavern and touched Palgrave's arm. It was Mary Garvey, the landlord's wife.

Leah had never seen a bodice cut so low. Mary's thick red hair was piled loosely on her head. *She never wears a cap or bonnet*, Leah silently rebuked. Then, standing on her toes with her hand resting lightly on his shoulder, Mary spoke into Palgrave's ear. He laughed and the pair bid each other good day. Leah clenched her jaw as her husband approached, teeth meshing like cogs.

'Not bad,' Palgrave said as he made his way over to his wife. He handed her a small coin purse and she placed it in her pocket. Palgrave shook the sack and the contents clanged loudly, making Joshua laugh. 'There's enough for a teapot, a few door handles ... and a candlestick or two,' he added, shooting Maria a wink.

'What are you hiding?' Leah demanded, catching the wink. 'Tell me.'

'I'd hoped to keep the secret longer,' he grinned, shaking his head at his own lack of resolution. 'The minister has commissioned a set of candlesticks for the meeting house. They should be worth at least six or seven pounds.'

Maria noticed the merest thread of a glance travel the short distance between husband and wife, part of an intricate tapestry she could not read. After a moment, the yarn was cut, tied off and neatly concealed.

'It's a wonder the minister can afford such luxuries as silver candlesticks,' Leah said.

'Why do you say that? He preaches of nothing else,' Palgrave replied.

The couple laughed quietly, continuing to weave a private joke.

Maria contained her amusement but she knew that it took a keen eye to see the light of God shining forth from Reverend Dent's pulpit.

'And there's our lodger,' Palgrave went on, basking, building on his sudden good fortune.

'Lodger?' Maria queried, surprised she'd heard no news of it.

'Aye, a tenant,' Palgrave said, 'just for the summer. He's sleeping in the barn.'

Palgrave was economical with words as well as gestures. Leah elaborated. 'He's a carpenter from England. He's helping to build the schoolhouse.'

'When did he arrive in Eastham?' Maria asked.

'Only the day before yesterday, although he arrived in the colonies some time earlier, I think,' Leah said. 'Palgrave came across him in the tavern. He needed somewhere to stay and I thought we could use another pound each month.'

'Although not a godly man,' Leah concluded, 'he appears a trustworthy sort.'

'What's your tenant's name?' Maria asked.

'Samuel Bellamy,' Palgrave said, 'the man who bested Judah at quarterstaff.'

'You watched the bout?' Leah turned to her sister.

'From the oak,' Maria answered. 'It took up all of the green. It was difficult to avoid. Besides, I was concerned for Judah.'

As Palgrave related the details of the fight to his wife, Maria remembered the black-haired man with the wide, provocative grin. Even though her demeanour showed no hint of it, Maria was thrilled that she now knew his name.

'He's not a godly man, you say?' Maria asked.

Palgrave shook his head. 'But neither am I. There are worse things that can be said of a person.'

'Shush.' Leah held her finger to her lip. 'You're seen at meeting every Sabbath.'

'My appearance there each Sunday is for the sake of you and the children. It has nothing to do with God.' He pulled his wife to him.

Chided, Leah squeezed Palgrave's hands in appreciation. Warp and weft interlaced, continuing to craft a picture delicate and tender. Maria directed her eyes to the ground.

'Bellamy will be joining us shortly. He's inside,' Palgrave said, indicating the tavern.

With this information, Maria's heart began to race. The children, bored by the adult conversation, had begun playing tag, running rings around her skirt. Maria was oblivious to their shrieks and activity, staring only at the tavern's entrance.

'Hush, children,' Leah said. 'You'll have Mister Earl here shortly. He'll wallop you with his staff.'

With a chorus of giggles, the children ran off to the oak tree that Maria had stood by earlier in the day and continued their game. She looked after them as they departed.

'Here comes Bellamy now,' Palgrave said.

Maria turned and watched as Samuel Bellamy made his way through the festivalgoers. He carried a mug of ale in each hand. He had washed his face of sweat and dirt and now wore a ruffled shirt, burgundy coat and black tricorn hat. Judah, who was standing among a group of friends, merrily called his name. Bellamy turned and nodded. His thick hair was secured at his neck by a wide, red ribbon. Among the muted browns and greys and sombre greens of Eastham, Bellamy shone like a beacon.

When the newcomer reached the trio, Palgrave began. 'Samuel Bellamy, I'd like you to meet my sister, Maria Hallett.'

Maria lowered her eyes to the ground and curtsied. She could detect from the amusement in his brown eyes that he recognised her immediately. Her cheeks grew hot and she was suddenly ashamed. Bellamy handed the mugs to Palgrave and took Maria's hand from where it hung at her side. He grasped her gloved fingertips in his own until Maria met his gaze.

'It's a pleasure to meet you, Mister Bellamy,' Maria said.

'I saw you watching the bout.'

'Bout, you say? All I saw were two boys playing at quarterstaff.'

'There was no playing about it,' Bellamy rebutted.

They laughed. Leah's eyes darted between them.

'It seemed to me that the match was a mere entertainment to you.'

'A mere entertainment!' Bellamy laughed loudly, rolling his 'r's gently. Then he conceded. 'Perhaps you're right. I'm hoping the townspeople will take to me.'

His voice was like nothing Maria had ever heard before. He spoke slowly, the words travelling fathoms from their origin deep at the base of his chest. Once they reached his throat, the sounds became textured, but not rough, like they'd passed through honeycomb on their way to the outside.

'Then perhaps you should have lost,' Maria finished.

Leah nudged her husband who was still holding the mugs.

'That would probably have been the wisest path,' Bellamy smiled, pleased he had incited such a response. He only released Maria's hand when a mug of ale was forced upon him by Palgrave.

THEY TOOK a picnic into the forest. The children ran ahead to Long Pond. Neither the earthy scent of the moss nor the plunging willows that surrounded the pond reminded Maria of her promise to Silas. Palgrave walked alongside Bellamy, ahead of the women. They spoke continuously. Occasionally Bellamy would turn his head and cast a momentary glimpse in Maria's direction as he conversed. These glimpses did not go unnoticed by Leah.

'Palgrave seems taken with Mister Bellamy,' Maria said to her sister.

'So do you.'

Maria shook her head and offered her sister a quiet laugh, an insufficient assurance she held no romantic feelings towards the outsider.

'It was just a game. His manner was so bold. There's nothing more to it than that.' Maria lied and then added after a pause, 'Perhaps I shouldn't have mocked him as I did.'

Maria was relieved Leah said nothing more on the matter. The truth was that this newcomer had provoked such a startling blend of feelings in her that she was now uncertain as to the proper way to proceed. She both feared and hoped that her earlier playfulness would be construed by Bellamy as affection, but as she concentrated on the soft crunch of leaves underfoot she doubted whether there was a suitable way forward. Her father would never consider an attachment to a man like Samuel Bellamy.

Yet as the sisters walked, Maria was drawn to the dialogue of the men. Bellamy spoke of his plans to complete the schoolhouse and then, with the money earned, buy some acres to farm. Even though he was a carpenter he spoke knowledgeably about farming, explaining that he hoped his crops would go beyond wheat and rye. He spoke of planting native yields that were more suited to the climate of Massachusetts Bay, such as cranberries and Indian maize. Palgrave nodded his head tentatively.

'But it seems to me,' Palgrave said, 'any person can walk into the woods and fill a basket full of cranberries. Why would anyone pay good money for them?'

'That may not be convenient for all people. The elderly or infirm, for example.' Bellamy replied. 'I would grow the bushes myself and package the berries by the pound. I could sell them from a storefront in the town, somewhere by the harbour.'

'But cranberries?' Palgrave said. 'You have some grand plans, my friend. How do you come up with such notions?'

Bellamy merely laughed. 'My hope is that my storefront will extend beyond cranberries to haberdashery, general merchandise, hardware, silverware and the like,' he explained. 'Why you, my friend, could sell your goods through my store as well as your own, thus doubling your profit! Eastham is a busy harbour. Seamen want to spend the money they've earned. There's no use for silver and gold on a godforsaken merchant pink.'

After a short walk through the wood, they reached a

birch that Palgrave suggested would be a suitable place to stop. Following a warning from their mother, the children removed their shoes and stockings and began to wade ankle deep into the water of the pond a short distance away. Joyous cries ensued when their feet sank into the mud. They were immediately joined on the bank by their watchful parents. Maria knelt on the cool ground and began unpacking the food from her basket, all the while aware of Bellamy's eyes on her.

'Your hair gleams in this light,' he remarked. 'I've never seen locks so beautiful. I would call them "flaxen".'

Maria, unsure of how to respond to a compliment made so brazenly, invited Bellamy to sit with a slight movement of her hand. Bellamy immediately took an apple from the basket and removed a small jackknife from the pocket of his breeches. He cut the apple and offered her a thin slice, holding it towards her between the blade and his thumb. When she made no sign of taking the fruit he edged his hand a little closer, prompting her to accept the token. She did and nibbled around the edges of the apple. It was an orange pippin from her father's orchard. Bellamy watched her closely.

'It's a farm you're after is it, Mister Bellamy?' Maria asked.

'You can call me Sam, or Samuel if you'd prefer,' he suggested. 'Aye, it's a farm I'm wanting.'

Maria nodded, rubbing the apple against her lips, wondering if putting down roots would suit a man like Bellamy.

'But it's more than that,' he went on. 'I want freedom enough to build a life here for myself.'

'Freedom. That's a curious word to use,' Maria couldn't stop herself saying. She took a second piece of apple.

'I'm from Devon, you see,' he explained. 'My father was a farmer, although not a very successful one. He struggled. My mam struggled. Always.' He paused as he wiped the knife clean on his breeches. 'They were trapped. My grandad was also a farmer, as was his father and so on and so on, back through the ages. But I wanted more, you see. So, when I was fourteen, I took myself off to London. Found an apprenticeship with a joiner.'

She nodded. 'Your mother must have missed you terribly.'

'I'm from a litter of eight. I wasn't missed.'

'I'm sure that's not true.'

Their eyes locked. Despite her inexperience in matters of the heart, Maria had no difficulty understanding the essence of their mutual contemplation. Time passed. Maria was uncertain how long they sat there like that, trapped in one another's orbit. Neither was aware of the laughter and chatter of the others as they made their way from the pond back to the birch tree.

AFTER THE GROUP HAD EATEN, Bellamy offered to take the children back to the pond. Before Leah could object, he had called for Maria's assistance. Leah opened her mouth but was hushed by her sister.

'We won't be long,' Maria advised as she stood hastily and flattened her skirt. As the couple herded the children in the direction of the pond, Leah looked on in concern.

'Don't worry so,' Palgrave said, as they watched them walk together. 'Sam's an honest man.'

'*Sam* now, is it?'

Leah twisted the thick silver ring on her finger. The

wedding band, made by Palgrave himself, was engraved with asters.

'Honesty and godliness are not the same thing,' she cautioned. 'There's nothing good that can come of such a match.'

'Maria is a sensible girl, but headstrong. She'll buck if you interfere.'

'There are so many men in this town. Boys she has grown up with ...' she said. 'Silas Dent loves her. Any fool can see that. He has a calling and a ministry. Why doesn't she know what's best?'

'Sam has a calling, too – a trade, plans for the future.'

'It's not the same thing!'

Palgrave placed his hand gently on his wife's thigh, rubbing soothingly. 'People marvelled at our marriage, have you forgotten? The beautiful daughter of the colony's most prosperous farmer marrying a poor, widowed silversmith twelve years her senior ...'

'You were so much more than that.' Leah responded before continuing. 'Besides ...'

'Besides nothing,' Palgrave cut in. '*My* godliness is a pretence, Leah. I wish it were not so, but that's the truth. You and the children are my calling. My only sin is the desire to provide you with more, and to make a life more worthy.'

Her husband's declaration stifled further argument. Leah rose to her knees and took his face in her hands. She kissed him longingly on the mouth, gratified she had made such a match.

'I want for nothing,' Leah whispered.

~

BELLAMY LOOKED at Maria in the stippled light under the overhanging willow. Her eyes were in shadow but the sun cut like a scythe across her mouth, her lips crimson with strawberry juice. The children had been splashing in the water for some time, yet neither Maria nor Bellamy had spoken. But when two-and-half-year-old Caleb threatened to topple face first into the water as he grasped for tadpoles, Maria raised her voice.

'Look to your brother, Joseph,' Maria shouted to the eldest child. The boy did not respond.

'Joseph!' she repeated. He turned. 'Take his hand so he doesn't fall.'

'They're a merry tribe,' Bellamy said.

'They keep my sister busy.'

'Palgrave and your sister seem well suited.'

'Aye, they are. Leah and Palgrave are still very much in love. It was that which restored him.'

Bellamy looked at her. 'How so?'

'Palgrave was troubled, deeply so. Leah made him want to live again.' Maria explained no further but leant towards him and plucked a leaf from the shrub he was seated beside. 'Just as this witch-hazel mends the body, Leah cured Palgrave's spirit.'

Maria offered him the pear-shaped leaf. 'My Aunt Margaret is a midwife and a healer of sorts. She tells me the woods are full of remedies; her knowledge is vast and much valued by our community.' She paused, glancing at Bellamy. 'Margaret has taught me a little, but I long to know more.'

'We call this "winterbloom" in England,' he said, fingering the leathery leaf.

'That's a kinder name.'

Bellamy took her hand and turned it skywards. As he placed the foliage in her palm he caught a glimpse of her wrist. It was speckled with paint. He pulled the sleeve of her dress a little towards her elbow.

'Are you an artist, Maria Hallett?' he asked, examining the sapphire blue marking her pale flesh.

'Painting, sketching ... they're amusements.'

'Are amusements not frowned upon?' There was humour in his eyes.

She nodded. 'That's why I must conceal it.'

'The colour ... it reminds me of the sea.'

As he cradled her hand in his he released the small pearl button that secured the glove and stroked the exposed flesh of her wrist tenderly. Maria closed her eyes, pleasuring in the sensation. Then he slowly raised her hand to his mouth. Maria opened her eyes and watched closely as he pressed his lips to her wrist. She did not protest as she thought she might in such a moment. When he drew her hand away from his lips he secured the fastening again. A scream was heard. Maria's eyes darted towards the children who were splashing each other furiously.

'Children,' she cried, rising 'Get back to your mother and father. You'll be drenched before long.' She turned to Bellamy.

'We should get back too.'

'When may I see you again?'

'There are things we must discuss first.'

'When?'

'Tomorrow,' she instructed. 'I'll meet you here, by this witch-hazel, after you've finished at the schoolhouse.'

'At five,' he said.

Maria started at the mention of time.

'What's the hour now?' she asked, remembering.

Bellamy produced his pocket watch. 'A minute or so after four.'

'I must go.' Maria lifted her skirt a little from the ground and turned to leave.

'I didn't mean to offend you.'

Returning to Bellamy, she took his hands in hers. 'You didn't. I ...' she sighed, closing her eyes for an instant before whispering, 'You didn't.'

Then she let his hand go and ran into the forest.

3

Maria made her way hastily through the forest to Boat Meadow River. Leaping over familiar logs and dodging ditches and stones, her movement through the trees was bold and confident. As she ran, she uttered a short prayer requesting Silas's forgiveness. She was disappointed in herself, disappointed she had been so wholly distracted. She had not given Silas Dent a thought since she left him at the oak hours before.

By the time she reached the willow, she was panting and perspiring. Her face burned. She gathered her hair together to cool her neck and scanned her surroundings. Silas was nowhere in sight. Letting her hair fall, she walked to the river and bent down on her knees by its edge and removed her bonnet. She splashed her face with water and then stared at her reflection for a moment as she considered how to proceed.

'Are you praying for forgiveness, Maria Hallett, or admiring your beauty?' It was Silas's voice.

Maria stood and turned.

'I can't tell from up here,' he continued.

She looked into the foliage of the willow. There sat Silas, perched on high, concealed by the leaves, in a cradle formed by branches at the centre of the tree more than fifteen feet above her.

'Neither,' she called and walked towards the tree. 'I was cooling my face. I ran here from Long Pond to meet you.'

'You're over an hour late,' he yelled down.

'I'm here now,' she said as she planted her foot firmly on a low branch and pulled herself up towards him. Within minutes she was beside him. They sat for a moment in silence, waiting for their emotions to settle.

'We've not climbed this willow for years,' she eventually said. 'But I can remember every foothold.'

He didn't respond. Maria examined his face, which was lowered to the ground.

'I'm sorry, Silas,' she said seriously, nestling into the fork of a branch.

She placed her hand over his. 'I'm ashamed of myself, heartily ashamed. Do you forgive me?'

Noting her sincerity and pained by her obvious sorrow, Silas said, 'Pay it no mind, dear Maria. It has been half a year since we last met. A further hour bore me no anguish. The wait only sweetened the anticipation.'

'You're my dearest friend. Thank you.'

The twenty-two-year-old considered her for a moment – her red face and the askew bonnet that she had hurriedly replaced before the climb. He straightened it gently. *How many times have we sat here on this branch?* he wondered. The ancient willow had been their meeting place as children. It had been their sanctuary. But it was in the highest branches of the gnarled tree where Silas and Maria had discovered their private haven. It was here where Maria had found him when his mother had died and had coaxed him down to the ground. It was here where he had consoled Maria when her sister had become estranged from her father's home after Palgrave Williams asked for her hand.

Silas looked again at Maria. She was his friend, his sister, his god; yet still, he wanted her to be so much more. And soon she would be.

'But tell me, what *is* your excuse for keeping me, your dearest friend, waiting?'

As he anticipated her response he noticed her lips part slightly and a shy smile form on them.

'You have piqued my interest,' he said. 'I have never seen you wear such a heavenly countenance.'

Her smile faded and Maria cast him an uneasy glance before speaking. Her cheeks reddened.

'Caleb fell in the pond,' she replied. 'Leah asked me to fetch dry clothes. It took longer than expected, that's all.'

'I see.' It was unlike Maria to lie, but there was a peculiarity in her manner.

Silas stared though the leaves to the river below. He had loved Maria always. Even as a boy he had loved her. Not as a brother might, or even as a friend, but as a man might with strange sensations of agony and rapture all at once. It was impossible not to forgive her. He had forgiven Maria for this and everything else she might do long ago.

Now was the time to speak. He cleared his throat and looked at her directly.

'It has been the expectation of many people, myself included, of course, that you and I would marry one day.' He spoke quickly, harnessing his courage. 'I can think of no better place than sitting in our favoured willow to ask ... well ... I believe that day has come.'

'Silas,' she said. 'I feared this might have been the reason for your return.'

'Feared?'

'Thought, I meant to say.'

He hesitated. 'Don't you love me?'

'It's not as simple as that.'

He looked away. 'For me, it is.'

Her chest tightened in regret. She hated seeing him disappointed. Maria stared into the water below and willed her feelings to change. Although it pained her to admit it, the encounter with Bellamy by the witch-hazel only confirmed what she'd always known. Silas was a friend and nothing more.

It was some minutes before she had courage enough to end the awkward silence.

'Yes, our marriage *has* been the expectation of many people. I knew it ... but it has never been mine,' she explained. 'I should have spoken before now. I wish you'd told me of your feelings sooner ... Silas, why didn't you?'

To speak the truth, to say that he believed she had always felt the same would make him appear foolish, a boy; nothing like the man of the world he had become while at Harvard.

Finally, he turned to face her. 'I wanted to make my mark in the world before we married. Your father has high expectations for you, Maria. I wanted to be able to meet them.'

This surprised her. 'You're the minister's son. Surely that holds you in good standing.'

'There's little love felt for my father in this town,' Silas said. 'I hoped to prove that the son could outshine his father. That's why I worked so diligently at Harvard.' He paused for a moment. 'It was only for you.'

When she didn't protest, when he saw her shoulders

slump and her brow pinch in thought, he sensed her weakening.

'I have such plans for us. With your father's blessing we could marry this summer then travel together to Beverly. Of course, I will begin as assistant to the Reverend Lyons but it's a fine house where we shall live. I've seen it. You will have your own sewing room and I my own study. There is even room enough for a child.'

'You have fine plans, Silas,' she said. 'But I must think on it. I'm not certain I would make a suitable wife to a minister.'

He was solemn, downcast by her reaction. Silas could not remember a time when their marriage had not been his only ambition. He could not understand why it hadn't been hers as well.

Before she could offer anything more, Silas climbed through the branches of the willow to the ground. As he was brushing his fine suit free of leaves, Maria leapt from the lowest branch. She stumbled but he did not offer his hand.

'Don't be cross. I'm only asking for a little time.'

Disappointment swelled in his throat and threatened to choke him. She waited for a response but he was unable to speak.

'You've turned pale,' she said, touching her palm to his cheek.

He pulled away and sat heavily on one of the knotted roots of the willow that bulged through the earth. Despite the sorrow she had caused him, he needed her close.

'May I hold your hand, Maria?'

They had held hands before, he realised, but in unceremonious ways. He had clasped her fingertips each time he had helped her across the brook. Once, he remembered, she had twisted her ankle in the forest and he had carried her the two miles to her home. The feeling of her flesh against his, even through her skirts, had stayed with him. It would forever.

She looked at him. 'Aye.' She unbuttoned her glove. She took a seat beside him. He clutched her hand quickly and firmly, as though attempting to erase her hesitancy through will alone.

Maria looked down at their locked hands, awkward and contorted. She carefully intertwined her fingers with his to assume a more comfortable grasp. Closing her eyes, she waited for the same sense of exhilaration to affect her as Bellamy's touch had. Listening to the low *kuk* of the herons by the river, she waited patiently, ever so patiently, to be overcome.

4

———

Leah moved around the table watchfully, listening to her husband and Bellamy speaking as she ladled the supper, a pottage made from the previous day's boiled pork and vegetables, into bowls. When the family arrived home, Leah had added a peck of barley and some herbs she had found in the forest to stretch the broth a little further. Palgrave's deep, thoughtful drawl had adopted a lightness, the tone of which she did not recognise. His voice skipped almost excitedly from one subject to the next and she registered a new expression on his face, one she had never noticed before. She was seeing him as he might have looked as a boy, when his dreams were still imaginable.

Bellamy spoke of a seaman he'd met in the tavern. Leah shushed her children. The sailor had related news of a Spanish fleet, 'a *treasure* fleet', that had been wrecked on the rocks off Florida's coast. Most of the sailors in Eastham were setting sail for Spanish territory the next day. He and Palgrave laughed at their folly. Ten-year-old Joseph joined in, striving to imitate Bellamy's assured tenor. The topic attracted the interest of the other children, who immediately began questioning Bellamy about the endeavour. Leah shushed them again. Palgrave navigated the discussion back to his guest's plans.

Bellamy was eager to begin work on the schoolhouse, eager to earn money, eager to buy enough acres for a farm. *Eager to wed my sister*, thought Leah. The entire exchange was worrying. However, as she studied her husband's curious manner, she couldn't reason whether her concern was rooted in doubts about Maria's future or her own.

Leah sat down and wordlessly spooned her supper from the bowl to her mouth. As she listened to the men, her contemplations drifted to the day in November ten years ago when she had first visited Palgrave Williams. On the instruction of her mother she and her sister had walked to his house, now her home. It was this house that Palgrave had built for his first family – Anne, Paul and Amy. Her father and other men from Eastham had aided Palgrave in the task. She recalled her father describing it as a 'middling sort of house', with a kitchen and parlour downstairs and two chambers above.

Those upstairs rooms now slept three of her children, as well as herself and her husband. Caleb's crib stood in the kitchen, closest to the hearth in winter, and her eldest son slept in the parlour. When they married, on Leah's advice, Palgrave had attached a store to the house. It was here that Leah sold and bartered the door locks, nails, hammers, gimlets and other hardware her husband manufactured.

On that day a decade ago, Leah had knocked on the door then stamped the snow from her feet as she waited for an answer. There was none. She knocked a second time, more firmly and looked down at her sister. Maria looked back, offering no solution, waiting for her older sister to resolve the matter. Leah wondered whether she should leave the basket and depart, but decided to knock once more. She gave the oak door a loud, vigorous pounding.

'Mister Williams! It's Leah Hallett, Joseph Hallett's daughter. I'm here with my sister. My mother has sent us with some food.'

Leah placed her ear to the door.

'Mister Williams, would you open the door? May we come in? It's mightily cold.'

Leah stood in the fog of her breath and measured her options. Her mother would be cross with her if she returned home with the basket. Yet, if she left it, and Mister Williams was not in, might it not be stolen or plundered by hungry racoons? Perhaps the occupant of the house was unwell, she considered, and could not come to the door. Her agitation increased. Leah looked about her, searching for a solution. Maria stood by her side silently, her hands pushed tightly into a grey fur muff. The notion that Palgrave Williams simply did not want to speak with anyone didn't cross the young woman's mind.

'Mister Williams ...' she said once more as the door suddenly opened.

The eighteen-year-old gasped as she was affronted by the stink of rum, tobacco and tallow, but it was the rank stench of staleness that she found most upsetting.

'You're persistent, Leah Hallett,' Williams said, not unpleasantly, glancing into the basket she held across her arm. A prayer book lay on top. 'Get on your way. I'm in need of neither your charity nor your prayers.' He shot each sister a curt nod.

Leah eyed the man in his entirety, from his bloodshot

eyes made red by despair, to his unshaven face, to his narrow, bare feet. 'I would argue otherwise.' He raised an eyebrow. Leah's focus turned to his chest and the sallowness of his skin. Williams hurriedly began to tie his shirt, conscious of his oversight.

Palgrave Williams was hard to recognise behind the whiskers and the brusqueness. Although Leah had had no dealings with him, her father had spoken well of the silversmith and she had admired both his orderly appearance and his untiring devotion each Sunday when she saw him at meeting. From her family's box at the foot of the altar, she would raise her eyes to the balcony and cautiously glance his way. Leah was quietly amused by his dedication to his prayer book and to Reverend Dent's sermon but respected his determination to win acceptance and make a home in Eastham. Only once had he inadvertently caught her eye and they had stared at each other for a moment before he nodded bashfully and returned his focus to his prayer book. She had mused upon his gaze for many days afterwards. There was something that moved her about his light blue eyes. They brimmed with hope.

Williams opened his mouth to speak but no words came. Instead he stepped back and opened the door wider, allowing the girls to pass. Leah took off her cloak and, bending to wrap it around her sister's shoulders, instructed, 'Wait here, Maria. I won't be long.'

When she entered the parlour, Leah scanned the modest room as best she could in the darkness of the afternoon. The shutters were closed. The only light to be seen was cast by a single candle. As her eyes adjusted to the dimly lit room, Leah could find no trace of liquor or tobacco. To her surprise, the sparsely furnished room was tidy, save for the books piled higgledy-piggledy on the bare wooden floor.

Noticing Leah take in her surroundings, Williams cleared his throat. 'I was waiting for my wife to arrive,' he said. 'She would have known better than I what a parlour needs.' He spoke cautiously, Leah noted, as though each utterance was weighed and assessed before leaving his mouth.

'You enjoy reading, Mister Williams?'

He nodded. She looked at him expectantly, but he elaborated no further.

'I have brought this for you.' Leah placed the basket on a stack of books that was piled between them. Williams stood with his back against the wall, hands stiff at his sides. It seemed such an unnatural pose for the lean, fluid man she remembered from meeting. 'My mother thought you may be in need ...'

She halted as she remembered his declaration upon opening the door.

'You can do what you like with the prayer book,' she said. 'But I baked the bread and had a hand in making the cheese. I can attest to the quality of both.'

Williams took a small step towards her and touched the handle of the basket. Leah believed she caught the glimmer of a smile through his sandy beard, but she couldn't be certain. His face was in shadow. She was confident, however, that his posture had softened a little.

'Thank you. I'm obliged.' Williams moved forward into the light and she considered his face. In his eyes, she now only saw loneliness.

'There's no need to be,' Leah said. 'I'll call again tomorrow at the same time. I will bring a pie for your supper and a pair of woollen stockings I intended for my father ...' she glanced at his feet then raised an eyebrow, '... but I think you are more in need of them.'

Without waiting for a response, she turned and walked to the door. Leah took her cloak from Maria who hurriedly followed her sister's departure. When Leah reached the woods she looked back. Williams stood at the entrance. He raised his hand before closing the door. The following day when she returned, he had bathed and attired himself in shoes and a coat she recognised from meeting. The books, too, were ordered more neatly around the perimeter of the parlour.

'Mama,' eight-year-old Elizabeth said now from the opposite side of the table, 'may I have some more?'

Leah nodded distractedly.

'Tell me about your sister, Leah,' Bellamy said, turning in his chair. 'How does she spend her time? Of what does she dream?'

Bellamy's question hovered annoyingly over the table like a persistent turkey gnat. The conversation's twist having stifled her appetite, Leah pushed her bowl towards her daughter more firmly than she had intended. The contents splashed the table. She sighed in consternation before looking at the lodger and answering.

'I'm not privy to my sister's dreams, Mister Bellamy.'

Caleb tugged at Leah's bodice, hoping for refreshment. She hastily brushed her son's small hand away from her breast.

'Aye, but you would know her as well as anyone ...'

'Finish your supper children,' Leah said, irritated. Her daughter looked to her mother in confusion. 'It's late and you all need your rest. You've had a very exciting day.'

She hurriedly ushered her children upstairs. Palgrave stood and walked slowly to the mantle where his pipe and its fixings were located. Once his pipe was filled and lit, he turned to his guest, a half-smile evident across his thin lips.

'Don't chase Maria,' Palgrave advised matter-of-factly. 'Joseph Hallett lost one daughter. He's not going to give over the other. When Leah married me, she severed herself from her family. It was a trying time for everyone and the sorrow it heaped on her mother brought on her death. Leah was devastated. She repents for it daily. I hear her prayers in the evening when she thinks no-one is listening.' Palgrave shook his head. 'Leah isn't going to aid you in your quest.'

'What is it about me that makes me so undesirable a prospect?' Bellamy asked.

Palgrave laughed. 'Everything. You're penniless, homeless and not of the church. What's more, you're a stranger. You might as well be an Indian.'

Bellamy frowned.

'If you want to have a life here, Sam, you must remember one thing,' Palgrave said. 'These people are cautious and untrusting. Fathers seek out the wisest match for their children, not the most passionate.

'Joseph Hallett is an honest man, but he ...' Palgrave searched his mind for an instant for the appropriate adjective, 'but he's elementary. The intricacies of the heart are beyond him. To him, marriage is as simple as animal husbandry.'

This appraisal forced a grin to Bellamy's lips.

'You and Leah,' Bellamy said after a moment. 'I can see passion there.'

'We're different,' Palgrave said.

'How?'

Palgrave cast a fleeting glance at the door before he began.

'I came to the colony twelve years ago. My wife and children were to follow when I'd established a home, a livelihood,' he explained. 'One year later I sent for them. All three perished on the voyage from England. I turned from God, turned from the town. Reverend Dent was threatening exile. Then Leah came to this house with a basket of food and her own prayer book. Within a few months we were married.'

Bellamy was silent, waiting for more. Palgrave was aware his tale was stark of detail and frustrating to the listener, but he couldn't expand further. There were aspects of his relationship with Leah that remained incomprehensible even to him.

'Men are crawling over each other for Maria's hand – young men who were born here, who will inherit farms. Or have found for themselves ministries in Beverly.'

'You mean Silas Dent?' Bellamy had heard the young minister's name mentioned a few times since arriving in Eastham. It was always with a tone of optimism.

'Aye,' Palgrave sat and crossed his willowy limbs. 'He's the most likely prospect. Maria's aware that her future was charted long ago. What's more, Reverend Dent, Silas's father, is a hard-hearted man whose congregation is shrinking. He will push for this marriage, hoping it will shore up his ministry.'

'Life is certainly complicated in Eastham.'

'You don't know the half of it, my friend,' Palgrave puffed on his pipe making contemplative smoke rings. 'Give up on her. It's a hopeless cause. When you have your farm, return to England and find yourself a wife if no-one else here appeals. It's the only sensible course.'

Bellamy was downcast and tapped his fingertips on the table as he considered Palgrave's counsel. He raised his head after a moment and looked squarely into the clear eyes of his confidante.

'Would you have given Leah up?'

Palgrave placed his pipe in his mouth and breathed in deeply. He expelled the smoke slowly before answering.

'Never. I would die for that woman. I owe her my life.'

5

———

'More pie,' Reverend Dent called to Abby without removing his eyes from his plate. 'More?' he questioned his son, tilting his head an inch.

'Nay, thank you, Abby,' Silas said, making a point of looking at the slave as he placed his spoon across his plate. 'The pie was lovely but I have no appetite.'

'What troubles you tonight?' she questioned, heaping another serving of pie onto the minister's plate.

She spoke perfect English in a deep, honeyed timbre. When the minister had brought Abby to Eastham from Providence years ago, Silas's mother had made it her business to teach the then nine-year-old Indian the tongue of the colony. Goody Dent would not suffer a savage in her home. If the child was going to be their house slave, she was to speak English. Three months later, through the kindness and understanding of Goody Dent, Abby was confidently reciting the psalms to her mistress each evening. 'You can't beat goodness into a child', she explained to her husband, who was fond of taking a leather strap to the child's legs when she had, at first, refused to speak.

'Well, Abby,' Silas took a deep breath and folded his napkin on the table. 'This concerns you as well as father.'

The minister raised his head but continued to eat. Silas prolonged the suspense a moment longer. Abby was proud of the young man she had raised. Neither of the minister's subsequent wives had felt the calling to assist in the rearing of their stepson. That suited her just fine. In a life made barren by circumstance, Silas was her greatest pleasure and achievement.

'I have asked Maria Hallett for her hand in marriage,' Silas said. Perhaps a little doubtfully, it seemed to Abby.

She walked to Silas and squeezed him gently on the shoulder with her broad, copper-coloured hand but waited to comment until the minister had had his say. Although Dent's house had been her home for thirty years, the minister never let Abby forgot she was still a slave.

'Well done, boy!' he exclaimed. 'She's a grand prize. There was that unfortunate business with her sister and the silversmith ... although that seems to have worked to our advantage. Maria Hallett is a fine girl and Joseph ...'

'I know, father,' Silas said, before the minister could state that Joseph Hallett was one of the wealthiest men in the colony. 'But I have asked for Maria's hand because I love her.' He paused, as if gathering strength.

'Because she is the only woman I will ever love.' Silas directed this heartfelt declaration more to Abby than his father.

'I'm sure that's the case,' Dent commented. 'But you cannot ignore breeding and the implications for the future.'

'I'm so pleased,' Abby said, tactically cutting short Dent's misplaced enthusiasm. 'Maria is a beautiful and pious young woman. She will make a splendid wife.' Silas placed his own hand on Abby's, which still rested on his shoulder.

'Have you spoken to Joseph Hallett?' Dent asked, resuming his supper.

Silas had called at the Hallett's farm before meeting Maria that afternoon. As was the custom to ease the way into courtship, Silas had purchased a gift for Hallett, a small book on the subject of plant hybridisation, an interest of the farmer's. Although friendly enough and mildly interested in Silas's Harvard studies, Hallett had eyed the young man's suit with caution and inquired about the cost. He had raised a doubtful eyebrow at Silas's reply, crushing the young man's nerve. Silas departed without accomplishing his objective, the book remaining concealed in his pocket.

Abby sensed Silas's shoulders stiffen as he removed his hand from hers, placing it back on the table. She rounded the ornately carved mahogany structure and stood facing the young man, her arms folded across her chest and her smooth brow wrinkled with concern. Silas stared at her before beginning.

'Maria did not accept,' he said. 'But I'm hopeful she will soon.'

Abby's tan bosom heaved with sympathy. There was very little Silas could conceal from her. She knew his disposition intimately and felt his confusion and distress.

Reverend Dent pushed away the remnants of his meal. Only a few crumbs remained on the surface of the Saint-Cloud plate that he had purchased on a recent trip to Boston. It was the plate's blue lambrequin edging that Silas fixed his attention on now.

'How *did* the girl reply?' Dent asked, brushing his cravat free of crumbs.

'She said that my plan was a fine one but that she must think on it first.'

Silas had considered and reconsidered the events at the

willow many times in the past few hours. He had measured and deliberated upon Maria's every turn of phrase, each word and the stress of each syllable with the same diligence he applied to his studies at Harvard College.

'What's there to think on?' Dent's right eye twitched momentarily. 'Maria Hallett could do no better than you.'

Abby held her tongue but her dark, almond-shaped eyes darted between father and son.

Silas struggled to remain buoyant in the face of his father's admonitions. 'I admit,' he went on, fingering the silverware in front of him. 'I had not planned to propose to her now but the events of the afternoon led me to that end. I believe the declaration of my love startled her, yes, but I am hopeful, confident, she will consent ... soon, if not imme-diately.'

Reverend Dent rose from the table.

'You must take what you believe is yours! She's a wilful one but you must break her. If Maria Hallett cannot see the path that is true and clear then you must show her God's way.'

Silas nodded, unconvinced. He could not remember ever being able to persuade Maria Hallett of anything. Furthermore, Maria was right – their betrothal was an assumption, incited and promoted by his father. The minister had discussed the union for so long that it had become fact for the young man and most of the town.

Abby silently began stacking the dishes on the table.

'There's no other way. At times the road is foggy, murky,' Dent said. 'Once it is illuminated for her, Maria Hallett will plainly see that to marry you is preordained by God.'

Silas watched Abby's steady movement around the parlour, comforted by her graceful progress from table to sideboard and back to table.

'What say you?' his father questioned. A series of deep creases appeared on his high, smooth brow.

'I will speak with Joseph Hallett tomorrow. I will show Maria the way.'

'That you will,' the minister stated.

Before he left the room, Dent looked conspicuously at both his son and slave, satisfied with the outcome of the exchange.

'Hasten with my tea, Abby,' the minister called from the hallway.

The slave and Silas glanced at each other quickly. Abby had fixed the minister a mug of chamomile tea every night since she was brought into the home. In fact, it was Silas's mother who had instructed the Indian in the making of the brew. She had advised that adding a few sprigs of lemon balm to the pot would aid the minister's digestion. In thirty years, Abby had not strayed from the recipe. In thirty years she could not recall the minister uttering a single 'thank you' for her efforts.

Once the tea was delivered, Abby continued with her chores while Silas meditated at the table. When the room began to darken he lit the candles fixed to the walls.

'What say you on this matter?' Silas asked.

Abby paused before responding, ordering her thoughts. The situation was not as clear-cut as the minister believed.

'I helped in the birthing of Maria Hallett,' Abby began. 'It was difficult. She had a twin brother who died without taking a breath. After Leah, her poor mother, Elizabeth, had such testing confinements. There was a boy who perished within hours of entering this world, and then another child who was born too soon. Maria was a true blessing from God.'

Silas waited for Abby to conclude.

'These deaths weigh heavily on the family, as does the passing of Elizabeth Hallett. Then, of course, there was Leah's marriage to the silversmith. Another loss...'

Abby wanted Silas to understand the undercurrents flowing through the Hallett family. Joseph Hallett cherished his daughters and had kept them close, Maria especially so. He raised them to be intelligent and strong-willed with the view to them marrying like-minded men who would, on Hallett's death, inherit his property. In truth, it did not surprise Abby that Maria needed time to consider the prospect of marrying Silas Dent.

Nothing was as simple as Silas hoped.

Abby sat and took Silas's hand. She examined his thin fingers then gently turned them so she could view his silken palm.

'You have never been tested, Silas,' Abby said. 'See clearly and choose wisely. The heart can be a trusted ally or a formidable enemy.'

'I will speak with Mister Hallett tomorrow.'

Silas stood and kissed Abby on the forehead before retiring. She watched him retreat from the kitchen then went on with her chores, fearing the paths Silas and his father had chosen were neither particularly clear nor true.

6

Maria appeared solemn as her father said grace. She bent her head and could feel the steam rising from the plate, dampening her face. The day's events had left her with a fierce hunger and she willed her father's thanks to be brief. She was flattered that a man like Samuel Bellamy had courted her favour. Eyes closed in prayer, she pictured his fingers manoeuvring the small knife around the apple as he sliced it and she recalled the welling fullness of his voice. Finally, when she heard her father murmur 'Amen' she quickly echoed his words and, breaking his grasp, began her supper.

Joseph Hallett, his daughter and their servant Hannah ate in silence for a moment until he rested his fork on the edge of his plate. He looked to Maria and forced his lips into a smile.

'What has made you so ravenous?' he asked.

'I went into town with Leah, just as I said. There was music and some games for the children. Then we had a picnic by Long Pond.'

The slightest trace of disapproval flashed across his ruddy

face, an expression that only a daughter accustomed to her father's peeves and moods would notice. There were many things of which Joseph Hallett did not approve – a public day of thanksgiving was one of them. Although he indulged Maria and permitted her to venture into town with her sister, he insisted on remaining on the farm to work. Although he had no contact with his other daughter, he trusted Leah's judgement where her sister was concerned. A straightforward farmer who had come to prosper late in life, Hallett found balancing clemency with Maria's moral integrity exhausting.

'I'm grateful for your permission,' Maria added. Aware that her father had also granted his labourers a day of rest to enjoy the festivities, she looked at him lovingly. Hallett cleared his throat in reply and looked at his plate.

'Silas Dent called by this afternoon,' Hallett said. Hannah's eyes left her plate as she glanced at her employer. Maria's expression darkened immediately. 'He described the bout between Judah Doane and a stranger, a seaman he thought. He mentioned he saw you.'

Maria nodded testily.

'Were you aware of his homecoming, Maria?' Hannah asked. 'Did he write you?'

The young woman shrugged as she forced one more spoonful of stew into her mouth. Maria did not want to think about Silas. His proposal and his visit were worrisome.

'Would you like another helping?' Hannah said. Maria replied that she did not and pushed her plate away, disappointed her appetite had so suddenly vanished.

'There was more he wanted to say, I could tell,' Hallett continued slowly, searching his daughter's face. Maria eyed him dispassionately.

'You make him anxious, that's all,' she said. 'It has always been so. You've never made a secret of your feelings towards his father.'

'He needs to grow a tougher hide,' Hallett returned to his meal. 'I have no objections to the boy.'

'He's a man now.'

Maria strummed her fingers gently on the sturdy oak table as she waited for her father and Hannah to finish. The second he laid his spoon across his plate she excused herself, fearful that the subject of Silas Dent would be revisited.

MARIA SAT in the middle of her bed and stared at the white wall opposite. Although she had attempted to push it from her thoughts, Silas's proposal troubled her greatly.

She reached out and picked up the Bible that lay by her bed. She handled the pages restlessly for a minute before replacing the book on the nightstand. With her palms together as if preparing to pray, she noticed the paint on her wrist. It was the ocean that she had been attempting to reproduce on paper – the roll of the water against Eastham's cliffs. Maria touched her lips softly with her fingertips. A faint knock sounded at her door.

'May I come in?'

Maria stood and opened the door. Hallett's expression was dour but not dispassionate. She permitted him entry.

'Has Silas Dent asked for your hand?' he asked without delay.

Maria studied his face for a moment, unsure how to respond. She did not consider Silas's request a formal proposal, and he had not sought her father's permission. Wasn't he merely flirting with the notion?

'Do not lie to me, Maria. Remember the Commandments, girl.'

Her father rarely used the Commandments as a child-rearing tool, preferring to believe that if God were in the hearts of His people, they wouldn't need reminding of their piety. Maria turned to her window. The sun was only now setting behind the barn. The sky was aflame with brilliant amber light. She had not forgotten her Commandments. She had never had any difficulty in abiding by the Ninth Commandment before. Why was speaking the truth so punishing today?

'Not in so many words,' she answered without turning from the window. 'He spoke of a future together, but there are matters I must dwell upon.'

Joseph Hallett emitted a low sound from his diaphragm, part sigh, part groan. Maria turned.

'What the devil is there to dwell upon?' he asked.

'I don't love Silas as a wife should.'

'But you do love him?' Hallett was struggling to make sense of her feelings.

'With all my heart, but as I would love a brother. I wish for something more.'

'It's enough,' he stated, hoping it would be the last word on the subject.

'It is not!' she cried without thinking. 'You have never hidden your dislike of Reverend Dent. Why is it paramount that I marry his son?'

'Do not raise your voice to me, child.' Maria immediately lowered her eyes.

'How do you know it's not enough?' Hallett said, more

gently. 'Silas Dent is a hard-working, God-fearing man and he loves you. Any fool can see that.'

She did not speak.

'You have known him your entire life, Maria. He has a ministry in Beverly. It's the best you can do. What more do you want?' her father, growing impatient again, demanded.

How could Maria articulate to her father all that was contained in Samuel Bellamy's kiss? It wasn't necessarily Samuel she pined for now, but feelings were stirred and an intoxicating spectrum of possibilities were sparked when his lips had met her skin. How could she explain that? Maria barely understood it herself.

Hallett raised his daughter's chin roughly in his exasperation. She flinched. 'Then it's settled. Once Silas Dent has requested your hand, I will allow his courtship of you to begin. Look to God to find your way. You are lost.'

Maria met her father's unrelenting scrutiny with tearless eyes. It was Joseph Hallett who broke their gaze when he departed. Father and daughter did not read from the scriptures, as was their evening ritual, that night.

7

When she heard the door shut at the back of the house, Maria raised her eyes from her sketch. She glanced at the lantern clock on the wall. *Tick tock*. It was too early for her father to be returning for dinner and she could hear the brush of Hannah's broom through the floorboards upstairs. Maria hastily rolled the paper, secured it with a piece of string and placed it in a basket along with her pastels. She had been working on the picture all morning. The vine of yellow starflowers creeping diagonally across the page was almost complete. Her private resolutions of the night before had come to naught and she had shared a strained breakfast with her father and Hannah in the morning. Retreating to the parlour when he had departed to the fields, Maria had attempted to ignore her father's demands. *Surely, he wouldn't force me to marry Silas*, she thought, as she counted down the minutes until her meeting with Mister Bellamy ... Samuel ... *Sam*. Nevertheless, the idea of marrying Silas Dent rested heavily with her.

When Joseph Hallett, Silas and Reverend Dent appeared in the doorway of the parlour Maria remained seated on the window seat, fearing her legs would buckle if she attempted to rise. The warmth from Silas's smile did little to soften the grimness of her father's expression. The men entered the room. Hallett moved within a few inches of his daughter. She rose cautiously, brushed her fingers down the front of her skirt and stood before him with her hands locked in front of her.

'Silas has asked for your hand,' Joseph Hallett stated. 'I have given my permission. You shall be married within the month.'

So quick.

Hallett rocked slightly on his feet, waiting for his daughter to raise her voice in protest, as though he were inviting her to challenge his authority. Maria looked from him to Silas who stood slightly behind, his hat clutched in his hands. Today he was dressed in more commonplace garb, a sober brown homespun suit. His eyes pleaded for her submission. Maria could discern nothing on the minister's face except the smug composure of one whose fiscal future was suddenly assured. His hopes of uniting his family with the Halletts had never been concealed.

Remaining outwardly collected, Maria was silent, the blow muddling her thoughts. Her father's perspicuous tone, the rigidity of his stance and his flint-like face showed her the futility in raising any objection, far more than any words he'd spoken. They remained in this impasse for some time as Maria refused to verbalise her acceptance. She could not. While she longed to please Silas with an utterance of enthusiasm for their marriage, even the smallest nod of agreement, she could not.

'It's settled then,' Hallett announced, turning to Silas and his father and shaking their hands. 'We will leave you alone now. The minister and I will discuss what's necessary.'

Without even a glance at Maria, the fathers decamped to negotiate her dowry and her nuptial lot. Her eyes narrowed with resentment as she imagined the minister haggling over Silas's share of her eventual inheritance.

Silas threw his hat on her mother's rocking chair and moved to Maria directly, taking her hands in his. 'I will make you happy, Maria. I promise.'

'I know you'll work tirelessly to that end, Silas,' Maria said, 'but why so fast? Are we to have no courtship?'

She pulled away from his grasp and walked to the window.

'It will be better this way.'

Maria looked at the fields beyond, heat rippling in the distance like a heaving sea, sensing herself being drawn, pulled towards a whirlpool.

'Oh, Silas,' she said, pleading. 'I'm not ready. You are not the one.'

Maria had said more than she should.

'How do you know?' he said, smiling, undeterred. 'Once we're established in Beverly you'll see differently. Then children will come ...'

Maria groaned in annoyance.

'I've been offered a glimpse of real feeling, a sensation in my heart, in my entire body, that I've never experienced with you.'

The remark stung. She saw his eyes flutter.

'I don't know if it's love or whether it will last, but how can I ignore it?'

'Who is the man?'

'It matters not.'

'It's merely a fancy,' Silas said, waving away the idea with a flick of his hand. 'When we're in Beverly your feelings will change.'

'What if they don't?' Maria said. 'Will you be content with a wife who has no wifely love for you?'

Silas didn't respond. Instead he walked to the fireplace and gently fingered the edge of the mantelpiece. *Tick tock.*

'I beg of you, Silas, as my oldest and dearest friend, release me from this union.' Maria stepped towards him. 'Tell your father now that we're not to be married!'

Silas turned and brushed her cheek with the back of his hand. Unwilling to free her but unable to stand firm, he echoed the words of his father. 'That will not do. I will show you the way that is true and clear. We will marry within the month.' His retreat to the door was halted when Maria clutched at his arm.

'I will not marry you.'

Ignoring her declaration, he pulled free of her grasp then walked to her basket and kicked it over. Her pastels spilled across the spotless wooden floor. He picked up the drawing over which she had laboured that morning and untied the fastening.

After studying the page for a moment he ordered, 'This will stop!' He forced the picture into her face, threatening and demeaning. It was thick with the scent of colour, oily against her lips. 'There'll be no more of this!' Then he hurled the paper to the ground and straightened his coat. It was almost comical to see Silas adopt such a tone, such mannerisms. He was play-acting, but badly. She almost felt sorry for him.

Equanimity seemingly restored, he strode from the room and slammed the door behind him.

Maria bent to her knees and serenely placed the pastels back in the basket then carefully examined her delicate illustration for smudges.

~

MARIA DIDN'T RAISE the subject of her marriage to Silas Dent with anyone for the next two days. In that period she did not leave the house nor did she sketch or paint. Instead she thought hard and prayed tirelessly on the union. Forgoing sleep, she had pored over her Bible, determined to find peace with her future. It was best for all if she conceded, she told herself. She wasn't as strong as Leah. Her efforts and contemplation were only interrupted by the presence of Reverend Dent in the parlour for an hour each day at ten o'clock. The idea irritated her that the rest of her life was being deliberated upon and designed by the two men downstairs. As she struggled to find peace with the notion, an image of Mister Bellamy waiting by the witch-hazel would intrude on her thoughts. The knowledge of what she was sacrificing gave force to unrestrained tears.

On the third day Reverend Dent and his son arrived promptly at ten. Maria was not expecting Silas to call and was told by her father to sit in the parlour with her intended while he discussed matters with the minister in the kitchen. Maria's reticence to discuss their marriage combined with Silas's enthusiasm for the subject made for an excruciating hour. At noontide Maria neither spoke to her father nor ate the rich pork pie Hannah had made for dinner.

~

JOSEPH HALLETT PLUNGED his knife into the pastry and meticulously cut the pie into quarters. He longed for the presence of his wife. He could not grasp the intricacies of a woman's heart. It was obvious his daughter was pained and, considering himself a practical father and not a cruel one, he saw no reason to punish her by dwelling on the situation. He believed staunchly that he was acting in her best interests and planned to wait until the following day before he mentioned the marriage again. She needed time to accept her fate, he figured. He would not see Maria married to a man like Palgrave Williams, a man with no prospects. He should have fought harder for Leah. He should have run Palgrave Williams from the town.

He glanced at his daughter, her hands folded in her lap, her pie untouched.

Returning to his meal, Hallett inventoried the reasons why Maria's marriage to Silas was the only course. He had lost one daughter and, in the process, five grandchildren. He knew he must tread delicately with his second but he lacked the emotional finesse to do so. Both of his daughters were wilful, he had raised them to be so, but it required a deft hand to control them.

As Hannah stacked the dishes, Maria asked her father if she might visit Leah. Hallett agreed, relieved that she might receive the womanly counsel that was beyond his reach. He was certain Leah would encourage her to marry Silas. Leah had followed her heart but she would urge her sister to be rational.

'Would you like to take the gig?' he asked gently.

Unwilling to appease his conscience with a polite response, she quietly rose and left the table.

WHEN MARIA STEPPED from the house, she was struck by the solid blanket of cloud that hung low in the sky. The sun was confined to the opposite side of the chalky shroud; a meagre, tawny haze the only evidence of its habitual rising.

The atmosphere was dense and the air still and noiseless. The only sound to be heard was the faint hum of crickets in the distance. She looked to the fields. No-one was working. Four labourers sat in a line with their backs against the wall of the barn. Nothing seemed natural about the day. Lying was the only action that seemed normal.

It wasn't Maria's intention to visit her sister. Leah, forever practical, would advise in favour of the union, a match that Maria could no longer consider. But Leah had been idealistic once. She walked slowly to the woods and remembered Silas's behaviour in the sitting room two days before. He had transformed into a grotesque imitation of his father. It galled and sickened her to see him so altered. Compassion, charity and affection had vanished from her friend in that instant. Yet today, he had been like the Silas of old and she wondered whether this duality was usual, part of God's puzzling design, or something else.

She discovered relief from the heat immediately upon setting foot in the forest. Maria stopped for a moment and breathed deeply of the damp, cool air before making her way to the willow.

THE YOUNG MINISTER had farewelled his father at the junction in the road about a mile from the Hallett home. Jumping from the carriage, he said he was going to walk the rest of the way into town. He watched his father's carriage continue down the left spike of the fork. Silas, setting foot along the right, soon found himself in the willow on the same branch that he had sat with Maria on the day of the celebrations.

On high, the faint suggestion of a breeze, not even

enough to stir the leaves, gradually cooled him and dried his clammy skin.

Silas was uncertain how many minutes he had been in the tree when he heard the soft crunch of leaves below him. Before long, he saw Maria come into view. Walking to the river she produced a small lace handkerchief from her shirt-sleeve then bent low to soak it in the water. When she rose she stood by the willow's trunk for a minute contemplating, he thought, whether or not to climb the tree. He wanted her to join him, but at the same time willed her not to. It had been awkward when he met with her that morning. Her anguish was clear. Despite his best efforts to ease her mind, he had noted a certain trepidation in her behaviour. He realised that she was afraid of him.

He regretted his loss of control. Thrusting the sketch into her face, raising his voice as he had was unforgivable. Silas identified desire as his provocateur. Unable to attain Maria, he had fallen upon his vilest instincts. What a fraud he was. In truth, he found Maria's sketches wonderful, a glimpse into her heart, a taste of her soul. But she was stubborn and he would have to limit her freedoms to break her. Only then could she be refashioned by his own hand.

Now she sat at the base of the tree, legs crossed, head resting against the bark. Wearing a light brown skirt and bodice, Maria unbuttoned the high collar of her blouse and eased the garment open to her shoulders. Silas watched her dab the ivory skin of her chest with the handkerchief. Then she sighed and closed her eyes. After a few minutes he noticed her head drop. He moved along the branch silently then climbed down several feet onto a platform formed by a number of intertwining branches. Here he sat and watched her sleep, noting the rise and fall of every breath, every twitch and quiver.

When Maria awoke, she stood quickly and checked a small, open-faced watch she retrieved from her pocket. Silas had never seen her with the timepiece before. *Tick tock.* Time was usually of no concern to Maria. Then she brushed the leaves from her skirt and hurried off in the direction of Long Pond.

After lowering himself to the ground, he checked his own watch. It was fifteen minutes to five. He wanted to call to her, explain his actions, hold her in his arms. But he didn't; suspicion gagged any kindly inclination. He wondered why she was heading further into the forest, in the opposite direction to her home. Silas left the willow and followed Maria silently through the trees.

8

'I knew you'd be here,' she said.

'I've been here every day at five o'clock. I was certain you'd come, eventually.'

'Everything's turned sour,' she said, gaining comfort in his arms. Although this was only their second encounter, it seemed to Maria they had grown closer during their separation.

Bellamy rested his head on hers and tightened his hold. But he soon raised his chin, startled by a noise coming from a dense thicket of milkweed a short distance away.

'What's wrong?' she asked.

'I heard something.' He took a step towards the thicket. 'A rustle.'

Maria moved into a position in front of Bellamy where she could see his view more clearly. She investigated the scene for a moment then turned back to him.

'It's nothing but a hummingbird supping from the milkweed. They hover just above the flower as they drink. Come.' She gestured for Bellamy to join her. 'See, it's just the flutter of its wings that caused the sound you heard.'

Bellamy studied the tiny bird's frantic efforts. 'By heavens! Those wings are going at a rate of knots!'

He examined the dusky-green-chested bird further. 'Surely it's wasted exertion. The wee thing would have to drink all day to gather energy enough to keep those wings moving at such a pace.'

'Aye,' Maria kept her eyes on the bird. It was no longer than her middle finger. 'My father once told me that a hummingbird is always only hours away from starvation even though it feeds endlessly.'

'Then it makes no sense. It would be wiser to rest and conserve energy...' Bellamy shook his head, puzzled. 'What a beautiful, strange little creature it is. But it defies nature. They defy death.'

'They are just one of God's miracles.'

Bellamy laughed. 'I would say they were more closely aligned with the Devil.'

'Indeed,' she agreed, nodding thoughtfully. She had never considered the bird's life unnatural. Despite living on the brink of death, a hummingbird's existence was a long one. Maria recalled her mother's claim that a crimson-breasted hummingbird visited the goldenrod that stood outside her kitchen daily for at least ten years. Maria, at six years of age, had questioned her mother, asking, 'How do you know it's the same bird?' Her mother had replied that the bird had told her so. The hummingbird had also informed her one springtide day how he loved the taste of the goldenrod's dark, sweet nectar best of all.

Maria watched the bird's flight to another section of the thicket. Bellamy took her hand. 'Now, little hummingbird, let's sit and you can tell me what troubles you.'

The couple settled in the same place they had first come together a few days before. Over the next few minutes Maria related to Bellamy everything that had occurred since their last meeting. With each word that passed her lips she reaped an extra grain of confidence and certainty in the direction of her future. Away from her father, Reverend Dent, Silas and the heavy burden of their demands, the prospect of marrying her childhood friend seemed ludicrous. She couldn't believe she'd even considered the match. *This* was now her reality; *this* was God's plan.

'I can't marry him. Yet, I can't see a way out.'

'Don't be daft,' Bellamy said. 'There is always a way out. Marry me instead.'

The surety in his tone made her smile. The curling of her lips seemed foreign; it was a sensation she had not experienced for a number of days.

'What amuses you?'

'Was that a marriage proposal, Samuel Bellamy?'

'It was.'

They sat together, each thinking their separate yet convergent thoughts, like intersecting currents at the shoreline. After a few minutes Maria was the first to speak.

'You're too impulsive. We barely know each other. We've not even spoken of love.'

'You're correct on all accounts.'

'But I cannot tarry or I'll be wed to Silas. I warrant Reverend Dent will already have the notice pinned to the meeting house door.'

'Palgrave described your father as practical,' Bellamy said after a moment, choosing his words as carefully as Williams had. 'We'll go to him. He may not approve of your marriage to me right now, but surely he'll not bind you to a man you do not, and cannot, love.'

Maria's heart lifted at the merest speck of hope that Bellamy's words offered her. It was only time that she would request from her father, nothing more. Time for her attachment to the newcomer to grow, and time for Samuel to buy an acreage and gain a foothold in Eastham. *But will father afford me that time?* Maria wondered. Since he had cast Leah from his home, she'd never seen him so resolute in a decision. Unlike her sister, Maria could not defy her father. The notion ran contrary to everything she had been taught to believe.

Silas watched Maria and Bellamy from behind a silky dogwood. He recognised the stranger immediately from the quarterstaff bout. In the still hush of the afternoon he had heard every word perfectly. The clarity of each syllable smarted. His artful design for the rest of his life was fast being erased and redrawn by the more adept hand of this dark-haired stranger. He struggled ineffectively to recall the confidence that had sat so comfortably alongside his thoughts on the journey from Cambridge to Eastham. Panic clawed at his throat. His knees dropped into the dirt. With his head lowered and hands clutched so tightly his knuckles turned white, he silently and viciously damned Samuel Bellamy for his arrival in Eastham and cursed Maria for her caprice. Rage burned in his chest and beads of sweat fell from his face, pitting the earth like the first solid raindrops preceding a storm. When he heard Maria's voice again he had no idea how long he had been gripped in this profane rendering of prayer.

'Or we could leave Eastham,' Maria suggested, turning to Bellamy. Silas raised his head and looked towards the couple. 'Perhaps travel to Boston or New York or even further ...'

Bellamy responded immediately, cutting short her proposal. 'If we're to do this, we shall do it properly. We shall go immediately and speak with your father. I've taken too many shortcuts in the past.'

'I doubt that Papa will listen to you. He's practical, that is a surety, but he's also obstinate.' Maria shook her head in hopelessness. 'I love my father and I have been taught to revere him.'

She rose. 'I fear my loyalty and my education will lead me into a marriage I cannot abide.'

'I can't leave Eastham,' Bellamy said after a moment's thought.

Maria turned to him. 'What do you mean?'

Bellamy exhaled loudly and stared for some minutes across the water before speaking. A mottled, beaver-coloured bittern loped through the shallows, systematically plunging its needle-like bill into the mud.

'It's true I'm a carpenter and it's a fact that I was born in Devon. I was also apprenticed to a joiner.' He paused. Maria could see the hesitance in his expression, yet he continued. 'Then when I was twenty, just one year from completing my apprenticeship, I joined the Royal Navy.'

'Why?'

Bellamy threw a stone carelessly into the lake. 'A carpenter's skills are highly prized on His Majesty's fleet, or so a pamphlet I found in a Billingsgate tavern told me. I thought I would see the world and line my pockets at the same time. That's what the pamphlet led me to believe. Five pounds a month I was promised. But as soon as the man-of-war set sail, it became clear what I had signed on for. Slavery. Yet, the king doesn't call it so when you're thrown a daily ration of salt beef crawling with maggots and a chunk of bread blue with mould.'

Maria didn't know how to respond. Without knowledge or experience of the world outside Eastham, words of comfort, or of consolation, would not come to her. Instead, she knelt beside him and took his hand.

'After a month on board I recall being taken to the captain, a pugnacious brute named Howe. I argued for my life. I argued that the *Royal Sovereign* would be my prison.'

Bellamy paused for a moment as he brought the captain's exact words to mind.

'Howe replied, "You're correct, lad. For being in a ship is being in a gaol, except with the chance of being drowned."'

Bellamy shrugged. Despite the anecdote Maria remained puzzled, struggling to believe that such a brand of cold-hearted barbarity existed in the world.

'Will you pray with me?'

'Your god would offer me no comfort. I've been alone in the world for a long time.'

'But now it's *us*.'

Bellamy rose and pulled Maria to her feet. 'My darling girl, I deserted the Royal Navy. I chose Eastham for its isolation. I daren't show my face in Boston or New York. There's likely a price on my head and it would be the gallows if I returned to England.'

Bellamy examined her expression closely, waiting for her to react but her face was as still as the pond before them. She stared into his eyes and deliberated on what further secrets he was hiding and whether she was brave enough to discover them. *Was this a sign?* she wondered. Samuel and Silas – the two men could not be more different.

'Kiss me again,' she said, finally.

He lifted her hands but she shook her head, stepping towards him and raising her face to his. Bellamy leant in and kissed her tenderly on the lips. Maria closed her eyes as the very essence of her soul ignited with possibility. Bellamy released her and kissed her gently on the forehead.

'We shall do as you suggest,' she said, 'and go to Papa. Now.'

As the two departed the pond and headed towards the home of Joseph Hallett, Silas emerged from behind the dogwood, his eyes ablaze with reborn optimism.

9

Bellamy and Maria stood in the parlour waiting for Hallett's response. Once Maria had finished outlining their situation and describing the only way she could see forward, Hallett drew his pipe from his shirt pocket, lit it and sat purposefully in the black cherry rocking chair he had crafted for Maria's mother. Bellamy's eyes journeyed from Maria's reassuring glances to Hallett's inscrutable mien to the lantern clock that hung on the wall above the mantelpiece. *Tick tock.* Bellamy shifted his position. Joseph Hallett could see that the young man wanted to speak and state his case – address him on an equal footing as any other man would. Hallett could tell this from Bellamy's clenched jaw and the perspiration on his upper lip. But, he judged, Maria would have warned the young man against such a confrontation. Hallett glanced at the clock. *Tick tock.*

Earlier, as Maria pleaded her case, her father had admired her grace and precision. Taking his hands and holding his gaze, Maria's tone was gentle and sincere, yet the words she chose were drenched with passion. But it was not of the overwrought, unreasonable sort. He realised then that she wasn't a headstrong girl any longer. She was a young woman, determined to find peace in her heart and home. And this realisation softened his initial outrage. Now, he shifted his gaze once more to the clock. *Tick tock.*

Hallett began to rock the chair gently. The unexpectedness of the movement garnered the attention of his daughter and Bellamy, but Joseph Hallett wasn't yet ready to speak. Despite his dislike of the minister, Silas Dent was the sensible choice. Maria's future would be secure as the esteemed wife of a respectable minister. Silas would neither stray nor abuse her. Hallett's obligations as a father would be fulfilled and he could rest knowing his daughter was well disposed and settled in the world.

Hallett drew deeply on his pipe. Yes, Silas loved his daughter, but there was no love on Maria's side. And, as a member of the church, he could not ignore his daughter's wishes and insist on a marriage in which she could not fulfil her duty of loving her mate. He looked at his daughter briefly. She bore little resemblance to her mother, unlike Leah. His eldest daughter resembled Elizabeth in both appearance and bearing. However, when Maria had fixed her gaze on him earlier and spoken so openly, his heart had welled with all the love he had only ever felt for his wife. He could not lose Maria as well.

Hallett stood and walked to the fireplace and tapped the contents of his pipe against the hearth's wall. Once he had placed the pipe back in his pocket he turned to the couple and took a deep breath.

'I will release you from your contract with the Dent boy,' he said, looking at the floor. Maria took a step forward. Hallett raised his hand and she halted. He now addressed Bellamy.

'Once you get your acreage, you may ask for my daughter's hand. In the meantime, you'll work for me here, from half five until supper. I won't pay you but I'll feed you and guide you through the Scriptures. You don't have any family that I know of and you need to be a part of one if you hope to remain in Eastham.'

Bellamy nodded his agreement.

'And you'll come to meeting with Maria and me every Sunday, without fail,' he added more severely, 'with the aim of one day being accepted into the church.'

'I understand,' Bellamy said. 'Thank you, Sir.'

'I will speak to Dent tomorrow,' Hallett went on and looked at the couple standing before him. 'That's all.'

Maria walked to her father and knelt at his feet. Kissing each of his roughened hands dutifully, she lowered her head. Hallett placed his palms on her sleek, golden crown.

THE MOON CAST a thin shaft of light across their naked bodies. Wordless, Leah and Palgrave lay in bed, the air close and damp, waiting for sleep to come.

'I wish you wouldn't do that,' Leah said.

'I won't release my seed in you, Leah. We have five children. It's enough. Be content with the pleasure you take from my body.'

Leah turned her face to the window. Palgrave knew she felt ashamed, embarrassed. It wasn't a wife's role to be *pleasured*. Risking another pregnancy was her penance, he supposed. He yawned and drew his wife to him, closing his eyes.

In the blissful oblivion between wake and sleep, Palgrave saw Leah, above him, her hands pressed to his chest and her hips gently rocking, steady and regular as a metronome. She had ridden from pleasure to rapture then off an invisible cliff. He hadn't realised a woman could cry out in ecstasy until Leah. He had never felt a woman constrict and pulse around him. It had never occurred to him that women were made to do so. Coupling with Anne had always been agreeable yet detached. Still and quiet as though it would be rude to disturb the other, trying hard to go unnoticed. When Leah was nursing Joseph, she'd asked him to suckle her breast, draw down her milk. He enjoyed the sweet and salty taste of her, the mutual nourishing. How could a woman be so composed, so self-contained, yet so passionate and uninhibited? It made him wonder what else she was capable of.

Palgrave opened his eyes and was in need of her once more. He put his mouth to her breast. She arched her back and sighed then his hand moved between her legs. She clutched his face between her hands and their lips met.

'I'm still nursing Joshua. It's safe.'

Palgrave shook his head in disagreement then settled his head on the pillow. That was no guarantee. He could control very little in this life but he could be master of this. It was custom for New England wives to have twelve or thirteen confinements, sometimes more. He had wanted no more children after the twins were born five years ago; Caleb had been 'an unexpected blessing', as Leah liked to remind him.

'It's a full moon. Fuller than I've ever seen it,' Palgrave said.

'You say that every full moon.' Leah turned to face her him. His sharp profile was vivid against the powerful glow.

Leah rolled onto her side and placed the flat of her hand on Palgrave's chest. Her callouses scratched his hairless skin. 'I've not heard Mister Bellamy yet. It's getting late.'

'It's not past ten. Perhaps he's cooling himself in the river ... with your sister.'

Leah attempted to raise her hand in protest but Palgrave grabbed it and lifted it to his mouth instead, kissing her fingertips softly. 'I'm joking. It's not long dark. He's likely working late.'

Leah shifted once more and pulled the sheet over her body. Within seconds she had kicked it away irritably.

'Be still. It's as though you cannot abide your own skin,' Palgrave said. 'What troubles you?'

'I worry for Maria. I worry ...'

'She'll repeat your mistakes.'

His remark prompted Leah to sit up and face her husband. 'I've made no mistakes, but Maria is different. Papa has coddled her. Her temperament is more suited to that of a minister's wife than a farmer's, despite what she may think.'

'Isn't that what your father said of you when you chose me over a man like Arthur Earl?'

'I never loved Arthur Earl. Marriage was never spoken of. He was ... is a friend, nothing more.'

'Perhaps you sell her short,' he said, running his hand down the length of her arm, admiring her breasts.

'I hope so.' Leah rested her head on the pillow. 'Everything seems out of sorts since Mister Bellamy arrived. He seems too large for Eastham. It's as though he has upset the balance of this tiny place.'

'How so?'

'The coupling of Maria and Silas ...' The whisper of a cooling breeze entered through the window touching Leah's skin, making it tingle.

'That was never set in stone. Their union was merely an expectation.'

'I had hoped when Silas returned they would wed.'

'You never told me this.'

Leah rolled towards her husband and allowed his arm to wrap around her. It was impossible to explain to Palgrave how she wanted something more for her sister without provoking a sense of his own inadequacy.

'You have changed as well,' Leah shared after a few minutes.

Palgrave remained silent but Leah felt his grip tighten on her arm. 'You've become spirited.'

'Was I not spirited before?' he asked. Leah could hear the humour in his tone.

'Aye, you were. But ...' Leah couldn't find the words to express her concerns. 'You shine when he speaks. I have never seen such ardour in you.'

'Jealous?'

'Afraid.'

Palgrave had recognised the change in himself. He had been foolish to entertain the possibility his wife might have remained ignorant to his altered humour.

'Sam has dreams, Leah. He has ambition. To taste that is enlivening, I confess. I have not experienced such vigour since ... for such a long time.'

A cloud passed in front of the moon, shading its brutal glare.

'Since you came to Eastham?'

'I arrived in Eastham with grand plans, with such optimism ...' He paused for a moment in thought. 'I still believe I could be a man of some significance, given the right opportunity. But I'm barely scratching together a livelihood ...'

Leah didn't speak, aware of her husband's frustrations.

'It was cruel fate.'

Palgrave rarely mentioned his first family, although she assumed he wanted to, at times. Occasionally, when she observed him watching their children, she would notice a look steal over his face, a look of recognition, an exchange of memories. Selfishly, Leah preferred to think of Palgrave's life beginning with her. The idea of another woman – and other children – he had once loved was terrifying.

Instead, Palgrave had spoken often to her of his own childhood. His father, a prosperous miller, was a man devoted to the care and education of his sons. He had been killed when Palgrave was barely a man. It troubled her to consider what might have been if he had lived. Palgrave would have become a man of great learning, she was certain.

She squeezed his hand tightly in an effort to reassure him. 'You've had your future taken from you twice. But God is testing you. We must be content with our lot, as it is now. God *will* see to us.'

'Your piety unnerves me, Leah' he said. 'It has always done so.'

He sensed her flinch.

'You saved me, my love, and I've allowed you to shoulder too much of this family's burden. I know you blame yourself for your mother's death ... I have wondered many times if you don't see this life as your atonement ...' He could feel Leah's body tense briefly, but she said nothing. 'The notion weighs heavily on me. Sam's enthusiasm is refreshing. That's all there is to it.'

'I'm content,' said Leah.

'I want you ecstatic.'

'Nobody is so.' Leah kissed her husband's chest tenderly.

Palgrave hugged his wife more closely and their legs entwined. Here they rested serenely for a moment until Palgrave cried out into the dark. 'Did you see it? The shooting star?' Releasing his wife, he sat upright, the air, like cool marble, came between their warm, slick bodies. He faced the window in anticipation. Leah stroked his back gently. When his head returned to the pillow he remarked mockingly, 'That *must* be a good portent. What would your people say?'

Leah manoeuvred their bodies into the same interlocked position they had held only moments before. 'Aye, it is,' she lied and nestled firmly against his side, suddenly fearful of what the future may bring.

MARIA STOOD in her chamber and watched Bellamy depart. It had only just grown dark but the moon bestowed a stark brilliance across the Hallett's yard and the road beyond. Hallett had invited Bellamy to join them for supper. Following the meal, the three had read from the scriptures at the same table at which they had eaten.

Then, instructed to bid one another good night, Maria and Bellamy nodded shyly to each other by the door before Maria took the stairs to her room and waited by her window for Bellamy's appearance.

He walked serenely across the yard, taking in the vibrant moon. When he reached the road he turned and viewed Maria framed in the window. He removed his hat and offered a grand, sweeping bow. She grinned and he raised his hand before he continued along the road in the direction of her sister's house. Leaning on the sill, she followed his journey as far as the lantern of the moon would allow before a dense blanket of cloud gently drifted into the foreground and snuffed out the light.

Maria sat heavily on her bed, awash with relief. After only a minute, she sprang to her feet once more and moved again to the window. *There will be no sleeping tonight,* she thought, restless and alert with happiness. The air had swiftly grown cool and she breathed deeply, basking in the freshness, taking in the blue-black sky and the minuscule specks of glistering radiance that bestrewed the heavens.

Then she saw it, her brow becoming threaded with unease. A shooting star, audacious in its intensity, blazed low and long across the night sky. Turning her back hastily on the outside, in case a second might follow, Maria's concern began to fester and her mind immediately turned to Silas.

His heart would be broken and she would be the cause. Pacing the length of the room, she contemplated how this situation might be softened for her dear friend. How might she counsel her father to cushion the blow? His forthright nature meant Hallett could be insensitive in such dealings and, despite his recent behaviour, she knew Silas possessed a fragile soul that felt even the slightest wound acutely, like a splinter beneath a fingernail. Maria resolved to advise her father in the morning. She heard the parlour clock strike ten then lay on her bed, certain there would be no sleep tonight.

10

The steady pulse of her hands against the dough was mesmerising. She was silent, thinking as she pushed, folded and rolled the dough. Leah liked silence. Always had. 'Join me, Leah,' I said after a while, still watching her knead. 'Just for a moment.'

She wiped her hands on a cloth then dried them on her apron and rolled down her sleeves. When she sat, I reached across the table and wiped a smudge of flour from her cheek.

'You're visiting early,' she said, laughing, pushing away my hand. 'Are you on your way to Boston?'

'I am.'

We sipped a little cider as I took in the setting around me. Elizabeth sat at the spinning wheel in the corner of the kitchen working wool into yarn. The twins, Joshua and Sarah, were beside one another at the table reading aloud from their primers; they were to start school in the fall. Using a wooden spoon, Caleb poked at a small piece of dough that Leah had given him. My godson Joseph had already left with his father for the workshop. My plan was to visit them there before leaving.

'It's a scene of industry and employment,' I remarked to my friend. 'They're a credit to you.'

Although she'd never admit it, Leah was proud of her accomplishments, the home she had created. Life was difficult at times; I could tell by the fine lines that webbed outwards from her eyes and the corners of her mouth.

'Can I bring you anything from Boston?'

Leah shook her head as she always did when I made the offer.

'A book for Palgrave, perhaps? An amusement for the twins? Would you like anything?'

'A fine strand of pearls.' Her expression didn't change.

I laughed at this. The children glanced at us and smiled briefly before returning their attention to their tasks. Leah gazed into her cup, thoughtful. I could almost see the question forming on her lips.

'How's your ... friend? The one in Boston, I mean?' Leah raised her eyebrows at me over the rim of her cup. Her interest surprised me.

'Charles is very well.'

'Charles,' she repeated, tracing his name in the flour dusted on the table with her finger. She glanced at her children then quietly inquired, 'Do you love him?'

Leah had never asked me that question before.

I nodded, looking at her squarely.

'The risk?'

'It would be worse not to have him.'

'Is he worthy of you?'

I nodded once more.

'I'm pleased. I should like to meet him one day.'

When I finally left the kitchen, I felt light, puffed, confident of my choice. Leah always asked the right questions. She had a knack for that.

~

'GOOD MORNING, MISTRESS HALLETT.' Arthur tipped the brim of his hat as he walked towards the road. 'Your sister is inside, engaged in the delicate art of bread making.'

Maria stopped, uncertain. She'd never heard Arthur Earl quite so jovial before. She wondered if he was attempting a jest.

'Leah *does* make a very fine loaf,' she replied. He laughed at this. 'You're in fine spirits today.'

'And you?'

She smiled, shrugging a shoulder. 'I'm none too sure.'

When Maria bid goodbye to Arthur it was not yet eight thirty. She had delighted in the walk to her sister's house, knowing she trod the same track Samuel had walked only the night before. Laughing quietly to herself, she vainly attempted to identify his footprints in the dirt. Yet her amusement was soon overshadowed by her distress over Silas. Her stomach twisted into knots when she remembered what was currently underway in the home of Reverend Dent. Joseph Hallett had departed early in the direction of Silas's home. As she had resolved, Maria instructed her father to be kind to the young man. Hallett had scoffed irritably at the advice.

To calm her nerves, she attempted to help Hannah with the baking, but her clumsy, distracted and impatient state eventually saw her shooed from the house with an order to visit Leah.

Without saying hello, she took a seat opposite the twins and assisted them in their study. Leah scrutinised her sister's manner closely. She was breathless and flushed and her eyes harboured a lively expectancy. While Maria stared at the boy and girl as they read, Leah recognised a preoccupation in her demeanour. It was as though, in thought, she was someplace else entirely. She had also dressed very carefully in a blue-grey skirt and laced bodice – an outfit more appropriate for meeting, or a baptism. Not everyday attire in Eastham. Maria's rope-like braid ran the length of her spine, coming to a stop at the small of her back. Leah rolled her sleeves to her elbows.

'When did you know you loved Palgrave?' Maria asked, startling her sister who was sifting flour over the table. It came down in a heavy snowfall.

Leah thought on her response carefully as she poured water into the well she had made in the mound.

'When he returned to meeting.' It was just a white lie. 'Do you recall?'

Maria nodded. 'Go ahead,' she instructed the twins.

'"The idle Fool is whipt at School",' Joshua read slowly. 'Is that the truth, Aunty?' he questioned after a moment's consideration, looking up at his aunt.

'Aye,' she replied. 'You must always work hard and never be lazy or you will be punished.' A brief flash of anxiety darkened the boy's expression but quickly vanished as his sister began on the next rhyme.

'"As runs the Glass, man's Life doth pass",' Sarah read, more confidently than her brother. 'I know what that means, Aunty.'

Maria eyed her seriously. 'Tell me.'

'It means that every man's time on this earth will run out and he will die.'

'Aye, you're correct,' Maria said.

'That's why we must seek God's grace in everything we do,' Leah interrupted. The children nodded solemnly.

'Now close your books and run to the workshop,' Leah said. 'Tell your father to call on Goody Blackman on his way to town to inform her that she will have turnips, a loaf and an eel pie by dinner time. She need not worry about leaving the house or her children.'

The twins leapt off their seats and headed out of the room. 'Four of them are poorly with the measles,' Leah explained to her sister. 'Little Amy is deathly ill.'

'I didn't know.'

Leah's concentration returned to the mound of dough on the table. Caleb coughed as flour billowed in a puff.

'Go after your brother and sister,' Leah said, looking down at her son as her right hand began to punch the dough. 'Ask them to fetch water before they return.'

Caleb left the house, still clutching the wooden spoon. Once the dough was flat Leah began to knead more vigorously. Maria watched her sister's hands as they pounded against the dough. Neither the sound of her sister's exertion nor the gentle hum of the bobbin as her niece worked at the spinning undermined her thoughts. With each assault the dough grew smoother and more pliable. Leah glanced quickly at her sister. Her countenance remained remote.

'Mister Bellamy was home late last evening,' Leah said when she had completed the kneading. 'He didn't return until half ten, perhaps even later.' Leah was still awake when she heard Bellamy arrive. He was whistling a lively tune.

Those words were all that were required for Maria to look at her sister, her gaze instantly attentive. Without further prompting she began to relate the exact events that had transpired since the afternoon of the picnic by the birch. An afternoon, she said, 'that seems centuries gone yet is only four days past.' Leah split the dough into four equal parts firmly with a long bladed knife and shaped them into perfect rounds as Maria spoke. Leah placed the loaves near the hearth and covered them with a cloth then began to clean the table. As she did so, she noticed Elizabeth in the corner, still at the wheel.

'Go, Elizabeth,' Leah said. 'Go and see to the twins and Caleb.' Discharged from her chore and sent to complete another, the girl departed the room reluctantly yet hastily; she knew better than to be sluggish following a direction from her mother.

Once Elizabeth had gone, Maria continued. 'I'm uncertain if what I feel for Samuel is love, but I need to find out.'

Maria stopped, her story finished. She waited for Leah to cease at her task and speak. Rolling down her sleeves and buttoning the cuffs, Leah took a position opposite her sister at the table and wiped her upper lip of the perspiration that had formed there during her labours.

'You're a fool,' she said. 'A selfish fool.'

Stung by the remark, Maria shifted in her chair.

'You've thrown away a prosperous future with a man who loves you and who you have known your entire life for the merest hint of something better with Bellamy. I cannot fathom you, Maria.' She bunched a wash clout between her fists. 'What's more, you've not even considered Reverend Dent in your scheme. To have his hopes dashed so ...'

She shook her head in disbelief and rose. 'He's a powerful man in Eastham and New England. Did you even consider what the consequences of making an enemy of Reverend Dent might be for Papa? Or for yourself? Especially now.'

Maria's eyes lowered to her lap. Leah walked to the spinning wheel and turned the bobbin harshly, breaking the thread. Maria had anticipated a mild word of caution but, considering Leah's own past, she had also expected understanding and support.

'For you to see yourself as a farmer's wife is absurd!'

Leah said, gaining momentum. Her voice was now raised to a fervent pitch. 'What do you know about keeping a house and a family?' She paused, fists on hips, demanding a response. 'Baking bread, seeing to livestock, tending a fire, killing a pig ...' She moved in closer towards her sister. Her tone grew cold. 'Do you know what it's like to grasp a beast by the snout and cut its throat? Could you even empty a chamber pot?'

Maria said nothing. Her composure returning, Leah sat down again.

'Papa has indulged you since Mother died, fearing your fate would be the same as my own.' Leah stared into Maria's guileless eyes. 'I don't regret my choice but it has been a hard road, Maria. I cannot believe you're suited to such a path. You mustn't give your youth away so freely.'

Leah paused, desperate for Maria to appreciate the reality of her choice. The only way forward, she realised, was to speak the truth.

'The penny pinching and the work and the daily struggles that seem endless ... sometimes, Maria ... sometimes I feel that my only ally in this world is God ...'

A firm tapping against the outside wall interrupted the exchange. The women raised their heads and saw Palgrave standing only inches from the doorway, taking in the scene. He wore a strange expression Leah did not recognise, a disconcerting patchwork of bewilderment and sorrow. His children hovered around him. Although they sensed the tension of the moment, they did not understand it.

Leah cleared her throat and stood. As the blood rose in his wife's cheeks, Palgrave's own expression was instantly wiped clean of any trace of distress. He greeted Maria with a carefree nod. 'I heard shouting. I came to see ...' He looked to his right. 'Caleb, stop that noise. Give that to me.' The child came into view and handed his father the wooden spoon he had been hammering against the wall.

'Everything is fine.' Leah looked at Palgrave squarely. 'Don't concern yourself.' As she moved towards her husband she hoped her veneer of cool assurance would be believed. Palgrave edged away. The gesture distressed her. She was certain he had never moved from her in that way before.

The twins offered her a full bucket; water lapped precariously against its sides. Leah smiled down at them, relieving them of their cargo. 'Joseph, have you collected the eggs this morning?' The boy ran to the hen house.

Palgrave watched his eldest son depart and the twins follow in his wake. Caleb trailed the threesome at an unsteady trot.

'Elizabeth,' Leah then directed. 'Get back to the spinning, please.' The girl moved into the house.

Order restored.

Leah stepped outside. Husband and wife stood alone in the yard, facing one another. In their silence they heard the faint scrape of the stool on the floor as their daughter took her place at the spinning wheel. Within seconds, the thrum of the treadle and whir of the bobbin became apparent. Palgrave stepped a foot closer to Leah and held out the wooden spoon. She smiled wanly. With her children no longer observing them, she was unable to conceal her remorse any longer. She grasped at the utensil. They both looked down at the object for a moment before Palgrave released his grip. His eyes rose to meet hers; they were desolate.

'The dough will have risen,' Leah said, slightly breathless, then added uncertainly, 'I should knead it again.'

Palgrave nodded with greater concern than the information warranted. He turned and walked towards the workshop.

When Leah returned indoors Maria had departed.

THE TIME WAS NEARING ten o'clock when Maria returned home. Despite the steadily rising heat of the day, the wretched confrontation with her sister forced the young woman into a desperate sprint along the road to her house.

She stopped in the yard, barely able to recall the two miles she had just run, and attempted to gather herself. She removed her hat. Her hair was wet. Moving into the shade offered by the gable, she fanned herself with her bonnet for some minutes until her face cooled and her panic grew more distant. When she finally entered the house she discovered her father sitting in the parlour. He had assumed the same position as the previous evening. *Tick tock.* Maria walked into the room and rounded the rocking chair. Joseph Hallett's hands gripped the arms of the rocker and his feet were planted firmly and evenly into the ground.

'Why didn't you tell me Samuel Bellamy had a price on his head?'

Maria's eyes widened as her chest began to hollow into a dismal cavern.

'Do not lie to me, girl!'

'I feared you would not agree to the match.' Maria eased herself into his line of vision. 'I was certain you would not agree.'

'Then you do not deny that he's a criminal?'

'I do not.' Maria spoke with a sincerity Hallett found disconcerting. 'But there are circumstances to consider.'

Hallett had been confident of the outcome of his

meeting with Dent. The minister could not hold him to a contract that was incomplete when it was obvious Maria wanted no part in the union. Hallett was not suggesting anything unreasonable. He even intended to pay Dent five pounds compensation. Endeavouring to be kind to the younger Dent, just as his daughter had advised, Hallett had tempered his words. But Reverend Dent was furious, crying for a larger sum in damages in the hope he might force Hallett's hand financially. The farmer had not budged. He made no mention of Samuel Bellamy until Silas raised the man's name himself.

As Silas spoke of Bellamy's past, Hallett watched both father and son closely, noting the identical glint of satisfaction in their eyes.

'How do you know this?' Hallett asked, masking his anger and shame with stony reserve.

Silas refused to respond.

Hallett had then grabbed him by the front of his shirt and forced his back against the wall. A small, decorative table that stood in the centre of the room was thrown sideways in the scramble. There was dread in the young man's eyes. Although their slave had run into the room on hearing the scuffle, the minister did not move to intervene. He merely raised his hand and gestured for the woman to leave them.

'Tell me! Who told you this? Why should you be believed?'

'I overheard them in the woods ...' he stammered. 'Maria and Bellamy. They met in the woods yesterday. It was late in the afternoon.'

Hallett thought for a moment on the boy's admission and the events of the day before and reasoned it was feasible. He released Silas.

'I'm sorry,' he said, looking at the boy. 'I allowed my fury to overcome my better nature. I apologise to you and your father.' He held out his hand to the young man. Silas shook it slowly then straightened his cravat. Before Hallett could offer his hand to the minister, Dent began to speak, pulling down his waistcoat.

'The way seems clear. Your daughter must marry my son. She cannot be bound to a criminal who will be hanging from gallows before long.'

Hallett nodded, deliberating on the appropriate course. He rubbed his whiskered chin deliberately.

'Aye, it's the truth. She cannot marry Bellamy. But the fact remains she does not love your son.' He fixed his attention on Silas. 'I'm mightily sorry, Silas. I know how you love her but my faith forbids me from tying her to a partner she has no wifely love for.'

Silas's jaw tightened. He hastily turned his back on the older men and affected an appearance of thoughtful self-possession by the window.

Hallett dug his hand deep into his pocket and produced five silver coins. He walked towards Reverend Dent and offered him the money. Fixed rigid in his position, Dent did not move. 'As you wish,' Hallett uttered then calmly righted the table he had overturned and placed the money on it. As he walked towards the door, Dent cried, 'I will have it known you are an antinomian, Sir. You are against the church!'

Hallett stopped in his tracks for an instant before leaving the dreadful scene.

Now Maria asked earnestly, 'Must I marry Silas?'

Hallett stood and took her by the hands. 'Would you do that?'

She nodded. 'If you ask that of me, I will.'

He shook his head. 'You don't care for him as you should. What's more, he might be a minister, but I do not hold with spying. It's the method of a coward.'

Maria exhaled slowly.

'But,' he continued, 'Mister Bellamy must leave Eastham at once. Alone.'

She raised her eyes to her father's. They were drenched with anguish.

'If I know Dent, he will have the authorities here before the week is out. If your Mister Bellamy has any chance of cheating the hangman's noose he must go immediately. I will send Thomas to warn him and fetch him to your sister's.'

11

Abby had been standing by the parlour entrance when Hallett left. He raised his hat to her as he coolly strode towards the door to the outside. Within seconds the minister appeared, red- faced and desperate. Abby instinctively stepped back. The slave had only gotten in the minister's way once when he was in such a fury. She was eleven when Dent had shoved her so hard against the wall that the wind had been completely knocked from her scrawny chest. It only took a moment to recover, but for a few terrifying seconds, she thought she had lost the ability to draw air.

Now Dent blustered across the hallway to his study.

She turned to the parlour and could see Silas standing by the window. Abby rapped softly on the doorjamb.

'Come in, Abby,' Silas said without turning. 'Did you hear?'

She nodded and approached him. 'I'm sorry the situation hasn't resolved as you'd hoped. Perhaps it is for the best.'

Silas sat heavily in the armchair and placed his head in his hands.

'There are other young ladies, here and in Beverly, who are worthy of your love. Your attachment to Maria Hallett will fade in time. Concentrate on your calling now.'

Silas lifted his head and she noticed his red eyes.

'I cannot see a time when I will not love her, Abby,' he muttered. '*She* is my calling.'

Abby walked to him then knelt by his feet and took his hands.

Silas had always been such a diligent person; even as a child, he was meticulous in his behaviour, appearance and studies. Aware from a young age of the low regard in which many held his father, Silas stood apart from the minister, to position himself more favourably in the eyes of the community. Everyone in the town had been disappointed when they learnt of his posting in Beverly, none more so than Abby herself. She wanted Silas close to her. Although she had not given birth to him, she believed the bond they shared was that of a mother and son.

'You cannot *make* Maria Hallett love you in the way you want,' she said now, mildly exasperated. 'Your heart is leading you astray.'

Silas rose and helped her to her feet. 'But Abby, all I have is my heart. I will let my love shine down upon Maria. I will overwhelm her with my love. She *will* be mine.'

The conviction in his voice made her tremble.

LEAH STOOD next to her husband in the barn as they watched Bellamy gather his few possessions and place them in a leather sling bag. Dressed in the attire he had worn on the day of the festival, he folded the clothes he had borrowed from Palgrave neatly and handed them to his erstwhile landlord. Palgrave received them with a nod.

'You have time,' Palgrave said quietly. 'Even if Dent sends word today, the nearest magistrate is in Boston.'

'Nay. Be quick,' Leah advised. 'There's nothing stopping the Reverend from forcing Arthur Earl to chain you in the pound until the magistrate arrives.' Neither her husband nor Bellamy knew what the minister was capable of.

Sensing Leah's alarm, Bellamy asked, 'Will Maria be safe?'

'Aye. Dent is powerful but my father is more so. He won't move against Maria.'

'I need to say goodbye to her,' Bellamy said. 'I want her to understand why I'm leaving.'

'You have no time. She'll understand,' Leah replied.

Bellamy sighed. 'I fear that she will not.'

'Where are you going?' Palgrave asked. 'You won't be able to remain in New England.'

'Florida,' Bellamy said. 'There's a ship leaving tonight.'

'In search of the Spanish treasure?' Palgrave asked.

'No-one will dare touch me when I return a gentleman.'

Leah looked at her husband. She could see he wasn't unsettled by the news. Yet wasn't this the kind of recklessness Bellamy and Palgrave had mocked only a few days before? Before she could protest, the trio heard the thunder of hooves approaching.

'Wait here,' Palgrave instructed as he walked out of the barn towards the house.

Bellamy crouched in a stall while Leah moved to the entrance and watched her husband hurry to the rider. It was Francis Jeffries, the deacon. He handed Palgrave a note and the men exchanged a few words before Jeffries rode off in the direction of the town. Leah studied her husband's expression as he examined the paper in his hands, but she could tell nothing from such a distance. He folded the note carefully and placed it in his shirt pocket.

'It's from Reverend Dent,' he informed the pair when he entered the barn. 'He no longer desires the candlesticks,' Palgrave said to his wife then turned to Bellamy. 'He made no mention of you.'

In light of the morning's events in the yard, Leah, deliberately optimistic, said 'It matters not. We will get by. We always do.' She took Palgrave's hand and clutched it firmly. Palgrave looked at their interlocked fingers, his expression grave.

'You should go now,' Leah then said to Bellamy. 'Don't take the road. Cut through the forest to the harbour. Will you find your way?'

Bellamy nodded slowly as he looked towards the doors. Palgrave and Leah turned. Maria stood in the entrance, flushed and breathless.

No-one spoke for some minutes. Leah eyed the occupants of the barn closely. An anxious longing passed between her sister and Bellamy. Then she turned and looked at her husband, whose hand she still grasped. There was no anxiety in his expression. In fact, when she thought on this moment later, she would describe him as reflective, with his eyes crinkled only slightly at their corners.

Eventually, Palgrave broke the silence. 'Come, Leah. We should leave them to say goodbye.'

Leah hesitated for an instant. Her eyes shot to her sister. Palgrave tightened his grip and drew her from the barn towards the house. Once they had departed, Maria and Bellamy came together. 'I will come back,' he assured her. 'When I have wealth enough.'

'I want to leave here and come with you. Papa has

released me. I am no longer pledged to Silas Dent,' She paused a moment. 'How can I go on living here?'

'You must, darling hummingbird,' he said. 'A ship is no place for a woman.'

'A ship?'

He nodded. 'Florida.'

Her expression darkened and she pulled away. 'I knew the shooting star last night was a dire sign.'

'You're talking nonsense. I'll come to no harm,' he went on. 'I survived five years on the *Royal Sovereign*.'

She shook her head in bewilderment and Bellamy took her hands.

'If I remain, Dent will see me hanging from a gibbet before the fall. I've no money and no power – I am at the mercy of men who do. My scruples, my good intentions matter not to men like Dent or the King. I'm of a sensible and honourable character but my purpose has been crippled, brutally and constantly, by those in authority. If men are denied the chance to live in freedom, they'll make their own freedom. I will come back, wealthy beyond your wildest dreams, Maria, I promise you. Then we'll marry.'

'But it changes nothing,' she protested. 'You will still be a criminal, a far worse criminal, wanted by the Spanish Crown as well.'

'That's true,' he responded calmly. 'But I will have gold and that tends to grant most men a pardon, regardless of their crimes. It's the only way.'

Maria hesitated. She barely knew this man. She wondered if she should believe him. He was a criminal, after all. Yet she found his confidence reassuring, a potent remedy for her misgivings. Perhaps it was her upbringing that had made her untrusting of things she did not know. Samuel was worldly, experienced in matters such as this.

Then she remembered their kiss. Her longing for him overcame all her doubts and fears. She nodded solemnly.

'Will you lie with me?' she asked, taking a step closer.

Bellamy considered her request for a moment before wrapping his arms around her waist.

'I will come back,' he whispered, leaning in to kiss her.

LEAH SAT QUIETLY on the edge of the bed as her husband made his way around their chamber, filling a sack with his belongings. Caleb sat on the floor by her feet playing with the alphabet blocks his oldest brother had crafted for him, babbling to himself all the while as he built a tower with them.

A is for apple so ripe and red.

Palgrave opened the top drawer of the chest and produced a razor. He examined it fondly for a few seconds before placing it in the sack. Then a pair of stockings Elizabeth had knitted him was added to the bag. Following this, a book – Swift, she noted. Palgrave gently pushed the drawer shut and placed his baggage on the floor. He sat beside his wife on the bed and took her hand.

'Are you deserting me?' she asked. They were the first words she had spoken since he told her of his plans. 'I know you overheard me this morning. I'm sorry. I was angry with Maria, not with you.'

B is the barrow that stands by the shed.

'I know. But it was the truth you spoke. I needed to hear you utter the words.'

She stared at her son on the ground and envied his blithe ignorance as he searched the blocks for the next letter.

C begins cow whose milk is sweet.

Leah wished Palgrave hadn't told her he was leaving with Bellamy. Surely it would be less painful if he'd simply fled in the night. When the couple had entered the house from the barn and Palgrave, still on the threshold, revealed his intentions she'd thought he was making fun. Such an announcement was inconceivable. Then he climbed the stairs and didn't turn back. Leah opened her mouth but no words came. It was the first time she could remember being speechless.

'Reconsider,' she pleaded now. 'It's such a rash decision.'

'I don't consider it rash. I've been thinking of making a change for some time. Sam merely has given me the impetus.'

Stunned by his admission, the colour drained from Leah's face.

D is for duck with the floppity feet.

'You have bolstered our family for far too long,' he explained. 'It's my turn to support you. I want you to have a maid and labourers and fine clothes.' He took her hands and examined her palms. 'Those callouses distress me so. They reflect on me poorly.' He kissed her fingertips.

She snatched her hands away.

'I don't need to tell you of the dangers, do I?' she said. 'You know nothing about life at sea. You are not a sailor, or a fortune hunter. You're the most tender of men.'

'I must provide you with more. For my own sake.'

Leah didn't want anything more than she had right at that moment. Palgrave sat by her side, his fingers clawed over the edge of the mattress as he focused on the baby.

E begins egg so smooth and white.

'Why did you come back that day?' he queried after a minute.

She looked at him, puzzled by his question.

'Why, when I was obviously troubled, not myself, why did you come back the next day?'

Leah recalled their second meeting so vividly, yet she thought for a time, choosing her words carefully. 'I saw something in your eyes – the smallest fleck of hope. I knew you weren't ready to give up. I believed all you needed was me to guide you out of the darkness.'

'Then it was merely compassion, Christian charity?'

She turned to him and clutched his arm. 'It was so much more.' Then she stopped, glancing at the stack of blocks. Despite his age, Caleb had a need for order. He carefully added another to the tower.

F is the fire that burns so bright.

Leah wanted to tell Palgrave how she had observed him each Sunday at meeting and how she had admired his dedication. She wanted to confide how his bashful manner and mild disposition had so appealed to her as a woman. She wanted to describe how closely she had watched him, how she waited for the moment meeting ended each Sabbath when he would stand and straighten his belt buckle, making sure it sat just so, in line with the buttons on his breeches. She wanted to tell him that this gesture made her feel that she knew him, that she knew him better than his wife, even better than he knew himself. She wanted to confess that she had fallen in love with him before they'd ever spoken, despite knowing he was wed. Leah longed to describe the sensation of joy that skipped over her heart when she had learnt of his wife's death.

But she was ashamed that she had glimpsed hope in the depths of his sorrow. The truth was she had wanted to save Palgrave Williams for her own sake. Her motive for visiting him the next day had been false. But Leah could not speak of her sin. It was an offence she still grappled with daily. She groaned faintly in frustration at her own weakness, prompting Palgrave to look at her briefly in search of something more.

'Dent cannot touch your sister or your father but he can ruin us. The candlesticks are proof of that,' he said after a moment.

G begins girl who sweeps the floor. Caleb admired the structure.

Palgrave was right. Reverend Dent would gnaw at her family like a rat at a bean. If he could not unite with the Halletts he would set about destroying them. *Still, there must be another way*, she thought. She and Palgrave would manage as they'd always done. As Leah searched her mind for a solution, Palgrave turned to her and said seriously, 'If I do not return I want you to marry Arthur Earl. He's well positioned in Eastham.'

Unnerved, she looked at him and cried, 'Nay!'

Caleb raised his face to her. Terror was etched upon his tiny brow and his tower collapsed. His face contorted with grief. Leah's heart beat frantically in her chest as she brought the sobbing child to her lap. As she struggled to prevent his departure, Palgrave was already talking about not coming back.

'I will not,' she stated. 'Your conscience will not be relieved in this way.'

'He loves you, Leah,' Palgrave said gently. 'He always has. Anyone can see it. Why do you think he has never married?'

'That has nothing to do with me!' Her outcry provoked a further gush of sobs from the baby and she wiped the child's face with her apron. She'd said more than she should. Caleb's tears had prompted her own and Leah rose from the bed and walked to the door, calling for Elizabeth. As she handed the child to her daughter, she spoke in hushed tones in the girl's ear. Once she had departed with Caleb, Leah turned to her husband.

'I cannot accept this.'

'You must.' He moved to her.

She shook her head, battling to stifle the tears that threatened to wear down her resolve.

He placed his arms around her and she shook them off and stormed to the window. Palgrave followed and spun her around to face him. She raised her hand to strike his face, but he caught her wrist then pinned her arms to her sides. As Leah fought his grasp, she began to cry. Pulling her closer, he attempted to kiss her but she resisted, turning her face away and closing her eyes.

'Go,' she muttered through the tears. 'If you're leaving, then leave. I can bear this no longer.'

He peppered her neck with soft kisses until he felt her anger begin to subside. When their lips eventually met, it was with a ferocity that neither of them had anticipated.

WHEN HE WAS ready to leave, Samuel knocked softly on Leah's front door. Palgrave emerged from the house, a cloth sack slung over his shoulder. Standing behind him in the darkness of the hallway was Leah.

'Would you like company?' Palgrave asked, walking across the threshold. Samuel eyed him thoughtfully for a moment before nodding his consent.

Maria turned instantly to her sister to gauge her reaction. Leah stepped into the sunlight. She was wearing a pained expression that Maria was not familiar with. Then they watched in silence as the men disappeared into the woods seventy yards in the distance. Neither Palgrave nor Leah said a word to each other. Goodbyes had already been voiced, Maria assumed. Then she turned and looked at her sister.

'Call on me tomorrow,' Leah said. 'I'm exhausted and I must take stock.'

'The children ...'

'They have gone to Aunty Margaret. She will send them back in the morning.'

Leah retreated and closed the door. Maria walked directly to the woods.

12

Maria raised her head and looked up high into the willow. The sun fell around the branches and through the leaves, creating an alluring medley of light and shadow. She immediately lifted her skirt and placed her foot on the lowest branch and steadily made her way to the top of the tree. She had bid farewell to Samuel Bellamy less than a half an hour before and a sense of apprehension had come to rest promptly in her heart. But nestled in the crook of a branch, she immediately began to feel more at ease. She considered that she had chosen the most difficult path. She was, however, certain that God would want her to remain true to her feelings. As she sat on high, Maria felt the nip of the sea's breeze, springing from the same wind that would carry Samuel away from Eastham. She raised her face into the sun and closed her eyes.

When she heard the rustle of leaves beneath her she knew it was Silas. Opening her eyes, she moved noiselessly to a lower branch and observed him through the boughs. He was standing, hands behind his back, gazing across the river. Hovering in the tree, she feared that, in the silence of the forest, the hammer in her chest would alert Silas to her whereabouts. Yet, if he glanced skywards, prompted by the liquid song of a wren or the jerky, fluttering flight of a butterfly, and spotted her, she would appear foolish. Eastham was too small a town to hide forever. Maria began to climb down. Not until she reached the lowest branches did he turn and face her.

'I thought I would find you here,' he remarked.

'Were you looking for me?'

'Aye.' He smiled.

She wondered if this meant he wanted to make amends. The sudden hoot of an owl startled her, making her flinch. She looked to the source of the sound but could not see the bird, hidden as it was in the boughs of an oak. Silas's self-possession had not been shaken by the unexpected noise. Although they had been friends for many years, she was not convinced the trials of the last few days could be forgotten.

He turned to speak to her. She took a step away.

'Maria, I won't give up on you. I am determined.'

Stunned by his coolness, his audacity, she had no words.

'Bellamy has gone, or will leave shortly, I imagine,' he continued, sitting on the bank. 'We will marry.'

'Silas, nay,' she said. 'What prevents you from understanding? I have prayed, Silas. I have begged God to guide the way to you. But we can never make each other happy.'

'Sit with me,' he said, patting the ground.

She shook her head.

'Please, Maria.'

She sighed, exhausted, exasperated.

'We have been each other's confidantes for so long,' he continued.

Maria cautiously moved closer then lowered herself beside him.

He grabbed her hand and gripped it tightly.

'Maria, I will show you the way.'

Infuriated by his stubbornness and her own stupidity, Maria attempted to pull her hand away and rise. Silas tightened his grasp and forced her back to the ground.

'Silas,' she managed to say firmly through her rising distress. 'Let me go. It saddens me, but if you will not leave off then our friendship must end.'

Silas pushed her shoulders to the ground and pressed his lips hard to hers. Maria writhed on the ground then raised her legs in an attempt to kick him away.

Within seconds she felt his entire body on her, pressing her flat into the cold, dead leaves. When their lips parted his hand tried to muffle her screams.

'Stop screaming, Maria. Please.'

She quietened. No-one could hear her. 'This is not the way,' she muttered, her voice breaking with the realisation of what was about to happen.

'It's the only way.'

He reached between them and lifted her skirts and shift. He hastily unbuttoned his fly. Maria emitted a muted cry as he pushed her legs apart with his body. 'Be still, Maria,' he whispered in her ear. 'Trust me. Unburden yourself.'

Then she was still.

He stared into her clear, dry eyes. Her gaze was intense and coloured with a disturbing palette of confusion, disappointment and acceptance. Unnerved for a moment, he looked beyond her to the base of the willow. When he entered her it was with a violent thrust he'd not expected. Maria shrieked. He glanced at her in concern and found her complexion ashen and her eyes rigidly fixed on his face in inquiry. Within only seconds of being inside her he released a low moan and his body quivered in unrestrained pleasure.

Then the minister's only child buried his head in her neck until he caught his breath. When he lifted himself from her, Maria began to tremble. She sobbed quietly. Silas drew down her skirts and carefully brushed them free of mud and leaves. Then he held her in his arms until she calmed.

PART II

NASSAU, NEW PROVIDENCE ISLAND
FALL 1716

13

———

Darling Leah,

After much Disappointment of our Expectations we find ourselves on New Providence, the largest of the Bahama Islands. I can imagine you reading this Letter, sitting at our Table by the Hearth with your Brow crumpled in great consternation, wondering to yourself what in blazes are they doing in such a place. I pray, do not hurl this Correspondence into the Fire until you have reached the conclusion of my Tale.

Bellamy and I reached Florida in good time on a Merchant Vessel, the William. Most of my Time was spent with Bellamy instructing me in the Art of knot tying. I have mastered twenty so far, and Bellamy informs me there are another dozen I should know among the thousands that exist. We landed in a place called Key Biscayne, a safe Inlet for Ships where a small Township has grown to serve the needs of the Seamen who lay Anchor there. Apart from those already mentioned, Key Biscayne has no outstanding Qualities that you would find of interest. The Journey was uneventful and the Captain was a reasonable type. However, my Companion did not take well to joining a Crew, protesting every apparent injustice he witnessed during the

Voyage. I warrant the Captain was well relieved when we finally dropped Anchor and he saw the last of Samuel Bellamy.

When we arrived we discovered the Spanish had already procured the Services of Indian and African Divers to retrieve the Treasure. What Items not looted by those living in the area were returned to the Hands of His Catholic Majesty King Phillip V. We learnt that three hundred and fifty thousand Spanish Dollars were being held in a Salvage Camp in Palmar de Ayz. That very Evening, by chance, we found Lodging at a local Tavern. Here we met Captain Henry Jennings, who Bellamy knew something of, both being involved in Queen Anne's War as they were. Jennings had been a Privateer during the conflict and, even though the War has been over these past two years, he still holds a particular grudge against the Crown's Foes. He refuses to Honour the Treaty of Utrecht and makes a living capturing Spanish and French Merchant Ships in the name of the Governor of Jamaica, Lord Hamilton.

Jennings seemed to be a Man of good understanding and good estate, despite his Appearance. He has small, pebble-sized Eyes and a beak-like Nose that calls to Mind the image of a Seagull. I could not guess at his Age. His Speech is even and well formed and his Eyes sprightly, yet silver Hair cascades down his Back in broad, even Waves. He had Commerce of sorts in the Town, rounding up a Crew to raid the Salvage Camp. Bellamy and he took to each other immediately and spoke easily about the War and other seafaring Business that meant naught to me. They are of similar Temperament. Cool headed and even tempered, yet hot as Mustard if there's a Prize at stake. With only sixty Men guarding the Treasure, Jennings was certain he could easily overwhelm them with his Band of two hundred. He had received this Intelligence from a Spaniard he had captured named Pedro de la Vega. While Bellamy and I declined his Invitation to join their Party, we did manage to secure Passage on his ship, the Barsheba.

Jennings sails in a Flotilla of three. The other two Vessels are the Discovery (the oldest, slowest and most wayward of the Trio) and the Cocoa Nut. Our Elizabeth, with her inclination for the unusual, would find the Name of the latter quite humorous, would she not?

It was a merry Voyage with Men from all Nations, it seemed. Negroes and Indians, Dutch, English and French, among others, all joined together in a free-spirited Brotherhood. I got on most well with a Negro from the Ivory Coast of Africa whom Jennings had rescued from a Slave Ship. His ebony Skin glistens in the sun and I find myself staring frequently at him, having never encountered anything as Black. Calm and good humoured, he is almost as tall as I but far more muscular. It is his Hope to make his way back to his Wife and Children. His People are Gold Miners who have worked and traded in the Material for Centuries. Perhaps our Affinity lies with our Trades. He speaks very little English and I, as you know, speak no Word of African. But through Hand Signals, elementary Sketches and vivid Gestures, we have managed to converse on a number of Occasions. I warrant, our Caleb would find a comfortable place in any one of our simple Exchanges. This Man, whose name is Ade, and I have learnt much about each other and have discovered, despite the hue of our Skin, that there is very little Difference between us.

The Town here, Nassau, stretches in a crescent Moon along the shore of the Harbour. It is a makeshift Village constructed of a few Manor Houses that have fallen into disrepair, and small a number of Stores, Shacks, Tents and Taverns. Much of the Town is cobbled together from Driftwood and the Canvas from Sails. Many of the Roofs I see are made from Palm Thatch. To study this Town you would never guess the Island is named for our own Providence in New England. Palm Trees and the most lush Vegetation I have ever encountered blanket the Hills and Mountains that make up the Hinterland of this Island. It is a vibrant

Harbour, brilliant in its busyness, although the Stench here belies its Appearance. They say the putrefying Stew of roasting Meat, Smoke, Rum, rotting Waste and unwashed Bodies can be smelt far out at Sea before the Island is even visible. Nevertheless, I see it as a Haven, a place where I can ply my Trade at a greater worth than I ever dreamt of in Eastham. There seems to be no lack of Sailors, Shipwrights and Traders in need of Tools and other such items. I have been told that a skilled Artisan can name his Price in Nassau.

Now I have made the loathsome Break, I will remain here for a Time until I can accrue a War Chest to bring Home to you all. I miss You and the Children dearly. There is not a Minute that passes that You or one of our Brood are not on my Mind. While Vexed, as I know you will be, think kindly on my Efforts and trust that I do Everything only for You.

Your devoted Husband,

Palgrave

STANDING on the sand looking towards the sea, Palgrave watched the sun's steady creep towards the horizon. It shot a bright orange streak across the water, a dazzling farewell that grew more intense each second. He imagined Leah preparing the children for bed, performing her elegant ballet of folding the clothes, washing faces and turning down the bedcovers, directing and comforting, organising and consoling. *She would soon lead the children in their prayers,* he thought – the skilfully executed coda to her day. He closed his eyes for an instant. How he longed to share an honest account of his exploits with her. It shamed him that he had skirted around the truth so easily, so skilfully, in his correspondence.

When he opened his eyes again he focused once more on the sunset and the beam of light that had now turned a remarkable shade of coral, even more striking than the flaming orange it had been only moments before. He noticed when the shaft reached the harbour its journey was abruptly interrupted by the hordes of galleys, sloops and frigates moored there, their hulls slapping the swell with a heavy 'thump'. With the sails down, the masts, yards and booms appeared to Palgrave like a dense, leafless forest. He did not hear Bellamy approach over the soft sand.

'This is for you.' Bellamy handed Palgrave a small, leather purse. 'Your share of the prize.'

Palgrave took the bag and eased apart the cord at the opening. Cupping the article in his hand, he counted the coins within.

'Twenty Spanish dollars,' Bellamy said. 'As part of the boarding party our share was more.'

'Enough to keep my family comfortably for a year.'

Bellamy nodded.

'This adventure we have embarked upon would be the dream of many young men,' Palgrave remarked.

It was difficult to determine whether Palgrave had uttered a question or a statement.

'That it would. But I take from your curious tone that it was never yours.'

'I dreamt of being a scholar, a learned man, when I was a boy.'

Bellamy looked at him.

'My father, you see,' Palgrave went on, staring towards the horizon, 'was a miller. He sent my brother and me to school. It was a grammar school – a cathedral school – where we wore black robes and crisp white cravats. When I was fifteen and my brother just thirteen, my father was killed, beaten to death by a mob of women who were driven to madness by hunger and fear for their children. He wasn't a greedy man. Just the opposite, in fact. These women killed him as he was dividing the last of his grain among them. Within the year, I was sent to live with a silversmith in Bristol named John Hoggett. And there I stayed until my twenty-first birthday.'

Bellamy remained silent, startled by the narrative.

'So, nay, it has never been my dream to go to sea.'

'We are more alike than I imagined.'

Palgrave raised an eyebrow.

'You kept a cool head about you during the raids. You surprised me.' Bellamy revised his observation. 'You surprise me in many ways.'

Palgrave didn't respond.

'I would have sworn you were accustomed to such assaults. You handled the half-pike expertly.'

'Hoggett taught me many skills. Smithing was only one of them. Bristol took some getting used to for a lad from a cathedral school.' Palgrave shrugged. 'I thought my battles were over when I married Anne.'

Bellamy thought on his friend's admission.

'Besides,' Palgrave returned to the assault. 'There were not sixty of them to two hundred of us.'

'But the *Gaviota*. Those seamen were prepared to do battle. You didn't flinch.'

The truth was that Palgrave's reaction had amazed even himself. On their way to New Providence Island from Florida, Jennings had encountered a Spanish ship, most likely bound for Havana. Hoisting the black flag, Jennings gave chase in his sloop, the *Barsheba,* which soon proved too fast for the heavily laden merchant ship. Within half a day, the *Barsheba* had come alongside the Spanish vessel and the chase was over. Palgrave knew not what had driven him to raise his hand when Jennings called for volunteers for the boarding party.

Using grappling hooks, they nestled close against the *Gaviota*. Not a soul was visible on deck. Once they'd hauled themselves over the railing and onto the Spanish ship, a crew of about thirty men emerged from below and from behind the rigging, each armed either with pistols and machetes, shortswords and daggers, or weaponry Palgrave did not recognise.

When the crew appeared, Palgrave felt fear, cold and virulent, volleying outwards in waves from his core. It was then that he recognised the peculiarity of his situation. Removed from his world, he had been released into another where fighting was his only option. He'd heard talk among the crew of battles. He knew violence might be coming and had thought he was ready for it; to meet it face to face was far different. He would have given anything to have it otherwise.

He remembered every detail of the incursion, movement by movement.

A cry had gone out in Spanish and the first shot was fired. He looked at Bellamy, who had shielded his face from the wooden shards that sprayed out when the shot hit the deck. Palgrave instinctively stormed into the fray, half-pike raised, and immediately beat a man's weapon from his hand. The young Spaniard had stared into Palgrave's face, shocked that his role had concluded so quickly. The sailor was barely a man. This realisation did not stop Palgrave from striking him hard on the side of his head and knocking him to the ground.

So resounding were the shouts, grunts and cries of pain on deck that they fuelled Palgrave's intent further still.

Next, a dark man with light green eyes heavy with terror came at him with an axe. Palgrave raised his weapon and swung, like he would a cricket bat, and caught him sharply on the ribcage. Palgrave felt the sailor's bones give way beneath the force of his pike; the dark man fell to the ground, clutching his side. Without a moment's meditation, Palgrave lifted his foot and kicked him convincingly in his injured side, then levelled him with a further swipe to the base of his skull.

Palgrave reasoned the skirmish lasted only a few minutes before it was over, before the Spanish captain positioned himself high on the quarterdeck and waved the white flag vigorously.

Now looking back on the battle with Bellamy, his actions gave him concern. It had been easy – too easy – for him to stave in a frightened man's head without a second's thought. He was ashamed of how enlivened he had felt afterwards, and a fierce blaze, one he was unaccustomed to, surged through his body along with the memory. He suddenly realised he had savoured the experience.

Bellamy turned and studied Palgrave's profile for a second. 'There's a pink, the *Rover*, leaving for Massachusetts Bay tonight. Take your twenty pieces of eight and go back to Leah. Living comfortably for a year is more than most men can boast.'

Palgrave still cupped the purse in his hand, weighing it meditatively for some minutes. 'A year is not enough.'

The sun had now set and there was only the merest glimmer of light emanating from the sky. Bellamy turned and looked towards the town. Palgrave followed suit. Torches and lanterns had been lit and the foreshore burned with activity. Storekeepers and traders went about their business as if it were morning. The sound of raucous singing coming from one of the many taverns could be heard on the beach, almost drowning out the sea's gentle lapping against the sand.

'We shall meet Jennings tonight and negotiate our terms for the next voyage,' Bellamy directed. 'But you must purchase some more fitting attire, my friend. You are already being called "The Puritan" among the crew.'

Palgrave shook his head and studied his sombre clothes. He removed his wide-brimmed felt hat and examined it for a moment. It was battered and dusty. 'I cannot change who I am.'

'Is *that* who you are?' Bellamy returned.

Palgrave shrugged and an inquisitive smile settled on his lips before the men walked across the sand towards the town.

Jennings seemed pleased to have both Bellamy and Palgrave join his crew for the Caribbean excursion. They agreed with a handshake in the tavern. The pair would be required to take the ship's articles the next day once aboard. The captain made ready to leave for his ship, citing their early morning departure, and advised Palgrave and Bellamy to follow suit.

When he and Bellamy were alone, Palgrave produced the compass he had purchased only an hour before from a fence called Mister Dugan. The enterprising salesman had set up shop in a tent next to the tavern. He was stout with a bilious look and wore a smart suit of clothes in a deep shade of burgundy, along with a powdered wig; it occurred to Palgrave, however, that even the most strikingly dressed men in Nassau appeared tarnished.

Dugan had regaled his customer with a lengthy, elaborate tale of how the silver-cased French mechanism had come into his possession. Their conversation meandered and twisted for almost an hour and eventually led them to Bristol, the bayside location of Dugan's birth. The fence was thrilled when he learnt of Palgrave's connection to the town and hastily sold him the compass for just one Spanish dollar, even though 'it pained him to do so', or so he had claimed.

Now Palgrave studied it more closely, turning the object this way and that as if to test its accuracy. *How my Joseph would like to toy with this*, he thought. He imagined his eldest son's delight in such a finely crafted object, the fascination bright in his eyes as he held a magnet sensitive to the earth's almighty pull.

14

____

Tamesine scanned the clientele of the the Three Jolly Irishmen from her position at the entrance. The smoke-filled tavern was thick with ship captains and sailors, mostly drunk, many of whom she recognised. Regular customers. By her side was a young boy. Taking his hand, she guided him through the patrons, nodding good evening to the musician who stood in the corner of the establishment playing _The King's Ballad_ on his fiddle. Brushing against Bellamy's seat, Tamesine stopped and curtseyed theatrically, one hand sweeping the dirt floor while the other held out the skirt of her pale blue mantua.

'Do beg pardon, Sir,' she said in an accent not dissimilar to Bellamy's.

'Pay it no mind,' said Bellamy as he and Palgrave rose from their seats.

As she lifted her face, her eyes locked momentarily with Bellamy's and she saw his gaze shift to her son and back again. Tamesine felt his look in every nerve of her body. Nodding politely at both men, she clutched her son's hand

and continued on her way to the back of the tavern and through a door to the outside. Here a canvas had been erected sheltering a galley, of sorts. A brick of a man with a bald head tussled the boy's hair playfully. The boy looked at the man and smiled affectionately.

'Be mindful of Tom,' Tamesine said as she turned towards the tavern.

'Turtle stew for supper, Johnny Boy?' Tom asked. He ladled a generous portion of steaming broth into a bowl from the cauldron that hung above an open fire.

Tamesine turned to her son a final time when she reached the door. A faint smile passed across her lips. Then she exhaled and walked back inside.

She strolled dispassionately in and around the tables. Most of the men were too drunk to notice her, indulging in their winnings from the Spanish raid. A barely discernible sneer darkened her pretty, open face for an instant.

The news of the raid had attracted a wave of rogues, adventurers and pirates from across the globe, yet Jennings was the only man with backbone enough to assemble a crew and sail northwards along the Florida coast to where it was stashed. Talk of him – and his two hundred men – rowing ashore at Palmar de Ayz was rampant on the island.

'Jennings marched three regiments along the beach,' Dugan had informed her yesterday. 'Each one was led by a flag-bearer and a drummer.'

Tamesine had nodded in interest, silently calculating the impact on her trade.

'Apparently the Spanish admiral strode, all pride and puff, along the beach to Jennings and asked, "Is this war?"' Dugan continued in an adequate Spanish accent.

'"Not at all," Jennings replied forcefully, not blinking an eye. "We have come to claim the mountain of wealth that was fished from the wrecks that you have buried in the sand." What gall! I've never heard of such swagger in all my time on this island. The admiral surrendered at once.'

Now Tamesine stopped and studied each table closely, seeking out that English captain. Disappointed by his absence, she continued on her saunter, smiling archly as men grabbed at her buttocks and thighs. A Spanish black lace fan concealed her revulsion. She halted for a moment and passed the time with the innkeeper, a cheerful Irish fellow named Garrett, brother of Tom the cook. The siblings had allowed Tamesine to pursue her ambitions in their tavern at no cost.

'What do you consider a fair cut?' she had asked when their deal was struck almost a decade before. Numerous taverns had sprouted in Nassau during the Spanish War. Tamesine had chosen this particular establishment because she had heard it was one of the only saloons not to offer the service of whores.

Garrett had looked down at the baby in her arms. 'How long has this little pup been in the world?'

'Not yet six months.'

'And you? You're but a babe yourself?' Garrett smiled.

'I've been here long enough,' she had replied coolly. 'I'm not green. How much?'

After a minute's consideration of both the mother and the baby he answered Tamesine's question. 'Why, nothing. The additional commerce your pretty presence will attract is payment enough.'

After her husband stranded her on New Providence Island, Tamesine realised she would have to fend for herself. Returning to England was not an option. She had run away with Lieutenant John King and, in doing so, had banished herself from her home and family.

It had never been her intention to tend to the clientele herself. She had a son, after all, and could not be cursed with syphilis or burdened with the cost of a beating. It struck her there was a larger sum to be had as the overseer of the operation. It was then but a simple task to attain the employment of three young women who, by hope or circumstance, had found themselves marooned on the island as well.

Back then, the custom had been mainly British Royal Navy seamen and the occasional officer who drank more, but also paid more, than a regular sailor. She soon learnt that was just their way; officers relished flaunting their rank, even if only to a whore. Now her trade was made up of pirates, or 'privateers' as many of them, reluctant to jettison their wartime credentials, preferred to be called.

The raucous laughter at a nearby table made her start.

'I fear it will be quiet for you this evening,' Garrett said. 'But tomorrow will be more profitable, once they've grown accustomed to their success and their sore heads hinder such imbibing as is taking place tonight.' He raised his bushy eyebrows and chuckled.

'There are those two over there,' he said, indicating Palgrave and Bellamy. 'Curious, they are. They've not yet finished one ale between them. The tall one, the one who resembles a farmer, is good humoured, although I warrant it is his chum who has the deeper pockets.'

Tamesine's brow furrowed as she pondered Garrett's words and recalled the concern that she and her son had provoked in the handsome man. She found them disturbing; their sobriety and poise were ill suited to this environment. However, casting her eye around the room, she thought they were the only likely prospects in a rank den of thieves and freebooters. She made her way slowly to their table.

Bellamy turned and appraised her when he felt her light touch on his shoulder. His eyes went to her mahogany curls, which she had piled loosely on the crown of her head. A rose-shaped pin helped secure the wayward locks. He waited for her to speak.

'Your dark eyes brim with sorrow,' she said, leaning closer to be heard above the din of the tavern.

'As do yours,' he replied.

'Let me brighten them.' She ran her fingertips the length of Bellamy's arm and took his hand. 'There is a girl,' she gestured towards a door with her head, 'in that room. A very pretty girl. If she does not take your fancy then there is another ...'

'You're from the south west aren't you?' Bellamy broke in, recognising her accent.

She nodded and looked at him suspiciously for a moment before remembering her purpose. 'You're a fine-looking man,' she continued.

'Thank you,' he replied, impressed with her persistence. 'But my friend here, Mister Williams, is a fine man all over – outside and in.'

Palgrave's eyes rolled in exasperation as Tamesine took him in. He wasn't an attractive man by any means – thin, angular face and long nose – but his pale blue eyes shone with kindness, buoying his appeal.

'When we set sail tomorrow morning it will be for a long time, many months perhaps,' Bellamy advised, lifting Tamesine's hand and offering it to his friend.

Without judgement, Palgrave shook his head casually and finished the remnants of his ale.

'I wish you both a pleasant evening,' he said, rising and

placing his hat on his head. 'I will see you at first light, Samuel.'

When he departed, Tamesine glided seamlessly into Palgrave's seat. 'So ... Samuel is your name. "Black Sam" I will call you,' she said, teasing.

'You have seen inside my soul and the colour of my heart,' he responded, smiling wryly.

'Nay,' she whispered. 'I speak of your eyes. They're pitch black. Your heart,' she continued softly, laying her palm on his chest, 'is the colour of sunlight. I can feel its warmth.'

Bellamy could feel her breath on his face. He glanced at her hand.

'You are mistaken good lady. The eyes are the window to the soul, are they not?' he offered, enjoying the exchange. 'My heart, if I may lay claim to one, is as dark as my visage – as black as coal.'

'I pray thee, allow me to spark that cold, hard rock that lies at your core.' She edged even closer.

Bellamy gazed into her hazel eyes and gently fixed one of her curls behind her ear. He laughed lightly, uncertainly, she thought. Then Tamesine felt the tingle of goosebumps on her bare arms. But when he abruptly removed her hand from his chest and asked after her boy, her face hardened.

Confused by the shift, she replied. 'A friend is watching over him.'

'What has brought you to Nassau?' Bellamy asked, leaning back in his chair.

'My husband. He was a sailor.'

'Was he killed?'

'That's what I tell his son.'

Bellamy nodded. He looked at her kindly. Then he rose and reached into his pocket and produced two Spanish dollars. He placed them in her hand, bending her fingers gently around the coins. 'That's for your time.'

'But ...' she began.

'Waste neither your wiles nor your wit on me,' he responded as he left the table. 'I have business to see to.'

15

___

Palgrave sat on the ship's deck playing at cards with Bellamy and Ade. It was a complex Spanish game of trickery and bidding called 'ombre'. Bellamy had taught them. To both Palgrave's and Bellamy's astonishment, Ade, who had only a rudimentary understanding of the English language, picked up the nuances of the game much faster than Palgrave. Even Bellamy, who had been taught the diversion years ago in the navy, found it difficult to trump the African.

Born under another nation's flag, Palgrave judged, Ade could be a man of immense learning and power – a magistrate, a doctor, or, more likely, a great soldier. Palgrave had been teaching the African to read using the Bible that Leah had desperately thrown into his bag on his departure. Ade proved an adept and critical student, frequently disputing the plausibility of the text. He remarked, however, that he 'found some worth in the Psalms', explaining he could 'hear' their music.

Unless Jennings issued specific orders to mend rigging or clean the weaponry, the crew were left to distract themselves. They played games of chance, or music on fiddles, lutes or accordions, while others drank or slept. In the weeks on board the *Barsheba*, criss-crossing Spanish shipping lanes around Cuba, Jennings had taken only one prize, a small French sloop en route to New Orleans from Havana carrying a cargo that Jennings roughly valued at a mere four thousand pounds. With rations and fresh water becoming scant, Bellamy and Palgrave feared they would soon be forced to turn back to New Providence or Jamaica.

Only a week ago they had come across an English frigate, the *Mary*. Jennings refused to take the ship, despite the captain, a young man called Stone, having great riches on board. Instead, Jennings paid Stone handsomely for the twenty gallons of rum that he and the crew filched from the *Mary*'s cargo.

Later, Bellamy had complained impatiently to Palgrave. 'He's cutting our opportunities by a third in his unwillingness to capture English ships!'

'He's a privateer working for the king,' Palgrave had reasoned.

'He's no privateer. He's a pirate through and through. The war is long finished. His friend Hamilton is no better. Despite his lofty title and fine home in Port Royal, he's happy to take his cut when Jennings comes to call.

'I want to return to Eastham quickly,' he went on. 'I promised Maria a year. At this rate it will take me at least five!'

'She'll wait. Maria is constant in her affections.'

Bellamy had glanced doubtfully at his friend. In truth, it was not Maria's affections that were of concern to him. Since departing Nassau, he had caught himself often recalling the woman from the tavern and their brief exchange. The sound of her warm, soft voice still echoed in his mind.

Now, tiring of the card game, he raised his eyes to the main mast then called to the boatswain. 'Mister Wilson, hand me your eyeglass!'

Clutching the telescope, Bellamy made his way speedily through the rigging to the masthead. He adjusted the instrument and peered in the direction of Cuba, which lay about two miles away.

Palgrave's eyes followed his friend closely while Ade rearranged their cards. Bellamy was restless. He needed to take action, even if the action was merely watching.

After a few minutes, Ade placed a card on the pile. Another winning hand. As Palgrave gathered the cards and began to shuffle, Bellamy called from his perch, 'Get Captain Jennings. There's a ship!'

Palgrave and Ade rose to the railing and gazed into the distance. Jennings arrived on deck and held his eyeglass to his face. He nodded slowly, confirming Bellamy's claim.

'You have an eagle's eye, Bellamy,' Jennings said as Bellamy climbed to the deck. 'Their colours aren't clear. Can you see anything?'

'Nay, but it's a ship ...' Bellamy looked at his captain keenly, his eyes as bright as two stars.

'It has anchored in Bahia Honda,' Jennings said. After a moment's thought he continued. 'We'll approach slowly, flying the Union flag. We'll anchor in the entrance of the harbour.'

JENNINGS'S SHIPS, the *Barsheba*, *Cocoa Nut* and *Discovery*, dropped anchor just outside the narrow entrance of the keyhole-shaped harbour of Bahia Honda. With the distance narrowed, Jennings was able to recognise that the vessel, named *Sainte Marie*, was a heavily armed French frigate, much larger than any of Jennings's slim, elegant sloops. The captain scrutinised the activity on the ship more closely from the quarterdeck, his silver hair blowing in the gusty offshore wind. Bellamy eyed him vigilantly, head cocked like a cat waiting for unseen prey.

Jennings requested the presence of the two other captains, Liddell and Carnegie, aboard the *Barsheba*. Bellamy ran to the bow and cried through funnelled hands in the direction of the *Discovery* and the *Cocoa Nut*.

While the captains weighed their options in Jennings's cabin, Bellamy paced the length of the deck, halting occasionally to stare at the *Sainte Marie*. The magnitude of the ship was awesome. *What a beauty*, Bellamy mused in wonder. The expanse of the glorious oak hull reminded him of a ship of the line, not a lacklustre merchant pink. The upper deck was painted a deep sky blue and the golden figurehead at the bow was a bare-breasted woman clutching a trident. Her grandeur was worthy of a flagship for the French Navy.

Bellamy looked at his pocket watch then snapped it closed with a loud exhalation of breath.

'Penny for your thoughts,' Palgrave said.

'It would mean death to us all to attack that frigate directly in this wind. We'd be sitting ducks once our intentions became clear,' Palgrave nodded as Bellamy crouched beside him. 'And it's impossible to tack at speed through the heads on a day like today. We might capture the ship, but it will not be achieved by force or speed. A deception is required.'

'A deception?'

Before Bellamy could continue, the three captains emerged on deck and assembled the crew of the *Barsheba*.

Bellamy noticed Liddell wore a strained expression on his smooth round face as he positioned his hat just so on his head. After outlining the dangers of a direct attack, Jennings turned to Bellamy.

'You first spied the frigate. Take two men in a rowboat to scout the situation,' he ordered. 'We need to know the number of crew, the number of guns and the extent of the cargo. Get as accurate a figure as possible.'

Bellamy nodded and invited Palgrave and Ade to join him.

~

THE THREE MEN covered the distance quickly. Once noticed by a member of the *Sainte Marie*'s crew, Bellamy requested permission for them to come aboard and talk with the captain.

'*Sainte Marie* is a beautiful ship,' Bellamy began after the men exchanged greetings.

'I was an Admiral in the war. I enjoy keeping my hand in, as you English like to say, even though I'm merely a merchant sailor now,' he explained modestly. 'I insist that my vessel is maintained to the highest standard.'

Captain D'Escoubet matched perfectly with his ship. He was broad of shoulder and belly, and had muscular, bronzed hands. He wore an immaculate suit the colour of cobalt that resembled an officer's uniform. After learning that the men had rowed twenty miles along the coast in search of water, he invited the trio to join him for supper. His English was faultless.

Bellamy explained he was a carpenter, part of the crew of an English merchant ship, the *Mary*. He told D'Escoubet that they had been travelling from Jamaica to Virginia, but had begun taking on water the day before yesterday. Consequently, their captain, a trader named Wainwright, guided the sloop into an inlet around Cabañas. Although the marshy cove was an ideal anchorage to make repairs, claimed Bellamy, they had found little by way of supplies. Wainwright had therefore tasked the three who now sat at D'Escoubet's table to embark on a search for fresh water.

'Why did you not seek aid from the English ships moored in the heads?' asked the captain at the completion of Bellamy's tale.

'Why, we did!' Palgrave answered. 'The captain refused to help us. He took us for pirates, I warrant.'

Bellamy and Ade, summoning an expression of surprise, added their agreement.

'What are you carrying?' the captain asked.

'Fifty hogsheads of sugar and less in tobacco,' Palgrave said without missing a beat, shovelling a spoonful of potatoes into his mouth.

'Africans? Slaves?' D'Escoubet queried.

'None,' Bellamy answered.

The captain looked at the stately African sitting opposite him.

'He's a free man,' Bellamy said.

'What's your cargo, Captain?' Palgrave asked. 'There may be some trade to be done.'

D'Escoubet shrugged. 'Much the same as you, I'm afraid. We departed Saint-Domingue last week with a little coffee and sugar, some tobacco.'

'But the *Sainte Marie* is heavily armed, is it not?'

'Sixteen guns and forty men is not excessive for these waters, Mister Williams,' D'Escoubet explained. 'I'm a quarter owner in this ship and all its cargo. It's in my best interests to see it arrive safely in La Nouvelle-Orléans.'

Palgrave shot Bellamy a glance. Both of them were certain a frigate as formidable as the *Sainte Marie* would be hauling cargo more lucrative. It wouldn't have surprised Bellamy to learn, in fact, that D'Escoubet himself was a privateer.

The sun had not yet set when the three men departed the *Sainte Maire* with four casks of fresh water and a crate of oranges.

BELLAMY INFORMED JENNINGS, Liddell and Carnegie of the exact details of their meeting with D'Escoubet, describing the capacity of the frigate and his belief that a direct attack would be disastrous.

'Our sloops would certainly be sunk,' Bellamy explained. 'D'Escoubet says his ship has only sixteen guns, but they're twelve-pounders and there might be more. There could be up to forty guns on board. I don't trust him.'

Nevertheless, Jennings was eager to take the ship, citing surprise as their most sure weapon. Carnegie was obsequious and self-seeking, and agreed with Jennings. Liddell opposed, most stringently, the proposal.

'I thought I made my position plain,' Liddell stated. His tone was even. 'The *Sainte Marie* is a trading ship on lawful occasion and D'Escoubet is an officer of some repute. It would be piracy to seize the ship unlawfully.'

'Then we label it a pirate ship and seize her,' Jennings put in. 'Bellamy believes D'Escoubet could very well be engaging in piracy himself.'

It did not concern Bellamy that Jennings was embroidering the account for the sake of his argument. He was hungry for the quarry.

'It's illegal!' Liddell cried, slapping his hand against the captain's table. 'Unless you have substantiated proof that the *Sainte Marie* is carrying English goods unlawfully neither I nor the crew of the *Cocoa Nut* will be party to your scheme.'

'By God man!' Jennings shouted, rising. 'What are you out here for? To look upon such a grand prize then return to shore with your fingers in your mouth?'

Palgrave glanced at Bellamy, both aware that Jennings was flying his true colours at last.

'You're a coward!' Jennings went on. 'You have been at my right hand during the *unlawful* capture of more than a dozen ships, and at the raid of Palmar de Ayz. Vanity and fear dictate we call ourselves privateers, but let us not conceal our better natures under the cloak of arrogance any longer. You and I, and all aboard this ship, are pirates.'

Jennings sat and poured out a single cup of madeira. He passed it across the table to Liddell. Once he was calm he continued.

'Granted, the frigate that lies within our grasp only two miles away in the harbour is a more daunting prospect than any of our previous snatches. This is no employment for the lily-livered or faint-hearted,' Jennings said. 'We will vote.'

The crew proved as hungry as Bellamy. Liddell was outvoted. He was transported, under guard, to his cabin aboard his ship while the details of the raid were discussed.

16

Three long boats, each crewed by twelve half-naked, ash-coated men, rowed across the bay to engage the *Sainte Marie*. The *Barsheba* and the *Discovery* sailed a half-mile's distance behind them. The wash of the oars and the muted sounds of their pilots' breath was the only indication of the imminent assault.

Under midnight's mantle, the boats approached their target. Never before involved in a battle in which the stakes had been so high, Bellamy's heart raced and he found it difficult to temper his breathing. At that moment, he realised he was terrified – not of death, but of failure. He wiped the perspiration from his upper lip and tasted ash. He corralled his wayward thoughts and instead attempted to focus on Maria – his real prize – and her golden hair, her wide blue eyes and the life they might soon share. But her ivory skin and the soft blush of her cheek were quickly thrust from his mind by the image of another woman – the madam from the tavern in Nassau. Bellamy closed his eyes tight for an instant, alarmed by the unsolicited thought. When he opened them again his dread had faded.

Not until his boat tapped against the ship's hull announcing its arrival was the nightwatchman aboard the *Sainte Maire* alerted. Leaning over the railing, the sailor was stunned by the sight before him. Unsure whether they were natives or phantoms, he called out in terror. 'Where are you going?!'

Bellamy was struck by the ridiculousness of the question and smirked.

'Aboard. Where do you think?'

A few seconds later, a fusillade of musket shot and an unruly chorus of howls and shrieks were discharged from the long boats. The sailor disappeared and D'Escoubet appeared on the quarterdeck. A blast of cannon fire immediately rang out from *Barsheba* and a cannonball tore over D'Escoubet's head, missing him by an inch, but splintering the mainmast. Bellamy threw the first grappling hook, landing it securely on the rail. He climbed the hull quickly, screaming like an Indian the entire time. Close behind was Ade who, balancing his long feet on the railing with half-pike held aloft, emitted a thunderous roar, horrifying the startled crew who thought Hell itself had been unleashed upon the vessel. The French crew dashed below decks or darted up masts in fear of their fates.

What Bellamy witnessed was a shambles. The bleary-eyed crew from the French ship ran directionless, gathering arms and loading muskets, terrified by the two dozen invading savages. Several seamen threw themselves into the water rather than confront the beasts. As Jennings's men intimidated the bewildered sailors into submission, Bellamy searched for D'Escoubet and leapt up the stairs to the quarterdeck. He looked about him for a moment.

'Do you surrender?' he called to the French crew.

A low grumble of voices that Bellamy took for assent followed.

He ordered Jennings's crew to tie the men up and search the lower decks for others. From his position on the raised platform, he cast his eye along the length of the ship and discovered the captain, towards the stern, heaving his substantial body over the side of the ship. Bellamy ran starboard and saw D'Escoubet and three officers lowering themselves into a rowboat.

'Mister Williams,' Bellamy shouted when he spotted Palgrave below, netting floundering sailors and hauling them into his long boat. 'D'Escoubet is escaping.'

Palgrave began to row in the French captain's direction. It wasn't long before D'Escoubet's small rowboat was overtaken and Bellamy watched as the Frenchman's hands flew into the sky. Bellamy exhaled and hastily reviewed the scene on deck. The *Sainte Marie* was theirs – and the French had not fired a single shot.

'THAT WAS QUITE A RUSE, Messieurs Bellamy and Williams,' D'Escoubet commented casually. He was tied alongside his officers to the mizzenmast of the *Sainte Marie*. Bellamy and Palgrave had cleaned themselves of soot and had dressed in garments found below deck among the crew's belongings.

'And Monsieur l'Afrique,' he looked at Ade who stood nearby, calmly tying his shirt. 'That was a splendid performance. Petrifying.'

Ade offered him a quizzical glance.

'Why did you concede?' Bellamy asked. 'You could have sunk the *Barsheba* and the *Discovery* with ease.'

The captain smiled ruefully. 'My men were in no state of

mind to load cannons and do battle. Surprise and fear are matchless weapons, are they not?'

Bellamy nodded and he and D'Escoubet measured one another for an instant.

'I think as well,' the captain went on thoughtfully. 'That, despite my naval history, I did not want to see her come to harm.'

'The mast was fractured,' Bellamy said.

The captain shrugged. 'It is nothing a skilled carpenter cannot mend.'

Bellamy considered the captain's words. Surprise. Fear. Terror. They were remarkable weapons indeed. Bellamy and the crew had gone into battle appearing as if they were capable of anything. As a result, they didn't have to do much at all and had managed to capture a well-armed frigate without serious damage to the ship, crew or cargo.

'It's a wonder you are English,' D'Escoubet continued. 'You showed great courage and enterprise.'

Bellamy and Palgrave grinned at the Frenchman's back-handed compliment.

JENNINGS'S QUARTERMASTER, Mister van der Heul, discovered vast treasure and cargo in the hull worth nearly forty thousand pounds. As he was directing its transfer from the *Saint Marie* to the *Barsheba*, D'Escoubet looked at Bellamy and shrugged. Bellamy found himself slightly vexed that such a character was now without a command. He would, no doubt, be put ashore with his men to find his way to France, tail between his legs, seeking clemency from his partners and compensation from his insurers in La Rochelle. Then Jennings appeared on board.

'Untie the captain and his crew, Mister Williams. Take four men and see them safely aboard the *Discovery*. The *Sainte Marie* will now be helmed by Captain Carnegie.'

It was not unusual for the vanquished to be left with a ship, typically that which is least favoured by the victor. However, Carnegie's appointment astonished all who heard Jennings's announcement.

Palgrave looked immediately at Bellamy. His chest heaved and his jaw was fixed tight. Then he turned to D'Escoubet. The colour had drained from his ruddy face.

'What's to become of Liddell?' Bellamy asked Jennings severely.

'He has seen the error of his ways. He now has command of the *Cocoa Nut*,' Jennings explained, eyeing Bellamy sharply before adding. 'I would advise you to temper your tone, Mister Bellamy.'

It was D'Escoubet who broke the strained silence as they rowed towards the *Discovery*. 'She should have been yours, Monsieur Bellamy. If there is any justice in this world, she should have been yours.'

17

When they anchored in Nassau at dusk, the plunder was divided and the crew quickly dispersed, disappearing into one of the waterfront taverns. All except Ade, who lay on the beach, an ebony starfish, gazing into the heavens. Often he would sleep on deck. It was his practice when in port to sleep outdoors. He relished the open air more than anyone Palgrave knew. Being chained in the hull of a slave ship for months on end, rarely glimpsing daylight, changed a man's perception of the world. Lying on the sand and taking in the night sky was all the celebration Ade required. Palgrave and Bellamy delayed their revelries, preferring a thorough wash with hot water and soap to any carousing. The pair soon located a bathhouse operating from an abandoned mansion that once had belonged to a governor, or so Dugan informed them.

They spent some time submerged in the iron tubs on the ground floor, side by side, silent. Other baths were positioned higgledy-piggledy around them. The clientele spoke in low voices. Palgrave sank his body into the water and examined his strange surrounds. Vines wove a path along the balustrade of an elaborate staircase, creeping along the walls and floor of the once grand home. The doors on the first storey opened and closed as whores and sailors entered and exited. Two fierce-looking Turks, armed with scimitars, stood guard on the mezzanine offering protection. Palgrave glimpsed the heavens through the vast holes in the roof, where doves nested in the exposed rafters. He found the occasional flap of their wings a comfort, reminding him of home.

As the water in the tubs cooled, young men with olive skin and bare feet sloshed through the shallow puddles on the floor to empty buckets of white-hot liquid onto them. A young black woman shaved them both with a razor so sharp, the edge glinted in the steamy surrounds. Palgrave rested his head against the cold rim of the tub as the woman manoeuvred the razor around the clefts and rises of his neck. She frowned slightly as she worked. Palgrave stared beyond the woman. Listening to the scratch of the razor against his skin reminded him of Leah's second visit all those years ago.

Distracted and perplexed by her return, he warmed cider on the hearth for them. Leah emptied her basket of a pork pie and a pair of woollen stockings. When he handed her the cup, the two sat for some minutes drinking in silence, her hands wrapped around the vessel to warm them. Palgrave stared into his mug as the steam rose around his face, uncertain and sheepish, but he remembered the excitement that had stirred in him when he sensed her eyes on him. He glanced at her and she spoke.

'Would you allow me to shave you, Mister Williams?' she asked, placing her mug on the table, gazing at him with her gentle blue eyes. 'Your beard does you an injustice.'

Surprised at the request, he made no answer.

'You needn't fear,' she said, seriously. 'I shave my father quite regularly and have drawn blood only once.'

Could he detect a note of irony in her level tone? There was a definite flash of humour in her eyes. He felt that she displayed a maturity far beyond her eighteen years.

'In fact, he boasts that he would go no further than his own kitchen for the finest shave in New England. I'm quite accomplished, I assure you.'

Then he laughed. It was a loud, deep chuckle. Then she laughed too, her cheeks growing pink. 'Aye. If it would amuse you, Leah Hallett.'

'It's not a question of amusement, Sir,' she remarked, rising, 'but one of necessity.'

Palgrave watched in wonderment as she brought together what was needed – a basin of water she warmed on the fire, a pair of scissors discovered in a small wooden box of tools, some soap and two white cloths she had found in the first cupboard she opened. She moved around the kitchen as though it were already hers. Palgrave fetched his razor.

She removed his coat and lay it across the back of a chair then instructed him to sit. One of the cloths she carefully tucked into the neck of his shirt. Her fingers were cold as they passed against his skin. Leah trimmed his whiskers with the scissors, examining the area and smiling occasionally as she did so. He could not identify a single imperfection in her features or complexion. The urge to burrow his face into her treacle-coloured hair was overpowering and he wondered if those locks would smell as sweet. She rolled her sleeves to her elbows and lathered the soap in the water. Then, standing behind his chair, she began to massage the suds along his jawline and down into his neck. Her touch was firm, purposeful. Palgrave exhaled slowly and his heart's rhythm quickened. After drying her hands on the second cloth, Leah lifted the razor and proceeded to shave him with even, deliberate strokes along the length of his neck. Conscious of the rise and fall of Leah's breathing, Palgrave considered why this beautiful creature had come back to him.

Was it merely charity or could he sense something more in the caress of her fingertips and the brush of her skirts against his body? Anne had been marked as 'plain'. She possessed a simple but loyal nature. In their brief, but contented, time as husband and wife Palgrave never recalled her moving him like this with a single touch, so that his skin tingled in delight. Anne had been devoted in her companionship and constant in her temper but their love for each other had never been desire. Palgrave hushed his concerns and closed his eyes, allowing himself a moment of undefined pleasure as Leah performed her task.

Once she had finished she gathered the towel from his neck and delicately patted his face dry, taking special care in the nooks around his nose and lips. Then Leah stepped back and smiled.

'That's better. More like the Mister Williams I remember.'

'Will you come again?' he asked, more eagerly than he intended.

'Of course,' she replied, without a moment's thought. 'Tomorrow. It shan't be until the afternoon. My mother needs me in the morning.' Before she departed Leah promised to make him a salve from elderberry for his skin and some bayberry candles. She would bring them with her the next day.

Occasionally, Leah still shaved him with the same diligence as she had shown then, but it was without the charge that distinguished the first time, the kind of exhilaration that can only be generated by such a remarkable and totally unexpected occurrence. He looked into the face again of the woman who stood above him. She nodded sulkily, an indication she was finished, then she wiped the razor on the towel that hung from the waistband of her skirt. Palgrave lowered himself into the water.

An hour later Bellamy and Palgrave were seated at the Three Jolly Irishmen. Despite the rowdiness of the establishment, the atmosphere at their table was markedly solemn. Bellamy had not recovered from Jennings's slight and he gazed around the tavern, sullenly, silently, as if seeking someone out.

What could Palgrave say to Bellamy to appease him? Years of sufferance and his even temper made it difficult to empathise with a man like Sam, hot-headed and bold; over-bold, Jennings would argue. Before Palgrave could speak, he was distracted by a fight that had broken out on the other side of the room. Daggers were soon drawn by the two men, who were much addled in their behaviour. Bellamy and Palgrave rose as the landlord propelled himself over the bar and into the heart of the fray. Sharply tapping the most afflicted of the combatants on the head with a cudgel, the landlord then dragged the unconscious seaman from the tavern and deposited him outside in the dirt.

Once the fracas had ended, Palgrave said, 'You're sorely disappointed.'

Bellamy nodded.

'Carnegie has been with Jennings for a very long time,' Palgrave said. 'We aren't privy to their history. No doubt, over the years, promises have been made ...'

'The *Sainte Marie* should have been mine. It was my

plan. I led the assault. If Jennings was a fair man, I would be captain of that ship.'

Palgrave frowned as he thought on Bellamy's complaint.

'Our capacities are being thwarted,' Bellamy continued. 'Palgrave, Maria is so far out of sight that I can't see a time when we will be together. It will not be the summer at this rate.'

'What do you suggest?' Palgrave asked.

'Leave Jennings. Find another captain who will take us on.'

Palgrave was struck by his use of the word 'us'. He supposed he and Bellamy were linked, knotted together, working towards a common purpose. Each saw to the other's welfare and aimed for a safe return to Eastham in the summer. The truth was Palgrave could not imagine separating from his friend. Perhaps Carnegie and Jennings shared a similar connection.

As Palgrave contemplated their partnership, he felt the stroke of a hand along his shoulders. He turned. It was the seductive madam from their previous visit to the tavern.

'I have just heard word of your exploits capturing the French ship.' She bent low and addressed Palgrave in a silken tone. 'Your daring is all that is spoken of.'

'It was my friend's ploy. He's the mastermind behind the siege,' Palgrave responded, skilfully averting his eye from her bosom.

Ignoring Bellamy, Tamesine went on. 'You're much changed. That buccaneer coat and shirt suit you well.'

Palgrave looked down at the pine-green jacket and ruffled blouse he had pilfered from the *Sainte Marie*. She ran her fingertip along his jawline, lifting his face. 'Your skin is like velvet.'

Bellamy viewed the exchange with a wry half-smile on his lips.

'I've been shaved,' Palgrave said, untroubled by her advances. He stood and offered Tamesine his seat. She primly fixed the folds of her rose-coloured gown and the lace around the neckline as Palgrave dragged a stool to the table. He continued. 'My wife would not find my new attire fitting.'

'You have a wife ...' she said in amazement. 'It's unlike Captain Jennings to take on married men.'

Palgrave raised an eyebrow as though he was unaware of the proviso. 'My wife, Leah, is in New England with our five children.'

'Surely not,' Tamesine exclaimed in mock surprise. 'Five children! You don't appear half as weary as you should.'

Palgrave laughed, amused by the seduction that had been set in play. He lifted his mug to his lips. When he lowered it again to the table, Tamesine took his hand and interlaced their fingers. Her lips parted and she beckoned him away from the table with a slight lean of her head. Palgrave stared at their hands seriously for a moment as he contemplated his response.

'Verily, I long for a woman's touch,' he explained, looking into her eyes. 'But neither you nor any of your young ladies are that woman.'

Tamesine removed her hand slowly as her pretty complexion darkened. Bellamy could not tell the cause; regret mixed with envy, or perhaps longing.

Bellamy rose.

'Would you care to take a stroll by the waterfront?' he asked.

Tamesine nodded tentatively as Bellamy took her gently by the elbow and led her outside.

~

'HAVE YOU MET HER?' Tamesine asked as Bellamy guided her towards the shoreline, weaving between the makeshift tents and shelters.

He looked at her inquiringly, drawing her nearer to the water and away from the occupants of the beach and all that escorted them – the cursing, the acrid stink of burnt fish and the occasional grunts and sighs of pleasure.

'Your friend's wife?'

He nodded. She stared at the moon in contemplation. It was a new moon, just a thin bright sickle against the black.

'He must love her very much. It's been so long since I've come across a faithful man,' she said after a while.

'Leah is beautiful. Younger than Palgrave, virtuous. She's forthright and hard-working. Palgrave told me once he would die for her ...' He stopped himself when he noticed goosebumps rising like prickles on her arms. 'But what's your name?' Bellamy looped her arm through his own, pulling her closer.

'Tamesine,' she answered.

'*Tamesine, Tamesine, Tamesine ...*' he sang, accompanied by the various tunes played on pipes and drums that drifted to them on the breeze. 'Where are you from?'

Her eyes narrowed and she pulled away. 'I cannot afford to be *strolling* with gentleman. I must see to my young ladies, especially in these times.'

'I'll pay you for the interruption to your occupation.'

Tamesine scoffed at his remark. As she was about to walk away, Bellamy asked hastily, 'Of what times do you speak?'

She halted but did not turn back. Bellamy approached her and lay his hand softly on her arm.

'Tell me.'

'In this last month everything has shifted in Nassau,' she began, turning to face him. 'A pirate, Benjamin Hornigold, has settled here. He's a brute, as is his crony, Edward Teach.'

Tamesine looked around her warily as though Hornigold or Teach might be within earshot.

'Surely two more brutes among that crowd,' Bellamy gestured towards the tavern, 'wouldn't account for such a change.'

'They're different. They've declared Nassau their dominion and all other pirates to be under their personal protection. There has been no authority in New Providence since the war, but a community of sorts has grown here. Malformed it might be, but it has functioned without excessive malice or menace very tidily. This pair, Hornigold and Teach, are demanding a share of the profits from all the businesses on the island, including the Three Jolly Irishmen. Garrett is hard. Why, you witnessed him tonight.' Bellamy recalled the landlord's quick, business-like handling of the brawl and nodded. 'But he can't take on the likes of Hornigold and Teach; both would run a man through to save the inconvenience of looking at him. What's more,' she went on breathlessly, 'they have mounted guns onto the fort in their own defence. The two saunter around town as if they own it.'

'It seems that they do.'

'Hornigold announced that he aims to create his own kingdom here – a kingdom where he is sole sovereign.'

Bellamy looked at her pensively, weighing up the idea.

'The cruellest among them call themselves the "Flying Gang",' Tamesine continued. 'All further associates of Hornigold. They have begun to accost law-abiding settlers and property owners in the street, stealing away their money and valuables. There are rumours that the few landowners who remain will flee New Providence Island, and with them will follow what little decency is left in this squalid pirate haven.'

'You should leave. Take your son and return to Cornwall.'

Tamesine looked at him, startled.

'Your name, the music in your voice, the colour in your cheek,' he explained, grinning. 'They smack of Cornwall.'

She smiled shyly.

'I can't,' she said after a moment. 'I can't leave Garrett and Tom.'

'You're attached in some way?'

Tamesine shook her head. 'They helped me once. There's no more to our friendship than that. What I earn now staves off Hornigold. Mine is the most profitable brothel on the island. Hornigold is hungry for a piece of the pie.'

Bellamy thought on her words for a moment. 'I'll deal with him.'

'You're handsome and courageous, Black Sam, but you're no match for the likes of Captain Hornigold and his cohorts.'

Then she touched her hand to his cheek, flattered by his concern and his gallantry. 'I can manage Hornigold,' she said. 'I built the brothel at the Three Jolly Irishmen from nothing and I have handled rougher trade than the likes of Captain Benjamin Hornigold,' she said in an attempt to reassure Bellamy of her credentials. 'I purchased a small holding behind the town five years ago. I built my house myself, hiring labourers and purchasing the materials all on my own.'

He looked towards the harbour. It was difficult to read his expression.

'Who is the third Irishman?' he eventually asked.

The question amused her. 'There is no third.'

Bellamy turned to her as she laughed, the light from the fires on the beach glinting off the water and lacing through her hair. His breath caught in his throat. Tamesine wasn't composed like Maria, she was brazen, quick-witted and often surly. Yet she was also kind and forgiving and devoted. She was quicksilver.

'Will you show me the house that you built?'

She nodded, her eyes not leaving the harbour.

BELLAMY WASN'T certain of the hour. His watch was in the pocket of his vest; the vest lay on the floor on the other side of Tamesine's small, neat chamber. He examined his surrounds in the half-light of the one candle they had left alight. On the chest next to the bed was a hairbrush with an ivory handle and mirrored back. This sat beside a golden box, embellished with ships. Bellamy assumed it played music and probably housed the charms and ornaments she wore when working. A cool breeze streamed through the window and Bellamy gingerly raised the quilt to Tamesine's shoulders. He rolled over and stared at her profile as she slept, delicately fingering her hair, which splayed over the pillow in unruly tendrils. Bellamy hadn't planned to bed her that night, but when he entered the house and witnessed her accomplishment – the glossy floor, the lace curtains, the gleaming, well-ordered stack of pots above the hearth and the homely smells of dust and fresh linen – the urge to know her overrode any thoughts of propriety or of Maria. Tamesine was so much more than she had at first appeared.

Bellamy had watched her closely as she moved around the kitchen lighting the candles, viewing her wholly for the first time. His heart welled. It was when she showed him the short pile of books she used to tutor her son.

'Where is he tonight?' Bellamy asked.

'Staying with a friend who runs a boarding house. It's not good for John to be with me at the Irishmen every night. Besides, Mistress Landry loves him like her own.'

When she went to move to the hutch, he leant towards her and kissed her lightly on the back of her neck. She turned, neither startled nor obliging, and solemnly raised her face to his; their lips met.

Now, shifting onto his back, he realised he had lost himself in her that evening. As he kissed her lips and neck and breasts and felt her warmth beneath him, Bellamy knew he was lost forever and he didn't care. Nassau was another world, a world where Maria had no place.

Tamesine awoke with a gasp and a single tear fell down her cheek.

'I was dreaming,' she said, staring at the ceiling. 'John was standing on the beach, just by the tavern, and a wave the size of a mountain was heading towards him. He was waving at me, happy, unaware, as I shouted at him to run, but he didn't. I tried to reach him but there were others, who I couldn't see, holding me back ...' She groaned. 'And then I woke.'

Bellamy took her in his arms and hugged her tightly to his chest. She was trembling.

'Our greatest fears haunt us always,' Bellamy said. He thought for a moment, deciding. He then cleared his throat in readiness to give voice to a memory he had attempted numerous times to muffle over the last few years.

'I was once a carpenter's mate in the Royal Navy. Not long after I had joined the ship, I was awoken one evening by the boatswain. He hauled me out of bed and ordered me to gather my tools. I was to meet him promptly at the Surgeon's quarters, although the *Royal Sovereign* had had no surgeon since I had been on board. Laid out on a table in the cabin was the gunner's mate, who I had seen from time to time about the ship. He was a merry, pleasant fellow, about the same age as I was then. The young man, whose name was Blake, bore no resemblance to the jolly shipmate I remembered – ghostly pale, he was. Although he had been plied with more than a quart of rum, his eyes were fearful ... You see, Blake knew what was about to happen before I.'

Bellamy paused, as if to steel himself.

'Go on,' Tamesine pressed gently.

'The boatswain ordered me to produce my saw. Puzzled as to why there might be a carpenter needed at that hour in the surgeon's quarters, I asked, "Which saw would that be?" The boatswain cuffed me hard about the head and shouted, "Whichever saw might cut through this!" He lifted back the blanket and it was then that I realised why I had been awoken. Blake's leg was coloured dark green from his knee to his foot. The skin was dry and puckered; the infected part of the limb seemed shrunken and malformed. The boatswain ordered I should begin cutting above the knee. He had experience with the particular ailment, it seemed. I withdrew my back-saw from my bag and stared at the leg for what seemed like an age. Then, his patience wearing thin, the boatswain ordered me to begin. He said he had time for neither idlers nor the lily-livered. I looked into Blake's eyes. They seemed forgiving, but I probably just told myself so.

Then the boatswain placed a rolled cloth, one that you might use to bind a wound, in the boy's mouth and two other men approached the table. I had not even noticed them in the cabin until that moment. They laid themselves across his body, one on either side of the table. The drink, the cloth, the weight of his shipmates provided not a jot of relief. Blake screamed and writhed when the blade met his skin. It seemed to me that death would have been preferable to the fellow than this. He pleaded with me to stop and I very nearly did, despite the consequences. Then he went limp. He'd fainted. I completed the task but he never woke up.'

Bellamy rubbed his face then stretched out his body – it had become knotted with tension. 'That memory remains with me still. In my mind, I often find myself returning to the surgeon's quarters aboard the *Sovereign*. I have relived that night many times. I can't seem to run far enough away to leave it behind.'

He had never given voice to that heinous experience before. There was something about this woman – her strength, her vulnerability – that made him feel comfortable enough to share it with her.

Tamesine nestled her head on his chest. She kissed his warm skin softly as he rested.

'You should leave here, Tamesine,' he said once more. 'I have some money now. I will see you and John on the next pink heading to England.'

She nestled into his side. 'I can't leave Garrett and Tom yet,' she explained. 'I have money too, but not quite enough. Once John's future is secure, we'll depart.'

'Future?'

She squirmed a little against him before beginning guardedly.

'My hope is for John to go to Eton College in Windsor. I have written the bursar. I have funds enough for his first year's tuition and a generous portion of land for myself nearby. A small but established estate.'

She waited for Bellamy to mock her scheme. When he didn't she continued more whimsically.

'I imagine a small grove of apple trees at the back. The fruit I shall use to brew cider and make jam. And from my sitting room window the only sight visible will be a host of green fields stretching as far as the eye can see. A stone wall, or a hedgerow here and there, will be but a minor interruption to their tranquil roll towards the horizon.'

'Go on,' he murmured. 'This is a far more agreeable dream than mine.'

'I will hire an overseer and labourers to work my land. My father was a fisherman, so I know nothing of landed work. But I will learn. The profits should be ample to see to John's schooling and a comfortable life for the two of us,' she explained. 'No-one need ever know how I went about gaining the capital for such a venture.'

'It's an admirable plan,' Bellamy said. 'You're admirable.'

Tamesine placed her arm over his chest. 'Do you have a wife or sweetheart, Samuel Bellamy?'

He considered his response carefully before answering. It would be easy for him to deceive her but he wanted his relationship with Tamesine to begin on a firm foundation of honesty. 'Aye,' he replied eventually.

Bellamy sensed her body stiffen. 'Then I'm merely a whore.'

'Nay,' he replied sincerely. 'You are my...' He wasn't certain what Tamesine was yet but he had allowed her into his heart.

Bellamy felt a tear on his chest.

'I must get back,' Tamesine said, raising herself from the bed. She shot him a hard look as she dressed. 'You should leave.'

'Would you prefer that I lie to you?'

'It matters not what I prefer.'

WHEN HE RETURNED TO TOWN, Bellamy found Palgrave and Ade at the southern end of the beach, away from the hubbub of the settlement. The men lay on their backs staring into the night sky. They had lit a small fire that was now growing weak. Bellamy took a piece of driftwood and began to poke it gently, awakening the flames, taking in the comforting, welcoming scent of wood smoke.

'That one there,' Palgrave said, pointing into the darkness, 'is called Orion. He was a great hunter.'

'Was he of your people?' Ade asked.

Palgrave grinned. 'Nay. He's from a story.'

'A Bible story?'

'A different story.'

Ade nodded. But Palgrave could tell from his creased brow that his friend was frustrated by the inadequate explanation. But how could he describe to Ade another people's gods when Palgrave didn't believe in his own?

Bellamy sat down heavily beside his friends and lay back on the sand. 'How do you know about the stars?'

'My Elizabeth has an interest in the heavens. She has a book – *Journey into the Night Sky: A Starwatcher's Companion to Constellations and Greek Mythology*,' Palgrave said. 'I bought it from a store in Salem for her seventh birthday. She has always had a vast mind and a healthy appetite for knowledge. Much to her mother's consternation, from early on, she could not be sated by the Bible. She's similar to me in that respect.' He paused, remembering. 'Joseph, on the other hand, finds contentment from another source. He's satisfied tinkering with a broken clock for weeks trying to mend it. I've never seen him grow frustrated in his efforts. He possesses the patience of Job and a thoroughly dogged spirit. Joseph resembles Leah in that way.'

'And the youngest three?' Bellamy asked.

'It's still too early to tell. But I hope they will follow Leah's path.'

Bellamy yawned then placed his hands behind his head. He groaned slightly as he did so.

'What troubles you?'

'I can barely picture her,' Bellamy confessed. 'The image grows fainter each day.'

'Maria?'

'Aye'.

'You've not known her long enough,' Palgrave explained. 'The two of you have had no time to meld into one. But you will.'

Bellamy turned his head towards his friend.

Palgrave explained. 'Occasionally, a stray thought will drift into my mind. Most times it's a notion or feeling unrelated to anything I'm doing at that moment or have, in fact, ever experienced before. Nevertheless, there it is, lodged like a burr.' Bellamy nodded. 'Then Leah will echo in words the very same idea and I realise what has wandered into my mind is a wayward thought from her own, drawn to a sympathetic home.

Palgrave closed his eyes. 'I can see Leah as vividly as if she were standing before me now.'

'My wife is everywhere,' Ade joined in. Palgrave and Bellamy turned to him immediately; neither had been aware the African was following their exchange. Ade stretched his arm to the sky and steadily lowered it in an arc to the sand. 'In the heavens, on the horizon, in the sea.'

Bellamy thought on the counsel of his companions for a minute then turned to Palgrave. 'Are you saying I don't love her?'

Palgrave shook his head and answered kindly. 'You simply don't know her.'

18

'Your attachment to this woman ...' Palgrave began uncertainly. 'It's she that you seek out now, is it not?'

Bellamy eyed him solemnly and nodded.

'Her name is Tamesine. I have not seen her here these past two days,' Bellamy responded absently as he looked towards the door, beyond the clientele, rough and monstrous. 'Our last meeting did not end well and I'm concerned.'

Jennings's flotilla had sailed that morning for Jamaica. Bellamy and Palgrave had taken their leave from the crew. Both men had attempted to convince Ade to join them in their search for another ship. The African had refused, explaining that although they were his friends, Jennings had been his saviour. He had promised to return Ade to his people.

'I'm certain that's a comparison of which Jennings would approve,' Bellamy had remarked dryly. Ade stared at him in confusion as Palgrave laughed quietly.

'There are greater riches to be had if you join us,' Palgrave said.

Ade shook his head. He wasn't to be persuaded. It wasn't a question of riches. When they parted, Ade had gripped each of them in turn by the shoulders and kissed them on both cheeks. Then he stepped into a long boat. Palgrave and Bellamy watched the boat head out into the mouth of the harbour. A lump rose in Palgrave's throat and he inhaled deeply.

'What do you suggest we do?' Palgrave asked now, bringing a cup to his lips and drawing in the yeasty, grassy smell of the ale.

'Find another captain without Jennings's ties to Jamaica,' Bellamy replied as he rose from the table. 'I'll see to another beer.'

As he stood, he caught sight of Tamesine in the entrance. She was dressed for her evening's employment in an emerald gown with a neckline that scooped low across her bosom. Although her expression remained composed, her eyes darted around the tavern. Two men were by her side. The shorter and stouter of the pair had unkempt ginger hair that jutted out from under his hat like taut ropes. An equally defiant beard hung to his broad chest. His companion was taller; taller than Palgrave, Bellamy judged. The menace Bellamy noted in his honed gaze and angular features marked him as the more formidable of the pair.

Once Tamesine spotted Bellamy, her eyes relaxed but he could still detect concern in her expression as she pointed towards him. The two men began to walk his way.

'Samuel Bellamy?' the ginger-haired man asked.

Bellamy nodded.

'Benjamin Hornigold.' He offered his hand. 'This is my associate Edward Teach.'

Bellamy shook Hornigold's hand. With an outstretched arm, he took a step towards Teach. Teach eyed him grimly before taking his hand. His sable-coloured beard, Bellamy noticed, grew from his cheekbones and hung to his belly. It had been twisted and tied in a number of places with black ribbons. Teach turned and beckoned to Garrett to bring them refreshments. His hair fell down his back in a plait, barely visible against the black of his coat. It was fashioned in the style of a Ramillie wig, with a large black bow securing the top of the braid and a smaller one tied at the bottom. He wore a naked cutlass in his belt. When he turned back to the group, Bellamy introduced Palgrave and the men sat. From the corner of his eye, Bellamy could detect Tamesine watching the conference from the bar.

'Damnation to him who ever lived to wear a halter!' Teach cried as the men raised their glasses.

'I've heard tell of your daring, Mister Bellamy,' said Hornigold after a moment.

Bellamy looked at him.

'And of yours, Mister Williams,' he added, turning to Palgrave. 'I've heard men speak of "The Puritan", yet your actions do not resemble those of a believer.'

'I hail from New England, Sir,' Palgrave explained. 'Perhaps this is how the moniker was born.'

'What are your plans?' asked Hornigold. 'Jennings sailed this morning, did he not?'

'Aye,' Bellamy replied.

'We need men like these two, wouldn't you agree Mister Teach?' Hornigold asked his companion.

Teach nodded sullenly into his beer.

'Gentlemen, I have a proposition,' continued Hornigold.

'Go on,' Palgrave said.

'Join my crew,' he suggested. 'I sail in a flotilla of three. The *Benjamin* is my own. The *Adventure* and the *Ranger* are helmed by men I trust, and who trust in me. Mister Teach and myself know Jennings from the war, being similarly occupied during the fray. You will discover, gentlemen, I'm a very different cut of captain.'

'You're a privateer no longer?' Bellamy asked.

'I sail under the prerogative of neither man nor God, and the Devil can have me if I falter in my resolve.' He paused before adding. 'I never consented to the articles of peace with the French and Spaniards. They're fair game, in my view. But we meddle not with the English or Dutch; I refuse to take plunder from English vessels and I doubt you will find a captain in these waters who will.'

Palgrave and Bellamy glanced at each other briefly.

'Yet you accost Englishman in the street and plunder the livelihoods of those that do business here on New Providence Island,' Bellamy remarked casually.

'Hear, hear!' cried a man who had been seated at the adjoining table. He was now standing with his mug raised, swaying slightly with the effort.

Hornigold turned to him with a sneer, feigning amusement. His laugh sounded like a rusty hinge. 'What say you, Levasseur?'

'Hear, hear, I say!' repeated the Frenchman, grinning. Dressed in a fine sapphire-coloured coat, the sailor gazed vaguely at Hornigold as the captain rose steadily to his feet.

'This, Messieurs Bellamy and Williams, is Olivier Levasseur, or "La Buse" – the buzzard,' Hornigold began affably. 'He was a naval officer during the war, you see, who then turned privateer. Why, he received a *lettre de marque* from King Louis himself! But he joined my disparate crew not six months ago when I rescued him from the gallows in Port Royal. Trussed up like a goose, he was. Despite him being French, I put my own neck on the line and killed three of the Royal Navy's finest in the process. An act of kindness, it was.'

With a restrained flourish, he put his hand on his heart before adding, 'I could not witness a brother tar undone in such a heinous way.'

'He saved me because I'm the finest sailing master in the Caribbean,' the Frenchman announced to the surrounding tables, eliciting shouts and a smattering of applause.

Hornigold ignored him.

'Now, La Buse believes he knows better than his captain.' Hornigold shook his head in disbelief. 'La Buse shares your opinions, Mister Bellamy. He has voiced them heartily on numerous occasions.'

'And I will voice them again!' the Frenchman cried.

Eyeing Levasseur, Hornigold paused and stood, placing his hands on his hips, as if considering the situation. Still smiling, La Buse mimicked his captain's stance and attitude. The others at his table grinned, and laughter erupted from the crowd.

Quick as a dart, Hornigold withdrew his cutlass from his belt and, in one movement, drew it deftly across the Frenchman's face. The noise in the tavern suddenly grew quiet; Bellamy could hear Tamesine gasp at the bar. Teach barely raised his eyes from his glass.

'Just deserves, La Buse,' said Hornigold calmly. 'You will *never* be free of me.'

The sweep of Hornigold's sword had seemed nothing more than the lick of a cat's tongue, but Levasseur's cup fell to the ground and his hand flew to his eye. A second later, he dropped to his knees in the sawdust, his brilliant blue coat stained with blood. Palgrave made to stand, but Bellamy gripped his arm. Hornigold resumed his place at the table as Levasseur was led outside by Garrett.

The noise in the tavern instantly returned to its usual rowdy cacophony.

'Now, Mister Bellamy, you were asking about my business dealings in New Providence, were you not?' Hornigold said as though he were not responsible for the blood beneath the sole of his cavalier boot. Bellamy nodded.

'I'm tax collecting, Mister Bellamy,' the captain explained. 'We are the authority now in Nassau and that incurs costs.'

'I see,' Bellamy said. The men glanced at one another before Hornigold continued more optimistically.

'Prove your mettle, impress me with your initiative, earn your place aboard the *Benjamin* and the first prize we capture will be yours. Am I good to my word, Mister Teach?'

'He is good to his word,' Teach responded wearily as he gestured for a further round of drinks.

IT WAS three in the morning before the landlord expelled the final stragglers from the Three Jolly Irishmen. Bellamy sat on the beach waiting for Tamesine, away from the excess of noise, sights and odours that defined the tavern. Instead, he imbibed the mild, briny breeze. When she emerged onto the road she held her son's hand. The boy yawned as he waved to the innkeeper then rubbed his eyes. His mother pressed him tight to her skirts and kissed the crown of his head before the pair walked on. Bellamy rose from his spot on the sand and jogged behind them.

'Good morning, Mister Bellamy.' Tamesine turned, unsurprised by his presence. 'To be walking the streets at this hour with the Flying Gang on the prowl ... Oh, but of course you are now a part of said crew, are you not?'

'You disapprove?'

She paused then shook her head. 'Not really. I understand.'

Before he could question her further, his attention was drawn to the child by her side. 'John King, I presume.' Bellamy held out his hand. 'My name is Sam Bellamy.'

The boy greeted the stranger with a firm grip and a confidence Bellamy had not anticipated in such a spindly youth.

'It's a pleasure to meet you, Sir.' His voice was deep and gravelly. Not that of a boy. His accent was nothing Bellamy had heard before.

The child was tanned like his mother but he did not possess her round, generous features. He had a man's face, Bellamy decided. It would take years for John's angular jaw and deep wide-set eyes to appear a natural fit. *He must resemble his father*, Bellamy thought, *in every trait save the hair*. Although it was cropped short, Bellamy could tell the child had inherited his mother's rich auburn mane.

'You appear tired. Would you prefer to ride home?' Bellamy asked the boy.

John thought over the proposal seriously for a moment before looking at his mother. She nodded.

'I'd be most grateful, Sir,' the boy replied.

Bellamy knelt on the ground and the nine-year-old climbed onto his back. When he stood, they began on their way. Bellamy could feel the child's warm breath against his neck.

'Are you a sailor?' John asked.

'Aye.'

'Which one is your ship?' the boy continued, gesturing to the vessels moored in the harbour.

'The *Benjamin*, it's called.'

'Are you the captain?'

'Hush, John!' his mother broke in. 'Allow Mister Bellamy some peace.'

'I'm not the captain,' Bellamy answered. 'But I hope to be the captain of a ship soon.'

'If I were the captain of a mightily armed sloop of war I would name her *The King's Maid*,' John began certainly, as Tamesine and Bellamy shot each other an amused glance.

'I have given it some thought and it's a very clever choice. It has a double meaning, you see. My name is John King and I am also the servant *of* the king but, as you know, all ships are women, so I could not name the ship the *King's Servant* ...'

Bellamy still couldn't pin down the boy's accent, mottled as it was. It was tinged with Irish melodies, the wholesome-ness of the West Country and a dash of patois.

'That's all, John,' Tamesine said sternly. It was the final word on the subject.

They walked in silence. Occasionally, man and woman would look at each other. Bellamy sensed the boy's body growing steadily heavier

'I've missed you, Tamesine,' Bellamy murmured. 'Mentioning Maria was thoughtless.'

'Mah-*rye*-uh,' she repeated. 'A pretty name. A biblical name.'

'I suppose it is.'

Tamesine sighed and walked on in silence until they reached her house. 'I have missed you as well. But you have another life that is clean and white and pure. I'm not that. Nassau is not that. Whatever happens between us here cannot sully our dreams.'

She paused for a moment before adding. 'And I cannot give myself over to another sailor.'

John was asleep when they arrived at her home. Bellamy manoeuvred the boy carefully onto the small trundle bed in the kitchen. Tamesine proceeded to remove his shoes and coat. Once she had pulled a coverlet up to his chin, she spoke.

'I'll pour you some cider,' she whispered as she released a number of pins from her hair. He admired her curls as they tumbled over her shoulders. Bellamy lit the candles on the table then sat. Tamesine wrapped a crimson shawl around her shoulders then wiped two cups thoroughly before pouring the cider.

'They made us a generous offer,' Bellamy said, once Tamesine had joined him at the table. 'Palgrave and I have joined Hornigold's crew, not the Flying Gang.'

She nodded and brought her cup to her lips.

'I too have entered into an arrangement, of sorts, with Captain Hornigold,' she admitted after a time.

Bellamy raised his eyes.

'I have agreed to pay him the sum of two hundred Spanish dollars. Once the money is delivered Tom, Garrett and myself will be free of him.'

'But your plans ...'

'They've been delayed, but only temporarily.'

Bellamy drained his cup then brought it down hard on the table. 'I fear we have both brokered with the Devil.'

'Shhhh ...' Tamesine turned to the sleeping child beside the table. 'There's no other way, Sam. Hornigold has become the law in Nassau,' she whispered. 'We cannot act on impulse; he is protected by the Flying Gang. All we can do is be ever cautious.'

'Honour among thieves?'

She smiled. 'Earn your prize. Then you will be free of him.'

He nodded, ill at ease.

'Your son is a credit to you,' he said after a moment.

Tamesine lowered her head and stared into her cider. Even in the dim glow of the candlelight, Bellamy noticed her blush.

'I enjoy your company, Tamesine,' he added.

'What about your sweetheart?' she asked, staring into his eyes.

He shook his head despairingly. 'I can barely recall her face.'

She leant across the table and took his hand, her eyes awash with compassion.

'You are so real,' he said, stroking her hand.

'Stay with me.'

Bellamy nodded.

Tamesine rose and gently blew out the candles then led Bellamy to her bed.

19

During the week before Hornigold's flotilla was due to set sail, Bellamy spent each evening with Tamesine. They didn't speak of the future. Instead, they, along with John, created their own private haven – a sanctuary, of sorts, removed from the world of Hornigold's Nassau, and of time itself. Tamesine's house was a pretty, unaffected little cottage and the walls were plastered and washed with many coats of lime. The house was a rich, creamy colour with a pitched, shingled roof and would not look out of place, Bellamy guessed, nestled in any Cornish hamlet. Even the vegetation surrounding the cottage was not greatly dissimilar to that of Cornwall's rugged coast.

When the ship finally set sail, they chose not to say 'goodbye'.

The following evening, the ship anchored in an inlet of Deadman's Cay. Palgrave and Bellamy, along with the rest of the eighty-man crew, were ordered below deck. The air was rank with smoke and rum, sweat and fart. A single lantern provided the only illumination. The crew hummed softly, a dirge Palgrave could not identify, as they waited for their captain and Teach to appear below decks. Most of the men, Palgrave reckoned, were younger than him by many years. He could easily detect their greenness through the stains and grime in which they were costumed. Bellamy and Palgrave were positioned on stools at the centre of a series of concentric circles formed by the one hundred or so men gathered there. The quartermaster, Mister Harjo, who Palgrave took for an Indian from his tawny skin and almond-shaped eyes, explained to them that the observance would begin once the sun had set.

Signing the ship's articles and swearing an oath to abide by the rules aboard had been a simple matter on the *Barsheba*. It was the routine act of reading and signing a contract in the captain's cabin. The deed had taken no longer than a few minutes. But Hornigold *had* stated he was a different cut of captain.

Here, the entire crew of the *Benjamin* had been gathered in the hull for over an hour, waiting until the sun descended below the horizon. Although Palgrave cared not for either Hornigold or Teach, he found himself anxious and craving acceptance from the disparate – and desperate – men who surrounded him.

As he waited, Palgrave wondered what Leah would make of this scene. A glint of a smile softened his tense lips. He was sure that his ever-sensible Leah, once she overcame her alarm over the situation, would recognise the spectacle of the moment.

He found himself evoking an earlier time when he had felt a similar apprehension. Leah, on her third visit to his home, had convinced Palgrave to return to meeting.

'Reverend Dent is demanding your expulsion from the town. He will not relent until you are seen at meeting. Will you not come?' Leah insisted urgently.

Palgrave shook his head gravely. 'It would be a lie,' he said and then added reluctantly, 'I no longer believe, Leah.'

She rose from her seat and walked to him by the hearth and took his hands. 'I understand.' She lowered her eyes for a moment before looking up into his face. 'Will you return for me?'

'The deception will not rest well with you.'

'I don't care.'

Palgrave could not grasp her motivation, neither could he deny her.

The following Sunday, Palgrave made certain he was the first to arrive at the meeting house. He took his usual seat in the balcony, a seat he had not occupied for many months. As the congregation filed through the wide oak doors, many looked up at him doubtfully. Their stares were as austere as the surrounds. Rumour and gossip were currency in East-ham. He could imagine what had been said about him since he'd retreated from life. He resolved to respond to each dubious glance with a pleasant, but solemn, 'good morning'.

When Leah and her family entered, they stopped below him on their way to the front box they occupied each week. Joseph Hallett looked at him and beckoned him down from the balcony with the hat he held in his hand. When Palgrave reached them, Hallett gripped his arm firmly.

'I'm heartened to see you have returned, Mister Williams,' Hallett declared for all to hear.

Palgrave glanced at Leah. Her eyes were wide and bright and her nose had coloured a vivid shade of ruby in the cold.

'Thank you, Sir,' Palgrave replied.

Joseph Hallett asked him to join his family in their box and Palgrave sat alone on the pew opposite Leah and her father. Maria and her mother sat to his right. The child's legs swung slowly back and forth and her feet brushed lightly across the floor. When the Reverend rose to his pulpit, he could not conceal his astonishment that the drunken idler and suspected infidel, Palgrave Williams, was seated with the most esteemed of Eastham's townsfolk. Palgrave met his reproving gaze, suddenly instilled with a dignity he could not recall. Neither could he recall, when meeting had concluded ninety minutes later, the contents of Dent's sermon. The minister's bluster had been muffled. It had taken all Palgrave's concentration to avert his gaze from the young lady sitting opposite him. The urge to examine her from that close distance, as one might study a work of art, was overwhelming. Palgrave had been aware of nothing throughout the duration of the service except his proximity to Leah Hallett.

Now it was Bellamy who sat opposite him. Palgrave squinted into the dim light of the sloop's rancid hull to register his expression. It was one of mild bemusement. Bellamy offered his friend a reassuring wink.

Eventually, as darkness flooded the hold, another lantern was lit and the crew's chant rose to a fervent pitch. It was then that Hornigold and Teach appeared below decks. The crew was hushed by Mister Harjo. Hornigold spoke.

'Mister Harjo. The articles and the looking glass, if you please.'

The quartermaster produced a scroll that he handed to the captain and a mirror each for Palgrave and Bellamy.

'An oath sworn to a looking glass is not to be taken lightly, gentleman,' Hornigold preached. 'It is the gateway into the next world. Deceive it at your peril.'

The captain proceeded to read from the scroll. Mister Harjo held a candle beside Hornigold's shoulder. The captain's rendering of the fourteen rules contained on the parchment was slow, theatrical and prompted frequent huzzahs from the inebriated crew.

During the reading of the articles Teach stood behind his captain with his hands knotted into tight fists. His eyes blazed fiercely and his chest heaved as he stared at the noviciates. He appeared otherworldly, as a demon let loose from hell might in a quest to seek out minions. It had not dawned on Palgrave until that moment the seriousness of the path he had chosen, the dark gateway he was about to enter. Jennings had been one type of pirate – a gentleman pirate. But it now occurred to Palgrave that Teach and Hornigold were another breed entirely. This was a startling recognition for an ordinary, honest man such as Palgrave; yet it did not alarm him. In fact, he experienced an odd sense of nobility as Hornigold concluded the ceremony.

'Gaze into the looking glass and swear the oath,' Hornigold ordered.

'I swear neither by heaven, nor by earth, nor by my head. I swear by this ship and those that hear my oath,' Hornigold declaimed then looked to the initiates who raised the mirrors to their faces and repeated the captain's words.

'Let the Devil cometh and take me, or worse, let my shipmates have their way, if I abide not by my solemn word and conduct contained within these articles.' Hornigold held the scroll aloft and the two men echoed the oath gravely.

This was followed by a deafening 'huzzah!' from the crew. Then Mister Teach stepped forward and produced a dagger from his belt. Moving to Palgrave first, he thundered, 'Give me your hand, Mister Williams.'

Palgrave offered his hand and Teach turned it palm upwards. A further supportive 'huzzah' issued from the spectators.

'This will hurt you more than it hurts me,' he continued in an undertone only Palgrave could hear. Palgrave raised his head hastily and stared at Teach. His manner had softened, Palgrave noticed, as Teach cautiously drew the blade across his palm. When Teach was finished, he wiped the blade clean and glanced at Palgrave for an instant. Palgrave could discern very little on Teach's whiskered face, save a distinct twinkle in the pirate's dark eyes.

By the time the blood began to surface through the shallow cut, Teach had executed the same deed on Bellamy. The pair were instructed to leave their bloody mark on the scroll on which the articles were written.

Observing the crosses, scratches and scrawls on the document, Palgrave dabbed a fingernail in his own blood and simply wrote his initials. Bellamy, however, wrote his entire name in a hand so neat Palgrave could have sworn he used quill and ink.

20

———

Once the articles had been sworn, the entire crew embarked on an evening of wild carousing and immense debauch, the likes of which Palgrave had never witnessed before. Palgrave drank more slowly than the rest of the crew, but Bellamy refused to indulge. Tense and unsettled, he retreated from the festivities early. Palgrave retired, slightly stewed, just before midnight. All hands drank until they were sick and then drank some more. Teach had guzzled rum so ferociously that he collapsed before ten. Palgrave was yet to discover what position Teach held on board the *Benjamin*. Although he sailed with Hornigold, Teach seemed to be independent of him.

Most of the men remained addled the next day. When Bellamy reported the sighting of a French sloop called '*Marianne*', even the captain himself was 'halfway to Concord', according to the boatswain, an Irishman from Boston named Mister Devlin.

Unaware of Hornigold's flotilla nestled in a cove only a mile away, the *Marianne* had come to rest off Crooked Island. 'Laying in wait' were the words the captain had used to describe his preferred stratagem before he returned below decks, bottle of madeira in hand. Bellamy had retired reluctantly, displeased by the captain's indifference. Palgrave could discern by his restlessness that he wanted to approach the ship immediately and take the small pink by surprise. Hornigold, however, decided to postpone an advance until his constitution returned 'halfway to sufferable'.

That evening, as the flotilla lay anchored in Deadman's Cay, Palgrave was assigned the night watch. The music of the *Marianne*'s French crew was carried to him by the salty wind. Palgrave could discern the sound of violins and pipes. It was a melancholy tune, accompanied by the sombre incantation of a verse Palgrave could not translate. He turned when he heard footsteps.

'Mister Williams,' Teach said as he lit a large briar wood pipe.

Palgrave responded with a nod, returning his gaze to the island.

'Your friend Mister Bellamy is anxious,' Teach remarked. 'Hornigold does not like to be rushed.'

'Sam's eager for the prize of his own ship. How do you gauge the situation?'

'Hornigold has set a heading for Isla de Tesoros, but he might let your friend have his way. Our captain is unpredictable.'

'Treasure Island?' Palgrave had gained a small insight into the Spanish language in recent months, but he was unsure of this translation.

Teach nodded.

'Why are you not captain to one of these ships, Mister Teach?'

'I don't believe I have the makings of a very fine captain,' he replied. 'My nature is capricious and I indulge too freely.

What's more, I enjoy the freedom that comes with being a regular seaman.'

'You don't appear to be a regular seaman.'

'I play my role.' He drew deeply on his pipe.

'I see.' Palgrave recalled Teach's involvement during the swearing of the articles.

'You are a married man, Mister Williams?'

'Aye, that I am. As are you, I hear,' Palgrave answered before adding disbelievingly, 'There's talk of fourteen wives?'

'It's more than talk,' Teach replied without humour. 'As I said, I indulge too freely.'

Palgrave looked at him and raised his eyebrows.

'They reside in Virginia and the Carolinas,' Teach continued.

'Together?' Palgrave asked, astonished at the unusual arrangement.

'Nay,' Teach released a rambunctious laugh. 'One knows not about the other. That would surely be my undoing. The sole time they shall meet, I pray, Mister Williams, will be at Hope Point on the Thames.'

Palgrave grinned at Teach's allusion to Execution Dock. 'You must have many children?'

'Aye,' Teach answered, seemingly unconcerned with what surely must be, Palgrave thought, a considerable brood.

'How?' Palgrave then inquired. 'Forgive me for asking, but how have you managed it? You have flouted the laws of the King and of God.'

'I believe in neither, Mister Williams,' Teach remarked without hesitation.

～

TEACH'S admission echoed in Palgrave's thoughts as he approached the *Marianne* in a large canoe. Although it grieved him to do so initially, Palgrave admitted there was very little separating him from Edward Teach, save his marital devotion. The cold truth was that Palgrave had abandoned his family. He mused tirelessly on his conversation with Teach. *What exactly do I believe in?* Palgrave asked himself. He had shunned God and it was plain, by his present occupation, he'd spurned authority as well. The very foundation of his life was Leah, yet he had deserted her.

'Mister Samuel Bellamy has free rein to seize the *Marianne*,' Hornigold had announced to the crew that morning. Bellamy had carefully strategised the attack on the French sloop over the course of the day. They would wait until midnight to proceed. He was promised the ship should the assault be successful. Bellamy had given command of one canoe to his friend while he helmed the other. Palgrave had selected Teach to join him and relied on him to choose the others who rowed alongside them now. Palgrave trusted the wild-eyed pirate sitting beside him; he had knowingly placed his wellbeing in the hands of a man who had faith in nothing except himself, yet, strangely, he was not uncomfortable with his decision.

Following Bellamy's instruction, the men had smudged their faces, necks and hands with coal. In the shadow of his black tricorn hat, Teach's expression was hardly visible. Occasionally, he drew deeply on the pipe. The burning tobacco shot an eerie glow across the lower part of his face. Palgrave noticed he had gone to some pains to decorate his beard with ribbons, tokens and good luck charms. He wore a bandolier slung over his shoulder fitted with three pistols. A naked cutlass was secured in his wide leather belt. He had also fixed a short length of cannon fuse under each side of his hat.

The boats slowed as they approached the sloop. Palgrave silently indicated for the crew to row around the stern to the port side. As they did so, Palgrave heard the grappling hooks of Bellamy's men clang against the rails of the ship. Before long the bell was rung and the clamour that ensued on deck was unmistakably that of sleepy, flustered sailors called to arms. Palgrave's dugout reached the port side and the men heaved their hooks on board. He and Teach climbed first and peered over the rail at the battle that was underway on the opposite side of the deck. Once on board, Palgrave signalled for the rest of the crew to follow and the men immediately began to scale the hull. Palgrave raised his sword and ran immediately into the heart of the conflict, while Teach lit the fuses under his hat then emitted an almighty howl that drew the attention of all those on board. The smoke and sparks from the fuses created a ghostly, luminescent vapour around the pirate's head. The skirmish halted as the French crewmen gaped at Teach.

Removing a pistol from his bandolier, Teach raised the weapon and took aim at a young seaman. Teach fired. Struck by the force of the shot, the boy, just a few years older than Joseph, was thrown against the foremast and collapsed at its base. Slumped over, limbs distorted, almost lifeless, he reminded Palgrave of a poppet Leah had sewn for Elizabeth. He had frequently discovered Molly in odd places around the house, barn or workshop, assuming the exact position that the youth did now. No-one moved towards the injured young man, terrified of the wrath they might incur.

'*Fixer vos bras!*' Palgrave heard the panicked cry ring out clearly in the silence. '*Fixer vos bras!*'

The French laid down their arms and placed their hands above their heads.

~

HORNIGOLD WAS true to his word and gifted Bellamy the *Marianne*. It wasn't a grand ship by any means, nothing like the *Sainte Marie*, but Bellamy was delighted and immediately began to assemble his crew. Levasseur, eager to be at arm's length from Hornigold, was a willing sailing master and Bellamy appointed Palgrave quartermaster. By the end of the day, the *Marianne* had a crew of about forty, including twelve of the captured French merchant seamen who Levasseur persuaded to adopt an alternative way of life. Although the pirate's appearance had changed much since the war, and he still wore a bandage over the right side of his face, the French sailors knew La Buse by reputation as a hero and were easily charmed by him.

Those that did not wish to join the crew were rowed to Crooked Island. All, that is, except the *Marianne*'s surgeon, a young Scotsman by the name of James Ferguson. He was discovered in the Surgeon's Quarters when Palgrave had assembled a party to search below decks. Palgrave thought he was an odd mix of a man, having a plump child-like face that sat strangely on a tall thickset body. Ferguson informed the boarding party that he had taken part in a failed Jacobite revolt against King George I while studying at the University of St Andrews. He was, it seemed, a fugitive as well.

Bellamy invited Ferguson, along with Palgrave and Levasseur, into the captain's cabin for supper. Palgrave had discovered a plentiful supply of chickens in the hold, along with a cow and two young pigs. Bellamy ordered that ten of the fowl be killed for the crew's first supper aboard the *Mari-*

anne. The men were pleased. For those who had sailed with Hornigold it was the first fresh meat they had eaten in weeks.

Palgrave watched the young surgeon closely during the meal, wondering why Bellamy had invited him. He was brash and obnoxious, but he wore his confidence like an ill-fitting waistcoat. Although Ferguson spoke of many a daring exploit during the revolt, his green eyes scurried between his three companions, as though he were expecting one of the dinner guests to leap out of their seat and run him through with their fork. Palgrave just couldn't imagine Ferguson raising arms against the might of the English king.

'What are your plans, Doctor Ferguson?' Bellamy asked.

'I plan to seek further employment in the Caribbean.'

'Would you consider joining my crew?'

'Ahh ...' Ferguson stammered, dismayed once again. 'I ...'

Palgrave looked briefly at his cohorts before addressing the doctor. 'Tell us the truth, lad. You seem a peculiar fit for a merchant vessel, let alone a political revolt.'

Ferguson's broad shoulders slumped. He placed his knife on the table.

'I was employed by the Dutch West India Company but this is no life for me. The advertisement mentioned nothing about pirates,' he sighed, looking at his dinner companions resignedly.

'And the revolt?' Palgrave asked. 'Are you a Jacobite?'

'I wrote a pamphlet in support of the Jacobite cause,' Ferguson explained. 'Although it was rather seditious, it was never actually printed. That's the extent of my involvement.'

The three bandits seated around the table laughed at the doctor's sudden candour, forcing Ferguson to join in as well. It was but a fleeting moment of repose for the doctor.

'Will you join the crew of *Marianne*?' Bellamy asked.

Palgrave rubbed his chin and wondered why Bellamy wanted to keep a surgeon on board. Very few captains engaged the services of a doctor.

Ferguson shook his head adamantly. 'I'm astonished, Mister Bellamy, that you would even ask!' He laughed. 'I'm little more than a coward. After today, I'm determined to return to Scotland.'

Bellamy nodded solemnly as Ferguson ate. As he lifted generous forkfuls to his mouth, a smile was evident on his cherubic face, brought by relief at his newfound liberty.

'I urge you to accept my offer ... willingly,' the captain said low-voiced, leaning across the table.

All laughter was instantly snuffed out. Ferguson swallowed his mouthful of food with an incredulous gulp, almost choking in the process.

As the surgeon coughed, Palgrave and Levasseur looked at each other, uncertain where their captain was heading.

Ferguson stiffened, his head snapping towards the door.

'What say you?' Bellamy pressed.

The doctor shifted and looked at the three men around him. He opened his mouth then hastily closed it again.

'You're free to speak,' Palgrave urged.

'Are you saying, Sir,' Ferguson addressed Bellamy, laying his fork on his plate, 'that if I don't agree to your offer freely, I will be kept prisoner aboard this ship?'

Bellamy rose and walked to the doctor. Ferguson recoiled slightly as the captain approached and lowered himself into the chair alongside the surgeon. Palgrave could see it took all the young man's nerve to look Bellamy in the eye.

'Just the opposite, Doctor,' Bellamy explained. 'I'm offering you freedom. Civilisation is your prison. Will you be content to toil for a shilling a day in a filthy hospital, tending ulcers and abscesses on the aged and impover-ished? Perhaps you see failing to heal children riddled with the pox a more satisfactory future for you? I'm offering you the world. The men on board this ship are kings of their own destiny.'

Ferguson shifted his eyes to the table. There was no choice.

'The *Marianne* needs a surgeon and here aboard this vessel you are to remain,' Bellamy said. 'You'll receive one and a half shares of all our plunder and a life free of tyranny. *That* is what I offer you, Doctor. Do you agree to it?'

Palgrave wondered what Bellamy would do if Ferguson called his bluff.

'I agree,' Ferguson uttered finally. Bellamy shook the surgeon's hand.

21

'I began to doubt your return,' Tamesine whispered, as she entered from the kitchen. She tiptoed briskly across the floor and slid into bed beside him. His skin was suntanned and she could see he had not shaved in his absence. The whiskers on his face were fast transforming into a thick, full beard. She ran her fingers through the hairs, attempting to untangle the knots. Soon the pintails began to whistle.

'You've been gone so long.'

'How long has it been,' Bellamy asked seriously, kissing her forehead, 'precisely?'

'Sixty-one days ... *precisely*,' she returned. Bellamy laughed softly. Tamesine pressed her body firmly against his.

'There was some news,' she went on hesitantly, 'of the trifling variety, imparted by several Frenchmen who managed to find their way to Nassau after you abandoned them on Crooked Island.'

'They were well seen to,' Bellamy explained. 'Those who refused to join my crew were left with rations and rum.

Many ships lay anchor off Crooked Island. It would not be such a great inconvenience to join another ship.'

She was silent for a moment as she attempted to word her next query. The mellow, nutty smell of chicory began to fill the cottage.

'One of them,' she said cautiously, 'an older gent who I took to be the captain, spoke of the "Diable Noir".'

Bellamy looked at her in confusion.

'A pitiless black devil who fired his pistol at the heart of a young sailor, a mere child, who'd not even raised a hand.'

His lips curled into a tender smile. 'You think I'm Diable Noir?'

'Perhaps.'

Neither of them spoke for a time.

'The coffee will be ready,' she said eventually, throwing back the covers.

Bellamy grabbed her arm, drawing her to his side. 'They speak of Teach. The shot was unexpected, to be sure, and fiendish, I will admit. But it prompted a surrender without further grievance.'

Tamesine stiffened at his choice of words.

'You think me callous.'

'I think of John. He speaks of nothing else since you last sailed except going to sea,' she said. 'That's not the life I have planned for him.'

'The sea is in his blood.'

'I won't have it.'

'Then take him to England now.'

'The time is not yet favourable.'

'I'll give you money.'

'I won't be bound to you in that way.'

She tugged her arm away and rose. When she reached the kitchen's hearth she crouched in front of the flames, hugging her knees to her chest. Despite the humidity that hung in the air like wet feathers, she was suddenly cold; her thin shift did nothing to warm her. John slept soundly on the trundle in the corner, the only evidence of his presence being the tawny curls that poked from the covers.

Although lively, her life in Nassau had been simple until the arrival of Samuel Bellamy. Now her mind was occupied constantly with concerns for his wellbeing and that of her son, who she now risked losing to the wretched sea.

Tamesine had heard much news of Bellamy since his departure, both of the trifling and noteworthy kind. It was difficult not be privy to such knowledge in a town like Nassau and, if she was truthful, she heartily relished every morsel, dropped like crumbs on the street. Pirates and their ilk regaled in tales of their own kind's audacity, cunning and cruelty. In the tavern, Tamesine would force herself away from discussions about Samuel Bellamy. Yet, without realising, she would soon find herself drawn back to the same conversation, lapping up every detail, hanging on the words of reprobates as though they were gospel. Despite her urge to know more, each scrap of information, no matter how minor, only served to distress her further. At the same time, she was comforted knowing he was alive and free. Exhausted by her constant deliberations, she would lie awake at night and recall his kind eyes and mannerly ways. Tamesine had wondered whether he was much altered.

She had been told of Bellamy's triumph as a captain, how he and Hornigold terrorised shipping lanes that connected Havana and the Spanish Main, New Orleans and France.

Then there was the tale about Black Sam that Mister Dugan, the fence, enjoyed recounting to all and sundry. Black Sam, a ruthless scoundrel who, flying a black flag featuring a death's head and crossbones, gave chase to a forty-gunned French frigate, engaging them in battle for over an hour. Eventually surrendering, the French captain had his throat cut forthwith by Black Sam himself. The cargo, more than thirty thousand pounds in silver and gold, was moved to the *Marianne*, and the crew were tied to the railings and masts, where upon Black Sam set the frigate alight.

The screams of the crew, Mister Dugan had been told, could be heard all the way to Rhode Island.

Tamesine knew Dugan well and was familiar with his tendency to embellish even the most trivial of occurrences, yet the particulars of the account were a grim pall that cast every memory of Bellamy in shadow.

During her contemplations the sun had risen and the chicory coffee bubbled furiously in the pot. She poured two cups and ventured into her chamber.

'I have dreamt of you,' she whispered, handing Bellamy the mug.

'Tell me.'

Embarrassed by her admission, she remained silent.

'I won't mock,' he said. 'I love to listen to your thoughts.'

She sat on the bed, crossing her legs.

'I have imagined you coming home to me, and of us keeping house together ... they're foolish thoughts,' she paused. 'Even brewing coffee for you makes me giddy with happiness.' She paused, staring into the black depths of her cup. 'Sometimes I wake and it's as if you've been lying right here next to me. I can sense your hands on my body and your scent on the pillow.'

Then she stopped.

'And ...' he urged.

'And sometimes I fear a change in you, that your character has altered. I worry that you have become like the rest of them.'

Bellamy frowned. 'I'll never become like the rest of them. That's not who I am.'

'What if you can't help it? The sea is in your blood too, is it not?'

'Nay!' he said, astonished at her claims. 'I'm a farmer.'

He sat up then, eager to make her know him. Crossing his legs, he became a reflection of her.

'I admit, I admire the workmanship and skill in a splendid galley or frigate, but I'm here with only one purpose. Freedom. When that's attained I'll come home to you.'

Tamesine hoped his promise was true, but she was still plagued by a feeling that, in the end, she would not be the woman Bellamy chose to go home to. Lieutenant John King had made the same vow.

'How's your friend Mister Williams?' she asked, desperate to change the subject.

'Very well,' Bellamy replied, sitting back against the pillow. He took a long sip of coffee then rested the cup on his thigh. 'He's my quartermaster. Palgrave has a hawk's eye for detail and a head for bookkeeping, which suit him to the position. He's also fearless, I've discovered, which is a handy trait for a quartermaster ... although his boldness does concern me.'

His face became grim, distracted by thoughts of his friend.

'Why are you so protective of him?'

Bellamy turned towards her, instantly lightening. 'You're an inquisitive one today, aren't you?'

'You two are strange bedfellows.'

'My departure from New England prompted his own. I

hope to safeguard his return. I value his friendship and his good sense. Nothing more.'

Bellamy took her mug, and placed it with his on the floor. Tamesine opened her mouth to speak, but he quieted her question with a kiss.

'Nothing more,' he repeated as he pulled her to him.

22

D ear Leah,

Commerce goes well. The Workshop and Store that I have established is steady in its trade and my Fears about our Future have been eased. When I return, it will be with Wealth enough to keep our Family content. My Thoughts are occupied solely by the Changes this will bring. You shall have a Servant and a pretty Dress of spring green, I think, to flatter your honeyed Hair. I will accompany Elizabeth to Salem where she may purchase all the Books she desires. Our Joseph will be schooled for as long as is his want and the twins will each receive a Horse. Beasts of burden they will not be. These fine Animals will be for the entertainment of our Twins and, rather than a Yoke, they shall wear fine Braids in their Manes. And finally, Baby Caleb shall have his Mother wholly. She will be released from all Concern. For myself, I dream of nothing more but this. You will scoff, I am certain, and say these things are nothing but Trifles – Trinkets of no real import. But to me, they are a Sign of something greater.

All variety of Character have I met here in Nassau. Some are unsavoury, it is true, and would not be made welcome at

Reverend Dent's Meeting House. But most are merry Fellows who share my humble ways and, like me, have been lured by Opportunity to the Region. One such Man, who has obtained my services and who has grown into a friend, is Edward Teach. He sports an impressive, ink-coloured Beard that he likes to adorn with Ribbons, Shells, Coins and the like. It resembles a Treasure Trove of found Objects, an illustrated Chronicle of his Adventures. He is superstitious, as are most of the Men here (even more so than your People), and each of the Charms in his Beard incite a particular (or peculiar) Memory. When I first caught sight of Edward Teach some months ago, he struck me as a fearsome Creature. But as our Attachment grows, I have come to view him as a melancholy, chary Soul, lost and bereft, if you will, of all foundation and hope. Yet he has great Skill as a Seaman and I warrant these Gifts will see him reach a position of great Prominence one day.

I find myself thinking of my Father and the injustice of his Death. It has recently occurred to me that his dying altered the Course of my Life. My Father made many Sacrifices for me, but, in the end, it was not enough. All the Good he did amounted to nothing in the face of angry, screaming Women hungry for the grain he had so little of.

I contemplate these questions endlessly. They turn over in my Mind and gather a frightening momentum in their progression. What heinous brand of Tyranny drove those Women to such brutality, to tear my father apart? How hungry must one Person be to kill another? If you were here, You would chastise me for my Misery, wouldn't You? And tell me how morose I am growing in my old age. You are right, of course, as always. I need You to lighten my Spirit.

November is upon us already and the Temperatures in New Providence remain clement. However, I can readily call to mind Snow falling. My Heart warms when I imagine You and the Chil-

dren by our Hearth in the Hour before Supper. You are seeing to the Meal, while Elizabeth lights Candles and attends to the Table. Joseph is still outside, of course, seeing the Animals into their Stalls and Pens. Caleb sits beneath the Window, all chubby Fingers and Consternation, as he struggles to set the Top I made him spinning. Or perhaps my earnest, kind-hearted Twins sit beside him, a Picture of frustration as they attempt to include their Baby Brother in a round of Knucklebones. I hear Laughter and Chatter and smell the earthy Bouquet of the Mushroom Soup you like to cook at this time of the Year. These Memories smart like a Spur and, like a Spur, incite me to achieve my Goal and come home hastily to my dear Family. By this time next Year, I will have joined you by our Hearth to enjoy the domestic scene I have just described.

The month also signifies an Anniversary, does it not? What a debased Individual I must have appeared when I opened the door that afternoon. You displayed the Courage of Esther when you decided to walk over the Threshold and enter my gloomy cave. Your Spirit lifted my own and I, for the first time since boyhood, was able to foresee an Existence that was Radiant and Inviting. I stand amazed at the Woman you have become.

Your devoted Husband,
Palgrave

～

'WHAT DO you write in those letters?' Bellamy asked as he approached.

Palgrave folded the paper and slipped it into his pocket. 'Nothing of you and your acquaintance,' Palgrave answered dryly, 'if that's your concern.'

Bellamy grinned. 'You're a clever man, Mister Williams, and have noted the overtone of my query.' Palgrave laughed.

'But what *do* you write in your letters to Leah?' The subject was of great interest to the younger man.

'Fact and fiction.' He then added. 'She's not replied to a single correspondence.'

'Are you concerned?'

Palgrave shrugged, gazing at the thunderheads in the distance. 'Leah is not one for writing letters. She abhors the way the written word can be misconstrued and prefers to confront a matter directly.'

'Then why do you continue in your labours? Surely, it must seem a wasted effort.'

'Not at all. I view these communications as a connection to Eastham, a link to my real life. If I cease, I fear I might lose myself forever.'

Bellamy thought on Palgrave's words for a moment.

'What are your plans when we return?' Palgrave asked. 'How does Tamesine figure into the life you hope to create with Maria?'

'I cannot envision a life away from Nassau with Tamesine. She has plans of her own that are independent of mine. But Maria ...' Bellamy ran his hands through his hair.

Palgrave could see his friend found the question worrisome.

'Maria belongs to another life,' Palgrave finished.

'Entirely.'

The desire to follow Tamesine to Windsor was overwhelming. Bellamy had come to know her and her son well. He loved them both. Powerful was the inclination to protect them and thrilling the notion of a future together. However, hadn't he held Maria in the same regard only a few months ago? He had proposed, after all. And although the proposal had not been ideal in its execution, it was sincere in its intent. Bellamy's brow creased as he considered the situation. He looked at Palgrave as his quartermaster removed the letter once more from his pocket. Bellamy had not shared a word of his journey with Maria. On not a single occasion had the tip of a quill dipped into an inkpot at his urging. And, although he had not spoken of love with Tamesine, promises had been made.

Bellamy stared towards the horizon and remembered his promise to Maria. Although sealed in the undignified surrounds of a stable, it had been a heartfelt oath spoken with conviction. Should he be bound to that pledge when he had neither signed his name in blood nor sworn his commitment into a looking glass? Circumstances had shifted so remarkably – so irrevocably – since that time in Eastham. *What exactly*, he wondered, *is holding me to that promise?*

'Think on it carefully, Sam,' Palgrave advised, as if reading his captain's mind. 'Obligation can be a millstone.'

PALGRAVE'S HAMMOCK swayed gently as he waited for sleep to arrive, the rhythmic creak of the beams under his weight a soothing lullaby. Bellamy had remained on deck when Palgrave retired. Sighting heavy clouds in the distance, he had awoken Levasseur and the ship's pilot, an Indian named John Julian. Julian had recently joined the crew in Florida when the *Marianne* had taken on supplies.

Ferguson had climbed into his berth shortly after Palgrave, wryly commenting on the unique aroma of ships, an odd combination of 'damp wood, braised onions and bodily excretions,' he said. Despite being forced to remain on the ship, the Scotsman took very easily to his role as Ship's Surgeon. Good-humoured and inherently intelligent (although he gave himself no credit for this) Ferguson also proved to be highly skilled at extemporising when confronted by the demands of an ill crew member. A large man, he could pull teeth with ease, although he preferred to offer the patient a tincture made from clove and ginger if no abscess had already formed on the gum. Ferguson chose not to prescribe opium as a treatment for pain or the flux, unless the man's condition was particularly intense. He also travelled with an abundant library, much of which Palgrave had read. The quartermaster enjoyed their discussions about books and other matters.

The surgeon was now curled onto his side, his hands tucked beneath his cheek like a babe. The pose reminded Palgrave of Joseph. It was becoming difficult to recall the image of his eldest child.

When the gale was spotted, Bellamy, Levasseur and Julian made hasty plans to skirt the storm to the east and, although Palgrave discerned by the light swing of his hammock and the gentle flap of the billowing canvas that they had been successful in their task, their berths remained empty.

The captain's cabin slept all the senior members of Bellamy's crew. Hammocks and makeshift bedding were out of place in the expansive, richly decorated chamber. Bellamy had insisted, according to his articles, that the captain should be given no special privilege. There was a large, rectangular table in the centre of the room made of walnut. Once a captain's dining table, it was now strewn with charts and tools of navigation. An ornate desk rested in the corner under a portrait of France's child king, Louis XV. Even though any of the crew were free to, it was only Palgrave and Ferguson who had ever used the desk. It was here Palgrave housed his notebooks. There were three leather-bound journals in which were written in neat, uniform columns a record of the plunder and the crew's shares. His quill, ink, paper, books and Leah's Bible rested on the bureau as well. It was also at this desk where Palgrave penned his carefully composed letters to his wife.

Listening to the muffled hum of snores and the night-time murmurs of his shipmate, Palgrave drifted close to sleep. *None of the crew have wives*, he thought. Bellamy denied married men a place on his ship. Most of them, he would wager, possessed neither family nor home. He was unique, he realised, the only truly fortunate man on board the ship. It was always thoughts of Leah that beckoned sleep. Even when the raucous din of his boozy shipmates or the squally sea threatened his slumber, it was memories of his wife that guided his journey to the land of nod.

Leah's fourth visit had taken place on a Monday morning.

'You're working again,' she said as she entered his work-shop. 'That's heartening to see.'

He turned and smiled. It was the first time he had seen her empty handed, it occurred to him. At meeting she always clutched a prayer book and when she visited previously, she had held a heavily laden basket. It was strange seeing her like that, unencumbered, hands clasped behind her back.

'What are you making there?' she asked, stepping closer.

'A goblet for the minister,' he answered. 'A "chalice", he called it.'

They caught each other in an amused glance.

'He visited me last night,' Palgrave explained. 'It seems my return to meeting and your father's hospitality have had a hand in the commission.'

'I'm pleased, so pleased,' she said moving further into

the shed. 'I've never been inside a silversmith's workshop.' She loosened her scarf. 'It's hot.'

'The forge ...' he began, indicating the fire.

'Might I have a little water? My throat's so dry.'

'It's the smoke. You're not used to it.' He hurried to the entrance. 'Come into the house.'

Entering the kitchen, Leah removed her cloak, hat and gloves then took a seat at the table. Palgrave washed his hands, ladled two cups of water from a pail and set them down. He took a seat opposite her.

Once Leah had taken a sip of her water she began. 'My father has forbidden me to visit you again. You're healed, he said, and require no further tending.'

Leah's manner when she came to his workshop had not pre-empted this.

'I see.' Palgrave placed his cup on the table.

'But I find myself drawn to you in a way I cannot grasp,' she said. 'Seeking out your presence every day, suffering intolerably when I'm not with you ... you have given me meaning.'

It was as though she were privy to his own thoughts. He leant towards her and took her hand. The skin was silky, bringing to mind the velvety cheeks of his children. Their eyes met.

'Might your feelings be merely a girlish fancy?' he asked, as a matter of course.

'I don't think so,' she answered, finding no offence in his query.

It was his turn to speak, he realised, to offer her counsel and tell her that her feelings would pass in time. Instead he rose and lifted her to her feet.

'I find myself suffering also when you're absent,' he

confided. 'But I'm in no position to offer myself to you, Leah.'

Then she stepped towards him and placed her cheek against his chest. He intuitively wrapped his arms around her body and closed his eyes. It was as though, up until that moment, a piece of him had been missing.

Leah raised her face to his. 'If you'll have me,' she began, 'my father can do nothing but consent. You're a godly man with an acreage and a business ... he admires your fortitude. He told you so yesterday, while you were seated at his table.'

Palgrave didn't react and gently eased her head against his chest once more. He knew Joseph Hallett would never consent to their marriage. To invite a widowed silversmith into your home as an act of Christian charity was vastly different to inviting that same man into your daughter's bed. Moreover, it would be the dowry and eventual inheritance that would be foremost in Hallett's mind. He strongly doubted Hallett would offer his daughter, dowry and half of his acreage to the likes of Palgrave Williams, even if he were a godly man. Although her optimism and conviction made it impossible for Leah to see it, marriage to Palgrave Williams would destroy everything she knew and had faith in. Yet, the idea of not having her was unendurable.

'Will you have me?' she asked quietly.

'Of course.'

Palgrave was still awake when Bellamy, Lambert and Julian came below decks an hour later.

23

It was the early hours of Sunday morning when they moored in the harbour of Puerto Plata. The bay overlooked a beach that stretched beyond the scope of Palgrave's pale-blue eyes. Apart from the watch, the crew were below decks, asleep. Waking at dawn on the Sabbath was a difficult custom for Palgrave to break.

A small township, similar in style to Nassau, was situated a little to the north of their current position. Palgrave picked up the eyeglass and peered towards the town. Not a soul was visible. How inviting even the most unseemly place appeared in dawn's first light. Each daybreak was like a brand new canvas. The sky was cloudless and coloured a most brilliant shade of pink. The morning was near perfect.

Still. Noiseless. *God is the friend of silence*, Leah would say.

Hornigold's flotilla would remain moored in Puerto Plata until the vessels were refitted and repaired. During the afternoon the captains gathered below decks on the *Benjamin*. By the time Bellamy returned to his ship, Palgrave sat alone at the great desk, scrutinising the figures in his journals.

Palgrave lifted his eyes when Bellamy entered. The captain nodded.

'The *Marianne* has taken more plunder than the rest of the fleet combined,' Palgrave said. 'Hornigold has seized just two ships in the past fortnight, neither of them carrying anything greater than a thousand pounds in cargo. We have captured twelve!'

Bellamy sat down heavily in the armchair facing Palgrave. It was upholstered in opulent gold fabric dotted with pink roses. Its twin sat at the opposite end of the room. Placed together each evening, they acted as a makeshift berth for the captain. Bellamy always slept lightly, conscious of each creak of the timbers.

'He's a drunk,' Bellamy remarked. 'He never has his wits about him.'

'Are we to give twenty-five per cent to said drunk?'

Bellamy closed his eyes and inhaled deeply. When he opened them again a few minutes later, he shook his head. Both of the men were weary. Striving to keep to a strict agenda, Bellamy had worked his crew hard over the past fortnight. Aware of their success, the plunder in the hold and the share they would receive at journey's end, not a single man had complained. And none of them had toiled more tirelessly than their captain.

Bellamy and Palgrave looked at each other for a time, both of them contemplating the same course, neither willing to commit to the deed by expressing it aloud.

'The dilemma is double-edged, is it not?' Palgrave asked. 'Seizing Hornigold's ships and captaincy is one thing. But it will also weaken his hold on Nassau.'

'Is that such a bad outcome?' Bellamy said, thinking of Tamesine. He rose and poured a small cup of madeira from a pitcher on the table.

'Nay, but it's a factor we must consider. You'll be snatching everything he owns, as well as his reputation. What's more, he was good to his word and furnished you with this ship.' Palgrave answered, before adding firmly. 'Regardless, Hornigold is a loathsome cretin who has neither your skill as a seaman nor your cunning and daring as a pirate.'

Bellamy eyed his friend curiously over the rim of his glass.

'I've never heard you speak with such passion, such vehemence. Your mettle has trebled since we left Eastham.' Bellamy drained his cup.

Offering a resigned shrug, Palgrave explained, 'I've discovered the joy of fighting back. You've been an excellent teacher.'

'Yet neither of us dare say the word that lies in our hearts. The word, the act, that will seal our fates forever.'

'Mutiny?' Palgrave asked.

'Mutiny,' Bellamy echoed softly.

Two DAYS later as they waited for the wind, Bellamy, Palgrave, Levasseur and four of the *Marianne's* crew boarded the *Benjamin*.

'What can I do for you, Mister Bellamy?' Hornigold shouted from the quarterdeck. Teach stood nearby, studying a chart.

Bellamy approached the quarterdeck and drew his pistol from the sling around his shoulder, aiming it at Hornigold's chest.

'I'm taking your ship, Sir,' Bellamy announced in an even voice.

The flamed-haired captain did not move, even though his pistol and sword were close at hand. The crew members from the *Marianne* moved towards Hornigold rapidly and tied him to the mizzenmast. Palgrave watched Levasseur approach the captain. The slash from Hornigold's blade had healed but La Buse was now mostly blind in his right eye. He had taken to wearing a black patch to conceal his disfigurement.

'Just deserves, Hornigold,' the Frenchman spat.

Hornigold shot the mutineers a venomous look. Bellamy displayed not a trace of agitation and the *Benjamin*'s crew made no effort to stop the rebellion that was underway. The young captain had gained a reputation as a hard but fair taskmaster whose unswerving focus guaranteed great riches.

Palgrave cast his gaze to Teach. Their eyes locked for an instant before Teach, without removing his gaze, reached slowly into his coat and produced his pipe.

'It'll be put to a vote,' Bellamy called. 'What say you, Sir?'

'Aye,' Hornigold said.

Once the men were assembled Bellamy rose to the quarterdeck and stood alongside Hornigold, whose hands were untied.

'Gentlemen,' Bellamy began. 'It has come to my attention that in the fortnight past, the *Marianne* has captured six times the number of prizes to that of the *Benjamin*. The plunder aboard my ship is greater than sixty thousand pounds. I'm made heartsick at the prospect of sharing this plunder with the likes of Captain Hornigold, who has earned a meagre two thousand pounds in the same time and under the same circumstances. I can vouch for these sums, gentlemen, and my quartermaster, Mister Williams has licence to produce the figures if any of you have an inkling to view them.'

Before he continued Bellamy scanned the grimy faces of the crew. Their regard of the twenty-seven-year-old was keen, but not suspicious. There was expectancy in their eyes, a belief in him as their leader. Their unstated support of his endeavour instantly filled Bellamy with fire. He continued with even greater conviction.

'I can expand the volume of our haul if I am free to capture English ships. I've no loyalty to any nation and those of you who know my tale will agree I suffered no great advantage sailing under the Union flag. I'm a free prince and have as much authority to make war on the whole world as he who has a hundred sail of ships at sea and an army of one hundred thousand men in the field.'

He paused and glanced at Palgrave. His quartermaster offered him an encouraging nod then shouted 'huzzah'.

Captured by the spirit of the moment, the entire crew chorused the triumphant cry. Then the men were suddenly quiet, anticipating Bellamy's next words.

'Hornigold, and all those who choose to stand with him, are nothing but hen-hearted numbskulls – cowardly whelps who will submit to laws that rich men have made for their own security, laws that have transformed strong men into weaklings. In turn, Hornigold has treated the township of Nassau with the same disrespect, turning free men and women into slaves. I declare that I'll plunder only the wealthy, from whichever nation they hail, under the protection of my own courage.'

A further resounding succession of huzzahs followed.

'WILL you sail in convoy with us, Mister Teach?' Palgrave inquired.

'Nay. The Carolinas are where I am heading,' Teach said. 'As you know, I have some interest in the region and, it occurs to me now, the Caribbean is too heavily pirated. It will not be long before it's policed. Particularly if Mister Bellamy strikes the terror on English shipping lanes that he has proposed.'

It had taken some convincing for Teach to captain one of the four sloops Bellamy had commandeered. Allegiance to Hornigold had not prompted his hesitation. It was an uncertainty in his skill as a leader. Teach had grown morose when Bellamy proposed the idea. However, both Bellamy and Palgrave pressed him until he eventually acquiesced. He chose the *Ranger* as his prize. They were obliged to Teach for not contesting the mutiny; Samuel Bellamy was a just, compelling captain whom the men respected, but it was Teach who held the winning hand if he had decided to challenge the revolt on Hornigold's behalf. With his volatile nature, there wasn't a man on board who did not live in fear of him.

Most of the crew decided to sail with either Bellamy or Teach. The handful that remained loyal to Hornigold were placed on board the *Benjamin*, along with their erstwhile captain, and given a few meagre rations along with some rum. The fourth and smallest ship of Hornigold's flotilla, the *Adventure*, was scuttled. Following Bellamy's address to the crew, Hornigold had not spoken. Neither had he resisted. Palgrave had been sceptical of his passiveness, anticipating a greater, more violent reaction from the captain. Bellamy had shrugged off his friend's concern.

'What's he to do? Even Teach did not raise a hand in his defence. Do not doubt our course now,' Bellamy declared, riding a wave of confidence. 'Nothing I did ran contrary to his own ship's articles. Every man is equal and any man among us was free to challenge his authority.'

Recalling Hornigold's demeanour, so coloured as it was with rancour and contempt, Palgrave failed to be reassured by his friend's words.

WHEN BELLAMY ARRIVED at Tamesine's house, the time had only recently passed noontide. He had made his way hastily through the streets of Nassau, liberally littered with most of his now one-hundred-and-thirty-man crew. They were diligently engaging in the revelries their captain had instructed them to pursue when they had disembarked. All except Palgrave, who had chosen to stay on board and adjust his ledgers following the payment of the crew.

He heard her voice as he approached the door of the cottage, instructing her son to pack up his books so she could serve dinner. Hesitating before knocking, Bellamy walked quietly to the side of the house and peeked in through the open window. The sunshine that tumbled through made mother and son difficult to see. He moved out of sight and squinted as his eyes adjusted. He caught the scent of the meal Tamesine had prepared. His stomach groaned softly. When he opened his eyes he furtively glanced in at the scene once more. She was wearing a plain blue dress with a lace collar and her hair fell down her back to her waist. It was held in check by a red ribbon. Bellamy admired her simple beauty, unadorned as she was at that moment by the trappings of her trade.

John closed his books and rose. When he returned, Tamesine instructed him to lay the table. As he did so,

Bellamy walked to the front door and knocked softly. It was opened by the boy within seconds. A smile that encompassed most of his thin face appeared instantly. Tamesine turned from the hearth towards the door. Laying down the plate and ladle, she moved to the entrance and took Bellamy's hand.

'Lay another place, please, John,' she said as she drew Bellamy into her home.

PART III

EASTHAM, MASSACHUSETTS
WINTER 1717

24

———

*T*he minute Goody Jeffries noticed that Palgrave Williams was gone to Boston, gossip spread like a viper in a bed. Palgrave doesn't have a brother; I'm certain he told me that he had no family in the colonies, another woman in Boston is more likely; Leah Williams is finally getting her comeuppance – full of conceit, just like her father; Why, it's a surprise Palgrave lasted as long as he did!

It was impossible to hush them. It was like trying to douse a wildfire with a thimble full of water. Leah remained stoic and sobersided in the face of it, but she gradually retreated. Pride was no shield against thorny looks and glances, or barbed whispers behind hands. I'd call by regularly. She wouldn't take my coin, so I took to bringing a pie my mother had 'burned' or a pail of milk that would 'spoil' if no-one drank it. She'd examine the pie and sniff the milk, both flawless, turn up her nose then thank me. I believe this charade was all that kept Leah standing.

There was a very fine line between kindness and charity, Leah taught me; but there was a line, nonetheless. Mary Garvey, from the ordinary, had even called by once with six jars of honey she had come across. I don't know how, payment from a luckless *card sharp, most likely. Leah refused the offering, saying she had more honey in her cellar than she knew what to do with, Mary told me. Mary wasn't offended, just confused, wondering how a woman in her predicament could afford to be so moral.*

Truth was, she couldn't. Tight-lipped as always, Leah never mentioned Palgrave's whereabouts to me. But I didn't believe the rumours. Palgrave loved her. That fact was as plain as a hat on a rack. It wasn't until the winter, around about November, when she told me. I didn't believe her at first. All my good feeling for Palgrave Williams drained away in that moment.

LEAH HELD Caleb's hand as she travelled the three miles to her father's home. Elizabeth walked by her side and the twins ran up ahead or behind, wherever their fancy took them. It had been many years since Leah had trod this path. Her father's acreage lay beyond the town at the end of a road that had no name. It didn't need one – everyone in Eastham knew where everybody else lived. Joseph walked ahead of his mother. She had dressed the child in his best clothes. A wan smile passed across her lips as she took him in. His trousers were too short, she realised as she examined her son's limber gait. They had been mended and patched more times than she could count. The boy had turned eleven in his father's absence and, in that time, had grown three inches. His fisted hands were pressed into the pockets of his coat. With his sandy-coloured hair, long limbs and shy bend to his back, he was a daily reminder of his father. Among her children, Leah sought out his presence most of all.

Snow covered the road, yet none of the children complained about the journey. Since their father's departure the family had unconsciously become closer, collared together in their anxiety and unease. They were so attuned to each other's moods and whimsies that even Caleb, now three years old, had an inkling of the humiliation his mother bore each day.

Leah despised herself for the lies. Any person of the town would offer her food, money or clothes, anything she required, if she told them the truth. But the thought of accepting charity was more degrading to Leah than her current situation scraping together a meagre living by trading eggs, cider, cheese or yarn. Nothing remained in Palgrave's workshop – she had sold everything already. The farm animals, one by one, would be next to go.

Palgrave had been gone almost five months.

'What's he like, Mama?' Elizabeth now asked. 'What's grandfather like?'

'You've seen him in meeting,' Leah replied.

'I know, but ... is he as mean as he looks?' the child asked.

'Nay, not at all,' Leah said with a smile. 'He's a very kind man, and he's wise. Your grandfather is godly, the most godly man in New England, I warrant, and a hard worker.

'Why do you not speak?'

'It matters not. What's done is done.'

Elizabeth nodded but her mouth twisted slightly.

'But our intention is not to visit your grandfather,' Leah went on, noting her daughter's displeasure. 'He may not want to see us, you understand. We're walking all this way to see your aunt.'

'Because she has been poorly?'

Leah nodded.

The day before, as Leah was raking clean the barn, Hannah, her father's servant, had called by.

'Good day to you, Goody Williams,' Hannah said evenly, her silhouette framed in the entrance.

Leah turned, startled, not recognising the voice.

'I'm concerned for your sister,' Hannah began immediately.

Joseph Hallett had found a servant in the aftermath of Leah's marriage to Palgrave and the death of Leah's beloved mother Elizabeth. When she arrived in the colonies after leaving Ireland, thirty-year-old Hannah White proved a perfect fit for Hallett and Maria. She had been in service in Cork and was able to read and write. By the time her indenture expired, Hannah was devoted to Hallett and Maria, so she stayed. Hannah cared greatly for the girl and the father and it wasn't long before Joseph Hallett trusted her with the accounts of both his household and his farm. 'Fair, able and dedicated' was how Maria most often described her.

Leah did not normally have dealings with the woman who always glanced at her coldly in passing when in town or in meeting. Her look as she approached Leah's home was no less frosty.

It had taken Leah a moment to gather herself. Hannah's visit was unexpected. She removed her gloves and wiped her face with the back of her hand.

'Good day, Hannah,' Leah replied. 'Shall we go into the house? I've some cider on the hearth.'

The older woman shook her head. Leah placed the rake against a stall then took a step closer to her visitor.

'What exactly is of concern to you?' Leah asked politely.

'It's your sister.'

Leah ached with guilt.

She had neglected Maria since Palgrave had left with Bellamy. She blamed neither Maria nor Samuel Bellamy for her husband's departure. If fault was to lie anywhere, it was with herself. Yet, on the occasions she had seen her sister since July, all the terrible feelings that were born and hastily buried on the afternoon of her husband's departure were instantly exhumed. Leah gained immense satisfaction from her resilience, but each time she was forced to recall Palgrave's final, abbreviated wave as he retreated into the woods like a savage, a small piece of her resolve was chipped away.

'Maria hasn't been herself since August. She is vague and forgetful, as if her mind is somewhere else,' Hannah explained in the same level tone, as though she were discussing the household budget or the frequency with which the hens were laying. 'But it has become worse recently. She's peevish much of the time, or takes to her bed and sleeps the day away. Except on the Sabbath, when she insists, without exception, on going to meeting. She has stopped painting and only sketches. She takes no enjoyment in nourishment, for the most part. When she does eat, it's with a ferocity I have never before seen in a young lady.' She faltered for a moment.

Leah glimpsed a flicker of concern cross Hannah's face.

'Then I hear moaning and whimpering from her chamber,' continued Hannah, 'as though she were ill.'

'Have you seen the contents of her chamber pot?' Leah asked.

'I have not,' Hannah answered before adding, deliberately, 'Maria takes care to empty that herself these days.'

'I see,' Leah remarked. 'I will visit her tomorrow after breakfast.'

'I don't know if you will be welcome in your father's home.'

'Then why did you come here and tell me this?' Leah

questioned. 'I can do nothing to help Maria if I do not see her.'

'I could bring Maria here ...'

'If Maria is ill she should remain where she is until we know more. Do not let my father's relationship with me be of concern to you,' Leah responded and noticed Hannah's lips tighten. 'Thank you for coming.'

For the final half mile, Leah carried Caleb on her hip. The child laughed as a light fall of snow dusted their noses and eyelashes. When they reached the gate of her father's property she studied the house closely, looking up at the window that was once her own then scanning the surrounding acreage that was blanketed white. There was no-one in sight. Typically, her father required only day labourers in winter. He would be mending fences or seeing to the livestock. Perhaps he was in the barn, tending to his seedlings – his 'experiments', as he and Leah had once joked in private – or grafting young apple trees together with the pocket knife he usually kept close. Leah would always be amazed when she watched her father so carefully see to the young plants, his knotted hands unexpectedly nimble as he sliced and peeled back the tender bark of the tree before nestling the scion underneath.

She checked herself. *Foolishness!* she thought. Those are chores for the spring.

They approached the house and Joseph rapped at the door. The group stamped their feet vigorously, ridding them of snow. The door was opened by Hannah within moments. She signalled for them to come inside.

'Your sister is in the parlour,' she said, waiting for them to remove their boots. 'I'll take the children into the kitchen. A batch of fat cakes have just come from the oven.'

The children looked to their mother as Leah placed

Caleb on the ground. 'Take off your coats and gloves, too,' Leah instructed. 'Then go with Hannah.'

Once they had disappeared down the hallway, Leah pushed the parlour door open slowly. Maria was positioned on the window seat with her legs raised. It was a position Leah herself had once enjoyed assuming when she was busy at needlework or mending. Maria wore thick stockings on her feet and her head was bare. Her blonde hair, which usually fell in sleek lengths over her shoulders, was bedraggled and dull. A sketching board rested on her lap. The room was cold and felt lifeless; the fire had all but died.

'Good morning, sister,' Leah said, closing the door behind her and walking to the hearth.

Maria looked up at her strangely. 'What an odd sight it is to see you in this house.'

Leah smiled uncertainly as she poked at the embers, encouraging heat. When she was satisfied with the strength of the blaze, she nestled another log in between the flames then, taking a taper, lit the candles in the sconces on the walls. Their flickering shadows only seemed to heighten the empty, echoing quality in the room.

'What are you drawing there?' Leah said, glancing at the board. 'Ah, the willow. You've done a fine job of capturing it in the wintertime. Just a season's difference can make such a change to its appearance, can it not?' Leah blew out the taper.

Maria continued with her task, carefully detailing the bleak, bare branches of the tree.

Leah sat opposite and studied her face. 'How are you feeling? Your colour has faded.'

'I'm feeling much better today.'

'Will you put your sketch down?' Leah asked. 'We haven't talked in so long.'

'You haven't been to meeting since September.' Maria placed the sketching board on the seat next to her then gazed at her sister peculiarly. 'Missing prayer service simply invites the Devil.'

'I've been remiss in many ways since Palgrave left.'

Leah was uncertain how to proceed. Her sister seemed much changed, pale and drained of energy, yet oddly serene in the same instance. After she thought for a moment on how she might temper her inquiries, Leah decided there was simply no way to soften such a thorny topic.

'Have you seen your flow these past months?' Leah asked.

'Nay,' Maria replied. 'Not since Samuel left.'

Maria picked up the board again and resumed her drawing.

'Stand for me, please,' Leah then instructed her, kindly, 'and unfasten your skirt.'

Maria did as her sister directed. Her skirt fell to the floor. Leah asked her sister to lie back on the window seat. She stood over Maria and pressed her abdomen firmly through her shift. Leah closed her eyes and moved her hands around Maria's belly. A smooth, apple-sized bulge was clearly evident. Then she asked her sister to stand and helped her dress. Taking Maria's hands in her own, she said gently, 'You're with child, Maria.'

'I thought as much.'

'Is the baby Mister Bellamy's?' Leah asked the question despite the certainty of the answer. She shouldn't have left them alone in the barn.

'Nay.'

Leah looked at her in confusion. The timing fit perfectly with Bellamy's departure. She gestured for Maria to sit.

'Then who is the father of your child?'

Maria sat back on the seat and looked at her sister squarely before she began.

Her expression brightened in wonder. 'I came across a little bird, a little hummingbird, in the woods. He was scarlet-breasted. He beckoned me to sit. It was a tiresome hot day in July and he said he would relieve me with his wings. I sat on the mossy bank by the willow and he fluttered so wildly about me that I soon became dizzy and lightheaded. "Lay down your head," he said. "Trust me. Unburden yourself. Lay down your head on the cool moss and close your eyes." I did as he told me and I fell asleep.' Maria paused and wet her lips. When she continued it was with even greater conviction. 'When I woke, the little bird lay on the ground beside me. His tiny chest heaved. He was exhausted and close to death. "I can evade death not a moment more. My burden will soon be lightened," he said. "But before I die I must tell you of your own fate," he said. "My burden has become yours. You have been blessed with my seed." Then he closed his eyes and drifted away.'

When she finished her account, Maria turned her face towards the window and gazed at the falling snow. Leah's mouth was dry and fear twisted and clumped in her stomach.

'Have you told anyone of this hummingbird?'

'Nay,' Maria replied. 'People would think me quite mad, would they not?'

Leah didn't react. Troubled by the admission, she stared at her sister for a minute then leant towards her and touched her cheek softly.

'You mustn't tell anyone what you told me,' Leah advised and kissed her sister on her forehead. 'Rest now. I'll find Papa.'

Maria returned her attention to the sketch.

When Leah entered the kitchen her children were stationed around the simple oak table her father had crafted when she was a child. They were indulging in the cakes and milk Hannah provided. She took in the scene for a minute. The room remained exactly as she remembered it, with the court cupboard her grandmother had brought with her from England standing opposite the entry. It housed the plates and jugs, bowls and silverware of her ancestors. Her mother's copper curfew sat at the side of the hearth. Leah remembered being mesmerised by the object as a child, running her hands daringly close to its boldly emblazoned surface and sensing the heat captured beneath.

'Where is my father?' Leah asked.

'Working. I didn't tell him of your visit.'

Leah nodded. 'Stay here children. I'll be back before long.'

Placing her cloak around her shoulders, Leah left the house in search of Joseph Hallett.

25

Hallett heard the soft crunch of footsteps on snow. He looked up briefly. It was his eldest daughter walking towards him. There was no mistaking Leah for her sister. Even though she was wearing a dark cloak and woollen bonnet pulled low over her brow, Hallett could plainly see who the young woman was – the way in which her chin was raised in curiosity and her hands were gripped behind her back was unmistakable. He returned his eyes to the beast he was tending.

The cow had not made her way back to the barn with the rest of the herd. Joseph Hallett bent low, examining the animal's hoof. He lifted the leg and rested it between his thighs, as a blacksmith might, then leant in for a closer inspection. The red cow bellowed as Hallett used pincers to remove an object from between the beast's toes. A nail. He dropped the leg and examined the offending item then placed it in his pocket along with the tongs.

'Do you regret not having a son?' he recalled Leah asking when she was twelve years old. They had stood in the same pasture together as the cows nibbled at spring's finest clover.

'Nay.'

Leah was never satisfied with his concise replies.

'But the farm,' she pressed. 'Would it not make more sense for your acreage to be passed on to a man? Is it not the law of New England that women are forbidden to inherit property?'

'It's the law that makes no sense,' he explained. 'You and Maria are my blood.'

He watched his daughter attempt to untangle his response. She frowned and looked up at him. Hallett tickled her cheek playfully with the end of one of her braids, making her giggle. Then he pointed to an animal and her calf. 'Go and see to that cow there. Tell me why she bawls so when the calf feeds.'

Leah made her way to the animal and patted her gently on her neck, leaning in and breathing deeply, taking in the cow's scent just as he had taught her. Then she knelt by the mother's side and examined her udder.

'It's red hot,' she called out to her father. 'And hard, as though a rock lies inside. She has the fever, I think.'

Leah rose.

'What's to be done, then?' he asked.

His daughter's brow furrowed before she began hesitantly. 'We should rub the udder with peppermint oil. Her calf will do the rest when he feeds.'

'Aye, good girl,' Hallett said.

Leah had smiled before following her father into the pasture to check on the other animals.

Hallett looked about him at that same field, now covered with white, then slapped the cow hard on the rump to send it on its way.

I should have acted sooner, he thought, walking through the thick snow towards his daughter. He'd witnessed the looks she and Palgrave had exchanged at meeting and read desire in them. But he had trusted Leah.

'Good day to you,' Leah said.

'Good morning,' he replied.

Then they were silent. Despite inhabiting the same town, attending the same meeting house and bearing the same measure of concern for Maria, it was the first time the pair had stood face to face in a decade. Breathing hard from the cold and trapped in the uncertainty of the moment, a sudden flurry of snow startled them into communication.

'Was it a rock?' Leah asked finally. Hallett looked at her. 'In the cow's hoof?'

He shook his head.

'A nail.' He produced the object from his pocket and handed it to his daughter. Leah studied it for a few seconds before handing it back.

'Strange the beast's foot found such a thing in all this snow,' Leah remarked.

Hallett took another look at the nail before pocketing it again.

'Might we go indoors ... Papa?' The word seemed alien and caught in her throat for an instant. 'There's a matter we must discuss.'

Leah turned and began to make her way towards the house. She stopped when she realised her father was not following her.

Hallett hadn't left his spot. He stared at her. 'You crushed me.'

She tilted her head in inquiry.

'You crushed me, child. Your mother too,' he explained. 'When you left ten years ago for Palgrave Williams.'

She had no words, no explanation. There was no argument, nothing she could articulate in response. Now she understood. Her father had spoken an undeniable truth.

HANNAH LEFT the remains of the cakes and poured two cups of cider for Leah and Hallett before escorting the children into the parlour to see their aunt.

Father and daughter sat at opposite ends of the long table. Leah placed her cup to her lips then lowered it again. She absently smoothed her skirt and checked the buttons and cuffs of her bodice before taking a further sip from her cup. Her hands came to rest in her lap before she spoke.

She began, looking at him squarely. 'Hannah called on me yesterday. She's worried for Maria.'

'There's a strangeness about her, it's true. She has not been well,' Hallett said, staring into his mug.

'She's with child.'

He raised his eyes to her in surprise then swirled the contents of his cup. Leah waited for the news to settle. She knew better than to rush her father.

'Mister Bellamy's, you think?' he finally asked.

Leah nodded. 'But it matters not. What's troubling is the odd tale, the dangerous tale, Maria has concocted about how she came to be this way.'

She took another sip of her cider before she began relating the story of Maria's hummingbird. As she spoke she witnessed her father's countenance alter from concern to dismay.

'The most unsettling part of the tale is her certainty in the episode. She hasn't invented the fiction to conceal her sin,' Leah said. 'She truly believes it.'

Hallett was silent. Leah could tell by his set jaw he was taking in the wider consequences of the situation.

'Hannah must take her away until the baby comes,' Leah advised cautiously. 'To Boston, or New York. Somewhere she'll not be noticed. When she returns, I'll take the child and raise it as my own. I doubt we'll ever see Bellamy again.'

Hallett stared at her, ill at ease. Leah took in his changed appearance. More weathered, leaner and with an air of feebleness she had not noticed from a distance. Her father was able and intelligent. She had witnessed him countless times devising remedies for sick animals or crops threatened by locust or black chaff, but she knew that he had neither the skill nor the wits to deal with this particular crisis.

'There'll be gossip, of course,' she continued. 'Palgrave has been gone since July ... but I can invent a tale of my own that people will believe or, at least, say they believe.'

'You've grown sceptical.'

Leah shrugged.

'I never had to worry about your faith.'

His daughter offered him a rueful smile. Hallett sat quietly for a number of minutes, gazing at his clenched hands on the table. Aware of her father's necessity to consider a matter from every angle, Leah waited quietly.

Finally Hallett rose and stroked his beard as he walked to the mantle and retrieved his pipe. 'Nay,' he uttered. 'The truth will out one day. It's better it is now.' He proceeded to fill the pipe, tamping down the tobacco confidently. 'You cannot bear your sister's sin, Leah.'

She stood abruptly, distressed by her father's decision and his composure. 'I'm content to endure anything I must for Maria. Reverend Dent will have her in irons otherwise.

And if her story comes to light he'll condemn her as a witch.'

Her father did not appear to understand.

'Papa, she'll be *hanged*.'

'Hush child. God will not spurn us,' he declared. 'I will not conceal her sin.'

'But you must!' Leah slapped her hands hard on the table. They stung in the cold. 'Dent's congregation is under threat of collapsing. He will use Maria to protect his position. You must remember what happened in Salem. Doubters rush back to the fold at the slightest mention of witchcraft ...'

Leah longed to tell her father about her own predicament and the Reverend's hand in it. But it would be pointless. Hallett knew the kind of man Dent was. Her father had tagged him as a hypocrite long ago.

She shook her head. 'Please, Papa ...'

He raised his hand to silence her.

'Might I spend some time with my grandchildren?' Hallett asked, ignoring her plea.

Leah sighed in frustration. 'Of course.'

Hallett left the room. Leah sat heavily on the wooden bench near the hearth. As she considered the various solutions to her sister's plight, she cast her eyes about the room and fixed them on the curfew once more. It was engraved with the image of a manticore, the emblem of her ancestors. Leah crouched beside the large copper shield and ran her hands gently over its emblazoned surface, now cool, and struggled to recapture the warmth and comfort it had once provided.

26

The following morning, Leah roused the children earlier than usual and prepared them for meeting. Washing their faces and hands, and trimming their nails, she polished her offspring until they sparkled. The girls' hair was brushed and plaited and fixed at the ends with small blue ribbons. She set out their best clothes for them to dress in. After the family had breakfasted and cleaned their teeth, Leah cast a final eye over their appearance. Their clothes were worn and their boots needed mending but they were handsome children in fine fettle. The glow of their spirits was obvious. Leah donned a dark green skirt and bodice and Elizabeth helped her fix her hair in braids that knitted around her head. Although she would not be seen that morning without her cap, Leah took pride in knowing her hair beneath was faultless.

'How do I look?' she had asked Elizabeth.

Her daughter examined her seriously for a number of seconds. 'Beautiful, Mama.'

Leah hugged her daughter to her, grateful for the falsehood. Leah knew she had aged years in the last five months.

When they arrived at the meeting house they climbed the stairs quickly and took their usual seats in the balcony. There was a certain comfort in being positioned above the town, surrounded by her children. Gradually, however, the parishioners noticed her return and she began to feel the first pricks. Pity, suspicion, contempt, like a thousand tiny darts, pierced her chest. She sat more erect and gripped the hand of Joseph, who was by her side. He looked at his mother then bent his head shyly before Leah felt his hand tighten around her own.

Leah resolved to meet each wretched gaze with a courteous nod. As she directed her eyes around the meeting house, she noticed Arthur Earl standing by the altar, straight-backed and noble, his attention fixed on her. She nodded, and his typically stern face gave in to a brief, but pleasing, smile. Her father and Maria were in their box, along with Hannah, who had joined the church at her employer's insistence some years ago.

Reverend Dent arrived at the altar wearing his cap and robes of office. He scanned the boxes and the balcony slowly, taking in the composition of his congregation. Dent called his sermon that Sabbath 'A Reminder' – a reminder of a time when heretics and antinomians threatened to depose 'the Puritan's holy experiment'. In particular, he spoke of Anne Hutchinson, the 'vile antinomian who scoffed at the legitimate ministers of the church who preached the commandments as essential for salvation'.

Leah looked at her father whose whiskered jaw seemed to jut defiantly towards the altar. Leah recalled him and her mother discussing Hutchinson and her condemnation of the covenant of works. It irritated her father that, according to most ministers at the time, God's salvation was 'wholly dependent' on one's shows of obedience and piety. Joseph and Elizabeth Hallett preferred the covenant of grace – the idea that eternal life would be granted to all those who had faith in God.

Had he ever made his views public? Leah wondered now.

Leah left the meeting house troubled by the true meaning of the sermon. Often times, when she and Palgrave were first married, she would depart meeting desperate to see the profounder meaning in Dent's address. Palgrave would laugh, amazed by her devotion, and inform her there simply was no deeper meaning.

'But surely ...' she would argue, certain there had to be the trace of a more weighty, philosophical notion concealed within Dent's tirade.

'He was preaching of a new robe, pure and simple,' Palgrave would say. 'Dent does not have the capacity for anything deeper.'

Leah reluctantly grew to accept this and began to use meeting for her own private reflections, meditation and prayer. Having become so adept at this, she had grown deaf to Dent's stentorian tones. But she was convinced this sermon was different. She was sure it was a poorly veiled attack on her father.

Leah watched as her children scattered over the green. 'Be mindful of your clothes,' she called after them, absently.

'Good day, Leah.' Arthur Earl removed his hat and pushed back his dark hair. 'Is there any news from Palgrave?'

'He writes but he doesn't say when he might return.'

'I see.' He turned his hat in his hands, smoothing out the brim. 'I was pleased to see you back at meeting.'

'Thank you.'

'Extremely pleased, indeed,' he added. He fixed his hat on his head, said goodbye but didn't move off.

'May I speak frankly, Leah?'

'Of course.'

'There are factions in this town,' he said in an undertone, his clear deep-set eyes revealing more than the words he spoke. 'Factions that would be much pleased to see your father ruined.'

She nodded. 'I knew as much.'

'His family, too.'

'I understand.' She looked around her, seeking out her children. The younger ones were playing near the whipping post with their friends while Joseph and Elizabeth stood by their grandfather and aunt.

'Take care, Leah.' She glanced at him. 'It would be wise for your husband to return swiftly.'

'I've no control over that.'

He lowered his eyes to the melting snow at his feet.

'Then, if there's any role which I might play ...' he said cautiously, raising his gaze to meet hers. 'A role which ... a role that might safeguard your family and preserve your happiness ...'

Leah stared seriously at him for a moment, considering the meaning of his offer.

'We talked of it once, I remember,' he added. 'We were sixteen.'

'I recall. We decided we weren't well-suited.'

'I *can* be a worthy husband.'

Leah took his hand and squeezed it tightly. Their eyes met as they considered the truth between them.

It would be simple to denounce her husband, to explain that Palgrave had deserted her. The entire town would support her. After all, Palgrave had suggested as much on the afternoon he departed. It would be the safest path but the betrayal would define her for eternity.

~

THERE WAS no snowfall on the day that Leah began to sob as she wiped clean the table after baking a fine sugar cake. The sugar had been given to her by her aunt, who claimed that 'a sixty-year-old widow was in no need of treats'. The realisation that there was nothing she could do struck her with such intensity that she had been forced to sit and bury her face in her hands. After a minute, she wiped her eyes and calmed herself, ashamed at her histrionics. Taking deep breaths, she wondered what Palgrave would counsel. Uncorrupted as he was by faith, guilt or obligation, it was her husband's rational guidance she now sought. She closed her eyes and waited for her resentment to ebb.

With the older children at school and Caleb resting, Leah took the stairs to her chamber. She opened her prayer book and removed Palgrave's letters. There were just four of them. Each page had been read so many times by herself and her children that she could swear the paper and ink were wearing thin. Even the crude seal Palgrave had used to secure the letters had been scrutinised tirelessly by Joseph and Elizabeth, as though the wax was likely to offer further testimony to their father's affairs. Examining his neat, exact hand as she put the pages in order, Leah didn't care that the words filled the children's heads with fanciful notions. She only viewed the correspondence as evidence of their relationship and the life they had shared.

She pressed the pages to her face, inhaling deeply, then lay down on the bed and began to read. When she finished, Leah closed her eyes for a moment before realising there was something she *was* able to do. She hastily folded Palgrave's letters and placed them in her prayer book. Then, moving to the small table near the window on which were stacked a number of her husband's books and an inkpot, Leah sat, took quill and paper in hand and began to write a correspondence of her own.

27

'I departed Beverly the moment I got your letter,' said Silas as Leah poured out cider and sliced the bread she had baked that morning.

'Thank you for making the journey,' Leah responded.

Silas watched as Leah carefully spread the slices with jam. Strawberry, he guessed. Leah Williams's strawberry jam was much prized in Eastham. *The remnants of a summer long-passed*, he mused. She then cut the bread into smaller pieces and laid them neatly on a dish. She edged it slowly across the table towards him before sitting down herself.

'Is your new position all that you hoped it would be?' Leah asked.

'Aye,' Silas responded. He paused for a moment as he cast his gaze around Leah's modest home. 'Reverend Cotton Mather visited Beverly in October. He delivered a rousing sermon to our congregation.'

'I know something of his reputation. Palgrave admires his mind.'

'He had supper with Reverend Talbot and myself,' he went on, pushing his spectacles along the bridge of his nose.

'Mather spoke very freely.' Leah nodded. 'Wouldn't that be something? To speak freely.'

Leah raised an eyebrow. 'Indeed. Mather has the power to do so.'

'Indeed,' Silas said.

Lost in his thoughts for a time, Silas finally roused when Leah refilled his cup.

'He possesses extremely liberal views on inoculation and the invisible world. He has been much maligned these twenty years past.'

'He's an extremely learned man. I'm certain you impressed him, Silas.'

Silas lowered his head, wondering how he could turn the conversation to Maria. But there was no need to.

'You're my final hope, Silas.'

He lifted his face. 'You said as much in your letter.'

Concise and stark of detail, the correspondence only mentioned Leah's 'unbridled fear for her sister's future'. She had been brief in her request for Silas's presence, as soon as possible, in Eastham. Nevertheless, those few words had restored his optimism in a possible marriage to Maria Hallett. Silas left immediately.

Following their joining by the willow in July, Silas was certain he had shown Maria the path that was true and clear. Yet, she stubbornly refused to speak with him. He waited by the willow for hours each day, anticipating her arrival. Each Sabbath he would will her to look at him as he sat beside the altar so near to her. Yet, not a single glance did she cast his way. Her eyes always remained calmly fixed on the stained glass window behind the altar. On one occasion, his final Sabbath in Eastham, his father had allowed Silas to deliver the sermon. Maria had closed her eyes for its entire duration, never once looking his way. He had wondered if she had been praying, or was the sight of him simply too odious for her to countenance?

In desperation, Silas had then asked Abby to deliver a note. It was a heartfelt apology for his actions that had taken him many days to pen. Abby complied, but returned within the hour bearing the letter, unopened. She begged him to cease in his quest. Finally, he departed Eastham melancholy and ashamed. Compelled to decline the position in Beverly, he raised the subject, indirectly, one evening with his father. The minister refused to be moved. Even Dent had given up on his son's marriage to Maria Hallett. Instead, he had become focused on the destruction of her father.

'How is Maria?' Silas asked. 'Is she unwell? The tone of your letter, your insistence that I come, concerned me ...'

Leah sipped her cider deliberately for a moment.

'The events of last summer were unfortunate,' Leah said. 'It had long been my hope my sister would marry you.'

'It had been my hope as well.'

Leah offered him a comforting smile. 'She treated you poorly, Silas, but it was unintentional. Her vision and her path were ... blurred.'

'By Samuel Bellamy.'

She nodded. 'But he is gone.'

Pausing, she looked at Silas sombrely. Her eyes flickered for a few seconds. She twisted her wedding band.

He took Leah's hand. She was trembling.

'What is it?' Silas urged in his kindest tone. 'Trust me. Confide in me. Unburden yourself.'

Leah parted her lips slightly then she lowered her head. When she raised her face again he could discern the wash of tears in her pure blue eyes.

'Maria is with child, Silas. Bellamy's child.'

Silas released her hand. He stiffened and stared at the

plate before him. The jam was vivid red and spread liberally on the bread. Its scent filled his nostrils. He inhaled deeply and closed his eyes, at once recalling and struggling to erase the memory of summer.

'The only solution I can see, Silas ...' Leah paused for a moment. 'Would you consider asking again for my sister's hand?'

He gripped his knees and closed his eyes.

'I'm aware of the immensity of what I ask you,' Leah continued. 'But I know you love her still. You wouldn't have come if it wasn't so.'

That afternoon by the willow he had lost sight of himself and his calling. He had sought God's forgiveness daily since. But he'd never lost sight of Maria. Now, it seemed God had excused his crime and had benevolently chosen to present him with an opportunity. He would become Maria's saviour and she would be his.

'Silas, are you praying?' Leah leant forward and touched his arm lightly.

He opened his eyes.

'It would not have to mean you sacrificing your good name.' She rose and moved to the hearth as she spoke. 'We could invent a story. That you and Maria married secretly in the summer, perhaps, and her condition ...'

Silas raised his hand when she turned.

'It matters not.' He stood, straightening his vest. 'You should speak with her directly and impress upon her the urgency of the situation. We must not tarry in this.'

Leah gasped and opened her mouth to speak.

'If the notion of marriage is favourable to her then I will visit your father and seek his permission at once,' he broke in.

Leah approached him, reached out and touched his

cheek delicately with her fingertips. 'Thank you, Silas. I will speak with Maria today.'

~

As Arthur approached the Williams's property, Silas thundered past him on Adagio, Dent's most handsome colt. There was no time to raise his hand or tip his hat. Quicker than an eyelid's beat, he was gone. Arthur pulled up his own horse, a black gelding named Joey, and looked behind him. Within seconds, horse and rider were out of sight along Backridge Road.

When he arrived at Leah's door, it was still open. His stomach balled into a knot and he made his way into the house quickly, scanning the parlour, listening for signs of her and Caleb. He found her in the kitchen, wiping down the table. Caleb was by her side, his face smeared with jam.

'The door was open,' he said.

'Oh.' It was all she said.

'Silas rode past me.' Arthur took a seat at the table, placing his palms on the well-worn wood, fingers spread wide. 'He was greased lightning on that new colt.'

Leah addressed her son. 'I'm certain there's more jam on your face than made it to your mouth.'

She went about scrubbing the child's face with a cloth then sent him on his way. Arthur soon heard him padding up the stairs. Leah busied herself at the hearth.

'What did he want?'

Leah wouldn't face him. 'He intends to ask for Maria's hand.'

'Again?'

Leah nodded.

'You're in agreement?'

'I am.'

Leah rose and turned to him, wiping her hands on her apron, chin raised.

'Just remember that the apple never falls far from the tree.' Arthur knew the words were wasted but they had to be said. Once Leah Hallett got a notion in her head, it was stuck there like cobbler's wax.

AFTER CALLING on her Aunty Margaret and leaving Joshua in her care, Leah walked to her father's home. The crisp air and clear sky gradually fortified her as she made her way along the road. She had concealed Maria's true condition from Silas. How could she tell the young minister that her sister was not right, that her spirit had been corrupted? Leah was hopeful she could convince Maria of the need to marry Silas. Surely, her fantasy was born from desperation. Once she was presented with the opportunity ... Leah buried her hands deeply in her muff and stared solemnly at the road ahead.

Seated in the parlour with her father and sister, Leah outlined the solution. Maria would marry Silas within the week then travel to Beverly where she would have the child. Silas would raise it as his own. She waited for them to respond.

Swaying gently in his rocking chair throughout the duration of Leah's proposal, her father's honed gaze and puckered lips told her he was considering the scheme. Maria, on the other hand, did not relinquish her sketch. Her hand travelled furiously over the page.

The incessant scratch of the pastel against the page prompted Leah to stand and distance herself as best she could from the sound. As she passed her sister, she glanced at the rendering Maria was so focused on. It was the same willow, but this version of the tree was dark and hostile. Rather than falling wistfully towards the ground, the gnarled branches stretched out viciously, as though seeking out quarry. The violence of the sketch made Leah stop as if struck in the face, waiting for the full burn of the slap to spread across her skin.

The lantern clock began its hourly chore. *Tick tock.* 'What say you, Maria?' her father asked.

Leah turned, startled.

Maria continued to draw. 'What will Samuel say when he returns?'

'But he may not return,' Leah advised sharply.

'I'll wait.'

Leah looked at her father in dismay. He remained composed.

'Reverend Dent's sermon,' Leah said. 'It was an outright slander, Papa. You must be aware ...'

Then Leah turned to her sister. 'Maria, you must be grateful for Silas's offer.'

Leah moved to her and sat by her side.

'Events are coming to a head,' she went on in despair. 'There are factions in this town ... there's no time to wait for Mister Bellamy.'

Her sister would not be moved and continued with her sketch.

'See sense,' Leah pleaded. 'Within weeks you'll be showing. Dent will move against us.'

Maria turned to the window, her eyes following the snowfall.

'Put down the sketch!'

Maria looked at her then laid down her pastel and

examined her work. As she wiped her blackened hand on her skirt she looked at her sister. Leah barely recognised her. She stared at her hard, searching for that which was absent. Maria cupped Leah's cheek in her hand.

'Hush, sister,' Maria whispered. 'Don't concern yourself. Samuel Bellamy will come back to me. I've spoken to Aunty Margaret about a potion.'

'What?'

'A potion, a brew to beckon Samuel back to me.'

'Margaret is a healer, not a witch!' Leah replied in exasperation. 'Are you to put her in harm's way as well?' She sighed and buried her head in her hands.

'Child, God is in our hearts and he will protect us,' Hallett said to Maria. 'This might be a sign. Your sister offers good counsel.'

'I will wait,' Maria responded, touching her belly. 'This child is a gift, chosen for me. The little hummingbird told me so. I've been blessed.' She resumed her sketching.

Leah's eyes darted to her father. 'Then you and Maria must leave at once.'

'Dent will not drive me from my home,' he said, softly. 'There's nothing more we can do, child.'

28

Abby knocked gently on Silas's door and entered. He was sitting at his table, neither reading nor writing.

'What was the purpose of Leah Williams's visit?' she asked as she picked up and folded the coat that had been thrown on the ground. She laid it across the foot of his bed. The young man didn't turn. 'She left so hastily.'

She moved further into the room and approached him. 'Silas.' She lay her hand on his shoulder.

'Maria is with child,' he said.

The slave gasped. Silas rose.

'Your child?'

'Nay,' he returned. Only Abby was capable of hearing the edge in his tone.

She followed Silas to his bed. When he sat, she gently touched his thick curls.

'A seaman who was in Eastham briefly, last summer,' he added.

Abby gripped his chin between her thumb and fore-finger and raised his face. She had held his face in this position many times when he was a child, to seek out a falsehood or check his pale skin for smudges and grime.

'Mister Roark says you took apples from his tree,' she had questioned when he was nine. 'He said he saw you take them. He saw the Doane boy as well.'

'I never did,' he had answered, dropping his eyes and attempting to pull away. 'Mister Roark is mistaken. He did not see me. Everyone knows he is half blind.'

'But God isn't. God sees everything, Silas Dent,' she had warned.

The boy had relented immediately and was sent to apologise to Mister Roark and offer, as repayment, his services during picking season.

She studied his expression now. His tired eyes were inscrutable. He held her gaze for only a few seconds before he eased his chin from her grasp.

'Leah Williams asked me to save her sister. To marry Maria and be a father to the child.'

She eased herself down next to him. He shifted along the bed.

'How could she request it?' Abby asked after a moment's thought. 'To risk your name ...'

'I'm happy to sacrifice my name. It means nothing.'

'Nay, Silas ...'

'Maria still won't have me,' he broke in. 'That's the reason Leah called today.'

'The seaman?'

Silas shrugged. 'Censure and chains are preferable to marrying me, it seems.'

Abby considered her counsel. The entire scenario was confusing. Apart from the occasional lapse as a child, Silas was not a liar. It was not an art that came to him naturally. But there was concealment in his manner. She recalled his declaration on the day Joseph Hallett had stymied his plans. His sureness had troubled her so. Likewise, his subsequent behaviour during summer was of concern. Ill-tempered one hour, miserable the next: neither state rendered him capable of finding enjoyment in anything. When he departed for Beverly she had hoped he would forget about Maria Hallett, hoped that finding his feet in a new position and unfamiliar town might preoccupy him.

Abby took his hand in her generous golden palms and asked herself why the family was so consumed by the Halletts. She tightened her grip. Forced to forgo and forget her entire life at the age of nine, Abby had never been able to conceive of this family's compulsion to have everything. Their godliness was all for show. Considering the care she'd taken with Silas, Abby found herself disappointed that he had not matured into a different man – a man without want.

After assuring Leah of his love for her sister, Silas returned to Beverly the following day. Confident her father would bend to Maria's ultimate decision, Leah worked doggedly to change her sister's mind over the ensuing fortnight. Each day, once the older children had gone to school, she walked the miles to her father's house to speak with Maria; each day the distance seemed to lengthen. Not long ago, Leah would have been spurred by her devotion, certain this trial was part of God's plan. But as the cold seeped through her boots and numbed her feet, she realised her only incentive was survival.

When she returned home each evening, Elizabeth and Sarah saw to a simple supper of broth and bread while Joseph, assisted by his younger brothers, tended to the few animals that remained. They would read Palgrave's letters and recite prayers together after dinner; Elizabeth had taken to warming her mother a footbath made of milk, honey and water. She'd brush her mother's hair as Leah soaked her aching feet in the sweet-smelling liquid. Then they'd slide into bed side by side, their mutual warmth reassuring to them both.

The kindness of her children each night was just enough to encourage Leah to make the journey again the next day.

It had come to the attention of Goody Holmes, who lived on the same road as Leah's aunt, Margaret Tompkins, that Leah Williams had left her youngest, Caleb, an unreasonable number of times with her aunt. Spying the child one morning as he fetched a bundle of kindling for his aunt, Goody Holmes donned her cloak and bonnet and hastened to Margaret's gate. Beckoning the boy to her she cried, 'Why are you calling on your aunt so often, Caleb Williams?'

The boy shrugged but didn't move towards her.

'Is your mother ill?' she pressed, walking closer to him. 'Or one of your brothers or sisters perhaps?'

He shook his head and wiped his nose along the sleeve of his coat.

'Why, she must be as busy as a bee since your father left,' she urged, gesturing the child closer.

Caleb remained fixed in his position, nursing the fagot of twigs.

'Where does she get to every day, Caleb Williams?' Goody Holmes finally said in exasperation as she approached the boy, wrapping a shawl around her shoulders.

'She calls on my grandfather and aunty,' he answered clearly, as if his mother's whereabouts were obvious.

'Is that so,' she murmured in astonishment.

'My Aunty Maria has been poorly.'

Wondering what had become of her charge, Goody Tompkins marched to her parlour window and glimpsed the exchange.

'Caleb, come back inside,' she called on opening the window. 'It's as cold as stone out there.'

Goody Holmes waved pleasantly to her neighbour as the boy turned and hurried back into the house. That afternoon Goody Holmes called on her sister, Catherine.

'Did you know Leah Williams has been welcomed back into the fold?' she asked her sister. It was clear from her tone that she knew her sister did not. Goody Holmes looked up from her cross-stitch briefly and caught Catherine's curious glance. Goody Holmes lowered her head once more and scrutinised her needlework casually.

'Nay. I did not, sister,' Catherine Jeffries proclaimed, laying down her needle and thread.

'Maria Hallett is ill, apparently.'

'Why, I saw her at meeting two Sundays past!' Goody Jeffries replied. 'She was as healthy as a horse.'

'Aye,' Goody Holmes said. 'A condition that strikes quite suddenly then. Would you agree, sister?'

Goody Jeffries nodded, her brow wrinkled as she passed her fine needle through the cloth.

When her husband, Francis Jeffries, came indoors an hour or two later, he groaned as he sat down and pulled off his boots. Besides attending to church business, the minister's deacon also worked a small croft he rented from Joseph

Hallett. He'd received an almighty kick from a disgruntled horse he had purchased from his landlord the week before. At four pounds, he had felt the beast was overpriced but Hallett was unwilling to negotiate. Jeffries's hip and his pride were still smarting from the blow.

The pain quickly vanished and his temper immediately improved when his wife relayed the news of Leah Hallett's daily visits to her sister. Jeffries smoothed his silver beard as he considered the significance of the news. Then he drew on his boots once more before heading out the door. Goody Jeffries heard her husband's favoured horse, Thomas, gallop past the house only minutes later.

WHEN LEAH ARRIVED at her father's house the following morning, she discovered a contingent of townspeople had preceded her. Joseph Hallett stood at the door. Hannah was visible behind him.

'Is it the pox, Hallett?' Jeffries called.

'My daughter is in good health.' Hallett pushed his fists firmly into the pockets of his coat.

As Leah worked her way through the throng she glanced at the anxious faces of those present and instantly the need to reach her father overwhelmed her. Jeffries had led Dent's most ardent supporters to her father's home. She glanced around briefly, searching for Arthur. He wasn't there. Shouldering a route around the horses and people, she finally found her father and stood by his side.

'Influenza struck my sister a few weeks ago,' Leah addressed the crowd. 'Why, isn't that so, Hannah?' The servant nodded grimly. 'But she's much recovered and in fine spirits.'

'Why do you still call here every day, Goody Williams?' Daniel Roberts called. Leah could not see Roberts but she recognised his gravelly voice.

'This is my family, Daniel Roberts,' Leah said. 'Has it become crime to call on one's family?'

'It's considered a suspicious turn of events when you have not set foot on this acreage for the last ten years,' he cried. 'Where's your husband, by the way, Goody Williams?'

She paused for an instant and wet her lips. 'You might remember, Daniel Roberts, how it was my husband who mended the rusted axles of your cart last spring and refused to accept nothing more than a kindly thank you in return.'

He did not respond. Leah wondered how her visits had become public.

'It's the hand of Providence that has seen your house stricken!'

Leah sharpened her gaze in an effort to locate the source of the declaration. Her eyes flicked over the crowd. She could hear her father's voice, and those of others – a hundred different voices – all trying to shout each other down. Leah couldn't make out any words.

'This house is not stricken,' Hallett called, his voice finally overwhelming the others.

'Perhaps your daughter has not been afflicted by a natural ailment, Hallett.'

'I can see you, Tobias Blackman,' Leah fumed and took a step towards the accuser. The man grimaced and attempted to move behind his horse. 'It was I who tended to your wife and children when they fell ill with measles last July, do you not recall? Was it Divine Providence that saved the lives of your entire family?'

Hallett turned swiftly to his daughter and touched her arm, gently easing her back to his side.

'Palgrave is well away from you Leah Williams,' Jeffries shouted. 'You're a fishwife and a scold.' The slur garnered a series of muffled sniggers. 'What's more, Hallett, that horse you sold me is a spiteful beast ...'

'You're a wily one, Francis Jeffries,' Leah responded. 'You decry my father in the hope of one day soon buying his land for a farthing.'

Her comments provoked outraged gasps from those assembled.

Striving to remain composed, Leah stood her ground and did not react to the heightened atmosphere. She glared at the deacon as she considered her best course. Then she turned to the parlour window. She wondered whether her sister now sat behind the glass sketching her willow, blithely oblivious to the hatred brewing only a few feet away. Leah raised her chin and stepped into the sweep of fury and loathing.

Hallett took his daughter's arm more firmly, pulling her back to his side.

'Nay, Leah. No more,' he said. 'I must be truthful. My God demands it.'

Leah parted her lips. Hallett responded with a stern shake of his head.

'My daughter has not been stricken with illness, either natural or unnatural. It is a fact she has been poorly and Leah has been tending to her,' Hallett cast his eye over the expectant, if unsympathetic gazes. 'My daughter is with child.'

Leah studied the reaction of the crowd. Some nodded as if not surprised, others appeared shocked that Maria Hallett had fallen so far. There was a distinct look of pleasure in the faces of Dent's most faithful.

'The father?' Jeffries asked.

'A sailor,' Hallett replied.

Further questions were not forthcoming as those assembled took in both the gravity of –and the possibility involved in – the situation.

'She must be examined.'

'The child will be born before Whitsuntide or thereabouts,' Leah announced.

'She must be examined by Reverend Dent and another impartial authority,' Jeffries cried.

'Dent? Impartial?' Leah said.

'Hush, Leah,' Hallett broke in and nodded. 'If she must.'

'She must,' Jeffries affirmed.

Leah never took the easy road. Not since we were children could I remember a time when she had acquiesced, given in without a fight. Even when I told her flatly, in as plain a way as I had courage to at sixteen, that I didn't want to marry her; that, in fact, I could never make her a fit husband. She had argued, of course, hammering me to bend and weld. I nearly did. She sees the world through a prism of black and white. For me, the world has always been murky.

This day was no different.

I ushered Maria into the meeting house, alone, as placid as a scarecrow, leaving Leah and her father in the snow, their frosty breath mingling with that of the horses that drew the cart. Leah had objected, of course, scoffed at the impartiality of the proceedings, demanding that her sister have an advocate present. Both Leah and her father knew Maria's time in the meeting house would be less examination and more inquisition, a trial of sorts. I closed the door on her, hoping Leah could read the chapters in such a fleeting glimpse.

But then Maria had mentioned the hummingbird and I knew

that even Leah, with her blazing spirit and iron will, could not temper that revelation.

~

LEAH STAMPED her feet in the snow. Hallett checked his watch. They glanced at each other uneasily.

'Where's your husband?' Hallett asked.

His tone was neither accusatory nor compassionate, yet Leah turned on him abruptly. He smiled sympathetically. The expression sat oddly on her father but she accepted it.

'Palgrave left with Mister Bellamy,' she replied, considering the snow at her feet. He was the only person outside her children and Arthur whom she had told of her husband's whereabouts. 'They're in New Providence.'

He raised his chin.

'It's an island near Florida.'

Hallett nodded more grimly than she could ever recall seeing and, instantly, a sharp pang in her chest heralded the arrival of a small, but sinister, spectre of doubt.

'Don't worry so, child.' Hallett stepped towards his daughter and took her hands. 'Your sister and your husband will be safe in God's hands.'

Leah wanted to believe. Once she would have. As she gripped her father's hands in the cold she struggled to overcome her uncertainty by seeking out the source of her faith. Not very long ago, the belief that God was ever-present in her soul burned so furiously that she had trouble believing in anything else. The surety of his protection was absolute. He had saved her twins during their birth. He was present when Joseph was struck down by measles. Leah had stared into her son's mottled face, praying until the fever passed. She had spoken and God had responded. Their relationship was unconditional. Even following her mother's unexpected death, she had believed that He had heard – and understood – her daily prayers for forgiveness.

Leah gently eased her hands from her father's grasp as she sensed the bitter sting of snow on her cheeks. She lifted her face towards the sky. But the desire to rouse her devotion was smothered by the awareness that there was nothing to awaken.

Once Leah's lips and fingers had grown numb, the doors of the meeting house finally opened and the pair was beckoned in by Arthur.

The dim glow of lamps proved no weapon against the biting cold of the meeting house. I was shivering in my heavy cloak, the chill creeping in through my boots and woollen hose clasped at my toes, now raw like a smashed thumb. The place reeked of burnt fat and soot from the candles. Goody Jeffries had been swapping the beeswax candles in the lamps for tallow when I arrived.

Leah made her way towards her sister, who was seated at the foot of the altar, and swept off her own cloak, laying it gently across Maria's shoulders. Leah shivered. There was no way to warn her, counsel her into submission.

'Your daughter has spoken of a hummingbird, Hallett.' Dent began from the pulpit. He was difficult to see in the weak light. A disembodied voice. 'It's a troubling admission.'

Hallett did not respond. I looked at Leah, her face as blank as death.

'Reverend,' Leah said, stepping a foot or two closer. 'It's clear my sister is not well. The anxiety this child has caused ...'

'Aye, the child,' Dent cut in. 'Your daughter is bastard-bellied. She has tarried with the Devil, Hallett. The child is proof of this.'

Leah's eyes stole around those assembled — Jeffries and his wife, Dent, myself. They rested on mine the longest.

'Surely, Sir,' Hallett broke in, 'you cannot believe my daughter is a heretic! Why, I helped raise this meeting house myself nearly thirty-five years ago when the old one burned to the ground. She comes to meeting every Sabbath ...'

'Even the most pious have turned their back on God, Joseph Hallett,' Dent replied. 'The Devil can confound any soul. He has come to her in the shape of a hummingbird.'

'Sir, I pray thee,' Leah said. 'You must see Maria is addle-brained. There was no hummingbird. To believe so is ludicrous.'

I could see her struggling with the logic. Leah would have believed as much herself not long ago.

'Yet, Goody Williams, we must believe your sister speaks the truth,' Dent explained. 'To think otherwise would be to deny the existence of God. God and Satan are opposite sides of an ever-spinning coin.'

Leah considered the predicament for a moment. It was a convoluted argument that made no rational sense, she saw now. She'd had similar disputes with Palgrave who believed in neither God nor the Devil.

'If we believe her mind is crippled then surely your argument is invalid,' Leah finally said. 'God and the Devil should play no part in this.'

'But what if she is not, Goody Williams?' Dent replied. 'How are we to know Maria Hallett is insane? By her own testimony she is not. Furthermore, your sister has stated in God's house that the father of her child is a mystery to her. She's only aware of the bird. Maria Hallett has been tempted and she has sinned in the most monstrous way. But what is most troubling is her lack of repentance.'

'Is this a trial?' Leah's voice grew harsh. 'Where is the jury and the magistrate?'

Leah took another step forward. Dent straightened his robes and looked at Jeffries. Leah was certain he backed away slightly.

'You have sinned as well, Goody Williams.'

Leah spun sharply. 'How so?'

'You lied. Telling us your sister had influenza was a lie,' Jeffries explained.

'Then you have been tempted as well.' Dent's nerve had returned. 'Your husband, Goody Williams, must have seen this in your nature. It hastened his departure, surely.'

Before Leah could remonstrate Jeffries continued.

'And I would like to give testimony about the horse Hallett sold me ...'

THE HYSTERIA CAUGHT AND SPREAD, sucking the air from the place. I'd seen it before.

'This is not a trial,' Leah cried, voice suddenly raspy. But it was too late. She was being swallowed by the void.

'Go on, Mister Jeffries,' Dent instructed.

'It's a hateful animal that'll not abide the halter. He kicks and bucks in the most unnatural way.'

'It is a sign,' Dent cried. 'A prodigious sign!'

'That horse is a fine animal,' Hallett argued. 'If he has grown tetchy since leaving my farm then you are to blame, Francis Jeffries.'

'Four pounds was a steep price to pay for such an unruly beast!'

'Then you should not have paid it,' Hallett said. 'Horses are expensive. That one was bought from Virginia. Your wish to rise above your station has always been your downfall, Francis Jeffries.'

'I can swear to the nature of the beast,' Goody Jeffries put in. 'Why, when I enter the barn he rears up and neighs in such a way ...' She shook her head. 'It's as though he knows there's a godly woman in his presence ...'

Goody Jeffries went on as only she can. I caught Leah's eyes, filled with panic. I stood and watched as she tried to swim against the current of a fast-flowing river and I even contemplated going to her, taking her arm and hauling her out of it, demanding that she realise there was no possibility of winning. But she would fight me. She would drown herself and me, her only ally.

LEAH TURNED INWARDS, shutting out the noise, and became aware of her own breathing. Short, shallow breaths that made her lungs ache with emptiness. Here she stood at a fork where there was no middle road and no turning back. But there must be an escape, a means of survival, she reckoned. After all, it wasn't only Maria standing trial.

'We should not be remiss and forget Maria Hallett's twin,' Dent put in, with increasing momentum. 'A boy who died in the womb.'

'What in the blazes has that got to do ...' Hallett began.

'And there were those others that died, as well,' Goody Jeffries added. 'The touch of the Devil has always been present in your home Joseph Hallett. Neither of your sons survived. I have often wondered what kinds of mischief your wife was up to with her sister and all her herbs and potions.'

'My wife was a godly woman, a saint! You cannot slander such a woman!'

'Your daughters, Joseph Hallett, have been tainted by the same brush!' Goody Jeffries said with increasing malice.

Leah looked at her sister. Maria didn't need saving, it occurred to her. She had time, only a little, but there was time. In her desperation to save her sister, Leah had overlooked the life she was carrying. Dent was determined to punish, but he could not condemn the unborn child.

As Goody Jeffries hurled accusations about her father and mother, and Dent thumped the altar vigorously, Leah forced herself to temper her breathing, to become conscious of the proceedings again. She needed to focus on the only direction she could take.

She stared at the altar then lowered her head. She waited a moment, readying herself, before raising her face to those present.

'LEAH, DON'T.' I moved towards her instinctively, as though she were walking too near a cliff edge. No-one reacted. I wonder now if I actually said the words, and whether or not I really reached out a hand.

'I have looked into my soul, Reverend Dent, and have seen God there,' Leah said, silencing Goody Jeffries's indictment. She looked at her father before she continued. 'The appearance of the hummingbird is foreboding. It would seem in the eyes of the church and the law that my sister has tarried with the Devil.'

Dent was doubtful, I could see. He had the angled mouth of a cynic – that look he got when someone sneezed during meeting – but Leah pressed on.

'My husband is in Boston, Sir. But he does not see to an ill

brother. He has abandoned me. My arrogance has prevented me from confessing this before. Pride has been my sin.'

'Leah,' Hallett said. 'Be mindful of what you're doing!'

'I could see my husband drifting from me. In my bitterness, I persuaded my sister to court the affections of the sailor, Samuel Bellamy, with a potion I fooled her into drinking.'

'To what end?'

'Does the Devil need a reason to spark chaos in the reverent?'

Leah lowered herself to her knees.

'I am stripped bare,' she said. 'Take mercy, Sir, on my sister and the blameless child growing inside her.'

'Then it is you who have sinned?' Dent asked, slightly astonished at the turn the proceedings had taken. 'You instigated your sister to couple with Satan?

'I have, Sir. I was tempted. I have looked into my heart and seen evil there. But I have cast Satan out. I fear the Devil, Sir, but I fear the wrath of God even more.'

Leah considered her words carefully, making sure she chose exactly those phrases that would appeal to Dent. It wasn't difficult for her. She was raised on his sermons, well schooled.

Dent stood above her for a long time, considering her statement. In the silence I closed my eyes and listened to the breathing around me, the whistle in Jeffries's chest and the creak of the boards when Dent shifted his weight.

THERE WAS some truth in her lie, she realised. She had courted evil over a decade ago when she had first spied Palgrave in meeting, then again when she abandoned her father and mother. The time had come to make amends.

Relieved to be free of her wrongdoings, Leah's eyes did not waver from the altar. Humiliation was Dent's goal.

Willing to shoulder her family's shame, Leah considered her contrition a small price to pay if she could secure some time to take stock.

Time to plan. Time for Palgrave to return. Time for her father to forgive her.

'Maria Hallett will be placed in prison until the time her child is born,' Dent finally declared.

Joseph Hallett released a muffled cry of anguish before striding to the altar. Leah rose quickly and gripped his arm. As he tried to throw her off and take the stairs that led to Dent, Leah clutched him about the neck and pressed her face to his.

'Trust me, Papa.'

He pulled back and stared at his daughter, her beauty contorted by the moment. When it was clear Hallett was calm, Dent went on.

'Once the child is delivered into the world we will consider events again.'

Leah turned to her sister. She had not moved. She did not protest her sentence nor move to speak the truth.

'In the light of your sister's condition and your own admissions, Goodwife Williams,' Dent's eyes flashed, 'you shall bear her whipping. Six strokes for her. Another six for you. I warrant you'll not be tempted again.'

Still holding the hand of her father, she felt his grip tighten. Sensing the first sting of tears, Leah clenched her teeth and lowered her head solemnly in deference.

LEAH'S PUNISHMENT was to take place at a quarter before eleven the following day. A notice was hung immediately on the meeting house door. Following consultation with Earl and considering the remorse she had displayed, Dent permitted Leah leave until then. She returned home and said nothing of the afternoon to her children. Leah instructed her father to inform her aunt of the whipping and that she should be ready with wraps for her back and barberry to treat infection. Word was sent to Arthur requesting that he deliver her to Margaret's home when the spectacle had concluded.

She asked her father to avoid the proceedings. She felt he should sit with Maria in the prison during the time it took to lay a whip twelve times across a woman's back. Hannah was to collect the children and their belongings in the morning and take them to the farm. There they would stay until Leah was well and, perhaps, after that. The children were to be kept from the schoolhouse and the village. Leah stressed they should not hear one word of her disgrace or her sister's. Her father was to tell them their mother had taken ill with the fever. Leah would stay with her aunt until able to see to her own recovery.

Once everything was settled to Leah's satisfaction, she placed her feet in the warm bath Elizabeth had poured and closed her eyes as her daughter brushed her hair in firm, even strokes.

30

Although unable to open her eyes, Leah believed she was conscious. She had been dozing for some time. Drifting in and out of sleep, her children's voices had echoed in her thoughts, as vivid as if the five were there beside her. She had also heard her aunt's gentle voice murmuring, 'Why? Why, child?'

Leah saw a vision of Maria at the willow and another of her father, gazing at her through rheumy eyes and muttering in prayer. Aware of nothing more now than a musty, woody aroma that filled the void around her, she would have guessed she was in the forest, her head resting on a pile of damp, fetid leaves.

She heard a crackle and a log shift among embers. Though the air in the room wasn't smoky, she could smell pine burning: the faint fragrance of reassurance.

The sudden crack of a whip made her flinch and her eyelids pinched tightly. A hand brushed her hair from her cheek. Forcing her eyes open, she was met by her aunt's kind green eyes. She squinted into the light. It was as though her aunt was shrouded in smoke.

'It was merely old Daniel Wendell driving his beasts to Barnstable,' Goody Tompkins soothed.

'Where am I?' Leah asked. Not a sound sprang from her lips. She tried again. 'Am I alive? I feel ...'

'You need water, Leah,' said Goody Tompkins, as she helped her patient manoeuvre onto her elbow. Despite her small frame, the older woman supported Leah's weight effortlessly. She held a cup to Leah's lips. After consuming a few sips, she took the cup away. Leah instinctively began to roll onto her back. Her aunt gripped her patient's shoulder and shook her head.

'On your side,' she advised.

Leah eased her head warily onto the pillow as she realised she was alive and in her aunt's house. Then before she could stop it, the recollection of being led to the whipping post took hold of her.

Those gathered on the green were people she had known her entire life. Her neighbours and friends, people she had gone to meeting with then chatted to on the green, complimenting them on their peach pie or their children's manners. Leah had birthed their babies, nursed them through illness and fed their children when their crops had failed. They had all provided her with similar kindnesses, at one time or another. But they all seemed like strangers as she passed by them on her way to the whipping post.

Silent tears wet the pillow beneath her cheek as she remembered their coldness.

The only one who had looked her way kindly had been the minister's slave, Abby. There had been a sadness in her eyes.

'What's that smell?' Leah asked as Goody Tompkins dabbed at her face with a damp cloth.

'Valerian root. I made you a tonic to help you sleep. The

cuts will heal faster if you can rest. That's why you feel so groggy.'

Leah winced as she attempted to move into a more comfortable position. It was William Mallick who had held the horsewhip. Praised by Dent for his even hand and keen eye, the heavy-set saddler performed all the whippings in Eastham. Only the week before, Leah had visited Mallick's shop with a harness she had no further use for. Mallick paid her two shillings, a sum far greater than the shabby item was worth.

'How are the children? My father?' Leah asked her aunt.

'Well. Your father visited this morning and stayed with you for some time. He's anxious.'

Leah moaned quietly as she shifted in the narrow bed.

'Hannah does well to care for them,' her aunt went on. 'The children continue with their schoolwork and young Joseph had been a great help on the farm ...'

As Leah had instructed, her father had not been on the green. When she was tied to the post, it was his familiar countenance she had longed for. She had wanted to cry out, demand his presence, but it had been too late. Goody Jeffries had unfastened Leah's loose robe, exposing her back. Despite the snow at her feet, Leah's skin had sensed nothing save the disapproving stares of all who surrounded her.

'The children have not been here?' Leah questioned, lifting her head an inch.

'Nay. They are concerned for you, but have been told they must be kept from you due to the fever.'

She lowered her head and closed her eyes.

'Palgrave should know of these events, Leah,' her aunt counselled. 'You should write him a letter. I could write him a letter. He would come back.'

Leah buried her head firmly into the pillow. It was true –

Leah needed Palgrave to return. Prayers were of no use to her now. She needed Palgrave, with his rational mind, to assume the responsibility she had denied him for so long. But she needed her husband's homecoming to be his desire as well.

'He'll never know about this,' Leah said.

'You cannot conceal this from your husband.' Goody Tompkins gestured to her patient's back.

'They're merely scars.'

Leah heard her aunt sigh. 'You're like your father in every way – stubborn as hammered iron. Your mother was much more amenable.' She sighed again. 'I must see to your wounds now.'

Goody Tompkins carefully eased the dressings away from the skin. 'How do they seem?' Leah asked.

'William Mallick was light-handed, I warrant. There'll be scars, but I've seen worse.'

'It hurt so.' Leah muttered into the pillow as the cool water touched her skin.

It had not felt as though Mallick had restrained himself. Leah had been shocked by the severity of the first lash. Her body had shuddered and her breath had caught in her throat for a moment before she began to gulp air frantically. By the time the second blow was laid across her naked back, only seconds later, the burn from the first had reached such an intensity that her legs threatened to give way beneath her. Involuntarily, Leah cried out, emitting a loud mew that provoked a succession of gasps from the spectators.

Whippings occurred frequently in Eastham, but Leah had witnessed only one. A farmer, James Ayres, had been condemned as an adulterer when Leah was fourteen. Typically a stoic and reserved man, Ayres had howled shamelessly when the lash had met his skin. Leah remembered her embarrassment on Ayres's behalf. She recalled looking away in shame. Her father had glanced at his daughter, concerned. It was not the sight of Ayres's flayed flesh that appalled her so. It was his humiliation that she had found so repulsive.

'Arthur Earl told me you fainted from the pain before Mallick had finished,' Goody Tompkins said, gently dabbing the gashes. 'That was two days past.'

'How many days until I'll have healed? I want to see my children and Maria.'

'There's been no inflammation or fever,' the older woman said, assessing her patient. 'Four or five days. Now, I'm putting on the barberry oil. It will smart.'

Leah cringed as her wounds protested the anointing. The stinging countered any lingering effects of the valerian. She began to consider the future and recalled again the sight of James Ayres on the whipping post. Although his wife forgave him for his sins, the town did not and Ayres had left Eastham soon after his punishment. It was impossible for Leah to entertain the prospect of a life for herself or her family in Eastham after this.

'Please bring me paper and ink, Margaret, and send word to my father. He's to collect me on Wednesday.'

Goody Tompkins grimaced. 'That's only three days.'

'There are matters I must see to.'

31

'Do you remember taking me to see James Ayres whipped?' Leah asked her father as she sat alongside him in the gig on the way back to the farm. Although Goody Tomkins had protested, Leah would not stay longer.

Many squelching wheels had made grooves in the snow, grooves that wove in and out of each other, crisscrossing, turning the road into a muddy, sodden patchwork.

'Aye. You were fourteen,' he replied without shifting his eyes from the road.

'Why did you?'

'You asked.' Leah spun her head towards him. She didn't recall the request. 'I thought it'd be favourable for you to view the townsfolk without the trappings of piety.'

Hallett glanced at her briefly then twisted the reins tightly around his knuckles. He stared ahead and offered no further explanation. *He was so similar to Palgrave,* Leah thought. She had only ever seen their differences before.

'The farmhands are gone,' he said, interrupting her thoughts. 'They were threatened with exile by Dent. When spring comes ... It's becoming more trying each day to do business in this town,' he explained, as though a matter of course. 'There is talk, too that your sister is a witch.'

Leah lowered her head and pulled her cloak around her firmly. She already knew that her own children could no longer attend school, teased and tormented as they were by their classmates. What was happening to her father was just the beginning of what was to come.

'We have to go,' Leah said. 'We have to leave Eastham before Maria has the child. I've written ...'

He shook his head.

'Papa ...' Leah pleaded.

'You're not to blame. Neither is your sister.'

Leah took little comfort in her father's assurances. 'Why remain? You'll lose everything.'

It took Hallett some moments to respond.

'Why did you break away from us all those years ago and marry Palgrave Williams against my wishes, against your mother's advice?'

Leah turned to him and stared, stunned by the question.

'You gave me no choice.'

'But I did.'

'It was no choice for me. I couldn't break from Palgrave.'

'But you could have.'

Studying his haggard profile in disbelief for a minute brought to her mind the morning she departed her father's house. The specifics of the day remained as imprecise as a poorly drawn portrait. Her father had raised his hand to strike her, she recalled, and her mother had released a strangled, panicked shriek. It was a sound so foreign to Leah that she had turned, alarmed more at the noise than the threat of being struck. Then Maria had fled the house, her golden train of hair trailing behind her as she ran through the snow towards the wood.

These images had stayed, but the words they had spoken were lost to her. All she was able to vividly remember were the emotions, threatening to burst like new bottles. Palgrave had begged her to leave Eastham that day. They could never make a life for themselves in the shadow of her dissent, he had argued. She refused. While she loved her father, she would not be tyrannised by him.

She shook her head. 'It's a sin,' said Leah. 'Your pride and mine. It's a sin.'

'According to Dent, but not to God,' replied Hallett. 'Will God deny me a place in heaven on Judgement Day?'

Leah shrugged. It seemed to her Judgement Day had already been and gone.

LEAH STRUGGLED to summon that pride as she approached the white-gabled house of Reverend Dent. She sat in her father's gig for some minutes with the reins gripped in her hands. The horse, unsure whether this was his final destination, moved back and forth uneasily, icy mud sloshing beneath his hooves. Finally, Leah stepped to the ground and tied the reins around a nearby post. The horse neighed softly and Leah stroked his muzzle for a moment before leaning her head against his neck. She took in the familiar smells of hay and dust, and the lingering odour of sweat. She stood erect and grimaced. The pain of her wounds still felt raw.

She had not told her father of her plans. He would have insisted on coming with her, stand by her side. But the handling of Dent required subtlety and strategy. The Reverend would not bend to her father's heavy-handed demands.

Abby opened the door before Leah could knock. She took Leah's elbow and led her gently into the parlour.

'I watched you waiting in the gig,' she said as she relieved Leah of her cloak and gloves.

Leah looked at her.

'How are your children?' Abby asked. 'Especially those twins.'

Leah smiled. Apart from her aunt, Abby was the most gifted midwife in Eastham. She had helped birth hundreds of babies, including Leah's own five.

'They're fine. All of them ... Do you remember Joshua and Sarah's birth?'

The slave nodded firmly. 'Better than any that I've had a hand in. The three of you came so near to death. You were being pulled so hard, but you refused to budge.'

Leah looked at the slave intensely, struggling to recall.

'Your aunt and I were torn, but you refused to let God take them.'

'It's all so foggy now.'

It was the first time she had spoken to Abby so intimately. As a slave, Abby hovered outside the circle of community in Eastham. Leah had never chatted to her as they spun wool together, or laughed with her as a wayward fly was scooped from the cider press.

'Palgrave, I know, urged you to save me ... to put me first. You can speak freely. Palgrave told me so.'

Abby closed her eyes briefly as though conjuring the memory of the day. 'Goody Tompkins and I agreed it was best to abide by your wishes. The mother always knows what's best and you were a strong one, Leah Williams. You *are* a strong one.'

Leah gazed at her fondly as she contemplated for the first time Abby's strange existence. She was trusted with the rearing of Silas, trusted to birth most of Eastham's babies, yet denied everything considered essential in life.

'Do you ever regret ... ?' Leah didn't quite know how to phrase the question she longed to ask.

'Silas has been a comfort.'

Leah moved to Abby and took her hands.

'I'm sorry,' Abby said.

'None of this is your doing.'

Abby's brow creased and her lips parted uncertainly. Before she was able to speak Leah said, 'I'm here to see Reverend Dent.'

'Of course.' Abby broke Leah's grasp. She walked to the door then faced Leah once more. Leah's eyes followed her. Seeing her again reminded her of the concern the slave had shown her on the day of the whipping.

Abby looked as though she was about to speak, but then turned and left the room without uttering another word.

When Dent entered, Leah was standing in the middle of the room facing the door. She had taken the position when Abby left her some twenty minutes before and had remained there, watching, waiting. Wetting her lips, she raised her head slightly and looked at Dent.

He stared at her through hard eyes, yet Leah noticed perspiration on his brow.

'I come seeking permission to visit my sister, Sir.'

'To what end?'

'Maria is carrying. I want to see to her wellbeing.'

'Goodwife Jeffries sees to that.'

'Goody Jeffries is no midwife,' Leah said. 'And she is childless. She has no experience in these matters. I'm best suited to the task.'

Reverend Dent smirked then walked to the hearth. 'Nay.'

'My aunt, then.'

Dent looked at her with a cold sneer. 'Your aunt? Her with her herbs and potions? I think not.'

Leah pressed her lips tightly closed. She could feel her anger rising, burning at a furious pace. Her skin bristled. Covering her face in her hands to conceal her fury, Leah considered her options. There were so few sympathetic to her family's predicament. Dent would not consent to any of them. Then she lowered her hands slowly and looked to Dent.

'Abby,' Leah said. 'Abby should accompany me. She is better acquainted than anyone with the women in my family. Surely you trust *her*.'

Walking to the hearth he stared into the flames for some minutes, considering the proposition. Leah studied his rounded back in revulsion, the way his pink, fleshy neck bulged over his collar. Her eyes darted to the metal poker, standing only inches to Dent's left.

'Aye,' he said eventually, without turning to meet Leah's hate-filled glare.

FRANCIS JEFFRIES UNLOCKED the iron-clamped oak door of the cell in which her sister had been housed for almost a week. As Jeffries manoeuvred the key in the lock, Leah noticed that the iron was rusty.

Abby handed him a note written in Dent's hurried hand.

Jeffries shook his head disapprovingly before handing the letter back to the slave. 'Such an unwarranted fuss,' he grumbled under his breath.

Despite the hearth that lay burning at the heart of the prison, Maria's cell was cold and Leah's senses were assailed by the many layers of stench within the cramped space. Her hand moved instinctively to cover her nose. The reek of urine barely masked a more disagreeable, fusty smell. Examining the cell, Leah easily spied the cause of both – mould veining blue and unbridled throughout the rough straw-plastered walls, and a makeshift chamber pot, almost full. It hadn't been emptied in days. Leah would empty it herself when they were finished.

Just two candles burnt in the dim chamber. Maria sat on her small pallet, her slim back as straight as one of the oaken beams supporting the walls of her jail. The pallet, along with a battered old stool, were the only pieces of furniture in the room. A thick, woollen shawl, which Leah recognised as one belonging to her mother, was draped over her sister's shoulders. A faded Bible lay on her lap. Maria looked up when Leah and Abby entered.

When Leah heard Jeffries lock the door behind him, she walked to her sister and, kneeling beside her, embraced her tightly.

'They'll let me have nothing but this Bible. I have requested my pastels and paper,' Maria began. 'They refuse. Reverend Dent insists I should do nothing but pray and think on my crimes.'

'Sins,' Leah corrected.

'Sins,' Maria echoed. 'Arthur Earl comes by three times each day to tend the fire. I don't think it is the beadle's responsibility. Is it?' She paused and looked at Leah, puzzled. 'He talks to me through the door. It's so thick I can barely hear him but it's nice of him to come.'

'Arthur's a kind and godly man.'

'Why, Abby,' Maria said, noticing the slave by the door, 'it is good of you to visit.'

Abby moved forwards and sat beside Maria, taking her hands.

'You're cold, Maria,' Abby said. 'You must keep warm, child. If you are cold, the baby is too.'

'I'll bring you mittens,' Leah said, 'and thick woollen stockings.

'Abby has come to see if you and the child are well.'

Maria nodded. She allowed the women to ease her back onto her pallet and untie her bodice and skirt. Abby knelt beside the bed and felt Maria's belly, pushing her hands hard into the pale flesh. Then she pressed her ear firmly into the side of Maria's abdomen. Leah edged away as Abby examined her sister, twisting her wedding band ruminatively as she waited.

Maria made no reaction. She stared at the ceiling. How strange and peaceful she seemed. It was a blessing, it occurred to Leah, that her sister had half lost her mind.

'Six months or thereabouts,' Abby said as she rose. Leah hurried forwards and helped her sister dress.

'I'll discuss the likelihood of having Maria return home to her father with Reverend Dent,' Abby said, more to herself than Leah. She stood, hands on hips staring down at the girl. 'This is no place for her to be.'

Leah wrapped her mother's shawl tightly around Maria's shoulders then sat beside her.

'To that end,' Leah began. 'I have written Silas.'

Maria raised her head and looked first at her sister then hastened her gaze to Abby. Abby shifted her eyes to the dusty, straw-covered floor.

'Silas is your friend,' Leah explained. 'He can convince the minister to release you. I've asked him to enlist the advice of Reverend Cotton Mather. He's a learned man with a robust, broad-minded intellect.'

Leah was aware this was a dangerous path to tread. Reverend Mather's support of the use of spectral evidence in

Salem led to the condemnation of many as witches. However, that was so long ago, Leah reasoned, more than twenty years. Palgrave believed Mather was a man of sense, now – one of the few rational minds in the church.

'My sketches, sister,' Maria said, rising feverishly. 'Will you bring my sketches and pastels?'

'I can but ask,' Leah replied.

Maria paced the length of the chamber. It took no more than four short steps for her to reach the opposite wall.

'I don't want to see Silas.' Maria's tone was adamant.

Leah looked at her. Maria's eyes were sharp and attentive.

'As you wish,' Leah replied. 'But will you meet with Reverend Mather, if he comes?'

Maria nodded.

32

'When can we return to school, Mama?' Elizabeth asked.

A plate Hannah was setting on the shelf fell from her hands and clanged against the floor. Leah and her daughter started.

'When the fever has passed,' Leah said. 'It's not safe to go into town.'

'But you do ...' Joshua began, laying his book on the table. She recognised it as *The Boston Ephemeris*, the farmer's almanac that was given to her by her father when she was a child. She wondered where Joshua had found it.

'Hush, boy,' Leah rebuked. 'I've recently been ill so I'm not susceptible.'

He looked at her, confused.

'I can't get sick again so soon.'

The child frowned then returned his attention to the book. He knew something was amiss. They all did. Virtually overnight, their small world had grown smaller, contracting within the boundaries of their grandfather's farm. The eldest, Joseph and Elizabeth, were more attuned to the mood of the town and noticed the scornful glares of passers by. Joseph was glad he couldn't hear their whispers, yet he knew they talked of witches. The children did not mention a word of their distress to their mother.

'It's best if we stay here, together,' Leah said, walking to her son and laying her hand on his shoulder. He looked up at her, the hurt beginning to drain from his eyes. She kissed his forehead. He smiled.

'I dreamt of Papa last night,' Elizabeth said all of a sudden, eyeing her mother warily.

Leah smiled. 'Tell me.'

'We were all bathing by the willow,' she began eagerly, laying down her quill. 'All of us. Papa and Joseph were jumping from the branches and ...' she stopped herself, uncertain. 'Never mind,' the girl finished hastily, returning her eyes to her writing.

'Go on,' Leah urged, nestling in beside her on the bench.

'It was a summer's day and so hot. I could feel the sting of the sun even in my sleep,' she said, turning to her mother. 'Joshua and Sarah were scooping up tadpoles in a net and little Caleb was splashing in the shallows. You know how he enjoys that. You, Mama, were standing by him with your skirt hitched up a little, the way you do when no-one but us are nearby, cooling your legs in the water.'

'What were you doing, my beautiful daughter?' Leah asked, stroking Elizabeth's honey-coloured hair.

'I was sitting on the bank relishing my good fortune,' she replied, the pleasure in her tone quickly fading.

Leah placed her hand around Elizabeth's shoulder and held her tightly. 'Summer is not long off.'

Leah could not sell the few remaining animals she possessed. No-one would have them, believing them tainted. Three pigs and a cluster of chickens were rounded up and loaded onto a cart with the assistance of Arthur Earl and transported to her father's farm.

The family had made the journey mostly in silence until they passed through the town. It was as though Leah could hear every vile thought directed her way. She turned to face Arthur.

'You should not be seen with me.'

'We have been friends since childhood, Leah Hallett,' he responded. 'I'll not turn from you now.'

'You're a good man, Arthur. The finest man in Massachusetts, I would argue.' Leah pressed the palms of her hands into her eyes for an instant.

Arthur looked ahead and hurried the horses with a sharp flick of the reins. 'My offer still stands. We could go to Boston.'

Leah wiped her eyes and nose with her hands then drew in a breath. 'I tried to kiss you once.' His mouth angled at the memory. 'You turned away. What has changed since then?'

'Nothing.' He flicked the reins to hurry their progress through the town. 'Everything.'

Hannah was the one who prepared one of Leah's fowl for dinner, a stew made with turnips. Although she had performed the task a hundred times before, that morning Leah hadn't been able to bring herself to wring the bird's neck. Hannah killed the chicken while Leah prepared the turnips.

At noontide Hallett and Joseph returned to the house. Leah examined her father as she served the meal. His cheeks were drawn and his eyes heavy with fatigue. At fifty-five, even with his grandson's ready assistance, he was too old to be doing the work of six farmhands.

'You say grace, Joseph,' Hallett said when Leah and Hannah had taken their seats.

The boy looked to his mother, uncertain. 'Go ahead,' she urged.

Joseph contemplated his words for a minute as he stared down at his clenched hands. It had always been Palgrave who muttered the mealtime prayer, despite his misgivings. And it had always been the same one.

'Almighty God, most merciful Father,' Joseph began hesitantly now, as if struggling in his nervousness to recall words so familiar, 'source of everything good, as we rejoice in your gifts we praise your name, through Jesus Christ our Lord. Amen.'

'Amen,' echoed the family.

~

ABBY WAS the last to take her seat at the table.

'Reverend Mather,' Dent began. 'Would you do us the honour of blessing our humble repast?'

Cotton Mather nodded respectfully at his host. 'This is your home, Sir. Perhaps your son might oblige,' Mather suggested, turning to Silas. 'Have you heard your son preach? The power of his sermons belies his youth and experience.'

The esteemed minister's dark hair was greying and pulled back at the base of his head. It was the first time Silas had seen him without his wig and robes of office. Instead, Mather wore simple russet-coloured breeches and coat, and sturdy leather riding boots that he had taken pains to clean before entering the house. Oddly, his nose did not appear as beak-like, nor his complexion as pallid, as Silas recalled.

Without the pomp of his position Mather looked more youthful.

Dent's only reaction to Mather's suggestion was a passing nod in the direction of his son. Mather looked at his young acquaintance, offering him a reassuring smile. Silas began on a cursory prayer. He had stomach for neither the food nor company this mealtime. He and Reverend Mather had arrived only an hour ago after travelling the one hundred miles from Boston.

During the journey to Eastham, Mather had questioned him ceaselessly regarding the Hallett family and the personalities of the different members of the household. It was a conversation fraught with peril. Silas found it a battle not to disclose his role in the predicament and his involvement with the Halletts. He had found himself wanting to. Instead, he spoke of Leah and Palgrave and Joseph Hallett. 'A certain fondness' he explained had developed between himself and the Halletts over the years, due to the proximity in age of the children and the nature of the Eastham community.

Despite his exhaustion on arrival, Silas had been eager to go to Maria. However, Abby had stopped him. She came to his room just as he was laying out his journal on his writing desk.

'She does not wish to see you, Silas,' Abby informed him immediately. Pulling back the drapes and tying them, she allowed the sunlight to trickle into the room. 'Maria has agreed to speak only with Reverend Mather.'

Silas moved quickly to the window. 'I despise this kind of light. It's weak, insipid.' he said, yanking the curtains closed. 'It might as well be dark.'

Unfazed, Abby proceeded to light the candles on the walls. 'Spring is in the air. I can feel it. Why, I can see it. Crocuses are already pushing up through the snow.'

Removing his spectacles, Silas pinched the bridge of his nose. 'But Leah's letter ...' he began. 'She begged me for my help. I assumed ... Have you seen Maria?'

'Aye. Despite her circumstances, she is well,' Abby answered, before adding pointedly, 'as is the child.'

Silas raised his head to look at the slave. 'Has she spoken of me?'

'Her mind is a muddle,' Abby continued, studying his reaction. 'Her humours changeable. Your father refuses to release her.'

'I see,' he replied. Despite his crime, and the multitude of sins he had committed in the name of love, Silas was certain Maria would not betray him. Although defiled and corrupted, every aspect of Maria Hallett remained unimpeachable.

Abby took his arm, turning him to face her. 'Silas' she said. 'Is it your child?'

He stared at her for a moment, eager to confess. If only he could simply unburden himself of his sins to Abby, seek her guidance as he had done countless times in the past, then surely a path would present itself. Questions ran through his mind. *Is there still time to save Maria? Perhaps he could remove her to Beverly or Boston, or a place even further?* Rocking slightly on his heels, he contemplated the consequences of such a route. If only Maria had agreed to marriage when it had been feasible.

'Nay,' he answered quietly. 'It is not.'

Now, as he poked the slices of roast beef on his plate, he quietly struggled to accept a future without Maria.

'I don't believe we have ever had such a noteworthy guest partaking of our modest offerings,' Dent began, keenly eyeing those seated. 'You, Sir, must be the most famed man in the colonies.'

'I would be satisfied with being the most devoted,' Mather said in a low voice, before adding thoughtfully, 'It's a fine sight to see your slave seated at the table, Sir. How long have you been with the family, Abby?'

'Since I was nine years old, Sir,' Abby replied.

'Are you a member of the church? Are you able to read and write?' Mather questioned.

'Aye, Sir,' Abby answered, straightening her back and laying her fork on the table. Before she spoke she cupped her hands in her lap. 'I took my first communion when I was thirteen.'

Mather nodded. 'Commendable.'

'Thank you, Sir,' Dent broke in. 'In my opinion, it's an individual's knowledge of the commandments and their presence at meeting each Sabbath that lifts them out of the dark morass of savagery.'

'I believe it's more a case of having God in one's heart,' Mather responded.

'Of course,' Dent muttered, returning his attention to his roast beef.

Silas lowered his eyes.

Abby cleared her throat. Reverend Mather put down his cup and looked at her through his wide brown eyes, waiting for her to speak. She realigned her fork along the grain of the timber.

'Go ahead,' Mather urged kindly. 'Is there something on your mind, Abby?'

The Indian smiled faintly in appreciation.

'Tell me, Sir. When would you like to interview Maria Hallett? I'm her midwife, you see, and she's quite troubled. I should come with you.'

Mather wiped his mouth with his napkin then folded it

carefully. 'I would like to speak with her father and sister first.'

Dent raised his head from his plate with a sudden jerk. 'Hallett is an antinomian; Leah Williams a confessed sinner.'

'There is no-one who is without sin, Sir. It's a noble act to confess it,' Mather put in.

Silas looked at his father. His face had grown red.

'Of course,' Dent said, shifting uncomfortably in his seat.

'My motives are twofold, I must admit,' Mather continued eagerly. 'I have a keen interest in Maria Hallett's ... *plight*.' Dent flinched. 'But I also have a keen interest in the hybridisation of corn. I understand Hallett has experienced some success in this area ...'

Dent relaxed and pushed his empty plate away. 'Hallett's success in all areas is waning with prodigious speed, as is his good standing in this town. His farmhands have turned from him and he struggles to make a living.'

Silas interrupted his father and responded to Mather's query. 'Aye, he has, Sir. Hybridisation of corn varieties has been a passion of Joseph Hallett's for many years.'

'Then you *are* well acquainted with the family?' Reverend Mather asked him, confused.

'Eastham is a prodigiously small town, Sir.'

Abby cast Silas a chary glance. He did not look at her.

Dent ignored his son's interjection and continued. 'What's more, he has one daughter in prison while the other has been abandoned by her husband, left penniless with five young children.'

Mather frowned. 'You possess a holding adjoining Hallett's farm, do you not?'

'Fourteen acres,' Dent replied. Mather gazed at him shrewdly for a moment.

'Silas alone will accompany me to the Hallett's farm tomorrow morning at eight,' Mather instructed. Dent grimaced and cleared his throat. Noting his host's discomfort, the minister added, 'Thank you for your hospitality, Sir. It was a *prodigiously* fine meal.'

33

Preferring to arrive unexpectedly, the minister had decided not to announce his visit to the Hallett farm. All but one of the children were in the kitchen with their mother, about to begin their lessons. The eldest was with his grandfather. Leah stood hastily and removed her apron. The maid, a robust woman of Irish extraction noticed the minister, guided the men through the house to the kitchen.

The young woman lowered her head and welcomed the visitors.

'Please excuse the intrusion, Goodwife Williams,' Mather began.

'It's no intrusion, Sir,' Leah replied calmly then turned to one of her children, a sturdy young man with hair the same shade of amber as his mother's. 'Joshua, please go and fetch your grandfather. Tell him the Reverend Cotton Mather has come to call.'

The child nodded and scurried out the door.

Mather then moved to Sarah who was seated at the table. 'I warrant you're one half of two.' He glanced at the page in her Bible the girl was diligently transcribing. She nodded. 'Two unique souls born into the world in magnificent chorus.'

Sarah looked up at the stranger and smiled.

'Twins are merely one of God's many miracles. I myself am father to twins. God took them from me when they were but seven weeks old.'

'I'm sorry to hear that, Sir,' Sarah murmured.

'I cherish the days they were mine and trust they are safe in heaven,' Mather went on matter-of-factly. 'I look forward to seeing them again come Judgement Day.'

Smiling gently, he touched the crown of the child's head lightly with his palm. Then Hallett entered, ushering Joshua and Joseph through the doorway ahead of him.

Standing with his hands on his hips, frowning, Hallett examined the scene in his kitchen, rubbing his beard with his fingertips. The farmer didn't appear disturbed by the presence of the stranger in his home, merely irritated, the minister thought, that his day's work had been disturbed. Hallett grunted softly when he had measured the situation to his satisfaction.

'Mister Hallett,' Silas stepped forward. 'May I introduce to you Reverend Cotton Mather. He has travelled a hundred miles from Boston to speak with you regarding your daughter.'

Removing his hat, Hallett reached his hand towards Mather but remained silent.

'Hannah,' Leah started when the men had shaken hands. 'Please show our guests to the parlour and bring us a little cider. Children, get on with your work.'

They sat in the parlour and waited for Hannah to bring refreshments. Reverend Mather took in his surroundings. The sparsely furnished room was spotless. Hallett rested without movement in the most exquisitely crafted rocking chair that the minister had ever laid eyes on. His daughter, a handsome woman in her late twenties, Mather guessed, sat perched on the edge of the window seat, her hands gripping her knees. The dispassion of her expression was at odds with the stiffness of her well-proportioned body. Occasionally she would look at Silas, who stood by the room's second window staring out at the snow-covered fields beyond. Then she would glance at her father and lean slightly forward, as though the urge to speak was utterly overpowering. Mather admired her restraint. It was a quality the pastor grappled with daily.

The lantern clock above the mantelpiece chimed the half hour. *Tick tock.* Mather raised his eyes to it. He offered Hallett and his daughter a courteous nod before beginning.

'I'm a great admirer of your farm, Mister Hallett,' Mather said. 'Your experiments with hybridisation are much talked about in Boston.'

'It's more dabbling,' Hallett responded, unfazed by the compliment. 'I'm ignorant of the science behind it. It just seems to me that two living things, despite their differences, might join and produce a hardier offspring that inherits the best qualities of both. Why, it's the most obvious, the most natural thing in the world, isn't it?'

'There are many in Boston who would disagree,' Mather smiled. 'They would argue, there's no place in God's natural world for science.'

Hallett shrugged and thought on the minister's words for a minute. 'It's always struck me, Reverend Mather, that God may desire us to improve on the world he created. Why else would he have seen fit to endow Man with intelligence and an inquiring spirit?'

'Papa ...' Leah began.

'Don't be alarmed. This is not a test of faith,' Mather

raised his palm. 'What think you, Goodwife Williams, of these matters?'

Leah's eyes darted to the minister then to her father, skittish. 'Speak Leah,' Hallett advised. 'The Reverend asked you a question.'

Her mouth puckered as she considered Mather's query. He was touched by the thoughtfulness of her gaze.

'At one time, Sir, my husband pressed me to seek out the services of a physician who could inoculate our children and ourselves against measles. Palgrave, my husband, had read a pamphlet you'd written on the subject. He urged me to read it also and I did. You presented a very persuasive argument.'

Mather nodded. He knew the pamphlet to which she referred. Grief-stricken and distraught, he had penned it only days after the disease had taken his wife, two-year-old daughter and newborn twins. It was vehemently worded and raised the ire of most of the colony's religious leaders.

Leah continued. Her tone was contemplative but firm. 'We had seen so many perish from sickness. In fact, I had only recently nursed my eldest through a bout of measles that left him hard of hearing. I prayed day and night, seeking God's charity and forgiveness for whatever sins Joseph or I were being punished. My son was saved and I chose to believe it was God who had saved him. I refused to agree to Palgrave's request.'

Leah rose as Hannah entered with a tray containing cups and a large beaker of cider. 'Sir, I believe if faced with a similar situation today, I might choose differently.'

She proceeded to help Hannah pour the cider.

Mather discerned from the young woman's pensive depiction of the memory that it was a decision with which she still struggled. This was the woman who, only three weeks past, had been whipped so stridently that she had collapsed at the post.

Dent depicted Leah Williams as fiery and sinful, a shrew of a woman who was not to be trusted. Silas had been vague in his portrayal, mentioning her only as a devoted mother, wife and sister, but had described her also as pious and unable to tell a lie, or so he believed. It was true that she had fallen, Silas had said, but she was a simple, devoted woman who would find her way back to God. 'Straightforward, ordinary, modest' were the terms Silas had used. But as Mather considered her careful response, he began to view Leah Williams through a more variegated spectrum.

'Where is your husband, Goodwife Williams?' Mather then asked mildly, relieving her of the tray. 'Please sit and take some cider yourself.'

Leah did as instructed. Silas edged closer to the exchange.

'Nassau, Sir,' Leah said. 'It's a town on New Providence Island.'

'I know of it.' Mather took a seat next to her by the window. 'Is he a seaman?'

'My husband is a silversmith, Sir.'

Hallett began to rock in the chair, gazing warmly at his daughter.

'Why did you lie regarding his whereabouts?'

Leah sipped her cider. 'Shame, pride, fear ...' She shook her head in bewilderment.

Mather took her hand.

'We were forced into a predicament,' Leah went on. Mather could see the first trickle of tears in her eyes. She blinked hard before continuing. 'If Palgrave did not seek work beyond New England we would have been penniless within months.'

'I understand,' Mather murmured. 'There's much wealth to be gained in the Caribbean by fair means ... and foul.'

'You speak of piracy, Sir?' Hallett asked.

'Aye,' Mather said, turning towards Hallett. 'My ministry in Boston presents all nature of challenges. I have been working with imprisoned pirates in order to bring them to repentance before their executions.'

Hallett looked at Leah. 'My husband is not a pirate, Sir. He has a gentle soul ... he is a silversmith,' she repeated the last quietly, almost to herself.

'Pirates stem from all walks of life, Madam. The sea is a school of vice,' Mather went on, rising. He pulled down his vest then removed a pipe from his pocket.

'Will you join me, Sir?' he asked his host. 'I'm aware it is early in the day, but such grave concerns prompt me ...'

Hallett nodded and rose. He produced his pipe and pouch of tobacco.

'You have many interests, Sir.' Hallett observed.

'Fascinations is a more fitting term.'

As the two men filled their pipes, Mather continued. 'There is a pirate that has been spoken of recently among the admiralty and the governor's circle. He's known only by the title, "Prince of the Sea", so opposed is he to authority and the like. He is cunning. So tainted with guile are his methods, he's said to have stolen treasure worth thousands of pounds and slaughtered many an innocent. Yet he is spoken of approvingly, even adoringly, by those who've known him. Men protect him with their refusal to divulge his name and appearance. What little is known about him is mere speculation. But he hails from the West Country – County Devon, they say.'

Leah and her father exchanged glances.

'What has happened to this man, I ask you, to induce such dissolute behaviour?' Mather mused.

'He is a lost soul.' Silas stepped forward. The minister turned, startled. He had almost forgotten the presence of the young pastor. 'The sooner he is brought to justice the better.'

Mather nodded vaguely in agreement before asking. 'Wouldn't it be wiser to discover the roots of this behaviour with the hope of salvaging his soul?'

Silas ignored the question. 'We should speak now of Maria Hallett,' he suggested with an insistence Mather would find affronting in a more experienced man.

'Of course,' the minister agreed. 'Reverend Dent has informed me of her unfortunate condition. We'll visit her tomorrow.' Mather turned to Leah. 'I've been told of your desire to see your sister released. I will recommend on that point after speaking with her.'

'Reverend,' Leah began. 'She is not of her right mind. The experiences of the past months have seen her much altered.'

'I am aware of this.'

He stared at Leah for a moment. He sensed her searching for signs. Her gentle gaze had turned dubious. Mather thought that it was unlikely that Leah Williams was not privy to his dealings with Ann Glover and the Goodwin children, even though she would have been a mere babe at the time. His experience with the Goodwin family and the hysteria it ignited in Salem all those years ago were a matter of public record, an enduring curse.

'I fear my sister will hang like Ann Glover,' Leah said, as if reading his mind. 'She was innocent, was she not? Accused of bewitching children because she spoke "the language of the Devil" when all she was guilty of was speaking Gaelic to two naughty children who decided to raise mischief.'

The lantern clock struck the hour. *Tick tock*. Mather heard an intake of breath. The Dent boy, suitably enraged. The rock of Hallett's chair did not break rhythm.

'Ann Glover was wrongly accused and falsely executed', said Mather quietly, voicing his error.

Apart from the murmurings of his own soul, it was the first time Mather had ever had his actions challenged directly.

'The events of Salem have afflicted my conscience for the past twenty-five years, Goodwife Williams. Myself and my family have been burdened with the marks of divine displeasure ever since.'

Mather watched her soften. She tilted her head and unlocked her clenched hands on her lap. Mather was pleased to detect a grain of trust from her.

'I'll intrude on your day no further,' Mather said after a moment, walking to the hearth and tapping his pipe against the stone of the surrounds. 'We will visit your sister tomorrow morning.'

'Maria does not wish to see Silas,' Leah broke in.

Mather looked at her sharply. 'For what reason?'

Leah paused and smoothed her skirt over her legs. 'She gave no reason.'

'She's confused, no doubt. Perhaps she muddles the son with the father,' Mather explained. 'I see no reason to go alone.'

'May I accompany you? Maria will be more at ease if I am present.'

Mather did not reply. He placed his pipe into the pocket of his coat.

'She has requested I bring her drawing materials,' Leah pressed. 'The distraction calms her.'

'Your sister sketches?' Mather asked, hopeful.

'Aye.'

'May I see her work?'

Leah hesitated, contemplating the request. She raised her chin slightly. 'Her sketches are private, Sir,' she said. 'To show you them would be a betrayal. Hasn't my sister been exposed enough?'

It occurred to Mather that it was he who had been exposed. To examine Maria Hallett's drawings with the intent of raking through her naked soul was exactly what he hoped for. The notion of glimpsing something intimate in the stroke of her brush, the press of her charcoal or her choice of subject appealed to the minister's fascination with human nature.

He nodded. Leah Williams had read him with a precision he found both distressing and captivating. 'She may have her drawing materials. I can see no harm in it.'

'And my presence tomorrow?' Leah asked as Mather headed to the door.

He paused, carefully fingering the felt brim of his hat as he weighed the request. 'We will meet you at the jail at nine.'

Once Mather and Silas had departed, Leah returned to the parlour and sat opposite her father. They looked at each other for a moment before Leah unbuttoned the collar of her blouse and leant back in the chair.

'It went very well, Leah. You did very well.'

'The pirate Mather spoke of ... could it be?'

'It's a possibility, I suppose.'

'He lodged with us. He seemed so ...' She paused. 'The brute Mather described ...'

'Hush, child,' Hallett said. 'There's no evidence. I'm certain there would be many seamen who hail from Devon and the West Country. I'm certain a handful of those have turned pirate since the Queen's War.'

Leah nodded but was unconvinced. Breathing fast, she closed her eyes for an instant. Life had become naught but a series of obstacles to overcome. The future appeared to be a never-ending mountain range waiting to be climbed.

Hannah entered to clear the cups. Leah opened her eyes briefly and caught the maid unawares, touching her father lightly yet deliberately on the shoulder as she passed. Nothing save the barest glimmer of a smile on her father's lips was proof of his gratitude. It was a routine gesture, Leah realised as she listened to Hannah stack the mugs on the tray, a commonplace sign of affection. Why did it surprise her? Her mother had passed ten years ago. It was out of the ordinary that her father had not since married again. She opened her eyes and studied them both. Hannah bustled around the room making the space appear as though Mather and Silas had never visited, while her father rocked gently in his chair, musing on the morning's events. Each was entirely comfortable in the presence of the other. Leah was thankful, she supposed, thankful her father had found a partner and was once again whole. A longing began to grow deep in Leah's chest.

She rose and began to busy herself before the pain worsened.

34

———

Hallett followed Hannah soon after she left the room. They were eager to get back to work, both yearning for the comfort of the everyday. Leah remained in the parlour, staring down at the window seat. She wasn't certain whether she wanted to open it and retrieve her sister's drawing materials. The impulse, so powerful, had only struck when she had witnessed Mather's eagerness. Now Leah was suddenly filled with dread.

Leah wasn't certain what she would find if she opened the hinged lid. On the one hand she hoped to discover the truth behind Maria's predicament. Leah had stopped believing in God and the Devil months ago. There was no hummingbird. Although certain Bellamy was the father of her sister's child, her fast-emerging rational mind demanded proof. Surely there were answers buried in Maria's sketches.

But what if there are no explanations in my sister's drawings? thought Leah. *What if the stroke of Maria's pastel attests to nothing except her madness?*

She knelt and brushed her hand over the cushion fixed

to the lid. Her fingers found the edge of the cushion where it butted against the wooden box beneath. Leah hesitated a moment before lifting the lid wide and staring into the contents of the box seat. The sketches were concealed within a black leather album fixed on one side with ribbon. Drawing it out, Leah sat on the floor and placed the album in front of her. She inhaled deeply before untying the ribbon and revealing the collection.

Each of the six pages was dated neatly in the bottom right-hand corner. Every page displayed the same likeness – Maria's beloved willow tree by Boat Meadow River. Leah laid each page flat on the floor in chronological order. What resulted was a shocking account of the last six months. On her hands and knees, Leah leant in closer to examine more carefully the horrifying transformation of the tree.

In July the tree was robust and vivid. Maria had chosen a palette of brilliant greens and yellows to highlight the abundance of life and light contained within the branches and leaves. The effect was warm and inviting. Following the willow's journey through autumn into winter, Leah was struck by the tree's decaying character. When she reached Maria's penultimate sketch, the one Leah had witnessed her so fiercely drawing, she saw that the tree had metamorphosed into a demon, the thick roots of the beast erupting through the surface of the forest floor. These were fiendish in their representation, as though endeavouring to escape from their earthly confines.

But then the final drawing ... Maria had used a different technique, one Leah remembered seeing her sister use before – a reverse method. Using her hands, Maria would blacken the entire page with charcoal then etch out her design with a small amount of India rubber. The technique lent images a ghostly effect. Leah stared into the branches of the willow. They appeared barren of all life, apart from a scarlet-breasted hummingbird hovering above the highest branch of the tree. It was the only colour on the page. Leah held it close to her face, examining the tiny bird as though it might speak to her and divulge the answers she was seeking. When nothing was forthcoming, Leah threw the page to the ground and rose. But as the paper landed, something caught her eye in the rendering – a man's face formed by the shape of the branches, threatening hostile eyes leering and twisted mouth snapping. It loomed out so obviously that Leah was amazed she had not noticed it before.

35

———

L eah was the first to arrive at the jail. She could hear movement inside the prison – Francis Jeffries, no doubt – yet the deacon failed to open the door and allow her to stand by the hearth. Leah clutched her sister's drawing materials under one arm. Townsfolk went about their business, avoiding her eye, berthing wide. She soon heard whispers from the corner of the gaol. Children peeking at her, then, turtle-like, pulling in their heads when she glanced their way. Leah turned from them and was immediately struck by a stone that skimmed her head. She barely felt it through her hair and cap, but she turned sharply from shock and anger. The children were gone. Bending, Leah scooped up the stone and examined it. A white river rock, no bigger than a farthing. She was placing it in her pocket when Abby arrived, alone. Mather and Silas made their way along the road a few minutes later.

Silas removed his hat and offered Leah greeting. He did not look at Abby. The minister remained simply dressed in the same clothes of russet he had worn the day before.

Mather knocked on the heavy door. Within seconds Francis Jeffries opened it and allowed the four visitors entry.

'She will not eat. She refuses sustenance,' Jeffries began urgently without offering any of the party greeting. Leah and Abby exchanged a concerned look. 'When my wife brought her food this morning, she pushed it away. When my wife pressed her to take nourishment, she threw the bowl against the wall.'

'Of whom do you speak, Mister Jeffries?' Mather asked.

Jeffries thought for a moment then pushed his hands into his pockets and looked at the floor before responding. 'Why, the girl, of course.'

'She has a name, Sir,'

'Mistress Hallett,' the deacon replied, reddening.

'How long has this been going on?' Mather then asked.

'Since yesterday evening when my wife told her ... the girl ... I mean Mistress Hallett, that she would be questioned today by the Reverend Mather and Silas Dent,' Jeffries stammered.

When the group entered Maria's chamber they found her lying on her pallet with her back towards them. Leah noticed the cornmeal mush had not been wiped clean from where it had been hurled. Now dry, it clung to the wall in clumps and streaks, adding another layer of rancidity to the foul space.

Leah touched her shoulder gently. 'Maria, Reverend Mather is here to speak with you. Please, sit up.'

Maria raised her head slightly and looked at her sister. 'I can feel *his* presence too,' she whispered.

'Of course, dear Sister. The minister has a powerful presence,' Leah remarked, oblivious to her sister's emphasis.

Maria shook her head slightly and closed her eyes. It was as if a mist had come to rest over her. Leah sensed it was not unlike the valerian fog that had settled over herself, ever so briefly, after the whipping. Leah recalled those days of being aware yet unaware. It was a kindness, it occurred to her, and a defence of sorts. Leah brushed Maria's hair from her face and helped her to rise. The young woman looked about her with an odd expression of bemusement. Mather turned to the mess on the floor.

'We shall speak in the antechamber,' he instructed before calling. 'Mister Jeffries!' The deacon appeared at the door. 'Clean up this mess, please.' Mather brushed past a disconcerted Jeffries as he ushered the rest of the group out.

Leah took her sister by the arm and walked with her the few steps to where Mather and the others were waiting. Silas allowed his eyes to travel immediately to Maria's mid-section before hastily averting them to the ground. His body stiffened and he placed his hands behind his back, staring beyond her to the flames in the hearth.

Leah led Maria to a stool by the fire. Silas had not offered her a single gesture of comfort or warmth. Leah wondered how the sight of Maria, the woman he once longed for so wholly, the woman he was willing to sacrifice his name for, could offend him so now.

While Leah was still pondering on Silas's behaviour, Maria rose from the stool and whispered in her sister's ear, then sat down once more. Leah turned to the shuttered window, puzzled.

'Be still. Hush,' Leah advised her sister in a murmur. 'Do not speak of such things.'

'But I can see him, Sister,' Maria persisted in a tone that all could hear. Mather took a step towards the women. 'It's the same hummingbird. He sits just above the window.' She pointed above Silas's head. 'I thought he had died.'

'The hummingbird is here now, you say?' Mather said, eager, kneeling by her side.

'He hovers above the window frame.'

'Does he speak?' Mather inquired.

Maria shook her head. 'He's laughing at you all.'

Mather responded, unruffled by Maria's behaviour. 'Why do we amuse him so?'

'He says you are foolish,' Maria replied, 'to look to unnatural causes.'

Leah raised her chin and took a step forward. Silas gripped her elbow. She turned to him, jerking her arm out of his grasp. His face was red, Leah noticed. Abby moved to her side and took her hand.

'So he speaks to you now?'

Maria nodded. 'I can hear his voice always.'

'Even when he is not present?'

Maria thought for a moment. 'It's as though his thoughts have become my own.'

'Will you speak to me of these thoughts?' Mather asked.

'The hummingbird tells me not to concern myself with all this,' Maria explained, waving her arm around the room. 'That I should trust him, confide in him and unburden myself.'

'Are you afraid?'

Maria closed her eyes and thought deeply on this. 'Nay. But I cannot trust him.'

'Because it's the Devil who speaks to you?' Mather hedged, touching her arm. Despite his even tone, Leah could see the minister was breathing fast in excitement.

The young woman looked to the window and then to her sister. Leah shook her head slightly. Then Maria looked directly at Silas.

'I believe so, Sir. It's God and the Devil at once.'

Mather rose with a start, as though propelled by the force of Maria's admission. Leah strode to her sister and took her shoulders in her arms, pulling her sister to her feet.

'Tell him, Maria,' Leah cried. 'Tell him you have not tarried with the Devil! Name the man who forwhored you … tell him that the child you are carrying is Samuel Bellamy's child … think of the gravity of your admission, Sister!'

The women looked at one another. Leah's grip on Maria's arms loosened. She suddenly recognised a small passage through the fog where her sister stood, distinct and unobscured.

'It must be the Devil, Leah,' Maria explained. 'I asked Samuel Bellamy to lie with me on the afternoon he departed Eastham.'

Leah dropped her hands to her side. Mather and Silas moved in on the young woman.

'He refused. He said he would not lie with me in the place where beasts are bed. Samuel said we should wait until we were married. He kissed me, nothing more.'

Leah witnessed tears forming in Maria's eyes. The first she had seen since this wretched encounter had started. She drew Maria into her arms and hugged her firmly. She did not need to ask whether she spoke the truth.

As they embraced, Leah thought on Maria's confessions of the morning, the hummingbird and also of her sketches of the willow. Mather stood aside and allowed the women this moment, knowing it may be their last. Leah rested her cheek against her sister's shoulder and closed her eyes. If not Bellamy, then who? Who was Maria protecting? *Trust me. Confide in me. Unburden yourself.* These phrases Maria had ascribed to the hummingbird. They were expressions she had repeated to Leah on a number of occasions.

When Leah released her sister, her eyes fell on Silas. He

met her gaze with an anguished stare. She thought of Maria's sketches. The willow had been Silas and Maria's special place, their haven. Suddenly, she recalled Silas uttering those solicitous words to her – *trust me, confide in me, unburden yourself* – on his return to Eastham, after she had appealed to him for help.

Stricken, Leah looked at Abby, whose expression was grim. As Leah opened her mouth to speak, she felt the light touch of Maria's fingertips on her lips.

'Be quiet, dear sister,' Maria said. 'Rest and accept my fate. This is a battle we cannot fight.'

'Maria is tired, Reverend,' Abby broke in. 'Is there anything else? Shall we conclude?'

Leah turned to the Indian. All concealment had dissolved. She observed the strain on Abby's face. Leah's mind raced. *How much did she owe the woman who had saved the life of her twins? What would she herself do to protect her own children?* She looked away.

'There is nothing else,' Mather responded. 'In the light of your sister's disclosures, Goodwife Williams, I cannot, with an easy heart, advise in favour of her release. She will be tried for witchcraft once the child is born.'

Leah moved to the bench on the opposite side of the room and sat down heavily. She lowered her head into her hands, exhausted. After a moment she looked at Mather. He was locked in a discussion with Silas regarding the battle between God and the Devil for Maria's soul. How fortunate it was that the young minister had witnessed, first-hand, that very confrontation, he said.

Leah had been hoodwinked by Mather's sincerity and intelligence. Mather's faith had blinded him.

Ultimately faith blinded everyone.

After a minute or two, she rose and thanked Mather for

travelling the one hundred miles to Eastham and for his efforts with her sister. She handed Maria her drawing materials, kissed her gently on the lips and walked towards the door. Before she departed, she turned and looked at Abby once more. What could she read in her dark eyes? Gratitude, regret, sorrow, relief? All were in the mix. Then she exited the miserable scene.

When Leah reached the centre of the meeting house green, she stopped and looked about her. Although covered with snow, she always thought the green appeared so much warmer and inviting in the winter. Leah inhaled deeply of the hollow, frigid air and began her journey to her father's farm, back to her children.

PART IV

SPRING 1717

36

TORTUGA ISLAND, HISPANIOLA
MARCH 1717

Their target fired off two chase guns. The crew ran starboard. Both shots missed the *Sultana* by at least ten feet. It had been a token display of boldness for the benefit of the ship's owners, Bellamy realised, when only moments later the captain appeared on the forecastle waving a white flag in wide arcs above his head. The eighteen guns mounted on the ship were merely a deterrent.

He turned to Palgrave and wiped his upper lip. 'Mister Williams, organise a boarding party.'

'Aye, Captain.' Palgrave moved off to gather men and arms.

Neither the obvious advantage the magnificent galley possessed nor the appearance of the King's Pennant on the flagpole proved an obstacle to Bellamy when he had first spied the ship three days before when she entered the Windward Passage.

'It's a slaver,' Bellamy had cried from the quarterdeck to the crew, 'in the middle passage, heading back to England. With the human cargo offloaded in Jamaica, its hold will be full of riches. It will be our greatest prize. Mark me! We must act now while we can harness this trade. It isn't much of a wind, I grant you, but we've gotten underway with less!'

Bellamy's words were the only prompt his brother sailors, who trusted their captain's judgement and acumen, required. The men issued a series of gutsy huzzahs, inciting Bellamy to call to the boatswain, a good-hearted Dubliner named Jeremiah Burke, to give chase. Burke gave the order to pull anchor and trim the sails and the *Sultana* instantly came alive. Men scurried up the ratlines. Others tended the lines at the base of the masts. Bellamy shouted orders from the quarterdeck to release all the sails. The ship's wings needed to seize every ounce of force from the feeble south-easterly breeze if the *Sultana* had any chance of catching the slaver. Palgrave looked aloft as he heard the creak of the timber masts.

Bellamy watched the men at work. How proud he was to have assembled this fine crew. As individuals, he could see that they were abrasive and crude, hopelessly ill-equipped in society. United on board the *Sultana*, these motley outcasts acted as one. With Bellamy as conductor, they were a finely tuned orchestra, perfectly balanced, in harmony with each other and the sea.

As the sails began to fill, Palgrave stood in the spray with Bellamy on the quarterdeck viewing their quarry, an outstanding three-hundred-ton galley.

'I've never seen a faster ship of that size. It's remarkable,' Palgrave observed as he handed the eyeglass to Bellamy. 'It must be a hundred feet if it's an inch.'

'It's faultless,' Bellamy replied.

'Will we catch her?'

'Raise the flag,' Bellamy cried in response, squinting into the sunlight in search of the boatswain.

Palgrave watched the death's head and bones speedily traverse the length of the foremast.

'Speed, Mister Burke?' Bellamy called into the mist.

'Seven-and-a-half knots,' the boatswain replied as he reeled in the chip log.

The captain smiled in satisfaction.

He and Palgrave had been sailing these waters for two months, since January, and had captured many a grand prize. The ship they gave chase in now, the *Sultana*, a first-rate galley, was but one of many they had taken. However, Bellamy had kept only two ships, preferring inconspicuousness over a great display of force. Levasseur, the Frenchman who had joined Bellamy's crew when the split with Hornigold had occurred, now helmed the *Marianne*. He proved as tenacious a seaman as Bellamy and now, when Palgrave looked to the stern, the Frenchman was sailing close behind them in the *Sultana*'s wake.

After spotting the ship, Bellamy had not rested. Instead, he chose to stand at the bow gazing at the ship ahead.

'He's a shrewd captain,' Bellamy had remarked, to Palgrave, referring to the captain of the slaver. 'But his crew are growing sluggish. Look how they come about.'

In the morning of the third day, the ship slowed near Long Key and the *Sultana* approached. Palgrave read its name through the eyeglass: *Whydah*. After the two shots were fired, the chase was done.

Bellamy had won his greatest prize of all.

'IT's a wicked trade you deal in, Mister Prince,' Bellamy commented, thinking of his friend Ade as he examined the ship. The captain had offered Bellamy a tour of the galley, joking that it was only fair, seeing that the *Whydah* now belonged to him. 'Selling people like goods and chattels ...'

Prince shrugged and his green, close-set eyes rolled towards the sky.

'The *Whydah* is an independent vessel and the owners pay me handsomely. Their insurers will cover the loss. The trade will go on, regardless of me. I'm aware my profession is mercenary,' he remarked casually as he shrugged once again.

'She is a beauty,' Bellamy remarked, stroking the knots and whorls of the glossy umber railing.

'She's constructed of oak, as you can see, Mister Bellamy,' Prince informed him as he led Bellamy through the vast ship. 'Custom made for the slave trade'

Bellamy followed the captain below decks.

'You're a gifted captain. Royal Navy?' Bellamy questioned.

Prince nodded. 'After the war I decided to take my leave in search of a more profitable occupation.'

'What I do is more profitable still,' Bellamy responded.

Prince laughed.

'But yours is not a law-abiding profession, Sir,' Prince remarked. 'I do not plan to finish my days at the business end of a gibbet on Boston Harbour.'

'You're treading a very fine line with that argument.'

'Perhaps. However, as it stands, slave trafficking does not run afoul of the King's laws.'

Palgrave appeared as Bellamy thought on Prince's comments.

'It's astounding. I've never seen such a haul,' He informed Bellamy. Prince yawned and leant against the ship's railing. 'Gold, silver, ivory, indigo, sugar, Jesuit's bark ...'

'Fifty thousand pounds worth in total,' Prince said. 'Approximately.'

Bellamy and Palgrave looked at each other. Both men shared the same thought. *Whydah*'s spoils, combined with what they had already accrued, meant they now had wealth enough to return to Eastham.

37

NASSAU, NEW PROVIDENCE ISLAND
MARCH 1717

Palgrave had not witnessed anything akin to the brand of jubilation that ensued once the *Whydah* had been captured. It was unusual for the captain and the quarter-master to join the men in celebration, but on their first night on the new ship, they did, albeit with less gusto than their shipmates. The *Whydah* was magnificent. Every man aboard knew it. She would rule the seas. They would be invincible. In light of this, Bellamy and Palgrave had agreed to remain in the Caribbean until the summer. But as the crew celebrated, the pair had grown pensive, brooding on the wider consequences of their decision.

'What ship's to your liking?' Bellamy asked Palgrave as they watched a lively, if somewhat unsteady, jig performed by Burke.

Palgrave, confused, shook his head.

'You'll be captain of one and I'll give the other to Levasseur. He's taking his leave with a heading for West Africa,' Bellamy said.

Palgrave was not surprised at Levasseur's decision, but Bellamy's had rendered him gobsmacked.

'Are you afflicted? I could never be a captain.'

'You underestimate yourself, my friend,' Bellamy said. 'Your education has been speedier than you realise. Your knowledge of the ocean, your confidence in dealing with the crew – both have grown. The men like you and trust you, for what that's worth.'

Palgrave raised his eyebrows, unconvinced.

'By agreeing to remain in these waters as we have,' Bellamy continued more seriously, 'we've chosen to fly extremely close to the sun. I've never been superstitious, but …

He understood precisely what Bellamy could not express. They both required a companion they could trust beyond all measure, a friend to keep them on a steady course. Success and complacency were deadly foes.

Palgrave chose the smaller of the two ships, the *Mari-anne*, while Levasseur departed in the *Sultana* along with Prince and half his crew. Bellamy's triumphs proved too tempting for the rest of Prince's men, who did not share their captain's fear of the noose.

For two weeks, the boats anchored off Long Key in Florida while the *Whydah*'s haul was offloaded and recorded by the quartermaster. Then the crew careened the ship on a deserted beach where the sand was as fine and yellow as cornmeal. The hull was scrubbed free of seaweed and barnacles. Tents were pitched. Water casks were filled with rainwater that the heavens relinquished each afternoon just before supper. Firewood was cut and grass was harvested for the twenty sheep discovered in the *Whydah*'s hold. The men lived like this for a fortnight.

Once the *Whydah* was back on the water, adjustments began to the interior. The cleaning had made the *Whydah* even faster, but it was still top heavy. Bellamy knew that in rough seas it would be unstable. He ordered for the ship to be cleared. The forecastle, pilot's cabin and most of the stern castle were removed and the quarterdeck was lowered. The area below decks where three hundred Africans had recently been crammed between narrow barricados was stripped, increasing the space for treasure and a larger crew. With the addition of ten of the *Sultana*'s swivel guns, Bellamy became captain of a formidable twenty-eight gun, three-masted galley. The captain was pleased with the efforts of his crew who worked tirelessly to have the *Whydah* ready as quickly as possible for another patrol. Such was their urgency to return to Nassau, fence their haul, buy supplies and return to sea, that none of the men had indulged heartily until the transformation was completed. They worked until sunset. Following supper, they would sit peaceably, almost drowsily on deck or on the beach playing cards and music in the moonlight.

For entertainment, there was Jack Driver, a stroller by profession. He had joined Bellamy's ranks after the *Whydah* had been seized. When Palgrave asked him how he had become a member of a slaving ship's crew, Driver responded by suggesting it was a means to an end, and certainly more gainful than strolling.

He was a whimsical fellow who seemed ill-suited to the life, but proved to be a boon to the crew. To much laughter and wild applause, Driver would put on airs and act out many performances, all fictitious and a few being of his own devising. On occasion, Palgrave had caught him in a quiet moment, frowning, as though the burdens of all men rested on his shoulders. He had a son, he explained, who he was forced to abandon to the care of his sister when the bailiff came knocking.

The crew's brief but beautiful idyll concluded once the

ships were anchored in Nassau. When Palgrave had paid the men they hastily made their way to the long boats and into the town to squander their coin.

Palgrave and Bellamy remained in the captain's cabin examining the charts they had discovered on the *Whydah*. The room began to darken and Palgrave glanced at the portholes. They had turned a deep shade of orange in the setting sun. He stared at the hovering dust illuminated by a beam of warm amber light reaching through the opening.

'Do you think you will return to Eastham?' asked Palgrave without turning his eyes away.

Bellamy moved the charts aside and lifted his head, sighing. 'Nay. I love Tamesine. I love her son.' He rubbed his face. 'I feel a duty to Maria, but that's not enough.'

Palgrave was not surprised by his response. 'Did you love her once?'

'I believe I would have grown to love her. There was an attraction, a definite spark.'

Palgrave nodded. His friend's words saddened him, more for himself than for Maria. There were any number of young men eager to wed her. He assured himself that Bellamy would be forgotten in a matter of weeks. But how would Palgrave continue without the companionship of Sam Bellamy?

'Tamesine is determined to return to England,' said Bellamy. 'I have decided to join her. With what we've seized, I have enough to buy a handsome property. John will go to school and be raised a gentleman's son.'

'You and the sea make such an easy match. It seems odd that you would have landed dreams.'

'You're the one who has taken so well to this life.' Bellamy rose, smiling. 'But it's no life for men such as us. As attractive as our existence may appear and as comely as this ship is, there's no substance to what we do here. A home, a wife, children ... those are what give us meaning.'

He squeezed Palgrave's shoulder fondly before departing. Within a few minutes, Palgrave heard his friend's feet against the hull as he clambered down a rope into a dinghy. The slight splash and rock of the small boat against the water became audible as Bellamy rowed towards shore, to his new life.

Gazing at the porthole in the darkening cabin, Palgrave considered his own plans in the light of Bellamy's. He lay his head across his folded arms and rested his eyes. Within minutes he was thinking of Leah and of that morning long ago.

The sun had not yet risen when he heard a frantic rap at the door. When he opened it, he was met by Leah, breathless and red-faced, standing ghost-like in the fog. Her body was shuddering violently. Despite the snow, she wore no cloak or gloves. He ushered her into his kitchen and removed his coat before cautiously threading her arms though the sleeves. Then he guided her to a stool by the hearth and snatched a cloth from the table. Standing behind her, drying her hair uncertainly, he wondered what had brought her to him in this state so early in the day.

The milk he had warmed for breakfast was still hot. He ladled some into a cup then knelt by Leah tentatively, holding the cup, waiting for her to cease shaking. Eventually, at his wit's end, Palgrave had taken her hands in his and rubbed them vigorously. Her fingertips were blue but he noticed her lips were slowly returning to their perfect pink.

Once she had taken a few sips of the milk, her trembling faded to a quiver and she began.

'I spoke to Papa about our desire to wed.'

Palgrave rose.

'That's my responsibility, Leah,' he said. 'It was I who should have broached that conversation.'

Palgrave had expected to discern an apologetic note in her manner. There was none. 'We could not wed, he said. He was adamant, so certain he knew what was best.'

Leah stood and placed her cheek against his chest.

Palgrave softened and instinctively placed his arms around her. He was instantly conscious of his body warming hers, the heavy rise and fall of her chest, the slender lines of her back and his own shortcomings.

'He raised his hand to strike me,' she went on, lifting her face to his.

'Your father struck you?'

She shook her head. 'But he was so near. I've never seen him so angry. I can't remember the words we exchanged, but we said too much. Both of us said too much.'

'I should take you home. You should seek his forgiveness.'

Leah had stared at him. There was a wild glint in her eyes. 'I cannot live in that house any longer. When I looked at Papa this morning, I saw myself through his eyes. I'm not a daughter, but a prize to be haggled over with the highest bidder. I'm free now, Palgrave.'

'Honour thy father and thy mother ...' Palgrave began, hoping to remind her of the wider consequences of her decision.

'I'm prepared to live with my sin if you'll have me.'

He embraced her firmly, not quite understanding her words.

She raised her face and kissed him tenderly on the lips, drawing him closer. He looked down at her, gazing at her flawlessness, her purity. Yet there was something else in her eyes, an insistence he had not seen before. Palgrave became aware at once that it was hopeless to resist. When he responded to her touch, she began to kiss him more hungrily, raising her hands to his shoulders. Leah's feet lifted from the ground as they clutched at each other, their desperation increasing. As she drew him down to the cold kitchen floor, he swept aside the stool on which she had been sitting. He watched her as she unfastened her bodice. The creamy skin beneath was irresistible.

When they eventually came together it was the greatest pleasure he had ever known.

PALGRAVE RAISED HIS HEAD. The cabin was dark. He rose and lit a candle then took quill and paper and began to write.

Dearest Leah,

Life goes on here in Nassau as usual. There is not a Day that passes that I do not Think of You, our Home and our Children. How I long to see You all again. My small Business has grown threefold in these past Months and I now see to the Needs of all sorts of Sailors and Shipwrights that are lured to this Place. The Children would find much to sate their Curiosity here. Strange Fish and Birds and Crabs as large as a man's hand. And the Turtles hauled from the Sea are boiled and eaten for Supper! There is even one Beast they call a Sea Cow that, in part, resembles a Cow, and in another, resembles an Elephant. For its size and inelegance, they are remarkably agile in Water, and I have witnessed these Creatures performing Rolls, Somersaults, and even swimming upside-down.

To bathe in the Sea is like plunging into a warm Bath. It is nothing like the biting Cape Cod Waters.

Palgrave placed the quill to rest and blotted his final words. He scanned the lines on the page. All he read was deceit. Lying was becoming increasingly difficult, he found. No truth remained in which he could base his falsehoods. He was no Jack Driver, gifted with the ability to invent a tale on a whim. While Bellamy's dreams were landed, Palgrave's own stretched far across the inconstant waters of the Caribbean to the horizon. His home, he realised, had become that vast expanse of greenish-blue.

While he yearned for Leah with an ache that was unbearable, Palgrave was aware that he would never be able to share his experiences. The scar on his chest received in his first fray; the absent tooth dislodged by a drunkard's fist; the monstrous wound on his belly that Bellamy had sealed with pitch; all these and the memories of the men he had killed, resting so lightly on his conscience, would have to be concealed behind an elaborately woven veil of lies. More profoundly, his newly restored confidence and conviction were not compatible with the pallid backdrop of his existence.

He removed his compass from his waistcoat and studied it carefully. His time at sea would bolster his life with Leah. They would never want for anything again. *Yet*, he wondered, *would not our union be undermined, weakened by what is hidden?*

Palgrave stretched and took a final look at the page before him. Then he crushed the paper into a tight ball and launched it through the porthole towards the horizon.

38

EASTHAM, MASSACHUSETTS
MARCH 1717

The idea came to Leah on the night the baby was born. She was awoken by Francis Jeffries's arrival at the farm at a quarter past midnight. Leah immediately gauged from his panicked stare and agitated stance that her sister's labour had begun.

But it can't be, she thought indignantly; it was not yet Maria's time.

'You can ride with me,' Joseph Hallett said to his daughter as he took the stairs to his chamber two at a time. 'It will be faster.'

'Fetch Abby,' Leah ordered the deacon. 'See her to the jail.'

When he did not respond immediately Leah repeated the instruction in an unrestrained scream. By the time Hannah had moved to her in the hope of guiding her back into the house, Jeffries was already riding from the property through the snow. When Leah and her father arrived at the jail Abby was positioned next to Maria's pallet with her ear pressed to her abdomen. Despite the cold in her cell, Maria was perspiring heavily. Leah placed a wet clout on her sister's forehead. The slave looked up and shook her head. Leah nodded in understanding.

'She was alone. When I got here she was all alone. Who knows when the pains began?' she said, rising and moving to the foot of the bed.

Tears welled in Leah's eyes before she checked herself and unbuttoned her sleeves.

'Papa, we'll need clean cloths and scissors and ...' Leah cried. 'Margaret will know what we need.'

The women heard Hallett's horse thunder along the road.

'It's too soon, Leah,' Maria said feebly, aware of Leah's arrival.

'Aye, it is that.' Leah moved to her side and took her hand. 'The baby will not survive.'

'It's best that way,' Maria said in a tone so coherent it made Leah hurt.

Maria screwed her face in pain and cried out. Leah leant in close and whispered, 'Take deep breaths, just like this.'

Maria focused on the gentle wash of Leah's breath against her cheek and soon her own breathing fell into rhythm with her sister's. But Maria rested for only a minute before she screamed out again. She gripped Leah's hand, turning her sister's fingertips pink. Leah winced.

Then Maria calmed again and stared hard into her sister's eyes as though seeking answers. Leah dabbed Maria's ashen face with a cloth and kissed her softly on each cheek. It was all she could offer.

Hallett soon returned and Leah retrieved what he'd collected from his sister.

'Wait outside,' Leah instructed. 'The baby is dead.'

Hallett nodded without emotion and left the jail.

Then Leah was beckoned back to the cell by a fearsome

howl. When she entered she saw an immense gush of fluid spill over Abby's hands. Leah resumed her position at her sister's side.

'I can see your baby's head,' Abby said. 'Maria, when the pain comes again, bear down. Push as hard as you can and breath out.'

In less than a minute Maria was overcome with agony once more. She did exactly as Abby said and, with a prolonged growl, pushed her baby into the world.

'It's a boy.' Abby began to wipe the child clean. She held her ear to its purpled, wrinkled chest. The shapeling was humanlike in form.

No larger than a loaf of bread, Leah thought.

Abby wrapped the body tightly in her shawl and stood.

'Would you like to hold him, Maria?' she asked.

Maria shook her head.

Abby studied the face of the child in her arms for a long time before finally turning to Leah.

Bitter and exhausted, Leah gazed at the aftermath of the child's birth. It was an event of such magnitude and consequence yet was all over in less than an hour. While Abby mournfully rocked the child in her arms, Maria wept quietly in her bed. Relief, sorrow; Leah knew not the source of her sister's tears. Now the child was born, Leah couldn't bear to face what lay next.

It was at that moment that her thoughts cleared, and the only way to survive first came to her.

Leah dismissed it quickly. *An insane thought*, she told herself, *born from desperation and fatigue.* But after a brief moment of consideration, the lunacy associated with the revelation began to fall away and what remained were a series of rational steps leading to freedom.

When Dent arrived at the jail, he forbade them from

burying the child next to its grandmother and uncles in the cemetery. How Leah had wanted to speak out, but it was still too early, she told herself, blunting her keenest impulse. The child was buried in the fields behind her father's house instead.

Before the children had risen, Joseph Hallett had planted his shovel in the ground and dug a deep hole by candlelight. Leah found herself terrified as she lay on her chest to place the shrouded package into the pit. She wondered in what kind of evil they were engaging. Leah wanted to lie down alongside the child, wrap him in her arms and feel the cold earth rain down upon her cheek. Then she remembered her vision. Hallett said a brief prayer. No gravestone was erected, leaving no proof of the damned child's existence.

IN THE AFTERNOON Leah walked into town and found Reverend Dent at home, alone. Leah knew not where Abby was. She didn't care. It made no difference to her plans.

When he opened the door, Leah spoke immediately.

'There are matters we must discuss,' she began. He'd looked at her incredulously. 'Matters that concern my sister and your son and the child born last night.'

Dent remained silent but Leah noticed his right eye flicker. He opened the door more fully. Leah raised her chin and passed by Dent into the parlour.

'Silas was the father of that child,' she said. 'It was your wretched grandchild who was buried without ceremony, like an animal, in the field behind my father's barn this morning.'

'It's a lie! You are wickedness itself, Leah Williams!' Dent protested immediately as though he had rehearsed the words. Leah wondered if he had suspected as much himself. The thought sickened her.

She went on evenly. 'I'm not sure how it came to be that they conceived a child together, and it matters not. Your son is the wicked one, Reverend. He has lied and watched the woman he loves condemned as a harlot and a witch. What's more, he has made me complicit in his crime.'

Leah's understanding of Silas's motives would be forever muddied by her certainty that he loved Maria. She had given up attempting to unravel the mystery that was Silas Dent. Affairs of greater importance now occupied her thoughts.

Dent turned his back on her then and moved to the hearth. Although she could not see his expression, Leah knew the minister was grappling with the facts, searching for an escape. When he faced her again his composure was restored.

'There's not a person in Eastham, why, in the whole of New England, who will believe the word of Maria Hallett, or her sister, over mine,' he responded.

'You're mistaken. The people of this town will latch onto any scandal or rumour. Eastham thrives on hearsay. It's the town's lifeblood.' Leah paused for an instant as she took in Dent's twitching eye. 'And you, Sir, your support is dwindling. You hope my family's downfall will shore up your ministry. But you're wrong. It will only destroy you.'

Dent cleared his throat but did not speak.

'Release my sister,' Leah pushed. 'My father will sell all his land, including that which is tenanted, to you for eighty pounds. Then we'll leave Eastham.'

'Why, that is blackmail!' Dent exclaimed.

'Yes, it is, Sir. I have drawn up the terms of our agreement.' She produced a document from her pocket and laid it on the table between them.

It took only a minute for Dent to concede and walk to the table. He lifted the sheet of paper and read it thoroughly.

'You're not to mention any of this,' Leah explained when Dent had finished.' My sister will be freed and, in a fortnight or perhaps longer, we'll leave Eastham forever. But my father must never know it was you who purchased his land.'

The minister placed the paper back on the table. 'The first point ...'

'It's nothing but the truth. Silas Dent is the father of Maria Hallett's dead infant.'

He nodded and left the room solemnly. When Dent returned to the parlour moments later he was clutching the money in his hand.

LEAH SOUGHT out Abby at the harbour. It was Friday morning; she knew the slave would be there along with every other Eastham woman. Leah watched her from the beach as she walked purposefully around the barrels and crates, oblivious to those around her. Occasionally, she would lift a fish to examine it more closely, taking in its briny scent, checking it for freshness.

Leah approached slowly over the sand, drawing hostile glances from the women around her. This had once been her Friday morning ritual. She had not purchased fish here since the summer. Although the scene was so familiar, Leah was aware of a change. She had become an outsider as well.

'Good day to you, Abby,' Leah said, laying her hand lightly on the Indian's shoulder.

The women had not spoken since the birth.

Abby turned, surprised. The slave clutched at Leah's fingertips, eager to speak.

'I need to talk with you,' Leah whispered before Abby could speak. She looked away, inspecting a tawny flounder, stroking its cold and waxy surface.

Then, feeling the eyes of every other woman in the marketplace on them, Leah added more loudly. 'Are you able to call by? My father and I would like to thank you for your help. This afternoon?'

Abby nodded, confused, her dark eyes searching for the truth behind Leah's invitation.

Leah leant in and kissed her on the cheek. She held her lips against Abby's warm skin for a few seconds before saying goodbye.

ONCE HER CHILDREN were in bed, Leah left the house and walked into town. She stood at the entrance to the tavern, the 'ordinary' as her father liked to call it. Music – a fast-paced jig – and the low grumble of voices could be heard from her position on the road only a few feet away. Leah had never stepped foot inside and she was wary of what might confront her when she did. She gathered her cloak around her shoulders before entering.

The door closed heavily behind her, alerting everyone to her arrival. Heads turned for an instant. The place was dense with smoke and her eyes stung as she sought out the landlord, Albert Garvey. Palgrave had had many dealings with Garvey in the past. Leah had disapproved of her husband's relationship with the tavern's owner. Now all her hopes rested upon it.

Leah recognised none of the men she passed by on her way to the bar. Seamen, she assumed. A few lifted their hats and nodded.

'You'll not find your husband in here, Goodwife,' one of them said, laughing.

Leah stopped and looked at him, an older man about her father's age with long grey whiskers and leathery skin.

'I'm not looking for my husband,' she said. 'I'm looking for the landlord, Mister Garvey.'

Not expecting such a firm reply, the man simply shrugged and returned his attention to his mug, unsure what he should say.

Then, from the corner of her eye, Leah glimpsed a woman approaching. It was the landlord's wife. Mary's face was powdered and the neckline of her scarlet gown was cut low. Her hair, Leah noticed for the first time, was beautiful. It fell in thick ginger lengths to her waist. Leah was instantly embarrassed by her own drab petticoat and bodice. She braced herself, tucking a stray strand of hair in her cap.

'Goody Williams,' she said, not unkindly. 'Such a pleasure.'

Leah nodded.

'Have you had word from Palgrave?' Mary asked. 'We're in need of some items. We daren't seek out the services of another smithy. Palgrave's work is the finest in New England.'

'Not recently,' Leah replied.

The women were silent for a moment. 'He will come back,' Mary said gently, reaching out and squeezing Leah's hand briefly.

The gesture surprised Leah. She found herself unable to speak.

Mary, sensing Leah's discomfort, broke the silence. 'How can I help you?'

'I wish to speak to your husband.'

'He's in Salem until Tuesday. Perhaps I can help?'

Leah sighed, suddenly losing her nerve. 'I ... I don't think ...'

Mary took her arm. 'Please, come with me. We can talk more freely in the back.'

Once Leah was seated in the landlord's office, Mary poured them both a drink.

'What's this?' Leah asked, peering into the depths of a cann her husband had made.

'Rum.'

Leah, perched on the edge of the chair, refused the refreshment.

'Think of it as a fortifying tonic,' Mary said, holding out the cup once more. 'You need it after what you've been through.'

Leah finally took the refreshment gratefully. The liquid burned as it travelled the length of her throat. She opened her mouth and inhaled deeply. She raised the cup to her lips again as her body became accustomed to the unfamiliar warmth settling in her chest.

'My family and I are in need of passage to Wellfleet,' Leah explained. 'I know there are ships which sail to Provincetown and Boston that take on cargo there. And I know, from what my husband has told me, that you are well acquainted with the captains of those ships.'

'But Wellfleet is not thirty miles by road ...'

'We must go by sea,' Leah said, so adamantly that Mary did not question her further. 'I have some money. I can pay the captain what the trip is worth. I can also pay you for your help ... and your discretion.'

Mary looked at Leah for a moment. 'Once it is arranged I will send word,' she said. She finished her drink in one gulp.

Leah closed her eyes briefly. Her posture relaxed. 'I've treated you poorly in the past, misjudged you.'

'You deserve a kindness,' Mary said. 'Palgrave is a friend.'

She searched her pocket for the money she'd carefully tied in a handkerchief before leaving the farm.

'I need no payment, Goody Williams.'

Leah rose and walked to the door. Before she exited, she turned and looked at the landlord's wife. 'Thank you, Mary,' she said. 'I ...' Leah knew of no way to adequately express her appreciation. '... your gown and your hair are very lovely.'

'I HAVE RECEIVED a reply from my aunt,' Arthur Earl informed her when he arrived at the farm ten days later. 'She's happy for you to lodge with her for a time.'

'I'll pay her ...' Leah said. 'My father has money.'

Arthur nodded. 'She'll refuse.'

Leah exhaled then slumped heavily onto the bench next to the hearth. 'Thank you, Arthur.' Her scheme hinged on finding a place to stay, a refuge of sorts. It was as though the anticipation of his aunt's response had been the only thing keeping her upright. Everything was now in place.

They sat together at the table for a time. The children were in the field with their grandfather, and Hannah was mending in the parlour.

'Palgrave will come back,' Arthur said.

Leah shrugged.

'It's a miserable admission I'm about to make, Arthur,' she said, 'but the distance that has formed between my husband and myself is immeasurable, much greater than the miles between Eastham and Nassau. Palgrave doesn't know a jot of what has occurred during his absence. I don't know, when ... *if* ... he returns whether that vastness can ever be bridged. How can I tell him what has gone on?'

He cleared his throat uncertainly. Leah turned to him. Arthur took her hands in his.

'You'll find a way. You always do.'

39

EASTHAM, MASSACHUSETTS
MARCH 1717

Abby did not waver when the day eventually arrived. In fact, she had been living in a state of readiness since the moment Leah had laid out her plan. The Indian woke in the morning to a bright, cloudless sky. *A perfect spring day*, she mused as she followed the flight of a downy woodpecker from the ground and into the branches of a nearby pine.

In the evening, when the minister asked for his tea, she calmly tipped the quantity of valerian root Leah had given her into his mug. She placed the empty vial in her pocket. Then she proceeded to add more lemon balm than was her custom in order to mask the taste, as Leah had advised. Leah had said she was not to be concerned with the amount of potion as it would take at least a gill to render a man of Dent's proportions unconscious. Abby gazed into the cup and swirled the concoction slowly before filling the vessel with boiling water.

She waited for the tea to cool a little, for the mixture to steep, before taking to the stairs and walking a deliberate path to the minister's bedchamber. When she delivered the tea, his back was to her. He sat at his desk under the window, the flame of his candle reflected in the window. Abby looked down at her hand as she placed the cup at his elbow. She was astounded there was no tremble evident. Dent did not acknowledge her.

She left the room and closed the door behind her. When she had taken five steps, as her foot had reached the stairway and her hand was on the bannister, she heard Dent cry out.

'Abby! This tea smells altered. Have you changed the recipe?'

All calm vanished. She clenched her hands into tight fists in order to stem their involuntary shake. Then, after inhaling three deep breaths, she returned to the room.

'I have, a little,' she began evenly. Dent stared at her accusingly, but Abby was gifted at remaining composed under the minister's scrutinising glare. 'Goody Jeffries suggested I use a dash of valerian root in the brew to beckon sleep more easily. It has a unique taste, I grant you, but she's concerned. She says you appear so weary each Sabbath. The Hallett affair weighs too heavily on you, she fears.'

Dent considered her explanation and his face softened. 'Goody Jeffries is a godly woman. She does well to be concerned for me.'

Abby waited a moment.

'You may go. I will pass on my thanks to Goody Jeffries tomorrow.'

Leah closed her eyes and listened to the quiet. The only sound evident was the dying crackle of the fire in the hearth. Leah wrapped her cloak more tightly around her shoulders.

When the candle in front of her had almost burnt down she did not bother to light another. The glow of the full moon was enough to see by. She assessed her emotions. There was an odd sensation in the base of her chest. She wondered if it was unease. *No, expectancy*, she quickly reasoned. Like awaiting the birth of a child.

She heard the lantern clock chime. *Tick tock*. One o'clock. The snort of a horse outside signalled Abby's arrival. Leah rose and made her way out of the kitchen door so no-one would be awakened.

Abby waited without dismounting while Leah took the small bundle of the slave's belongings and ran with it back to the kitchen. Minutes later, when Leah took Abby's hand and raised herself onto the horse, the slave commented in a low murmur, 'It is done.'

Leah nodded and Abby lifted the reins gently. The horse began its journey along the road. The women travelled slowly, without speaking. There was nothing that remained to be said. They had discussed this night for many weeks. When they arrived at the town, Abby slowed the horse's jog to a saunter, hoping not to invite notice. It seemed to Leah that during the quarter mile through town both of them held their breath. She glanced around her at the homes. Their shutters were drawn. Her aunt's house came into view and Leah smiled fondly. Margaret knew nothing of her niece's plan. When Leah had swiftly pocketed the vial that stood on her aunt's hutch, Margaret thought her niece had been retrieving a button that Caleb had lost the week before. Before Leah departed she had hugged her aunt warmly and thanked her for all she had done.

The horse brayed and Leah's thoughts returned to the present. The only light visible came from the tavern. She briefly wondered whether her captain was inside, the man who had agreed to transport her family to Wellfleet.

When they passed by Arthur Earl's home the urge to stop and bid him goodbye was overwhelming. She wondered if Arthur would suspect when awoken by the shouts of the men, by the ruckus the town would surely make.

ABBY DROVE the horse into the darkened stable at the rear of Dent's house. The women worked together to unbridle the mare and give her water. Before they shut the stable door they examined the interior, ensuring their presence had vanished. All was dark when they entered the house. Leah trailed Abby into the kitchen taking light, brisk steps. The smells of supper lingered in the air – onions and smoked pork. Abby opened the shutters, allowing the moonlight to cascade through the window. The slave lit two candles from the embers in the hearth.

'Before I left I shook him hard by the shoulder but he did not stir,' Abby murmured.

'Did you use all the valerian root I gave you?'

'Every drop.'

From behind the closed door of Dent's bedchamber they could hear the minister's throaty snore. The women glanced at each other quickly then Abby clutched the handle and twisted. They approached the bed and looked down at the slumbering pastor, instinctively aware of the other's thoughts. It was as though at that moment they were something greater, a more powerful entity, than mere co-conspirators.

Abby and Leah flinched at the hoot of a barn owl, their

heads turning immediately to their slumbering prey. He did not stir. Abby produced a document from her pocket. Leah noticed the age of the paper and the crude seal. She looked at the slave.

'My bill of sale.' Abby placed the document on Dent's pillow.

Leah nodded and moved to the opposite side of the minister's bed.

Then the women bent low and moved around the bed holding their candles to the bedclothes. Once the minister's quilt was alight, they did the same to the elegant drapery surrounding his window. Still Reverend Dent did not stir.

THEY DID NOT LOOK BACK at the funeral pyre of the house until they were halfway through the woods. A billowing haze, lit by a red-orange glow, was visible in the sky. Although gasping and exhausted, Leah and Abby continued at a steady trot until they reached the Hallett farm. When they arrived, dawn's first light was visible above the roof of the barn.

Hurrying inside, Leah found her father already seated at the table. Hannah was preparing breakfast. Despite the absence of crops and animals – both had dwindled away over the terrible months of Maria's confinement – arising at daybreak to begin his day's work was a habit Joseph Hallett could not alter. He stared at his daughter and her companion for a moment, taking in their fevered appearance and breathlessness.

'Abby, will you please wake Maria and the children and see them dressed?' Leah asked, her heart still pounding in her throat. 'They each have a bag with their belongings at the foot of their beds. We must hasten.'

Joseph Hallett looked at his daughter. 'Must hasten?'

'We're leaving,' Leah explained gently. 'So are you. I've secured passage on a ship travelling to Wellfleet where we will lodge for a time with Rebecca Earl, Arthur's aunt. You've met her on occasion, I recall.'

Hallett turned to Hannah. She shrugged and shook her head.

'You will come too, Hannah,' Leah advised.

'What are you up to, child?' Hallett said, rising. 'What have you done?'

'I have safeguarded our future, nothing more. But we must leave. Now.'

'Leah, my patience wears thin,' Hallett said. Leah noted the edge of frustration in his tone. 'I'm not leaving my farm.'

Leah looked at Hannah, seeking assistance. The woman did not budge. Her face was steely.

'It's all over. Your good name, as well as mine, is ruined in this town. Maria cannot step foot outside this property without being mocked and jeered and called a witch. Her spirit is forever altered. This farm, once prosperous and fertile, is barren. Eastham has become our prison. I can't abide it. This life is no life for any of us.'

Leah paused. The ship would be sailing in less than an hour; she did not have time to convince her father. She had thought that when presented with an alternative he would finally surrender. After all, there was nothing left to fight for in Eastham.

'I've money enough to buy another acreage north of here. Please.' She went to him and embraced him. His arms hung stiffly by his side.

'Where did you come by this money?' Hallett inquired, breaking free of her grasp.

'Palgrave,' Leah lied. 'He sent me seventy pounds.'

Hannah snuffed the candles as the morning sun began to brighten the room. Leah gazed at her father pleadingly. He shook his head firmly and returned to his breakfast.

'Papa, I beg you ...'

Hallett silenced his daughter and held out his hand for her. She walked to his side. 'I don't need saving, Leah. God will see to us.'

Leah stood by her father, motionless. Hannah went about her chores. Her father ate his bread and sipped his warm milk. A moment later, Leah stepped away.

As she and Abby were departing, Maria and the children in tow, she offered her father twenty pounds.

'God will provide for me, daughter,' was all he uttered by way of a farewell.

It was not until the seven émigrés were safe aboard the *Oracle*, packed into the meagre berth the captain had offered them, that Leah began to cry. Fat beads of tears dropped onto her lap.

'Are you crying or laughing, Mama?' Elizabeth asked when she spotted her mother slumped on the ground.

'Both,' Leah answered, holding out her arms for her daughter.

40

NASSAU, NEW PROVIDENCE ISLAND
MARCH 1717

Tamesine eyed Bellamy cautiously from across the table as they ate dinner.

'A slaver you say,' John mused. 'Did you see the Africans?'

Each time Samuel Bellamy returned, it was as though she were seeing him for the very first time. His hair was longer, she noticed. It was matted together by salt water and grime into thick vines that crept down his back and across his shoulders. His skin was now so thoroughly bronzed, he might be mistaken for a savage. He'd also allowed a dark beard to take hold of his face that blackened his appearance even further. He wore an indigo-coloured sash around his waist and a string of beads around his neck, the kind that an Indian might wear. She had seen neither until this day. He appeared quite terrifying, it occurred to Tamesine, wild in every way. Yet, when he spoke, she was comforted to hear that his voice maintained its gentle, measured richness.

'I did not,' Bellamy answered. 'They'd been offloaded in Jamaica.'

'What was the haul worth then, would you say?' the child continued.

'Sixty thousand pounds is my quartermaster's estimate.'

'John,' Tamesine interrupted. 'Stop prattling on! Finish your dinner.'

The boy's attention returned to his meal for only a moment. 'Mister Williams is your quartermaster, is he not? May I meet him?'

'I dare say you may,' Bellamy answered. 'He has a son about your age.'

'But you don't take married men in your crew!' John shot back. He remembered every detail about Captain Bellamy and his practices.

'Palgrave is the exception,' Bellamy smiled. 'But he's no longer my quartermaster. He's captain of the *Marianne* now.'

Bellamy was at odds with Tamasine's crisp white parlour. He needed to bathe. His fingernails were black with dirt. In the months he'd been absent, it were as though filth, sweat and salt had formed a thick crust on his body, a putrid camouflage.

'*Whydah*?' John mused. 'Where does that name come from? Do you know?'

'It's African, I believe, or so the captain told me. Its namesake is a trading port in Africa,' Bellamy explained.

'John grew these potatoes himself,' Tamesine broke in, attempting to change the course of the conversation.

'They're fine potatoes,' Bellamy responded seriously. 'You're also the proud owners of some livestock, I see.' He pointed in the direction of Tamesine's tidy garden.

'Just a few chickens, Sam,' John said with a grin. 'Was there much livestock on *Whydah* when you seized her?'

'A goat for milk, and chickens ...' Bellamy began to inventory the animals on board.

Tamesine rolled her eyes, allowing the males their exchange.

'I've never been on board anything larger than Tom's skiff,' John said deliberately after a minute.

Bellamy looked at Tamesine. She raised an eyebrow.

'There's not much to see, John,' Bellamy explained casually. 'I fear you'd be disappointed.'

John nodded thoughtfully and looked down at his plate. However, Tamesine did not relax. She knew her son better than to think the matter done with.

'Perhaps, Sam,' John said then, 'you might take me aboard some time ... soon.'

'Perhaps.'

'Mama?' John asked.

Tamesine looked from her son to Bellamy.

'I'm scheduled for the watch this evening,' Bellamy said. 'John could join me on board. I would welcome the company. He would also have the opportunity to meet Palgrave.'

'Mama?' John said, more desperately.

There was nothing that John wanted more. His face was tense in anticipation and he looked at her pleadingly. Bellamy had been correct. The sea was in his blood. But to allow him to set foot aboard a grand ship like the *Whydah* might seal his fate forever.

'John can help me with my duties,' Bellamy went on with a pointed wink. 'The decks are in dire need of a scrubbing. There's also a dozen or more sails that need mending. He'll be kept busy.'

He raised his eyebrows and smiled.

Tamesine nodded, joining in Bellamy's ruse. 'Might I join you? I've never been aboard either and I'm very handy with a needle and thread ...'

'Mama!' John cut in, horrified. 'Women aboard invite bad luck!'

'Is that so?' she replied, rising to clear the plates from the table. 'If you can cease going on so, I'll consider it.'

John agreed, but was only able to hold his tongue for a minute, before he asked, 'Well?'

Tamesine laughed, amused at her son's clockwork impatience. John's enthusiasm for life and new experiences was contagious, it seemed. 'Just for tonight, and I want you home at daybreak.'

John's fist flew into the air. This was accompanied by a loud 'huzzah!' that made the adults flinch.

'Now off with you,' Tamesine instructed when her son had finished his meal. 'Tom is expecting you at the harbour and *I'm* expecting at least half a dozen fresh jacks for our supper.'

Once John had departed, Tamesine was silent as she wiped surfaces and stacked plates.

'Are you cross?' Bellamy asked.

She shook her head. 'You're right. Once John sees what life on board a ship demands he might be rid of the urge. But I worry for him. My instincts tell me to keep him close, always, but I know that isn't good for a young man.'

Bellamy's arrival at her house had been a surprise, one she was still reeling from. Now Hornigold and the Flying Gang were gone, she was free to depart. There was enough in the locked chest buried beneath where her chickens roosted to afford her a comfortable life in England and John the education he deserved. She had even given up her business at the tavern. Once the idea of leaving was real in Tamesine's mind, the thought of the douchings that needed administering and the wounds that needed tending each evening repulsed her. Agatha, who had been with Tamesine from the beginning, was now responsible for the young ladies.

Bellamy had thrown her carefully laid plans into turmoil. Tamesine realised that she couldn't envisage a life without him, but to fight for him meant abandoning her own dreams.

'You are even more beautiful than when I last saw you, Tamesine,' he remarked. 'The colour of your blouse – wheat, I think? – becomes you so.'

It was the embroidery on the silk blouse that had caught her eye. Pink roses, the size of her smallest fingernail, bordered the neckline and ran the length of the button-holes. Dugan had informed her it had been looted from a Portuguese ship called *Cor-de-rosa*. Tamesine doubted the accuracy of the trader's information but she was taken with the garment nonetheless. Although it had 'pained' him to do so, Dugan sold it to Tamesine for just one Spanish dollar.

She could feel Bellamy's gaze on her now as she moved about the kitchen carrying out the routine duties of her day.

'Why do you blush?' he asked

She shrugged and smiled, her face reddening even further.

'May I bathe?

'Bonefish Pond is about a quarter mile from here.' She pointed north.

'Will you show me?'

'I'll fetch what we need.'

'IT'S GETTING LATE,' Tamesine moved to rise from the bed. 'John will be home soon with fish for supper.'

Bellamy clutched her hand and drew her closer. She looked at his contented face. He was clean and shaven. His hair remained in knots but he was beginning to resemble the Sam Bellamy she had fallen in love with. Earlier, he had stood waist deep in the tepid, still water of Bonefish Pond as Tamesine observed him washing, her eyes on his body, now pitted and grazed like one of the gnarled potatoes in John's garden. She examined the dents, scars and bruises, wondering where he had come by them. But they were of no concern. Each one would eventually disappear, washed away by less trying times.

Once clean he had sat beside her on the grassy bank. 'Less the pirate now,' she had said.

'Pirate,' he echoed, taking her hand, rubbing his thumb across her knuckles. 'Is that the only way you see me? As a pirate?'

Tamesine thought hard on his question. Studying his battle-weary body and unruly appearance, it was difficult for her to see him in any other way. Then she focused on the tender caress of his hands and the well of kindness apparent in his eyes, and she was instantly able to see through his pirate's veneer.

'You're a friend, a sailor ... and a merchant, of sorts, I suppose.' She paused before adding. 'A lover, too.'

'Could you ever see me as a husband?' he asked.

'I ... of course, but I hadn't entertained the notion,' she began. 'Your Puritan lady in New England ...'

'My plans are to join you and John in Windsor,' Bellamy explained. 'If you'll have me.'

He leant towards her and kissed her softly on her cheek. 'I love you, Tamesine.'

She nodded and her throat tightened. 'Of course I'll have you.'

A pintail skimmed across the surface of the water. They both started.

'Palgrave and I will stay out here 'til summer,' he continued as the ripples smoothed. 'By then I should have amassed enough for the three of us to live like kings.'

'Is that what you want?'

'I want to be free.'

'I understand,' she said. 'Then let's go now. We've enough. Why, you said the haul from the *Whydah* alone was worth sixty thousand pounds.'

'Until the summer.' Bellamy replied. 'The *Whydah* is capable of so much more.'

'You've been so lucky,' she went on. 'I worry ...'

'You're concerned I'm like a hummingbird.' She glanced at him, uncertain as to his meaning. 'I'm constantly defying death. You worry that my good fortune won't last.'

She nodded.

'One more hunt,' Bellamy assured her. 'Then you and I and John sail to England.'

His promises hadn't eased her mind but she told him she would wait for him. Now, held in his arms as she was, the sense of foreboding had faded.

'Come here,' he said, sitting up. 'Bring me my coat, if you will.'

Tamesine did as requested. Bellamy searched deep in the pocket before producing a gold ring.

'I want to be married tomorrow...' He paused. 'Will *you* marry me tomorrow?' he corrected, placing the ring on her finger. 'As there's no priest or minister on this godless island, I'll ask Palgrave if he will oblige.'

Tamesine examined the thick band on her finger. It was the brightest gold she had ever seen. So golden it was yellow.

'I found it among the treasures on the *Whydah*,' Bellamy said when she did not answer. 'It is Akan gold, I was to learn. Ade ... do you remember our friend Ade?' She nodded without taking her eyes off the ring. 'Ade mined for this gold and worked it into jewellery ... in Africa ... that was his trade ...'

Tamesine was aware he was rambling in his nervousness and that she should reply, but she wanted to ensure the moment was real and not one of her dreams.

'Tamesine,' he said finally, if a little apprehensively. 'What's your answer?'

She looked at him and smiled. 'Tomorrow morn,' she said in agreement. 'Bring Mister Williams here tomorrow morning and we shall be wed.'

41

NASSAU, NEW PROVIDENCE ISLAND

MARCH 1717

By dawn's first light, John had cleaned the decks, aided Bellamy in the repair of the mizzen stay and polished the ship's bell. The captain had even taught the child the hours of the watch. The boy carried out each task with delight. As he did so, Bellamy's heart swelled as a father's might, and he wondered how Palgrave bore the absence of one family and the loss of another so well. His friend had weathered a hard road.

By the time John rang six bells, Doctor Ferguson had appeared on deck to relieve Bellamy of his duty. Palgrave had also joined them, his own watch on board the *Marianne* completed.

When no job proved too tiresome for John, Bellamy, resigned to the idea that the boy's veins just might run with seawater, had produced a deck of cards. The four sat playing whist by lamplight on the quarterdeck for another two hours. It was at this time, as the sun was making its first appearance above the horizon, that Palgrave stood, alerted to the sound of a billowing sail off the port side.

'Hand me the eyeglass, John,' he called.

The boy promptly produced the object and handed it to the captain.

'It's the *Benjamin*, Sam.' Bellamy rose and moved to his friend's side. Hornigold's ship had just weighed anchor and was heading east towards Rose Island.

'I didn't see it in the harbour when we arrived yesterday,' Palgrave said. 'Did you?'

Bellamy shook his head. The men looked at each other for a moment, uneasy.

'The *Benjamin*?' John said. 'Were you not a member of the crew for some time, Sam?'

'You've a sound memory, John.' Bellamy handed the child the eyeglass.

'Captain Hornigold' Ferguson said. 'I assumed he'd been captured. There's been no word of him since the mutiny.'

Bellamy did not respond. Palgrave grimaced slightly.

'Mutiny?' John repeated, overwhelmed by the possibility.

Bellamy resumed his seat next to Ferguson, but Palgrave remained fixed at the rail, following the ship's course. 'It was months ago. If Hornigold was going to retaliate, he would have done so by now.'

'Do you believe that?' Palgrave retorted.

'Don't be concerned,' Bellamy said as he examined his cards. 'Most likely, Hornigold learnt of our presence in Nassau and decided to weigh anchor immediately. It would be the wisest course, would it not?'

'Hornigold isn't wise,' Palgrave said. 'He's impulsive and reckless ...' His eyes went to the boy who was hanging on their every word.

'Put your worries to rest,' Bellamy said. 'Hornigold has sailed.'

~

JOHN WAS sad to be leaving the *Whydah*. He would happily sail away on her if Bellamy would have him on his crew. But it was quite clear in Bellamy's articles that 'no boy is to be brought aboard.' Bellamy had been reticent when John had questioned him over exactly when he would no longer be considered a boy. His mother wanted him to go to school in England, but John considered that the sea would provide him with a far broader and more exciting education.

'What will you tell Leah of this day when you return?' Bellamy asked as Palgrave and John made their way to Tamesine's home.

John walked between the pair and looked from one to the other as they exchanged words. He wondered who Leah might be.

'Don't concern yourself with the Halletts. You couldn't have foreseen your attachment to Tamesine. Be content with the choice you have made.'

Save the crunch of boots on gravel, there was no noise, not the usual buzz of mosquitoes nor the song of the grasshoppers. Although unaware of his mother's intended marriage to Bellamy, the child sensed an import in the journey and thought it wise to join the men in their silence.

John heard the low, hollow coo of a quail dove and turned in the direction of the noise. The men stopped. John had frequently heard this small bird, but on only a couple of occasions had he seen the striking creature. An iridescent blend of green, bronze, purple and grey, the bird seemed to change colours in flight. He looked hard now into the scrub. As he did so, Bellamy and Palgrave removed their hats and fanned themselves in the still heat while they waited. He wondered what birds he would find in England. Although he was English, he was born in New Providence and had never visited the island of his mother's and father's birth. When he failed to locate the bird, he walked on. His companions followed in his wake.

Mister Williams clutched a book in his hand. John believed it was the Bible, although he could not be certain. He wondered whether Williams was a religious man. Bellamy's friend appeared quite learned and respectful, and spoke with a precision that was new to the child's ear. He and Sam Bellamy were vastly different to the other men in Nassau. Even Tom and Garret, who were kind and humorous, did not hold with graces. His mother scolded them frequently for their careless use of language around him.

As they approached the house, John could see that the door was open. Since quitting her job at the tavern, he and his mother had taken to rising early, eating a small breakfast of bread and milk then tending to the chickens, as well as the patch of vegetables he had planted. His mother said it was a habit they would have to adapt to, as farmers rose before dawn in England. New Providence was a peculiar place, she told him. It was not rooted in history, tradition or custom. People did as their pleasures dictated. But that was no way to live. After doing the chores, they would eat a more substantial meal before beginning on his lessons. His mother had begun trading their eggs and vegetables for milk and meat with two of the landowners who still lived in the hinterland. He and his mother rarely ventured into town any more. John loved the woman his mother had become.

$\sim$

PALGRAVE WAS the first to notice that the open door lay askew, off its hinges. He dropped Leah's Bible into the dirt.

'Wait here.' He ran towards the house.

He heard Bellamy follow. Palgrave turned, snapping sharply. 'Wait here with the boy!'

The colour drained from his friend's face. Palgrave eyed John. Bellamy nodded in consent.

Palgrave entered the kitchen. Chairs, a small bed and a hutch lay overturned. Books were splayed on the ground alongside pots, pans and what, Palgrave assumed, had been the contents of the hutch. Even the cinders from the hearth had been kicked across the floor. Palgrave noticed the foot-prints of a man embedded in the ashes. He looked more closely. Although there were many, they were all the same boot.

He quickly checked Bellamy and the boy. They were positioned where he had left them. Bellamy was crouching by the boy's side, holding his hand. When he turned back he ventured further into the room and opened the shutters. It was then that he noticed the blood on the door that opened into the next room.

Palgrave licked his lips and, feeling like an intruder, removed his hat, as though the small gesture of civility might erase whatever ghastly crime had occurred there the night before. He nudged the door open slightly with his shoulder.

Tamesine sat slumped on the ground. Although her back was against the bed, her head hung to one side. Her face could not be seen through her thick curtain of hair. He was reminded again of his daughter's poppet Molly, and his throat tightened.

He stopped in the doorway for a number of minutes, struck by the smell. It was a familiar odour. Raw iron and earth, the tinny scent of his workshop; the scent of blood. It had pooled around her in large, ruddy puddles.

An image of Leah rushed into his mind. When his wife had been labouring with the twins, the door of their chamber had been left ajar by accident. He had glimpsed her in passing, seeing her splayed animal-like in the straw that had been laid thickly on the ground in preparation for the birth. Her thighs were smeared with blood, dark and coppery. His throat had seized; he had wanted to scream in fear, rage and helplessness. But he had had Joseph and Elizabeth to see to. After he put the children into their bed, he had walked down the stairs to the kitchen, and sat silently sobbing until he was told that Leah had survived.

Palgrave moved closer to Tamesine's body. Her arms, thighs and chest had been cut deeply in many places with a dagger. He bent beside her and raised her head, brushing aside her splendid auburn hair, now mottled with blood.

She had been severely beaten. Her pretty face was nothing but gruesome pulp. Although there was no need for caution, Palgrave lifted her gently and laid her on her bed. He closed her blouse and pulled her skirts down to her ankles.

Since arriving in the Caribbean, Palgrave had been in countless battles. He had slain men and had witnessed numerous indignities. Yet there was nothing he had experienced thus far that equalled the repugnance of the scene before him.

Then he looked about the room. It too had been upended, and the same ashy footprints, made bloody by the evening's events, were visible on the ground.

42

NASSAU, NEW PROVIDENCE ISLAND
MARCH 1717

Bellamy took John back to the *Whydah* while Palgrave ventured into town. He informed Garrett and Tom of the circumstances. The brothers had gripped each other in a gentle embrace and wept quietly together.

When they broke apart they looked at each other for a moment before nodding in agreement.

'Hornigold,' Garrett said. 'That bastard is responsible for this.

Palgrave declined a drink, although Tom poured himself and his brother two large cups of rum.

'I suspected as much,' Palgrave agreed. 'We watched him sail this morning.'

Tom cleared his throat and wiped his eyes before speaking. 'He was in here yesterday. Throwing about his weight, demanding to see Tamesine and wanting to know about your Captain Bellamy's whereabouts. We told him Tamesine had left the island and sailed to England a fortnight ago. I never thought ...

'He has not been in Nassau in months.' Tom blinked

hard and wiped his nose on his apron. 'It seems he acquired another crew along the way.'

'Nothing like the Flying Gang, I grant you,' Garrett put in, before adding 'but a loathsome pack of buggers, nonetheless.'

'Sam should have scuttled his ship when he had the chance,' Tom finished vehemently.

'Teach?' Palgrave inquired, wondering whether his erstwhile friend had played a part in the tragedy.

The brothers shook their head. 'Blackbeard? We haven't laid eyes on that stone-hearted devil since the winter. Word has it he's terrorising the coastline of Virginia and the Carolinas.'

Palgrave nodded thoughtfully.

'Hornigold was searching for something,' Palgrave went on. 'Every room had been overturned.'

'Money,' Garrett responded immediately. 'Hornigold was claiming that Tamesine owed him a hundred dollars.'

'When she gave up the business here,' Tom put in, blowing his nose on a ratty handkerchief, 'she told us all her debts had been settled. Tamesine was always straight.'

'Hornigold hasn't seized a prize worth thruppence since the mutiny,' Garrett went on. 'His reputation and his standing in Nassau took a beating. His new crew was beginning to turn also ...'

'He was desperate,' Tom added, 'and he knew that Tamesine had money. I don't know where she might have stashed it, though.'

Palgrave nodded. He recalled the image of Tamesine's body as he had found her. The beast had gone to Tamesine's house with the intention of killing her. Torturing her to locate the money had been an unexpected pleasure and a message to

Bellamy. Hornigold wasn't to know it would not be Bellamy who found the body. Too cowardly to confront Bellamy directly, Hornigold had meted out revenge on the woman Bellamy loved. It was fortunate John had spent the night on the *Whydah*.

'Do you know his course?' Palgrave asked.

Garrett and Tom shrugged. 'Cuba is his most likely destination. There've been rumours of another Spanish treasure fleet.'

Before he departed, the pair assured Palgrave they would see to Tamesine and the house immediately.

Bellamy stared curiously at the child asleep in his cabin. He rocked the hammock gently. Before he had eventually fallen asleep, John had asked many questions about his mother and her whereabouts. But surely she must have died of something, some kind of illness, he had queried seriously. God wouldn't just take her, he argued. Never being schooled in religion, he hadn't accepted Palgrave's explanation that God sometimes unexpectedly took the wisest and kindest of his flock. Bellamy could offer him nothing more satisfactory. God and heaven were a ready and comforting lie.

While the child sought solace through answers, Bellamy had willed him to cease, seeking his own solace in the silence of his despair and the fury that was swelling inside him like thunder. Bellamy was intent on seeking out the brute Hornigold and killing him. It was an odd sensation to harbour such hate towards another man, it occurred to him. It was compelling, intoxicating, and had overtaken him completely – the relentless burn of vengeance. No doubt it was the identical feeling that had driven Hornigold to murder Tamesine. *Am I no better than that tyrant?* thought Bellamy. He did not care to search for an answer.

Then, just as John's eyes were almost closed, he had murmured, 'Will you take me with you, Sam?'

Bellamy sank lower in his chair and considered his path. They would leave Nassau immediately. He and Palgrave would sell a portion of their cargo to Dugan for supplies. It was likely Dugan would not have enough ready cash to purchase all the treasure aboard the *Whydah*. Palgrave would take John with him on the *Marianne* and start towards New England. They would rendezvous in Virginia and fence the remaining plunder, or later in Boston. Meanwhile, Bellamy would hunt Hornigold. He wouldn't be difficult to locate. Hornigold was a tornado.

Once he was done with him, Bellamy would follow the *Marianne*'s course to Virginia and sail north along the coastline towards Boston. Here the crew would be paid and farewelled. Bellamy cared not what became of the *Whydah* or the *Marianne*; they could be scuttled or burned for all he cared. He and John would travel to Connecticut or Maine where John would begin school. Bellamy would finally purchase his farm.

'LET HORNIGOLD BE,' Palgrave counselled when he heard of Bellamy's plan. 'We should both return to the colonies immediately.'

The pair stood on the deck of the *Whydah*. John remained asleep in the captain's cabin.

'Did Garrett and Tom know his heading?' Bellamy asked, ignoring Palgrave's protest.

Palgrave shook his head.

'What good can come of chasing Hornigold?' Palgrave pressed. 'Listen to reason, Sam!'

When Bellamy didn't concede, Palgrave went on. 'I've never believed in signs.' Bellamy looked at him inquiringly. Palgrave knew it wasn't a rational argument but he was beginning to finally recognise what Leah always had. 'Portents of good and evil. This is one, I'm certain. Tamesine ... your guardianship of John. Take stock before you act.'

'Hornigold will never be brought to justice for the crime he's committed. Even if one day he *is* captured by the authorities, he will be hung for piracy. Nothing more than that,' Bellamy said. 'I want him to know why he's dying.'

'It's a rash decision,' Palgrave went on. 'He'll come to justice sooner than you know, Tom and Garrett have been led to believe that his latest crew are already turning on him. He'll meet his end one way or the other.'

Palgrave considered his argument for a moment before he continued. The ship rolled gently over the waves. It was unusually choppy, Palgrave thought absently. A gale raged somewhere out there, he mused, turning his face towards the horizon for a moment.

'Be practical, Sam,' Palgrave tried to reason. 'The boy needs a family. He needs a mother. Come with me to Eastham.'

'Maria?' Bellamy queried.

Palgrave turned. 'My sister has a kind and forgiving spirit. Maria could give John all the love and care he requires.'

Bellamy leant on the railing as he considered Palgrave's advice.

Maria. Poor Maria. He had barely thought of her in recent months.

Eventually he shook his head.

'I'm responsible, don't you see? The mutiny, my disregard of a reprisal ... I should have anticipated his actions. I should have gone to Tamesine immediately when we spotted his ship. Perhaps *they* were the signs I was blind to.

'I must do this, Palgrave,' he continued. 'Will you take John to Virginia?' Bellamy asked, laying his hand on his friend's shoulder.

Palgrave nodded. 'Hornigold is heading for Cuba.'

The reluctant admission did nothing to dispel the feeling of patent disquiet manifesting so uncomfortably in his stomach.

43

WELLFLEET, MASSACHUSETTS
APRIL 1717

Leah, Maria and Abby stood in front of a house by the harbour in Wellfleet, their petticoats billowing around their legs in the strong breeze. Positioned so that the front faced the bay, the house became known to Leah through Arthur's 'friend', Charles. Until recently the white clapboard residence had belonged to Martha Clifford, Charles's mother. Being her only child, he alone inherited the dwelling but, as a lawyer in Boston, had no need for it. Arthur suggested it for Leah. Charles Clifford was ready to sell the home, its contents and the attached six acres for fifty pounds.

The women walked the perimeter of the property. To the rear lay a compact barn that would be ample to house the few animals that Leah required – two or three pigs that would soon multiply into more, a cow for milk and a horse to pull the plough. Leah couldn't envisage a need for a cart or gig. Wellfleet contained everything they needed. Charles had informed her that the land hadn't been worked since his father had passed seven years ago, but it was a fine holding nonetheless. He had returned to his practice in Boston and was now awaiting Leah's decision.

'Arthur told me of your unusual situation, Goody Hallett,' he had said after she inspected the house. Leah judged him to be of a similar age to her. She thought he had an extremely genial manner for a lawyer. He wore a dark hat and suit that was plain but finely tailored. 'It's the law of Massachusetts that a woman can neither buy nor sell property.'

'I am aware,' Leah stated mildly, ushering her children outside. 'My husband has given me his proxy to act on his behalf.'

Leah produced a letter from her pocket that she had written herself. She had found the exertion of forging Palgrave's exacting hand consoling. Channelling his spirit through a task she had watched him perform a thousand times before – signing a document, writing a correspondence – had stirred her profoundly. The longer he was absent, the more she seemed to crave him. Physically, the need for him was ever-present, like a thirst impossible to quench. On occasion, it felt as though a part of her had been ripped away.

Charles scrutinised the paper closely, nodding, engaging convincingly in the deception.

'I can offer you slightly more than the property is worth if this causes you any inconvenience, Mister Clifford.'

'That won't be necessary. Fifty pounds is ample,' he said, lifting his eyes to her, warm and dark. 'In Arthur's opinion, you're irreproachable. That's enough for me. If the property meets with your approval I will be happy to carry out the transaction with you ... on your husband's behalf, of course.'

It seemed to be the first stroke of good fortune she had come by since Palgrave's departure.

Now, as she examined the property again, she wondered about the relationship between Arthur and Charles. They had taken gambles of their own, staking their freedom to be together.

'What do you think?' Leah asked Abby and her sister.

'It's a handsome house, Leah,' Abby observed.

'I appreciate the position,' Maria added, gesturing towards the ocean.

Leah nodded, wondering when ... if her sister would ever be restored.

Since they had arrived in Wellfleet three weeks ago, Maria had taken to walking along the shorefront or cliffs daily, anticipating Samuel Bellamy's return. She would be gone for hours and refused to tolerate an escort. At her wit's end with concern, Leah began sending Joseph and Elizabeth to follow their aunt. One night, she had followed Maria herself when she heard her footsteps on the stairs. Leah had found her sister on the beach during a waxing moon. A red ribbon was tied about her hair and she was on her knees as if in prayer. *Know I call to you. Think of me. Think of me. So mote it be.* Leah heard her incant the words a hundred times over until the sun's first rays crept over the horizon. Filled with anxiety, Leah had run away from the scene.

However, in a way Leah envied her sister's blind, inscrutable hope. It was when Palgrave's letters had ceased that Leah lost faith in his return.

They pulled open the heavy door leading into the barn and Leah examined the plough and other tools she found there. *It will be a beginning*, she thought. Joseph, Abby, Maria and herself would have to work fast to ready the ground, but they had time to plant enough seed to see them through the winter. It would be a hard toil. Leah moved to the barn door.

Looking outside, she saw that there was an apple tree, and a lemon tree too.

'There's a well,' Abby said as she approached, 'on the other side of the house.'

Leah gazed towards the sea for a moment. It did not please her that she would have to use Palgrave's name in the transaction, but there was no other way.

She nodded to Abby. 'I will purchase this property then,' Leah stated. 'I will write to Mister Clifford immediately.'

44

NORFOLK, VIRGINIA
APRIL 1717

'How long do you intend to wait for Bellamy?' Ferguson asked on entering the captain's cabin.

'Until he arrives,' Palgrave said, glancing briefly at the surgeon. Palgrave was studying charts of the Atlantic coastline. He had no control over the weather's fickle temperament in this part of the world, but he aimed to ensure he was familiar with every inch of the perilous seaboard.

'We've been here three days,' Ferguson went on.

'And we will wait three days longer and three days after that if needs be,' Palgrave remarked, taking his eyes from the charts. 'What's your hurry?'

Ferguson raised his eyebrows.

'The crew want their share,' the doctor explained. 'They're aware you've fenced everything.'

'Not everything. They'll get paid when we reach Massachusetts,' Palgrave advised. 'Otherwise, I'll not have a crew to get us there. If they doubt my integrity they are free to leave the *Marianne* and join another captain.'

Ferguson walked further into the cabin and took a seat opposite Palgrave at the table.

'The crew also worry that it's Bellamy's fixation with Hornigold that'll lead to their undoing. He's their captain as well as yours. Revenge is a wasted effort.'

'Finding Hornigold is something he must do,' Palgrave stated, unrolling another chart. 'We wait.'

'What if it's Hornigold who walks away from their confrontation?' Ferguson then asked gravely.

Palgrave grinned, instantly recalling the summer morning when Bellamy fought Judah Doane in a quarter-staff bout. Bellamy's confidence and skill had astounded Palgrave. It seemed to him that in that moment, Bellamy was the best of all men blended into one – assertive, courageous, ambitious, enterprising. He had displayed all the qualities Palgrave believed that he lacked himself. He could not imagine any man besting Sam Bellamy, especially not the drunkard Benjamin Hornigold.

'I guarantee you, Doctor,' Palgrave responded, 'that will not be the outcome of their meeting.'

'You and Bellamy are strange companions,' Ferguson observed. 'It's quite plain that you rather ... for want of a better word, *idolise* one another.'

The surgeon settled into his chair and poured a glass of madeira for them both.

Palgrave supposed he did revere Bellamy, in the same way he had once revered Leah. But he'd never considered his friend's feelings towards himself. *What qualities could I possess for Bellamy to admire?* Palgrave pondered.

'I suppose, and these are merely my observations, that you are Bellamy's compass,' Ferguson remarked thought-fully as he sipped his wine.

'Yes, you're the man Bellamy hopes to be one day,' the doctor concluded, nodding, pleased with his supposition.

Palgrave stared at the charts, taking in the doctor's

thoughts. Bellamy yearned for freedom, a family and an acreage – everything Palgrave had once enjoyed. He shook his head in wonder, amazed by Ferguson's insight as well as his own blindness. Instantly, a desire that had been absent for a very long period overcame him. He smiled, as if being acquainted with a cherished, long-lost friend.

'How did you two come to meet?' the doctor then asked.

Palgrave laughed. 'It was in another lifetime, Doctor. I can barely recall.'

'When I arrived in Cuba, Hornigold had already sailed,' Bellamy informed Palgrave as he ate. 'I learnt from a tavern owner he was heading to Chesapeake Bay, hoping to reunite with Teach.' He spoke feverishly, with the energy of the retribution that drove him forward. Without it, he would surely collapse from exhaustion.

Palgrave stared at John for a moment. The boy was eating heartily of his meal. Then he looked back to Bellamy.

'Interesting,' Palgrave remarked. 'Teach has become the most profitable captain in the Atlantic. It's no wonder Hornigold hopes to join with him again.'

'The landlord told me Teach uses the seclusion on the eastern shore to prepare his ship,' Bellamy went on.

'Can your landlord be believed?'

'I paid him for his trouble,' Bellamy explained.

'The Chesapeake is fraught with narrow entrances and uncharted sandbars,' Palgrave said. 'Hornigold could have concealed himself anywhere along its two hundred miles. It would be suicide to ...'

Bellamy's eyes darted to John. The boy looked at both

men, his eyes wide. Bellamy then smiled and pushed away his plate. 'We should discuss these matters on deck.'

~

WHEN THE MEN departed the cabin, John lay down his fork and removed a brass button from the pocket of his vest. His mother had given it to him on the evening he left for the watch with Bellamy. It was a 'Lieutenant's button', she told him. It would 'keep him safe from harm.' Studying the embossed crown on its surface, sparking gold in the lamp-light, he regretted having taken it from her. If he hadn't perhaps it would be she who was safe now.

John had refused to leave Nassau with Mister Williams, seeking the comfort of the man his mother loved, the man who was to become his father. Bellamy had not discussed the *Whydah*'s heading, but the boy assumed Sam was on the trail of the man who had killed his mother. He knew that God had not 'taken' her; he had heard enough to realise the truth. Now the child was concerned for his guardian. John could not recall Sam resting since his mother's death.

Each evening as John struggled to find sleep, Sam would offer him a magical account of their life together once they reached the colonies. The house where they would live, the farm they would own, even the school he was to attend, were painted in vivid, alluring colours. Sam's deep, soothing tones seemed to travel directly from the ocean's depths. They flowed over him, dulling his pain and inducing his eyes to close. It was then that the brilliant landscape Sam had conceived of would come to life in his mind. But, as the days had worn on, John had become worried that the vision that sustained him was no longer Sam's dream. If it were, he told himself, surely they would be sailing north. If their future was a lie created to distract, then what remained?

He trusted Sam and loved him, but he wanted his mother so desperately that, at times, he couldn't breathe. Standing at the bow as the ship cut through the water, he would often contemplate joining her. Diving into the heaving white spray of the bow wave would be simple. God was welcome to him.

Pushing aside the remains of his supper, John folded his arms and rested his head, the button pressed firmly in his fist. He yawned then let the tears come.

PALGRAVE STARED AT THE HORIZON, considering Bellamy's proposal. The wind had picked up since the afternoon. White peaks sharpened the water's surface. Noticing something in the distance, he climbed to the quarterdeck for a closer inspection through the eyeglass.

'There's a storm out there, a wily gale,' he informed Bellamy. 'We don't have a day. We must weigh anchor tonight.'

'I will hunt Hornigold alone. Take one of the dugouts ...' Bellamy joined his friend on the quarterdeck.

'It's too dangerous. If we depart now we can harness this southerly. We can outrun the storm and it will have us in New England in a week.'

Since Tamesine's murder and his conversation with Ferguson, Palgrave's urgency to return to Leah had become overpowering. To risk being isolated in Norfolk while they waited for the storm to pass was unthinkable. What's more, there was no certainty Hornigold was holed up with Teach in the bay. And if he were, Bellamy would be forced to contend with the likes of Blackbeard as well.

Searching his mind for a way to make Bellamy see reason, he recalled the surgeon's words.

'You told me once, Sam, that we had to be each other's guide, one another's compass, if you like,' he said calmly, endeavouring to contain his anxiety. 'Your obsession to capture Hornigold is madness. You say you desire freedom, but it's your desire for revenge that has enslaved you. Relent. Find peace with John ... and perchance Maria.'

Bellamy thought for a moment. Palgrave examined his tangled mess of hair, his dusky skin and the fierce look in his eyes.

'One day is all I need. If I don't capture Hornigold in one day, I'll follow immediately.'

Palgrave looked at the man who had become his greatest friend, his most trusted companion, confidante and ally during their time at sea. He nodded then held out his hand, aware of the banality of the gesture.

Bellamy clutched it then drew Palgrave to him. The men, gripped for some time in an embrace that expressed many emotions, eventually broke apart.

'Set sail, my friend, I will see you in New England in a fortnight,' Bellamy remarked, leaving Palgrave on the quarterdeck.

45

EASTHAM, MASSACHUSETTS

APRIL 1717

Silas was perspiring when he reached the tree. He had not intended to beat such an urgent path, but once he had collected what was needed he could see no point in delaying any further.

He stood at the base of the willow and looked up into the familiar canopy. He loosened his cravat then removed his hat and robe, placing them on the ground before making his way through the labyrinth of branches that he had become intimate with over the years. Spring's first gold-green leaves brushed against his face. They were so smooth and cold in their freshness that they felt wet against his cheeks. Cushioned in the boughs, he closed his eyes and sighed deeply. That morning, he had performed the rites of his father's funeral with detachment. The words had sprung from his mouth effortlessly. It was as if he had unknowingly been preparing for the ceremony for years.

When he had returned to Eastham following news of his father's death, he had stood by his house. It had been reduced to ashes. Nothing could be salvaged. There was nothing he wanted to salvage. Francis Jeffries and some others were crying out for the Indian to be brought to justice, contemplating her most likely escape route from the town, and describing her trial and subsequent hanging. Silas had assured them, with little effort, that Abby was not responsible. His father was careless with candles and his pipe. That was that. Abby's body was probably among the ruins, he told them, if they cared to seek it out as proof. The men had shaken their heads shamefully. None of them cared for his father. They were concerned only with the comforts and power their association with him had brought. Now that Silas was being mooted as his father's successor in Eastham, he could see them striving to win his favour.

Silas believed not a word he told the townsfolk. His father was not careless. Although he could not imagine Abby committing murder, perhaps she had. He had seen his father strike her on occasion. More likely, it was Leah Williams's hand that had set his father's bed alight. But it mattered not. No-one but himself should be punished.

It was a shock to the small community when the Reverend had released Maria so soon after the birth of her child. Many believed she had bewitched him, yet no-one was courageous enough to question his decision. All were disappointed that they would not see Maria trialled and hanged for her crimes.

Now Maria Hallett had *disappeared*, they told Silas, along with her sister. He winced. Joseph Hallett remained on his farm struggling to rebuild his existence. When Jeffries and his wife had sneered at Maria and called her a witch, he told them to leave the family be.

He thought it was time they had some peace.

When Silas received Leah Williams's letter telling him of the birth of his dead son, he had read the correspondence many times. She had untangled every sordid knot in his dealings with Maria. Her words were emotionless. When he examined his sins as she had laid them out so meticulously on the page, Silas struggled to gauge his crimes. He could not believe it was he who had transgressed so heinously. Through her crisp, dispassionate writing, Leah Williams had sketched a terrifyingly accurate portrait. The three brief paragraphs offered Silas an honest depiction of himself for the very first time.

Leah had closed with just two lines:

'I will never speak of this. No-one would believe it. But believe me when I write that I will kill you if you come near Maria again.'

Silas had read the letter many times over in the days leading up to his father's death. Then he had burnt it. The purpose of the correspondence had been achieved.

Now he took the coil of rope he had taken from his father's stable and tied one end tightly around the branch of the tree on which he perched. Tying the other end around his neck in a crudely fashioned noose, he glanced around him at his surrounds. Nothing had altered. The willow, Boat Meadow River, the scent of the sea and dogwoods carried by the breeze – it was as though he were a boy once more. He pictured his Maria sitting beside him.

Then, with the briefest of smiles, he slid from the branch.

46

NORFOLK, VIRGINIA

APRIL 1717

For two hours Bellamy had sat on deck, contemplating the best course to secure the capture of Hornigold. He watched as the *Marianne* prepared to finally set sail. Palgrave waved, then turned and did not look back. Bellamy tracked the ship's hasty course out of the harbour towards the open sea. By the time the ship reached the opening to the bay, a light rain had begun falling and all sails on the *Marianne* had been loosed to capture the brisk southerly. Bellamy guessed the ship's speed to be eight knots. At that rate, Palgrave would be in Eastham before the week was out.

Once the ship was out of sight, Bellamy went below decks. He found John asleep at the table where he and Palgrave had left him. As he observed the boy, his mind turned to his plan. He would take five men in a dugout and venture further into the bay, into the inlets and narrows. He was certain that it would be there he would find Hornigold, concealed in the swamps. As he gathered what was needed, John woke.

'Don't go, Sam,' he murmured. His eyes were still closed.

'Shhh,' Bellamy whispered, rubbing the child's hair. 'I'll be back tomorrow by sunset. Mister Julian will see to you while I'm gone.'

The captain continued to move around the cabin. The boy stood and approached Bellamy. He stared at him earnestly and gripped his forearms, forcing him to listen.

'Mister Williams was right. We should weigh anchor immediately!' the boy asserted. 'Hornigold will run you through to save the inconvenience of looking at you.'

Bellamy looked fondly at his charge.

It was Tamesine's turn of phrase he had just uttered. He sank into a chair, sensing his resolve wearing thin, and pulled the boy onto his lap. For the first time, he recognised Tamesine in her son. His hair had grown longer in the weeks they'd been on Hornigold's trail. It now framed his features with the same velvety curl. Because of it, his thin face appeared fuller, rounder, like his mother's. It wouldn't be long before he would begin tying his hair with a ribbon at the base of his neck. The boy had already taken to wearing a tricorn hat discovered in the hold of the *Whydah*. While John's resemblance to his mother was growing, under his care, the child was drifting steadily away from her vision for him. *How would Tamesine consider this turn of events?* thought Bellamy.

'What would you have me do?' Bellamy asked quietly.

'Set sail for Massachusetts straight away,' he responded matter-of-factly. 'Buy our farm. I will begin school.'

Bellamy made no reply. He realised he had lost sight of Tamesine's dream.

'My mother is dead, Sam,' John explained gravely, taking Bellamy's rough and blackened hand in his and looking into his tired eyes. 'She'll never return.'

John paused for a minute, thinking. His brow furrowed as he attempted to comprehend matters of life, death and love – matters far beyond his realm of understanding. He struggled to find the right words to make Sam understand.

Finally, he uttered the only thing he knew for certain. 'I know she loved us both.'

Bellamy nodded. 'Aye, that she did.'

Bellamy's arms wrapped around the youth's skinny frame and John's knees went to his chest. He knew not whether John was too old for this brand of comfort, but it was the kind of consolation Bellamy himself needed at that moment.

'We'll set sail for Massachusetts in the morning, once the storm has passed,' Bellamy murmured. He felt John's body slacken in his arms, the relief washing over both of them.

BY SUNRISE there was no sign of the gale that had battered the *Whydah* during the night. The ship had rolled violently, making it impossible for John to sleep. Despite Bellamy's assurances that the *Whydah* was secured by four half-ton anchors in a deep, safe harbour, John was terrified the boat would be dashed on the rocks. Bellamy had laughed, informing the boy that he had a vivid imagination just like his mother. John had finally fallen asleep a little after midnight. Bellamy, however, remained alert, listening to the creak of the masts. If one were to snap, their hopes of weighing anchor the following morning would be scuttled.

When he judged that the storm had passed, Bellamy advised the crew of his plans. The hunt was over. There would be no more prizes. The *Whydah* was setting sail for Massachusetts directly. Those who wished to remain in Virginia would be paid handsomely for their service. Those who wished to continue north aboard the *Whydah* would be paid once they had reached their destination. Bellamy lost only twelve of his crew of one hundred and sixty men.

At dawn, Bellamy set about inspecting the hull for fractures and leaks. Then he climbed on deck and put the crew to work examining the masts for cracks and the sails for any tears they might have endured. By ten o'clock, Bellamy was satisfied the *Whydah* was fit to make sail.

THE *WHYDAH* RODE a gentle warm front along the coastline over the next week. The relaxed pace did not bother the captain. A sanguine atmosphere was apparent on board. Many of the crew had believed they'd earned more than enough from capturing the *Whydah* and had begun to harbour thoughts of concluding their careers at sea. In the nine days it took the ship to reach Block Island, the boatswain, Mister Burke, had not issued a single punishment. The crew was content, as was Bellamy. Dreams of his own began to enter his thoughts as he slept and he found himself anticipating the future at last.

John spent the days with Bellamy on the quarterdeck. The boy proved a gifted sailor. Bellamy taught him to read charts, measure the depth of the ocean and calculate the speed of the ship using a chip log. John learnt these skills with very little effort, becoming a valued member of the crew.

Such was the cheerfulness of all those on board during the *Whydah*'s journey north that Jack Driver recommenced his evening performances. These off-the-cuff recitals had not taken place since the *Whydah* had first been seized. John took great delight in the actor's shows, which were usually comic or musical. The captain would not tolerate the re-enactment of a tragic tale.

After taking on fresh water at Block Island, the *Whydah* began the final leg of her journey. Within a day they had reached Nantucket Sound and, by the following evening, they were approaching Cape Cod's Atlantic coast.

BELLAMY STARED hard at Eastham's cliffs and wondered if Palgrave had arrived. He thought about the last time he had viewed that same ridge. It was as he was sailing south towards Florida. Last summer seemed a lifetime ago.

So did Maria. He wondered if she might still be waiting for him.

It was suppertime before he issued new orders to the ship's pilot, Mister Julian. The *Whydah* was to stay the course and continue to Boston.

THEY WERE SETTLING in below deck after one of Mister Driver's performances when Bellamy noticed John shiver. He then heard a powerful lap of water against the ship's hull. There was no watch that evening; Bellamy rose, glancing through the porthole at his left.

A dense fog had rolled in from the north.

The dreadful crack of thunder that ensued made John quake. Leaving his plate and cup, Bellamy hastened to the quarterdeck. John trailed behind. A flash of lightning diverted his gaze for an instant.

The front the *Whydah* had harnessed from the Caribbean was luring a glacial arctic wind into its warm embrace.

'All hands on deck,' Bellamy cried immediately, assessing the magnitude of the storm. 'Raise sail!'

If the captain did not act immediately, the *Whydah* would be trapped in the union of two of nature's most opposing and unrelenting forces and hurled against the cliffs.

John alighted the steps to the quarterdeck immediately.

'Get below!' Bellamy ordered. 'We must skirt the storm.'

Motionless, the child whimpered when lightning struck the bowsprit.

'Now!' Bellamy yelled to the child before scooping John into his arms and rushing below to deposit him promptly into the captain's cabin.

'Stay here,' Bellamy said, striving for a level tone. 'I'll be back before long.'

By the time Bellamy appeared again on deck, a huge swell was pounding the hull and water was washing over the deck. Mountainous waves, almost forty feet high, were thrusting them towards the breakers. The *Whydah* rose skyward on a towering crest then crashed into a yawning chasm. Bellamy screamed orders from the quarterdeck, but it was difficult for the crew to hear above the din of the squall. John Julian, his pilot, stood with the helmsman battling against the wind as they attempted to turn the obstinate wheel and bring the ship's bow face-to-face with the wind.

Caught in the grips of the deadly nor-'easter, Bellamy quickly realised it was impossible to sail away from the coast or stay their course. Their only hope lay in dropping all of the ship's anchors.

Bellamy gave the order as another wave, almost half the height of the mainmast, crashed against the *Whydah*'s hull, sweeping four men over the side and into the bitter sea. A moment later, the foremast snapped like a twig. Jack Driver screamed out in agony, crushed under the fallen rigging. Bellamy ran to his aid but was washed to the port side by a further gush of water.

Still being propelled inexorably towards the crashing surf of the shoreline, the *Whydah*'s timbers groaned in exhaustion. As lightning flashed around him, Bellamy caught momentary glimpses of the cliffs of Eastham one hundred feet above him and the waves crashing into its rocky face.

'Drop anchor!' Bellamy yelled into the mayhem.

All four windlasses unwound at a manic rate. When the final windlass ceased its movement there was a moment's silence, a fleeting moment of respite on board as the *Whydah* stopped its relentless drift towards the foamy chaos of the beach. The men waited for the lines to go taut, for the anchors to take hold.

A minute passed.

They felt the anchors dragging.

Bellamy gave the command immediately.

'Cut the anchor cables!' Bellamy cried over the din of the thrashing wind, rain and thunder. 'Bring her all the way back around. Bring her face first into the beach.'

Their final chance at survival, the captain realised, was to bring *Whydah* aground on the beach, bow first. Then the strongest of swimmers might have a chance of being washed to safety before a wave dashed them against the rocks or the cold took them.

Julian did as Bellamy ordered but the ship did not turn. Bellamy rushed to his side and began to heave on the mighty wheel. It would not budge. The rudder had been damaged. Instead, the force of the sea sent the *Whydah* spinning backwards. Thirty foot waves pushed her towards the cliffs.

The force of the jolt with which the *Whydah* ran aground sent rigging crashing to the deck. Men were hurled overboard. The mainmast toppled into the sea like a felled tree. The cannons, broken free of their tackle, swept the length of the deck, pulverising any man in their path. With nothing left to do, Bellamy rushed below to the captain's cabin.

John trembled beneath the table. Lifting him into his arms, Bellamy hugged him tightly. He could feel the boy's tiny heart beating rapidly through his blouse, like a frightened rabbit. Bellamy hurried out of the cabin and up the ladder to the deck. Desperate to save themselves, seamen leapt overboard, instantly lost in the spume once they hit the water.

'Do you trust me?' Bellamy cried into John's ear.

Tears filled the boy's eyes but his jaw was tense. He nodded seriously.

'Hold tight,' Bellamy directed.

John locked his legs around Bellamy's waist and his arms around his neck.

As the timbers of the hull began to break apart, Bellamy hauled them both onto the railing. He looked John in the eye and smiled.

Deaf to the bedlam, only man and boy existed in that moment.

'Take a deep breath and close your eyes,' Bellamy said softly. 'Picture your mother.'

John shut his eyes tight. 'Do you see her?' Bellamy asked.

He nodded.

'So do I,' Bellamy said.

Hugging John to him, Bellamy leapt from the *Whydah* and plunged into the ocean.

47

WELLFLEET, MASSACHUSETTS

APRIL 1717

Leah raised her face into the sunlight and closed her eyes. It was difficult to believe that a storm so fierce to have blown shingles from the roof had battered the coastline only the night before. The time was not yet seven o'clock, but the sun already had a bite.

Rain had leaked through the ceiling and into the room Leah shared with Elizabeth and Abby. Her daughter was now tending to the mess, cleaning the floor and washing the bedclothes. *It will take her hours*, Leah thought, *with little Caleb in tow to help.* Leah had sent Sarah and Joshua to Goody Earl's with eggs to be traded for milk. As yet, Leah had not come by a cow that was to her liking.

Leah breathed in deeply before opening her eyes to survey the scene. She would see to the roof once she had tended to their small collection of crops. There was a ladder in the barn.

'The seedlings took a lashing,' Abby remarked, inspecting the bedraggled and damaged smatterings of green at her feet.

'It's a dire shame,' Maria said in consternation, shaking her head. 'So much work wasted ...'

'We'll save what we can then plant more,' Leah responded unemotionally. 'I have others in the barn.'

The women then looked at each other and, with a simultaneous sigh, sank into the dirt on their knees. Laughing quietly, they began on the task.

'Joseph,' Leah said, raising her head for an instant. 'Go see to the seedlings in the barn. Bring us those you think are strong enough.'

The young man left them. Leah looked after him. *He has grown taller still*, she thought. Her heart tightened. He was a constant reminder of his father.

The three women worked in silence for some time.

'I watched the storm from the window for a time,' remarked Maria as they toiled. 'Then I went out onto the beach,' she added, almost as an afterthought.

'Maria!' Leah said, straightening. 'You might've been killed!'

'It was past midnight,' Maria went on casually, unconcerned. 'The wind had all but passed.'

Leah frowned before returning to her task.

'While I was there, I called for Samuel's protection,' Maria continued. Leah and Abby glanced at each other. 'He was out there. I saw him.'

Leah offered her sister a meagre smile, hoping one day her mind would be righted.

When she was happy with the progress they were making, Leah rose and wiped her forehead with the back of her hand.

'I'll fetch water,' she informed the women.

As she made her way to the well, she heard the panicked

cries of her twins as they came towards her along the beach. Milk splashed against the sides of the pail that hung between them.

Leah ran to them.

'A man is coming, Mama,' Sarah said breathlessly. 'A horrid-looking man with a beard so long ...' Her daughter signalled to her knees.

'It's the Devil to be sure,' Joshua added, eyes wide. 'And he has a horse. A white horse.'

Leah relieved them of the pail that was all but empty then looked down the beach in the direction of the town. About a hundred yards away there was a figure walking beside a horse. Although not to his knees, his beard was indeed long. As he was walking into the sun, his head hung low and his hat was pulled over his brow.

'Hush, child! It's not the Devil,' Leah said amused, squinting into the distance. 'More likely just a beggar hoping for a shilling. But he will only find disappointment here. I've not a penny for him.'

'But he was dressed in fancy clothes,' Joshua argued. 'A buccaneer's coat of emerald green and a black hat with a shiny gold buckle.'

'And his horse was laden with heavy saddlebags. Two on each side,' Sarah added.

'Then perhaps he is a bagman ...' Leah began to explain.

'And he wanted to talk to us, Mama,' Sarah continued. 'He gestured us to him on our way out of the town.'

Leah frowned. 'Did he speak?'

The twins shook their heads adamantly.

Leah looked towards the stranger once more. When he was about fifty yards away, he stopped and removed his hat, taking in his surrounds. Then he replaced it carefully on his head and continued on his way. Looking into the sun, he could not see the woman and children standing on the beach before him.

But in the brief moment his hat was by his side Leah had seen the man clearly.

Standing as if frozen, Leah felt her heart begin to pound. She absently sought out her wedding band before picturing it on the shelf above the hearth.

She took a few steps towards him along the sand.

Certain now, Leah swallowed, sensing the hardness that had grown inside her soften, the obstinate knot that had tied around her heart begin to loosen. Tears formed behind her eyes. She wiped them hastily away with her apron.

'It's your father, children,' she stated. Sarah and Joshua moved to her side.

She waited, feet rooted in the sand, sweat trickling down between her breasts.

Within a minute, Palgrave was before them. He removed his hat to reveal a crimson scarf tied about his head. It was designed to keep his errant locks in check. His sandy hair appeared much lighter than Leah remembered and his pale skin was sun-kissed.

'My children do not recognise me,' he remarked with a grin.

'Your appearance is much altered,' Leah responded flatly, looking into his eyes. 'You've been gone a long time. Young children forget so quickly.'

Palgrave nodded. 'And you?'

Leah didn't answer. She looked away towards the ocean, unsure, needing a moment's respite.

'You've dirt on your cheek.' He reached out to touch her face. Leah took a step back, but returned her gaze to him.

'How did you find us?' she asked.

'I found our house deserted. I went to your father. He told me you had gone to Wellfleet with Maria and the children. That was all he said.'

They are Palgrave's eyes, thought Leah. *It is his dignified voice.*

A wave washed up the beach towards them, the water almost reaching their feet. As one, the group took a step sideways. Palgrave stroked his horse's neck gently then looked up at the house.

'I haven't forgotten,' said Leah quietly.

Palgrave instantly refocused his attention onto his wife. Leah flicked her eyes to the ocean again then looked back to her husband.

Yet she did not step closer.

'Those shutters are in need of repair', she said, gesturing to the house. 'The storm last night was brutal.'

'I will see to them for you ...' he said, still uncertain.

Before he could say more a cry came from the barn.

'Papa!' Joseph ran to the beach and launched himself into Palgrave's arms. Abby and Maria trailed the boy at a more sedate pace, allowing the family their reunion.

Palgrave peppered his son's face with kisses and laughed. Leah could see both were weeping. Then Sarah and Joshua moved forwards and approached their father cautiously. Palgrave knelt in front of them and they fell into his arms.

'You look like a pirate, Papa,' Joshua whispered into his father's ear.

'Joshua thought you were the Devil,' Sarah broke in.

Palgrave laughed and kissed them all. When he rose he held a twin in each arm.

'Mister Williams,' Abby said calmly. 'I'm so happy you've returned safely.'

'Thank you,' Palgrave replied. Leah could see her husband was confused by the Indian's presence and his family's move to Wellfleet. He noticed Maria and nodded.

Maria offered her brother-in-law a brief curtsey before hastening to the water's edge.

'Mister Bellamy?' Leah inquired.

'He follows in a few days, at most,' Palgrave replied.

Leah nodded.

'Tell Elizabeth and Caleb their father is home,' she instructed the twins. Palgrave lowered the boy and girl to the ground and they scurried towards the house.

'Come, Joseph,' Abby said. 'We should see to a meal. Your father will be hungry.'

'This horse is hungry too, Joseph,' Palgrave put in. 'Will you see to him for me?'

The boy smiled, eagerly taking the reins so he could lead the horse along the beach and towards the barn.

'And take care with those saddlebags, Joseph,' Palgrave called after his son. The boy's hand rose in acknowledgement.

He turned to Leah. 'They contain our future,' he said simply. His words seemed both a statement and an offering.

Alone on the sand, husband and wife stared at each other for some time. Palgrave seemed so foreign to her, nothing like the man who had walked into the woods then sailed away all those months ago. She wondered what he saw when he looked at her.

What will happen now? she mused. She had begun to build a *future* without him ...

Many minutes passed before she took two deliberate steps in his direction, until the toes of their boots met. She lifted her hand and touched his thick, tangled whiskers.

'Would you allow me to shave you, Mister Williams?' she

asked, raising her eyes to his. 'Your beard does you an injustice.'

Palgrave's mouth slowly widened into a broad smile.

'Aye. If it would amuse you, Leah Hallett.'

AFTERWORD

The Hummingbird and the Sea is inspired by a true story but is, however, a work of imagination. In 2014, I was in Washington DC with my family researching my second novel, *The President's Lunch*. My son Sam was six at the time and was fascinated by pirates. One afternoon as we strolled past the National Geographic Museum he alerted our attention to the exhibition on show, called *Real Pirates: The Untold Story of the Whydah from Slave Ship to Pirate Ship*. We bought our tickets and ventured inside.

It was here that I discovered the tale of 'Black Sam' Bellamy and his ill-fated captaincy of the *Whydah*. The wreckage of the ship was discovered off the coast of Cape Cod in 1984, buried under at least fifteen metres of sand. Underwater archaeology is still being carried out on the site. To date, more than 200,000 artefacts have been retrieved. What was found in the wreckage – tools, coins and, most notably, the ship's bell – became part of the touring exhibition we visited.

Samuel Bellamy's story gripped me instantly. A lowly, but honourable, English seaman, he turned to piracy when his sweetheart's father, a New England Puritan, denied his attempts at courtship with his daughter, Maria Hallett. Bellamy had no prospects. In the eyes of Maria's father, he was not a worthy partner. Determined to earn Hallett's favour, Bellamy decided to return to the sea – but not as a servant of the Royal Navy. He deserted and, funded by local goldsmith Palgrave Williams, who joined Bellamy on the journey, renamed himself 'Black Sam'.

Due to the amount of plunder he accrued in the short time he was terrorising the Caribbean (approximately nine months), 'Black Sam' is considered the most successful pirate of the era known as the 'Golden Age of Piracy' (1630–1750).

This success was largely due to his capture of the *Whydah*, an impressive, purpose-built slave and cargo ship. When Bellamy seized the ship on the return trip of her maiden voyage, he discovered approximately £60,000 worth of cargo in her hold. But on her homeward-bound journey in 1717, the *Whydah* was caught in a gale near Eastham, Massachusetts. Only nine of the 146-man crew survived. Six were hung for piracy. Partial human remains were also unearthed from the ocean floor, including an eleven-inch fibula still encased in a silk stocking and a shoe. These were originally thought to belong to a small man. Later, in 2006, scientists attributed them to a young boy aged between eight and eleven, likely John King. King was probably a 'powder monkey' – a young boy charged with hauling gunpowder from the ship's magazine to the cannons.

What I found most interesting was that while the English were expanding their empire into the American colonies and the Puritans were laying roots in Mass-achusetts Bay, the likes of William 'Captain' Kidd, 'Calico' Jack Rackham, Edward 'Blackbeard' Teach, Benjamin

Hornigold and 'Black Sam' Bellamy were terrorising the shipping lanes in the Caribbean. The Puritan Era and the Golden Age of Piracy coexisted side by side and occasionally these two points in history intersected.

I used these as my foundations for weaving a more expansive tale than the one I came across at the National Geographic Museum's exhibition. *The Hummingbird and the Sea* became a story that explored the real lives of both Puritans and pirates, and examined the ways their lives converged. In creating characters such as Leah, Tamesine, Silas and Reverend Dent, I sought to humanise the story that gripped me, to add greater meaning, tension, drama and complexity to an already fascinating tale, and to bring these two opposing worlds to life for a contemporary audience.

ACKNOWLEDGMENTS

Thank you so much for reading the story of Samuel Bellamy and the young woman he left behind. I hope you found the journeys of Sam, Palgrave, Leah and Maria engaging and exciting.

I am so grateful to Barry Clifford, the "history hunter" who discovered the wreck of the Whydah after a gruelling 12-month search. Without his remarkable salvage mission, I would never have been introduced to the incredible story of "Black Sam" Bellamy.

As always, I would like to give great thanks to my editor, Sylvia Balog. Sylvia's affinity for historical fiction has been invaluable. Her feel for the genre is remarkable. Likewise, huge thanks also go to my friend and proofreader, Jo Egan. Her eagle eyes and appreciation of detail cannot be equalled. And finally, my husband Chris, whose ongoing support, encouragement and IT know-how always astounds me.

ALSO BY JENNY BOND

HISTORICAL FICTION AVAILABLE AT
WWW.JENNYBONDBOOKS.COM

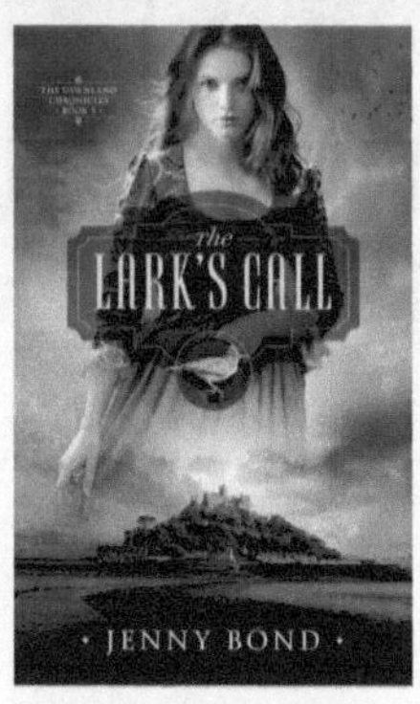

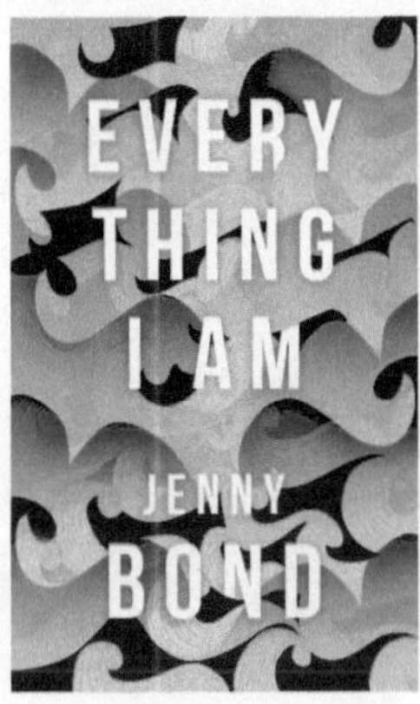
EVERY
THING
I AM
JENNY
BOND

ENJOYED THE HUMMINGBIRD AND THE SEA?

Thanks for reading *The Hummingbird and the Sea*. If you enjoyed the story, share a review where you bought the book, on Goodreads, or contact me at jennybondbooks.com and share your thoughts.

BONUS EPILOGUE
THE HUMMINGBIRD AND THE SEA

Get a free copy of the epilogue, *Strangers* when you sign up
for my newsletter via this link:
https://BookHip.com/MHTASSA

You'll also be notified of giveaways and new releases and
receive updates of my author journey

SAIL FURTHER INTO THE WORLD OF THE HUMMINGBIRD AND THE SEA

Check out my Pinterest board - images that provided inspiration and information during the writing process.

~

Listen to the Spotify playlist of the novel. Music, past and present, aimed to reflect the themes and atmosphere of the story.

~

To access either of the above, on the relevant platform search 'jennybondbooks'.

Tabby was led to her place next to the magistrates' bench. Her seat, an exceedingly uncomfortable straight-backed chair made of pine, was as hard as a ploughman's palm. *Crafted by an ill-skilled carpenter*, she guessed. She half hoped it would not be a lengthy trial for her back would not endure, although in truth she was willing to bear the discomfort for as long as was necessary. Her life was at stake, after all.

She had taken the counsel of friends and worn a simple, pale-green bodice and skirt. Both were borrowed, of course, as were the delicate pins that held her wild red hair in check. Scanning the faces in the courtroom, her gaze fell upon those most familiar, yet their sympathetic expressions did nothing to still the waves of unease ebbing and swelling in her belly.

Dummer and the other magistrates entered wearing their robes of office, their powdered wigs. 'Pomp and circumstance,' her father might have scoffed once. Recalling the sound of his voice as it had been all those years ago was a comfort to her now.

Tabby and the spectators rose at the magistrates' arrival, then sat, following their lead.

She waited as the men shuffled their documents and conferred about various points of interest. It was a torture of sorts, as though being probed and examined by a thousand eyes, a thousand whispers, a thousand suspicions: *Did she do it? A healer? Everyone knows ruddies have fiery tempers. Anything is possible.*

Attempting to inhale a deep, bolstering breath of air, she found herself hampered by the stay she was wearing. She fidgeted in her seat for a moment, twisting her torso left to right as a bear would seeking relief for an itchy back against a tree trunk. No trees here. No bears, either, although she would wager Governor Dummer was just as fierce.

Dummer seemed to be eyeing her with a curious, disapproving stare. She watched as he turned to the onlookers, waiting for them to silence before proceeding.

'Mistress Post, you have been charged with murder.'

A murmur went through the courtroom.

'During this trial, the Crown will present the facts of your crime and your motives for committing such a heinous and unwarranted act. If we can find no circumstances under which your crime was justified then, as you are aware, the penalty is death. You have refused your right to representation, arguing that it is only yourself who can tell your story. Is this correct, Mistress Post?'

She looked at Dummer squarely. 'I believe that is the only way my truth will out, for who knows but me and the dead man precisely what happened on that day?'

Dummer raised an eyebrow. 'A simple "yes" would suffice, Mistress Post.'

A bible rested on the arm of her chair. She had anticipated this moment during the week she spent in prison in the lead up to the trial, and before that as she travelled to Boston from Moosehead Lake. What would she do when called to swear on God's Holy Book? She decided she would not know until the moment was upon her. Now, as fast as a jack rabbit in front of a prairie fire, the moment had arrived. Tabby decided that if there were a God, she would rather have him for her than against. She placed her hand on the book and repeated the oath after Dummer.

Then came the question all present were waiting for.

'How do you plead?' Dummer asked.

A shadow passed across her blue eyes for an instant before she looked directly at the governor.

'Guilty,' she responded.

Available at www.jennybondbooks.com

ABOUT THE AUTHOR

I'm an author of contemporary fiction, historical fiction and non-fiction. I have published my books in Australia, New Zealand, USA and Europe.

I'm also an English teacher and I've been lucky enough to introduce the love of language to many students around the world.

I guess this also planted the seed of an idea that I should give writing a go, myself

Sydney, Australia, is where I was born and raised, but prior to my reinvention as a writer (which had something to do with a friendly argument with my husband!), I held the position of Head of English at Eaton House The Manor in London's Clapham Common. I also taught English and Drama for eight years at a selective high school in Sydney, and for five years at a private girls' college in Canberra.

Whether I've been at home, living and working in another country, or travelling for the sake of adventure, I have never spent a single day without a book by my side. This meant slipping from the act of reading into the act of writing didn't actually seem that much of a change.

I've long been a fan of great historical fiction writers such as Hilary Mantel, but I also spend quality time with books by authors from other genres, such as Margaret Atwood, Kate Atkinson, Tim Winton, Ian McEwan, Jane Austen, John Irving and E. Annie Proulx.

When I'm not writing, I enjoy keeping fit and love to

travel. I live in Canberra, Australia with my husband, two sons, and a lively Staffordshire Bull Terrier named Mick.

I enjoy running, swimming and yoga daily, as I believe staying active is an integral component of a happy writing life. You can visit me at www.jennybondbooks.com.

Jenny